Indulg...
fr...

Penny
Jordan

Secrets & the Virgin

featuring two classic stories

The Perfect Match?

The Perfect Lover

Also available

Seduction & the Mistress

featuring the classic novels,

The Perfect Seduction

Perfect Marriage Material

Penny Jordan has been writing for more than twenty years and has an outstanding record with over one hundred and thirty novels published, as well as hitting *The Sunday Times* and *New York Times* bestseller lists. Penny Jordan was born in Preston, Lancashire, and now lives in rural Cheshire.

Secrets & the Virgin

featuring

The Perfect Match?
The Perfect Lover

by

Penny Jordan

M&B™ and M&B™ with the Rose Device
are trademarks of the publisher.

First published in Great Britain 1997. This edition 2008.
Harlequin Mills & Boon Limited, Eton House,
18-24 Paradise Road,
Richmond, Surrey TW9 1SR

SECRETS & THE VIRGIN © by Harlequin Books SA 2008

The Perfect Match? © Penny Jordan 1997
The Perfect Lover © Penny Jordan 1997

ISBN: 978 0 263 86674 2

10-0608

Printed and bound in Spain
by Litografia Rosés S.A., Barcelona

The Perfect Match?

CHAPTER ONE

'AND you're sure you don't mind going to Haslewich to sort out everything…?'

'No, Mum, I don't mind at all,' Chrissie assured her mother quietly, exchanging looks over her head with her father as she did so.

It was no secret in their small, close-knit family unit just how much her younger brother's irresponsible behaviour and alcoholic lifestyle had upset Chrissie's mother.

In the early years of her marriage she had tried her best to help Charles, naïvely believing that he was genuinely trying to mend his ways. But eight years ago, following a short custodial sentence after he had been convicted of stealing several small items from the home of an acquaintance, which he had later sold to pay for the drink on which he was by then dependent, Chrissie's mother had decided that enough was enough and had cut herself off from him completely.

Chrissie understood just why she had felt compelled to do so.

Her father was a hard-working heart surgeon in a busy local hospital in the small Scottish border town where they lived and her mother was a member of the local town council and involved in several local charities.

Her brother's unsavoury reputation and dishonest behaviour was so completely opposite to her own way of life that it was very hard for her to deal with the situation.

Now though, Uncle Charles was dead and someone, *one* of them, would have to travel to Cheshire to sort things out, dispose of the small property he had owned in the centre of the town of Haslewich—all that was left from his share of the farmhouse and land that he and Chrissie's mother had inherited from their parents, and Chrissie had volunteered to take on the task.

'Heaven knows what kind of state the house will be in.' Chrissie's mother gave a small shudder. 'The last time I was there the whole place was filthy and you couldn't open a single cupboard door without an empty bottle falling out.

'I just wish I knew why he…' She closed her eyes. 'Even as a child he was different…awkward…self-destructive, very different from our father. He was such a kind, gentle man like my grandfather, but Charles… We were never very close as children, perhaps because of the big age gap between us.' She shook her head.

'I feel guilty about letting you go down to Haslewich on your own but we've got this conference in Mexico followed by your father's lecture tour.'

'Look, Mum, it's all right,' Chrissie reiterated. 'I don't mind, honestly, and it isn't as though I don't have the time.'

There was a big reshuffle going on in the English department of the school where Chrissie worked as a teacher and she had already warned her parents she had heard on the grapevine that the department was looking to cut costs and shed some staff.

'Well, I'm not entirely happy about your having to stay in Charles's house,' her mother told her.

'But that *is* the whole point of my going,' Chrissie reminded her wryly. 'The house has to be sold to help pay off Uncle Charles's debts and you said yourself that there was no way it could be put on the market until it had been cleaned from top to bottom.'

'I know. Which reminds me, I'll have to get in touch with the bank and the solicitors to make sure you've got my authority to deal with all the necessary paperwork.'

Once again Chrissie and her father shared a look over her mother's head.

Charles Platt had not just left behind him an untidy house and an unsavoury reputation; there was also a large number of outstanding debts.

In truth, she wasn't particularly looking forward to being the one to sort out the mess Uncle Charles had left behind, Chrissie admitted, but someone had to do it and she certainly wasn't going to let her mother be even more upset than she was already by letting her see her own distaste for the task.

The last time she had visited Haslewich had been following her grandmother's death, and her memories of the occasion and the area were coloured by her mother's grief.

Her Uncle Charles had been living with his mother in the old Cheshire farmhouse that had been passed down through many generations of their family, but her grandfather, disappointed in his son and well aware of his weakness, had sold off the land to another farmer, and following his wife's death the farmhouse itself had been sold, as well.

She could still remember the searing shame she had felt on seeing her Uncle Charles staggering from one of the town's many public houses whilst she had been shopping there with her mother. When a group of children had jeered at him and mocked him, her mother had drawn a quick, sharp breath and gone white before turning round and abruptly walking Chrissie off in the opposite direction.

That had been the first time she had become aware of the reason for the pain in her mother's face and voice whenever she mentioned her brother.

Now, as an adult, Chrissie was, of course, fully *au fait* with the history of her uncle's addiction to alcohol and gambling.

Weak and vain, he was something of a misfit in the local farming community in which he had grown up, and it had been obvious even before he reached his teens that he was not going to follow in the family tradition of farming.

'He broke my father's heart,' Chrissie's mother had once told her sadly. 'Dad did his best, selling off small pieces of land so that he could give Charles an allowance. He tried to understand and support him when he said that he wanted to be an actor. But it was all just an excuse to get money out of Dad and spend his time gambling and drinking, initially in Chester and then, when his cronies there got wise to him, back in Haslewich.'

And as they had talked, Chrissie had recognised how hurt her grandparents and her mother had been by her uncle's behaviour, how his attitudes to life, which were so very different from theirs, confused them. How impossible they found it to understand how he could so easily and carelessly flout the moral laws they lived their lives by and, most painful of all perhaps, how shamed they felt by him.

And now he was dead and with him had died a small piece of Haslewich history. Platts had farmed the land around Haslewich for over three centuries as the headstones on their graves in Haslewich's churchyard testified, but no longer.

'Don't get upset,' Chrissie urged her mother, going over to put her arm round her and kiss her.

Facially they were very similar, with wide-set, almond-shaped eyes and high cheek-bones in a delicately feminine face, but where her mother was small, barely five foot two and softly rounded, Chrissie had inherited her father's height and leaner body frame.

She also had, quite mysteriously since both her parents were dark-haired, hair the colour of richly polished chestnuts, thick and straight and healthily glossy.

At twenty-seven going on twenty-eight, she considered herself mature enough to be above being flattered by those men who did a double take when they saw her for the first time, plainly expecting her to feel complimented by their admiration of her face and body without having bothered to take the time to learn anything about her, the person. Physical attractiveness was not, in her opinion, the prime factor in motivating a new relationship. For her there had to be something far more compelling than that. For her there had to be a sense of being instinctively drawn to the other person, 'knowing' that the magnetic pull between the two of them was too overwhelming, too powerful, to be ignored. She was, in short, a true romantic, although she was very loath to admit it.

'It's not fair,' one of her friends had told her mockcrossly the previous summer.

'If I had your looks I know I'd make much better use of them than you do. You don't *know* how lucky you are.'

'True beauty comes from within,' Chrissie had told her gently—and meant it.

Whilst she had been at university, she had been approached by a talent scout for a modelling agency but had refused to take them seriously.

There were those who had wondered if her irrepressible sense of humour was quite the thing one wanted in a schoolteacher, but Chrissie had proved that the ability to see and laugh at the humorous side of life was no bar to being able to teach—and to teach well.

'I'm still not entirely happy about the idea of your staying in Charles's house,' her mother repeated.

Chrissie sat down opposite her.

'Mum…we've already been through all this,' she reminded her. 'The whole point of my going to Haslewich is to prepare the house for sale and the best way I can do that is if I'm living there.'

'Yes, you're right, of course. But knowing how Charles lived…' Her mother gave a small shudder.

She was a meticulous housewife, a wonderful cook, the true daughter of ancestors who had spent their lives scrubbing dairies and stone floors, polishing, washing and waging war on dirt in all its many forms.

'I've got my own bedding and my own towels and utensils,' Chrissie reminded her mother.

'I should be doing this,' Rose Oldham protested. 'Charles is…was my brother….'

'And *my* uncle,' Chrissie pointed out, adding, 'And besides, you can't. You don't have the time right now and I do.'

Although she wasn't going to say as much to her mother who she knew, despite her modern outlook on life, was still eagerly waiting for the day when Chrissie became a wife and mother, she had been rather glad of the excuse of having to go to Haslewich. It had enabled her to turn down an invitation from a fellow teacher who had been pursuing her all term to join him and a group of friends in Provence for the summer.

Provence had been very tempting, but the teacher had not. Privately, Chrissie had always been a little wary of her weakness for men of a distinctly swashbuckling and impetuous nature and more suited to the pages of an historical romance than modern-day society and it was one she very firmly squashed whenever she felt it stirring.

The fellow teacher had not come anywhere near creating any kind of stir within her and would, no doubt, have made excellent husband and father material, but he certainly wouldn't have done anything to satisfy that quirky and rather regrettable feminine desire she knew she had for a man who would excite and entice her, a man who would challenge her, match her, a man with a capital *M*.

Well, one thing was for sure, she certainly wasn't

likely to find him in Haslewich, which by all her reckoning was a sleepy little market town, a quiet backwater where nothing much ever happened.

CHAPTER TWO

'I TAKE it they still haven't caught whoever broke into Queensmead?' Guy Cooke asked Jenny Crighton as she came into the small antiques shop in which they were co-partners.

'No,' Jenny told him, shaking her head as she responded to his enquiry about the recent theft and break-in at her father-in-law's home.

She smiled warmly at Guy as she spoke. He really was the most extraordinarily good-looking man and if she wasn't so firmly and happily married to her own husband she had to admit that it could have been all too easy to join the long queue of women who sighed dreamily over Guy's very masculine blend of a virilely powerful and tautly muscled male body—the kind of body that would have allowed him to pose for a trendily provocative jeans advert any day of the week—allied to enigmatically hooded eyes set above high cheek-bones and a certain way of looking at you that was completely irresistible, virtually resulting in a complete meltdown. Add to that highly sensual cocktail the intensely masculine genes he had inherited from his Gypsy forebears and the reputation that went with them and it was easy to understand why the word 'sexy' accompanied by a longing look was the way most of her sex would quite freely have described him.

Not that Jenny was totally immune to Guy's looks or the unexpected and even more dangerous generosity and warmth of character that went with them, but she loved Jon and she thought it was very sad that with all he had to offer a woman, Guy had not yet found the right one for him.

'At least they didn't harm Ben,' she added. 'But it has shaken him. You know how stubborn he can be normally and how hard Jon and I have found it to try to persuade him to have someone to live in.'

'Tell me about it,' Guy invited. 'When I went up there to do a valuation on the antiques for his insurance company, he practically hit the roof when I told him that he was going to need to have an alarm system installed. I take it he never did?'

'Well, you know Ben,' Jenny sighed. 'Luckily they didn't take very much and the police think they must have been disturbed either by the phone ringing or by someone arriving at the house.'

'It's so hard to contemplate that someone would actually break in in broad daylight and calmly proceed to remove not just small items but actual pieces of furniture, as well.'

'The police did warn us that there's very little chance of our getting anything back. Apparently there's been a spate of these kinds of robberies recently and they think it's gangs coming out from the city wanting to make money to buy drugs. The new motorways, of course, facilitate a quick getaway and make them and the stolen property so much harder to trace.'

'But you've managed to persuade the old boy to have someone living in?' Guy questioned her as he started to check through the contents of a large packing case that contained goods from a house clearance. Junk in the main, he suspected, but you never knew….

'Well, unfortunately, no,' Jenny replied. 'But Maddy is due to arrive at the end of the week. You know she always comes up from London to spend a few weeks here in the summer.'

'Will Max be coming with her?' Guy asked, referring to Jon and Jenny's elder son and Maddy's husband.

Jenny bit her lip. 'No…no, he won't. It seems he's heavily involved on a case at the moment and he's going to have to fly out to Spain to see his client. She's got a yacht that's apparently in a marina out there.'

Max was a barrister working from a prestigious set of chambers in London. He specialised in divorce work and it hadn't escaped Guy's notice that most of his clients were women. Max liked women, or rather he liked the boost to his ego that deceiving them gave him.

Guy did not have a very high opinion of Max but he cared far too much for Jenny to let her know it.

Life hadn't always been easy for Jenny and although she and her husband, Jon, were happy together now…

Unlike Max, Guy genuinely did like women, all women, but some women especially so. Women like Jenny—warm, gentle, womanly women with quiet, understated beauty. Their more flashy, visually eye-catching counterparts held very little allure for Guy. He was a physically good-looking man himself and well knew how worthless mere good looks could be. A warm, loving, caring nature, though, now *that* was something that time could never erode, something enduring and worthy of loving, cherishing…

But he had long ago come to accept that Jenny was not for him; that she loved her husband and would never see him as anything more than a friend. 'A much younger friend' as she had once stressed to him, reminding him of the age gap between them. At thirty-nine Guy no longer considered himself to be particularly 'young'.

'Apart from the shock of the burglary itself, the thing that's upset Ben the most,' Jenny was saying, 'is losing the little yew desk. His father apparently had it copied from the French original that belonged to *his* grand-mother. It was a very pretty little piece, but being a copy, not really of any great financial value.'

'But a good deal of sentimental value,' Guy suggested.

'Very much so,' Jenny concurred. 'When I was talking to Luke about it the other day, he told me that the Chester side of the family owned a matching pair of the original from which Ben's desk was copied and that they had been gifts brought back from France for the twin daughters of the Crighton who bought them. His father now has one of them and his uncle the other.'

'Mmm…well, perhaps the thief or thieves didn't realise Ben's was a copy.'

'Maybe not, although the police seem to think they probably took it because it was in the hallway and easy to move like the silver and jewellery they took.

'Ruth and I had to spend virtually a whole day checking over the house and listing what was missing. Ben certainly wasn't in any fit state to help and although, of course, I had some knowledge of what should have been there, Ruth, as Ben's sister, was naturally much more accurate.'

'She's back from the States, then?'

'Yes, she and Grant flew in on Saturday.' Jenny laughed. 'I think it's wonderful how the two of them have stuck to their agreement to spend alternate three months in one another's countries.'

'It's lovely to see them together. They're so much in love, even now.'

'Well, I imagine all that they've been through must make the time they're having together now all the more precious.'

'I agree. Real confirmation that fact can be stranger than fiction.'

'And real love so strong that nothing can diminish or destroy it,' Jenny added softly. 'In all the years they were apart, neither of them was ever tempted to marry someone else.'

'But at least they're together now and so deeply in love that Bobbie complains that despite the fact that they were all married at the same time, Ruth and Grant are a far more romantic couple than her and Luke.'

'Well, Bobbie and Luke do have a young child and two busy careers,' Guy commented, 'while her grandparents are both retired and free to concentrate exclusively on one another.'

'They may both be retired but Ruth is still on half a

dozen local committees as well as running her single-parent units,' Jenny reminded him. 'And Grant has an extraordinary spread of business interests to keep him busy. I sometimes feel exhausted just listening to what they've been doing. I can't help comparing their energy and the enjoyment they get out of life with Ben's growing lack of interest in everything.'

Jenny's forehead pleated in a worried frown as she reflected on her father-in-law.

'Is he still going ahead with his hip-joint replacement operation?' Guy asked her.

'I hope so,' Jenny told him feelingly. 'It's scheduled for the end of the summer and the plan was that Maddy would be there when he comes out of hospital to look after him. He responds far better to her than he does to any of us, partially because she's Max's wife, of course, and so far as Ben is concerned, Max can do no wrong.'

'But not so far as you, Max's mother, are concerned,' Guy offered shrewdly.

Jenny shook her head. 'Ben has always spoiled Max and Max has never needed any encouragement to believe he deserves to receive preferential treatment. I did hope that when he and Maddy married...' She stopped and shook her head, changing the subject to ask, 'Anything interesting in that lot?'

'Not really,' Guy replied, taking his cue from her and letting the subject drop, switching from discussing personal matters to their shared business interests. 'I've had a call to do another house clearance this morning although I doubt that there'll be anything there of any interest. Charlie Platt,' he added grimly.

'Charlie Platt?' Jenny queried, frowning again, then her expression clearing. 'Oh yes, I know who you mean.'

'Yes,' Guy went on. 'By all accounts he virtually drank himself to death.'

'Oh, poor man,' Jenny sympathised compassionately.

'Poor man nothing,' Guy told her grimly. 'He was the biggest con man in town. His parents publicly disowned him. He died leaving debts all over the place.'

From the tone of his voice, Jenny wondered if Guy was one of the people he had owed money to. If so, she doubted that Guy would admit, even to her, that he had been taken advantage of.

Normally an easygoing, compassionate man, generally inclined to judge others gently rather than harshly, he also possessed a surprisingly fierce streak of pride, accentuated, Jenny suspected, by the fact that his family, the Cooke clan, various members of whom were spread throughout the town, had originated, so local history had it, from the unsanctified union of one of a band of travelling Romany Gypsies and the naïvely innocent daughter of a town schoolmaster. They were generally held in a mixture of awe and contempt by their less enterprising and energetic peers.

The girl had been married off in haste and disgrace to a local widowed tavern keeper desperately in need of someone to take charge of his sprawling brood of existing children.

Dependent upon where you stood in the local hierarchy, there was a tendency to regard the activities of the Cooke clan, both professionally and privately, as extremely suspect or extremely enviable.

Over the generations, the name Cooke had become synonymous, not just with the local taverns and public houses that they ran, but also with such disparate activities as poaching, gaming and other enterprising methods of increasing their income, a habit the more God-fearing local folk were inclined to put down to the genes they had inherited from their roving-eyed Gypsy forebears.

Not that any members of the family went in for poaching or its equivalent these days. *That* practice had died out with his grandfather's generation, Guy had once wryly told Jenny, along with the bulk of his then-adult male relatives, most of whom had been with the Cheshire Regiment during the First World War.

'But that kind of reputation is hard to lose,' Guy had told Jenny. 'Once a Cooke, always a Cooke!'

'And having those brigandish dark good looks of yours doesn't help,' Jenny had teased him gently.

'No,' Guy had agreed shortly. He had lost count of the number of fathers who had sternly admonished their daughters against dating him when he had been younger. He thought now that he must have been the only teenage boy in the locality to have gained the reputation of being wild and dangerous whilst still possessing his virginity.

It was half-day closing, and after Jenny had left and Guy had locked up the shop, he went home to work on his other business interests, which ranged from a half share in the very popular local restaurant owned by one of his sisters and her husband to a smaller share in a firm of local builders owned by yet another relative.

He had recently been considering the validity of investing in small local properties that could be renovated and then let out on short-term leases to employees of one of the large multinationals that had recently started to move into the area.

Antiques, especially furniture, were his first love but the business he shared with Jenny was hardly sufficient to keep him fully occupied.

He frowned as he studied the post. He and Jenny were the prime motivators behind the Antiques Fair that was due to be held at Fitzburgh Place the following month, a combined event to promote the area and hopefully raise money for Jenny and Ruth's pet charity, the single mothers homes scheme, which Ruth had started as a result of her own experiences as an unmarried mother.

As Guy started to check off the list of exhibitors to the fair against the list of invitation letters he had sent out, he remembered what Jenny had said about Charlie Platt.

He and Charlie had been at school together…just. Guy had entered the school just as Charlie was on the verge of leaving it to move up to the seniors.

A thin, pale boy, who had suffered badly from child-hood asthma, which thankfully he had later outgrown, Guy had shown no signs then of the fact that as an adult male he would grow up to be strong and muscular. He had been small and vulnerable-looking, the youngest of his mother's brood, a quiet, studious boy whom his female siblings had mothered and whom Charlie Platt had immediately and instinctively focused on as an ideal victim for his practice of blackmailing the vulnerable into parting with their dinner money.

Guy had tried to resist, refusing trenchantly to hand

over the money—he was, after all, well used to being cuffed and teased by his much larger and far more bois-terous male cousins—but he had had one fear he kept hidden from his family and that was of water. Because of his asthma, he had never been allowed to learn to swim or to play in the river that bounded the town in case the cold water brought on an attack.

Charlie Platt had very quickly discovered Guy's fear, both of the river and, even more importantly, of other people's discovering how he felt. Predictably he had made use of it.

Guy knew he would never forget the day Charlie Platt had held him under the water for so long that Guy had really believed he was going to die, probably would have died if one of his bigger and older cousins hadn't happened to come along, seen what was happening and treated Charlie Platt to the kind of rough justice that boys of that age could mete out to one another, blacking his eye, bruising his pride and putting an end to Guy's torment.

That summer, Guy had taught himself to swim, and after Charlie had left the school Guy hadn't come across him again until they were both adults, by which time Charlie was already drinking heavily and gaining some-thing of an unsavoury reputation for himself.

And now Charlie was dead. Guy couldn't feel sur-prised, nor sorry, and he certainly had no desire to ac-commodate the terse telephone instructions he had received via his answerphone from the young woman who had announced herself as Chrissie Oldham.

Who exactly was she? She had sounded too crisp and businesslike to be one of the steady stream of women who, at one time or another, had shared Charlie's roof. She must have been employed to sort out the estate.

Guy's frown deepened. One thing Charlie's death had done was to focus his own mind on the fact that he was close to forty with little to show for his life other than a healthy bank balance and a small group of friends.

Avril, his next to eldest sister, had complained to him at Christmas that it was high time he got married and produced a family of his own, as she watched him playing with her own grandchildren. Grandchildren!! But then Avril *was* fifteen years his senior.

He had no plans to follow her advice, though. There was no way he could share his life, commit his life…his self to another person without loving her to the point where life without her would quite simply be an untenable option.

And he had only once come even close to feeling like that and she… He got up and walked across to the window, then stood staring out at the view in front of him.

He had moved to his present house six months earlier. In a prestigious part of town, it was one in a small close of similar properties originally built to house local members of the clergy. Ruth, Jenny's aunt-in-law, lived there, three doors down; several high-ranking executives from the town's largest corporate employer, Aarlston-Becker, owned adjacent properties.

There were those who, Guy suspected even now, felt that such a house was far too grand, far too good, for a mere Cooke, even one like himself who had gone from grammar school to university and from there to all the art capitals of Europe before returning home to set up in business.

He glanced at his watch. He still had another hour before he needed to leave for Charlie Platt's house, but he had a good two hours' worth of paperwork on his desk in front of him, he reminded himself sternly.

Chrissie groaned as she straightened up and her aching back muscles protested. She had spent virtually the whole of her time since arriving in Haslewich cleaning her late uncle's small house, a task she could only relate, in terms of stress levels, to the mythical job of cleansing the Augean stables.

Every racing paper that Charlie had bought during his tenure in the house—and there had been many of them—instead of being thrown away had simply been tossed in an untidy pile on the spare-bedroom floor. This was the very room that Chrissie had planned to occupy during her hopefully brief stay. And that was just for starters. Letters, bills, in the main unpaid, junk mail, you name it—Uncle Charles had kept it.

Chrissie suspected they must have grave doubts about her at the local supermarket when she had very nearly cleaned them out of their supply of rolls of black plastic refuse sacks.

Her initial idea had been to burn the waste paper on a bonfire in the terraced cottage's small back garden, but she had soon recognised that there was far too much of it for such easy disposal and instead she had been forced to apply to the local authority for their advice and assistance on its disposal.

This morning, a couple of friendly workmen plus an open lorry had arrived in the street to remove the sacks of paper she had prepared for them.

The cottage was one of a terrace of similar properties built into what had originally been one of the town's boundary walls using, Chrissie suspected, stone 'reclaimed' from the walls themselves and the castle, which had been virtually destroyed during the Civil War.

It could, she admitted judiciously, with a little imagination and an awful lot of determined hard work, be turned into a very attractive home for a single person or a young childless couple.

Several of the other cottages in the street had already undergone or were undergoing this process and the shiny brightness of their painted front doors highlighted the air of shabby neglect that hallmarked her uncle's cottage.

Now that she had emptied the small second bedroom, she did at least have somewhere to sleep. Her mother would have been grimly approving, no doubt, had she seen the fervour with which she had scrubbed and sanitized both the bathroom and kitchen before allowing herself to use them. She still had her reservations, though, about the wisdom of using the ancient fridge, which had formerly been home to various, thankfully unidentifiable, mouldy pieces of food.

But the worst ordeal of her visit still lay ahead of her and that was her appointment tomorrow with her late uncle's solicitors.

His clothes she had already consigned to another much smaller collection of plastic liners ready for collection by a representative of a local charity.

The house had, as she and her parents had already guessed, revealed no material assets likely to provide enough money to help to settle his debts, with the exception of a rather attractive small yew desk.

When Chrissie had mentioned this item to her mother, she had said instantly that the desk had originally belonged to her grandmother, Chrissie's great grandmother.

'Don't arrange for it to be sold, Chrissie,' she had begged her daughter. 'We'll have it valued instead and I'll buy it from the estate. I asked Charles what had happened to it after Mother died and he said he didn't know.' She had given a small sigh. 'I suppose I ought to have guessed that he'd keep it for himself. I'm just glad that he didn't actually sell it. I suppose it's too much to hope that he kept Nan's Staffordshire figures, as well?'

'I'm sorry, Mum, but they're definitely not here,' Chrissie had told her, promising that she would have the desk appraised independently as well as by the dealer she had arranged to come and value the small, and she suspected, mainly worthless bits and pieces she had found round the house.

The desk certainly was a very attractive piece, all the more so now that she had cleaned and polished it; sturdily made it was, at the same time, very prettily feminine.

Chrissie glanced at her watch. The dealer she had been recommended to contact by her late uncle's solicitors would be here any minute. Once he had checked over and removed the bits and pieces she had placed on one side along with all the cottage's furniture—apart from the desk that was in the front room—she could arrange for the estate agent to view the cottage and put it on the market.

Tiredly she stretched her body but at least she had the satisfaction of knowing that every single nook and cranny of the small house was now clean. She still had the remnants of some of the cobwebs on her person to prove it, she acknowledged ruefully as she caught sight of the small grubby mark on her once pristine white T-shirt.

CHAPTER THREE

GUY knocked briefly on the cottage door and then waited. Knowing the way Charlie Platt had lived, he had deliberately changed into a pair of faded, well-worn jeans and an equally faded and now rather close-fitting T-shirt. The days when he had been considered an under-sized weakling were now long past. It had caused him a certain amount of wry amusement when he attended antique fairs to be mistaken for one of the helpers brought in to carry the heavier pieces of furniture.

Chrissie heard the knock on the door and went to open it. Guy started to glance at her with brief disinter-est, preparatory to introducing himself, and then looked at her again whilst Chrissie returned his look with the same shocked intensity.

She had heard, of course—who hadn't?—of 'love at first sight' but had always wryly dismissed it as a fairy-tale fantasy.

Surely no one in these modern times could possibly be stricken so instantly, so totally, in the space of less than a minute, or know immediately that *this* was the one, the *only* person with whom they could spend the rest of their lives.

But none of these admirably logical and sensible thoughts came anywhere near entering her head now as she simply stood and returned the intensity of Guy's silent visual contact with her.

Outside in the street, in the rest of the world, people went about their normal daily business, but the two of them were as far removed from that kind of mundanity as it was possible to be, transported to a world of their own where only the two of them existed.

Chrissie could feel her pulse jumping, her heart beating with frantic haste, her breathing growing far too fast and shallow, as she and Guy continued to search one another's face, the recognition between them both instant and compelling.

That he was good-looking and very physically male she had noted automatically when she opened the door, but her reaction to him now went deeper than that, much, much deeper. It encompassed not just his outward appearance, his physical attributes, but his deeper inner self, as well.

It was almost as though there was some psychic, soul-deep bond between them that both of them had instantly recognised and responded to. There could surely be no other reason for the sheer intensity of their shared sense of recognition and awareness, Chrissie reasoned as she mechanically stepped back into the cottage knowing that Guy would follow her in.

Guy couldn't believe what was happening to him. He knew there was a story within the family that along with the physical genes inherited from their wild Gypsy ancestor, there were those Cookes who also inherited some of his more spiritual and psychic gifts, but *he* had never had any occasion in the past to consider himself one of those so gifted, nor indeed to put very much credence in their existence.

He was far too much a modern twenty-first-century man for that, and yet he was intensely aware of that startling moment of unexpected insight he had experienced when the cottage door opened and he had seen *her* standing there, had known the moment he looked at her that he was confronting his own fate. Somehow he already knew just how that wonderful waterfall of dark red hair would feel slipping through his hands, against his body…how *she* would feel, how she would taste, how she would smell and even how she would look… cry out in the moment of their shared physical coming together. He knew…he knew…

He could hear the blood pulsing in his ears and feel the rapid-fire volley of his heartbeat that sounded like a warning drum roll. He knew as he looked at her that she was *the* woman, the *one* woman, who would make his life—him—complete. He knew, too, that if he were to stretch out his hand to her now, she would put her own into it and silently follow him; allow him to lead her…*take* her, in every sense of the word, but she was no dependent, naïve clinging vine. On the contrary, he recognised that she was an extremely well-grounded and femininely powerful woman.

As he stepped into the hallway and closed the door behind him, he reached out instinctively to touch her face. Immediately Chrissie turned her head and pressed her mouth to the hard palm of his hand.

Guy heard himself groan as he drew her towards him with his other hand. Her body fitted perfectly within his, as he would fit perfectly within hers.

He didn't know which of them was trembling harder as he bent his head and replaced the hard warmth of his palm against her lips with the even harder warmth of his mouth. He only knew that the tiny, agonized sound of delight she made beneath his kiss was echoed a thousandfold deep within his own body.

Chrissie could feel herself trembling violently as she gave herself over not just to Guy's kiss, but to the new role that fate had devised for her. She had never imagined minutes ago when she opened the door to him that she was opening the door to her future. She had never been the kind of woman to rush into any kind of physical intimacy—just the opposite—yet here she was, knowing that no matter how far the intimacy went between the two of them, it could be nowhere near as intense as the silent, emotional bonding they had already shared.

Never had she imagined that she could react like this to a man's touch, to his kiss, that she could want him so immediately and so overwhelmingly, that she could feel the urgent almost violent desire within him to tear aside the barriers of their clothing and know her utterly and completely and to share that desire, to know just how much he ached for the feel of her skin against his, beneath his, and how much she shared and returned that ache.

She could hear him whispering beneath their shared hungry kisses how much he wanted her, how much he had longed for her in his life—unintelligible, disjointed words that ran together from a raw trickle of sound into a sensual flood.

How long they stood there, kissing, touching… *wanting,* Chrissie had no idea; she only knew that when he finally released her, she was trembling so much she could hardly stand up, that her mouth felt swollen and bruised, that his mouth looked…looked…

She swallowed as she looked at him and he reached reassuringly for her hand, then held it tenderly in the firm, warm grip of his own. '*Coup de foudre*, I believe the French call it.'

'They would,' Chrissie replied shakily. She ached to be back in his arms. She ached all over for him, she admitted, inside and out, and it was nothing like the aches and pains she had been suffering because of her hard physical work cleaning up the cottage, nothing at all.

God, but he wanted her, Guy recognised. He wanted her so much that he didn't know how he was managing to keep his hands off her. He had never considered himself to be a highly sexed man, but right now…

'I've never experienced anything like this before,' Chrissie confessed.

'Good,' Guy told her tautly, adding rawly, 'I think I'd want to kill any other man who might have—'

Chrissie stopped him, shaking her head, but she knew what he meant. She felt equally savage and uncharacteristically jealous of any other woman who might have had the same effect on him as she quite obviously had had.

She took a deep breath and forced herself to try to come back down to normality, but it was almost impossible. 'I want you so much,' she admitted shakily. Then Guy was bridging the small gap between them and taking her back in his arms.

For several long minutes, the only sound was that of their increasingly passionate kisses and strained breathing. Chrissie had no idea which of them it was who lifted Guy's hand to her breast; she only knew that the sensation of his holding her, touching her *there*, made her whole body jerk in a frenzy of physical need, a sensation like a jolt of electricity running straight from her breast to her womb, convulsing her whole body with a deep-rooted, aching need.

'Please don't, please don't,' she whispered huskily, even though she was the one who arched back against him, guiding his hand whilst he rubbed the tip of his thumb over and over her T-shirt-covered nipple until she was pleading frantically with him to soothe her aching flesh with the healing suckle of his mouth.

Chrissie had never pleaded with a man to make love to her before or imagined she might want to, but this whole situation was a world apart from anything she had experienced before, completely foreign territory to her, a place where the old rules, the old guidelines, meant nothing and where the only things she had to guide her were her own senses and needs and his.

When Guy tugged up her T-shirt in response to her frenzied pleas and fastened his mouth on the hard, swollen tip of her breast, Chrissie almost felt she might faint from the intensity of her pleasure.

She could hear his soft murmurs as he caressed her and could feel the need in his body. She ached to touch him, to explore him, to know him, and suddenly the fierce suckling of his mouth against her breast wasn't enough to satisfy the urgent clamour of her physical response to him. Only one thing, one person, could satisfy and silence that.

Her hands trembling, she lifted them to cup his face and gently ease him away from her body. As he looked into her eyes, she dropped her hands and held one of them out to him and started to walk towards the stairs.

Her hand felt small and delicate, almost lost within the grip of his as he let her lead him, but as they started to mount the stairs, she felt him pull back slightly from her.

'You don't have to do this, you know,' she heard him telling her rustily.

Silently Chrissie searched his face before telling him with quiet dignity, 'Yes, I do, but if *you* would rather not…'

Her honest directness made Guy's heart ache for her. She was so trusting, so giving, so…so perfect.

'You shouldn't need to ask,' he told her huskily, adding with a rueful, self-derogatory laugh as he looked briefly down at his own body, 'The answer is, I'm afraid to say, rather too obvious.'

Chrissie couldn't help it. She followed his gaze, her eyes widening in betrayal of her female response to the evidence of his male desire for her. A tiny kick of pleasure pushed up her heart rate and the temptation to reach out and run her fingertips exploratively along the hard ridge of his arousal was one she had to fight hard to resist, but her body language had already given her away and Guy's visual reciprocal inspection of her was every bit as revealing of his own need.

For the first time in her life, Chrissie suddenly knew what it meant to feel sexually proud of her body, to know within the most inner core of herself that when she stood naked before Guy, it would be with pride and in the knowledge that her body, her femininity, her womanliness, would fill him with silent awe, with reverence, with arousal and need. As his nakedness would her.

She could feel his hand trembling slightly as she led the way to the small empty bedroom she was using.

Just for a second and only for a second as she opened the door and led him inside, she regretted the bareness of the scrubbed walls and floor, the plainness of the inflatable mattress with its simple white covering of bed linen she had brought from home. What, after all, did they need with the gaudy trappings of romance, with satin sheets and four-poster beds, rich brocades and thick carpets? They had all the richness, all the luxury, all the sensuality, they would need in one another.

Guy surveyed the plain bare room in silence. It smelled of fresh air and cleanliness and something far less easy to pigeon-hole—a scent, a perfume, an essence, which he recognised was hers.

'You're actually staying here?' he commented, frowning slightly as he did so. The house was in one of the poorer parts of town, and whilst Haslewich was, generally speaking, a safe enough place to live and safer than most, there had been several incidents lately of youths brawling in the streets in this part of town and it was only a couple of streets away trouble had erupted recently with youngsters apparently buying drugs outside a local nightclub.

'It seemed to be the most sensible thing to do,' Chrissie told him.

Was he perhaps put out by the starkness of the room and its setting or did he perhaps think that she was being too forward and usurping his role? He wasn't to know, after all, how unique this whole situation was for her, how unique her desire for him and her responsiveness to him were, how unique he was.

'If you'd rather…' she began hesitantly, but Guy didn't let her finish.

He gathered her up in his arms as he told her softly, 'No. this is perfect…*you* are perfect. This is how love should be, not contrived or forced, achievable only with the right backcloth, the right props, the right setting, but simply instinctive and natural, wholesome and clean. We don't need any of the trappings of seduction, because this isn't seduction. And besides, no setting however beautiful could anywhere near match your beauty or the beauty of what we're going to share, to create.'

Chrissie felt her eyes start to fill with emotional tears. It was almost as though he could read her mind, as though he shared her thoughts, as though the two of them were so much in harmony that they were already almost a part of one another.

Unsteadily she lifted her hand to his face, touching her fingertips to his mouth, trembling as she explored the difference between the slightly rough flesh above his lip where he shaved with the sensual smoothness of his mouth.

'Chrissie.'

Slowly, one by one, he sucked her fingers into his mouth as he looked deep into her eyes.

As she looked equally intensely back at him, Chrissie had no awareness of the soft keening sound of pleasure she gave in response to the sensation caused by the sensually rhythmic movement of his mouth and tongue as they caressed her fingers.

Deep within her body, she could feel herself starting to ache and melt, to experience feelings and needs as old as humankind itself. Her body suddenly felt as though it were weighted down with heavy, inhibiting armour, her clothes a chafing restriction against which her skin and her senses rebelled.

In the past, sexual intimacy for Chrissie had always been a fairly passive activity with the man taking the lead. She had certainly never envisaged a situation where she might do as she was doing now and start to tug impatiently at her own irritatingly unyielding clothes in her yearning hunger to experience a man's hands on her body. But then, this was different…this was… Her small moans of frustration gave way to voluptuous sighs of pleasure as Guy started to help her remove her recalcitrant garments.

It shocked her a little at first to recognise when she finally stood naked before him that the unfamiliar scent of her body was the scent of her arousal, her desire for him, but if she found the realisation unexpected and slightly shocking, Guy, it seemed, viewed it in a totally different way and had no inhibitions about telling and showing her.

As he nuzzled the hollow between her breasts, he told her appreciatively, 'You smell so good. Just like a woman should.'

'I...there is a shower,' she began to suggest, but as though he guessed what she was thinking, Guy smiled slowly at her, then shook his head and told her firmly, 'No. Don't you know how erotic it is...how erotic you are...how much the scent of you makes me want to touch you, taste you, explore and know every inch of you?'

For the first time since that initial contact when they had looked into one another's eyes and known, Chrissie felt slightly flustered and uncertain.

'I don't want you all washed and antiseptic,' Guy added meaningfully. 'I want you the way you are now. A woman, warm and aroused, wanting me and scented by...tasting of that wanting...and I want you to want me in the same way,' he finished rawly.

'I do,' Chrissie whispered back, and she knew as she said it that it was true and that already she ached for the scent of him in her nostrils, the taste of him on her mouth.

Once again her eyes gave her away and Guy muttered hoarsely to her, 'You know what I mean, don't you?'

The only thing she needed to do was simply to nod her head and watch in trembling anticipation as he swiftly removed his own clothes. His body was taut and athletic, all clean lines and strong muscles. The sight of the soft, dark body hair that lay in silken whirls against his skin seized her body with a pang of female appreciation and made her curl her toes in sensual response to such masculinity.

Again in direct contradiction to her previous and admittedly rather prosaic and mundane sexual experience, she discovered that with Guy she actually wanted to look at his body, to explore it visually with an open-eyed female curiosity, not just to know its differentness but, she suspected with a small sense of shock, to inspect and judge its male ability to satisfy the hunger that she knew she wasn't going to be able to control for much longer.

She hadn't realised quite how long she had been studying him or quite how hard she was frowning until she heard Guy asking her with rueful light-heartedness, 'Do I pass?'

Thoroughly mortified, Chrissie started to look away, nodding her head as self-consciousness began to overwhelm her, but Guy simply laughed and hugged her reassuringly.

'It's all right,' he told her warmly. 'You have every right to look and judge. There mustn't be any barriers between us, Chrissie, or any inhibitions or murky areas that can't be touched. That isn't what you and I are about. Of course you want to look at me. Just as I want to look at you. After all, doesn't half the pleasure in enjoying a meal come from its visual presentation, and doesn't that presentation stimulate and increase our appetite for it, just as looking at you is stimulating my appetite for you?' he asked her softly.

And then, before she could make any response, he bent his head to kiss her.

Gently at first, almost too gently, Chrissie decided, she started to press herself closer to him whilst she tried to prolong and deepen each kiss like a fish chasing a lure, not realising that *she* was the one being lured until

Guy's arms snapped tightly round her and then the tongue she had been trying yearningly to caress and coax with hers was suddenly no longer teasingly tempting her into his but instead thrusting powerfully and sensually within her own, causing her whole body to jerk against Guy's in a shudder of pleasure she was completely unable to control.

Not, or so it seemed from Guy's approving reaction, that he wanted her to control it, or anything else, she recognised as his hands swept her body and cupped her buttocks, pulling her tightly against him whilst he murmured against her mouth how much he wanted her, how much he ached for her.

No more than she wanted and ached for him, Chrissie knew, but she wasn't aware of having whispered the words against his mouth until Guy picked her up in his arms and carried her across to the bed.

As he placed her on it, she could feel the warmth of his breath against the skin of her midriff. Shakily she closed her eyes as she felt herself starting to quiver and then tensed as she felt Guy's mouth brush lightly against her body, his tongue tracing round her navel.

Once and then again, a thousand tiny darts of sensual pleasure exploded inside her like the seeds of a puff-ball exploding in the summer sunshine, the sensation at one and the same time so delicate and yet so powerful that it shocked her into speechless wonder.

'Is it good?' she heard Guy questioning her thickly. 'Do you like that?'

Like it? The only reaction Chrissie could manage was a soft groan followed by a sharply indrawn breath as his mouth started to move downwards across her stomach towards her hip-bone in a series of caresses so light that they barely seemed to graze the surface of her skin and yet so sensually erotic that what lay beneath that skin was already reacting to them with a rhythmic urgency that couldn't be ignored.

Not even the sensation of his hand gently and protectively covering her sex could detract from the effect the delicate, tender exploration of his mouth was having on her body.

Which, she decided later, had to be the reason why she finally opened her eyes and saw Guy kneeling between her thighs, his whole concentration focused on the feminine heart of her as he slid his hands beneath her and gently tilted her body upwards so that he could have complete and total access to her intimacy. She felt no sense of inhibition or false modesty, no need to cover herself or push him away, but instead a strong awareness of the rightness, the perfection of his intimate, loving possession of her as his tongue probed the moist mystery of her body whilst she lay still and watchful, her breathing shallow but steady until he found what he was seeking and started to caress it with increasingly sensual strokes. Then her body trembled and jerked wildly in response to him, so wildly that she could feel the hard grip of his fingers biting possessively into her flesh as he continued to hold her beneath his mouth whilst she writhed and arched frantically beneath him, not sure if she wanted to pull away and bring her sweet torture to an end or arch up greedily against him and demand even more of the shocking pleasure he was giving her.

Her body, though, was perfectly sure of what *it* wanted, needed, craved, and the high female sound of arousal that sobbed from her throat made sure that Guy knew, as well.

'No. No more, please don't,' Chrissie panted deliriously as the hot quivers of pleasure darted through her body, convulsing her womb with tiny warning spasms of what lay ahead of her, making her shiver in a mixture of awe that she could feel such intense pleasure and a self-protective fear of the inevitable loss of self-control, of *self* that would come with it.

It was Guy who now controlled her body and her reactions and not her.

'Stop,' she begged him, adding unintentionally, 'I'm afraid…'

'Of what?' Guy asked her rawly. 'This?' He watched her face as she trembled against his touch.

'It's all so overpowering, so…so unfamiliar to me,' Chrissie admitted unwillingly. 'I don't…I haven't…'

'You've given yourself physically before,' Guy guessed for her, 'but not like this, not totally, completely, physically, emotionally and mentally, the way it is now between us. I feel just as afraid,' he told her simply, 'afraid of not matching up to your expectations, of disappointing you, of spoiling what we have been given.'

'You couldn't do that,' Chrissie told him softly, and as she said it she knew it was true and she knew something else, as well. 'I want you, Guy,' she told him emotionally, reaching out towards him, her body trembling as she met the burning look of physical desire in his eyes.

Unable to stop herself, she reached out and touched

the tip of his erect manhood with her fingertips and then ran them slowly and a little hesitantly along the shaft.

Now it was his turn to tremble and groan, the sound emerging from deep within his chest as he closed his eyes and told her thickly, 'God, that feels so good, too good.' He suddenly tensed and groaned again, then bent his head and cupped her breast with his hand, drawing her nipple into his mouth and sucking fiercely on it, not just to give her pleasure, Chrissie recognised with a sharp kick of female power, but also because it was what he wanted. He needed to feel the soft warmth of her breast within his mouth, to draw on it and from it in just the same way that she now ached to feel him within her.

'Now, now, please, Guy, now,' she pleaded, whispering the impassioned words between the frantic kisses, her earlier fear of losing control completely forgotten, overwhelmed by a far more urgent and important need—the need to complete the cycle they had both set in motion, to be fulfilled, to be—

Chrissie gave a sharp, piercing cry of relief as she felt Guy's first deep thrust within her body.

'You feel wonderful,' she heard Guy telling her thickly. 'We fit together perfectly, perfectly.'

Chrissie couldn't make any verbal response but she knew there was no need, the way her body was already responding to the rhythmic movement of his told him everything he needed to know.

She had never imagined that physical intimacy could be like this; that two bodies could be so well matched, fit together so perfectly that they together made one perfect whole; so completely in harmony with one another that Chrissie actually felt as though she could physically feel the ripples of pleasure that ran through Guy's body with each movement he made within her own, and she sensed that he, too, could feel hers, that he knew exactly the second when she needed the more urgent movement of his body within hers, the heartbeat of time precisely even before she cried out to him that she ached for him, craved him, had to have him, deep, deep within the most secret part of her body.

And she could feel through the strong contractions of her own release the thick pulse of his.

'Oh, Guy,' Chrissie wept emotionally as he held her in his arms.

'I know. I know,' he soothed her tenderly, gently brushing the tears from her face as he bent his head to kiss her mouth lingeringly. He drew her deep into the protective warmth of his own body, stroking her skin as though he couldn't bear the thought of letting her go.

'You feel so good, so right,' he told her emotively. 'Oh God, you feel so good.'

'I still can't quite believe what's happened,' Chrissie confessed, suddenly a little shy. 'It's not...I don't...'

'Do you think I don't *know* that?' Guy interrupted her gruffly, taking hold of her hand and lifting it to his lips whilst he placed a kiss in her palm and then closed her fingers over it. 'And besides, what you and I have goes way, way beyond anything like any coy, false need to play games with one another. What we have...what we *can* have...' He broke off and shook his head. As she looked at him, Chrissie saw that his own eyes were filled with moisture.

'Oh, Guy,' she protested shakily. It was her turn now to comfort him, so she kissed his mouth with all the love she felt for him.

'We need to make time to talk to one another properly,' Guy told her unsteadily when she had released his mouth. 'No, not here,' he told her, reading her mind. 'If I stay here with you…' He groaned and closed his eyes. 'Have dinner with me tonight. My sister and her husband own a small restaurant. We could meet there. I daren't offer to pick you up,' he told her softly, 'because if I do…' He looked expressively at her still-naked body, warm and relaxed from his lovemaking, satiated…now…

But Guy was right. They *did* need to talk. There was so much she wanted to know about him, so much she wanted to discover.

'How ironic that I should meet you here of all places, in the house that belonged to Charlie Platt,' Guy murmured to her. When he saw Chrissie start to frown, he explained, 'We never got on.'

'You didn't like him,' Chrissie supplied, turning away slightly so that he couldn't see her face.

'No, I *didn't* like him,' Guy agreed grimly. 'In fact…' He stopped and shook his head. 'Let's not talk about Charlie Platt. He doesn't mean anything to either of us, thank God.'

Chrissie opened her mouth to tell him, correct him. 'Guy,' she began, but then got no further.

'I love the way you say my name,' he told her lovingly. 'It makes me want to kiss you like this….'

'You still haven't looked at the furniture,' Chrissie managed to remind him breathlessly, ten minutes later.

'I'll go through everything another time,' Guy responded, his expression suddenly changing, his eyes becoming dark and almost brooding as he asked her huskily, 'There *will* be another time, won't there, my Chrissie, and another and another and…?' Then he was kissing her again, and between those kisses Chrissie somehow found the breath to reassure him that their times together would stretch to eternity and beyond.

It took them over an hour to shower and dress and finally manage to say goodbye.

Chrissie had written down the address of his sister's restaurant, and after he had gone she simply sat and looked at it, already counting the minutes and the seconds until they could be together again.

The telephone rang whilst she was still engrossed in her day-dream, still floating on a cloud of pure golden bliss.

She smiled dreamily into the telephone as she picked up the receiver and responded to her mother's hello.

'You sound happy,' her mother commented.

'I am,' Chrissie told her simply and then proceeded to give her a very edited version of the events of the afternoon.

Chrissie was very close to her parents and kept no secrets from them, but she was just beginning to discover that some things were so precious, so sacred that they couldn't be shared with anyone other than the person they most closely concerned.

'I know it sounds incredible,' Chrissie told her mother, 'and I have to admit that if anyone had told me that Guy and I were going to fall in love at first sight, I probably wouldn't have believed them but—'

'Oh, Chrissie, are you sure…I don't think…' her mother interrupted her uncertainly. 'He sounds wonderful, darling, and of course I'm thrilled for you, but…'

'He's wonderful,' Chrissie assured her mother. 'He's more than wonderful,' she added softly, more to herself than to her parent. 'He knew Uncle Charles, by the way, although I got the impression that he didn't much care for him.'

'Did you tell him that Charles was your uncle?' her mother asked her anxiously.

'No. I didn't get the chance,' Chrissie told her. 'He's taking me out to dinner tonight, though, so I shall probably tell him then.'

There was a small pause before her mother queried doubtfully, 'Do you think that's wise, darling? I hate to pour cold water on things, but you said yourself that he didn't seem to have a very good opinion of your uncle and it might be wise not to say too much about your…your relationship with him, at least until the two of you get to know one another a little better.'

'You mean I should lie to Guy?' Chrissie questioned her mother, a little shocked.

'Well, no, of course not…at any rate not directly,' her mother responded. She paused. 'I should hate to think that your uncle's bad reputation might cast a shadow on your happiness, darling, and perhaps I shouldn't even suggest such a thing, but people do tend to make judgements. Of course, once your Guy has got to know you a little better, then…'

'Are you trying to say that Guy might reject me

because of who…because of Uncle Charles?' Chrissie
asked her mother slowly.

'I don't know, darling. I would hope not, but…well,
your uncle…'

She didn't say any more; she didn't need to. Her uncle,
as Chrissie well knew, had been a liar, a cheat and a thief.

'But I've upset you,' Chrissie heard her mother saying
sadly, 'and that was the last thing I wanted to do….'

'No, no, it isn't that,' Chrissie tried to reassure her.
'It's just…well, I hate the thought of being deceit-
ful…dishonest with anyone, but most especially with
Guy.' But the idea that anything, anything at all, might
cast the smallest shadow on her happiness filled her
with such anguish, made her so fearful for the vulnerability of her newly born love that she instinctively
wanted to protect it from anything and everything that
might threaten or damage it.

'Did you ask your Guy to value the desk,' her mother
prompted her whilst Chrissie blushed, remembering
just why she hadn't even thought about mentioning the
desk to him.

'No…no, I didn't,' she admitted. 'But perhaps under
the circumstances it might be better to ask someone
else to value it,' she suggested. 'I wouldn't want Guy or
anyone else to think that I wanted him to value it in our
favour because of…well, you understand what I mean,'
she tried to explain.

'Yes, yes, of course,' her mother agreed. 'And you're
quite right. It's the sentimental value of the desk that
makes it so valuable to me and your father. We both
agree we want to pay its full market value into the estate,

even though by law I suspect that it's half my property anyway. Of course, it might be hard to prove as much. However, when I think of all those poor people your uncle defrauded…'

Chrissie didn't say anything. She already knew of her parents' decision to obtain via the solicitors acting for her deceased uncle a list of all her uncle's creditors so that these could be reimbursed—from her parents' own pocket in all probability. Chrissie doubted that even after the sale of the house and paying off the mortgages on it there would be enough to pay his debts.

'So anyway,' her mother teased gently as Chrissie started to bring their conversation to a close, 'when are we going to meet your Guy?'

'Not yet,' Chrissie told her firmly. 'Not until you get back from your trip—I'll be thinking about you tomorrow when you fly out.' She was glad that her mother couldn't see her flushed face as she acknowledged that whilst it was natural and automatic for her to discuss her feelings for Guy with her mother, they were still too new, he was still too new in her life, for her to want to share him publicly with anyone else.

'A table for two… What happens if I say we don't have one?' Frances Sorter teased her brother.

She had been a little uncertain at first just how things would work out between her husband and her brother when Guy had first offered to help finance their restaurant business. Both of them were in their own quiet way rather dominant, the kind of males who were used to being in control and taking command. But as she acknowledged now, she needn't have worried.

The two men got along just fine and there was no doubt that Guy contributed some valuable input into the business and not just in terms of money or even the business he brought in. It had been Guy who had encouraged them to expand and extend the dining room when they had been a little wary of taking on the extra financial commitment, and Guy, too, who had backed his faith in them with the money to do so. And he had been right. The plain, old-fashioned but superbly cooked country food that her husband specialised in had very quickly met with local approval and they were already gaining an equally good reputation farther afield, as well.

Roy, her husband, insisted on using only top-quality ingredients, organically grown vegetables and livestock reared by traditional methods rather than factory farmed. His beefsteak pie had male customers salivating in anticipation and their wives complaining that they were tired of having their home cooking compared to its detriment with Roy's.

'Paul even told me that Roy's pastry was better than his mother's,' one wife had confided ruefully to Frances.

Both their sons were now at catering college and hopefully would eventually come into the business with them, while Miranda, their daughter, had set up her own ancillary sideline, catering for private dinner parties and the like and keeping to the family tradition of serving wholesome country food.

'Is it a business dinner?' Frances asked, pausing delicately.

Guy looked at her. 'No,' he told her quietly.

'No...? It's a woman,' Frances guessed.

'She's a woman,' Guy agreed, only just resisting the temptation to tell his sister she was *THE* woman. However, he knew her too well and he knew also that once he had said that, every member of the Cooke clan would know by this time tomorrow what he had told her and he wasn't ready for that, not quite yet. He wanted her to himself far too much right now to want to share her with anyone else, much less his inquisitive, gregarious and sociable family.

'Oh, I almost forgot to tell you,' Frances exclaimed. 'There's been another break-in—at The Limes this time. Apparently the police suspect that a professional gang's at work.'

Guy knew that his sister's husband's cousin was a police inspector based in Chester and so he listened frowningly as she provided him with details.

'The police suspect that the gang moves into an area and picks it clean before moving on. They're not going for the really valuable stuff—that's too heavily protected and alarmed—but apparently they do seem to know what they're looking for. Chester, of course, with all its antiques shops and its visitors is an ideal place for them to get rid of what they've stolen by offloading it to dealers before the police can circulate a description of what's gone.'

'Mmm. It's every dealer's nightmare,' Guy agreed, 'to find out that what you've bought in good faith turns out to be stolen property.'

'How are things going for the Antiques Fair?' Frances asked him, changing the subject.

'Fine,' Guy responded, adding with a grin, 'Almost too well at the moment, in fact. So far, my major problem is finding enough space for everyone who wants to participate and I've actually had to turn down quite a few.'

'A bit different from the first one you organised three years ago,' his sister reminded him. 'Then, you were virtually having to plead with people to come.'

'Don't remind me,' Guy told her wryly.

'You still made a success of it, though,' she pointed out. 'And a good profit, plus what was donated to local charities. Will you be doing that again this year?'

'Oh yes, I don't think that either Jenny or Ruth would let me get away with not doing.'

Frances laughed. 'Ruth Crighton's homes for single mothers is a very worthwhile cause,' she pointed out to her brother, 'and because it's small and local I think that people do feel more inclined to want to help. Ruth was telling me the last time she and Grant were here that they're actually starting to train their own counsellors and planning to provide an after-care service for their mothers and babies.'

'Tell me about it,' Guy groaned. 'It's begun to take over so much of Jenny's time that I've got a feeling it won't be long before she decides to give up her share of the business.'

Frances gave him a sharp look. Guy and Jenny Crighton had been in business together for many years now, although she knew that for Jenny the antiques shop they both ran had never been more than a part-time sideline. She had occasionally wondered over the years about the exact nature of the relationship between her brother and Jenny, for although it was obvious that Jenny was devoted to her husband, Jon Crighton, the senior partner in the family's local legal practice, it was also obvious, to Frances at least, that Guy was extremely fond of and protective towards his business partner. Now though, totally unexpectedly it seemed, there was a new woman in Guy's life.

Frances was no fool. She was well aware that her brother had not exactly lived the life of a monk and that in his twenties in particular he had dated a string of stunningly attractive young women. But he was close to forty now and so far as she knew, there had been no one special in his life for quite some time. So who was this new woman and where had Guy met her? she wondered curiously. She would have to make some enquiries via the family grapevine, she decided vigorously, whilst giving her brother a dulcetly innocent smile.

CHAPTER FOUR

CHRISSIE had just stepped out of the bath when she heard someone knock on the door. Pulling on her towelling robe, she hurried downstairs and then paused warily before checking the safety catch and opening the door, her small frown of uncertainty dissolving in the heat of her delighted smile as she saw Guy standing on the doorstep, his arms full of flowers.

'You said we should meet at the restaurant,' she reminded him huskily after she had let him in and laughingly admonished him for the extravagance of the enormous armful of flowers he had given her.

'I know,' he agreed tenderly, giving her a look that made her toes curl and her body go hot.

'You said that if we didn't, that you…that we…' she began as she took the flowers into the kitchen where they totally filled the small sink.

'I know *exactly* what I said and why,' Guy asserted. As Chrissie turned round, he caught her in his arms and added gruffly, 'And I was right, too. God, I've missed you.'

'You can't have,' Chrissie protested shakily. 'It's only been a few hours and—'

'A few hours, a few minutes, it doesn't matter how long it is…any amount of time spent away from you is too long,' Guy interrupted her passionately.

It must be because she hadn't had anything to eat since this morning that she felt so light-headed and dizzy, Chrissie told herself. Either that or…

'We'll be late for dinner,' she warned Guy as he started to kiss her, unfastening her robe so that he could slide his hands inside it and slowly caress her naked and still-damp body.

'Do you care?' he asked her throatily.

Chrissie shook her head.

This time, because she knew what to expect, she somehow assumed that her response would be less intense, the emotion between them not quite as magical, but she quickly discovered she was wrong. If anything, their response to one another, their need for one another, was even more total and overwhelming than it had been before, their bodies moving in perfect harmony with one another.

'I've never known anything like this,' Guy whispered rawly to her as he held her in the aftermath of their loving.

'Neither have I,' Chrissie agreed. 'It…it frightens me a little bit,' she told him quietly. 'It's almost…too perfect….'

'*Too* perfect!' Guy laughed. 'How *can* it be?' he teased her.

Chrissie laughed as well, her laughter turning to a wide-eyed look of shaken passion as Guy started to make love to her again, bending his head to gently kiss and then caress the naked tip of her breast, slowly and delicately drawing the sensitive, responsive flesh into his mouth whilst Chrissie gasped in helpless pleasure, reaching out for him, clinging to him as she felt herself start to be caught up in the powerful undertow of the desire he was arousing within her.

'I'm never going to want to let you go now, you know that, don't you?' Guy told her tenderly after they had made love.

'I don't think I'm ever going to want you to let go,' Chrissie admitted honestly, closing her eyes, caught halfway between tears and laughter as her emotions overwhelmed her. 'I still can't quite believe that all this is happening,' she added. 'I only came to Haslewich to sort out my…things here.'

'You came because fate had already decreed that we should meet,' Guy corrected her softly.

'I…I wouldn't even *be* here if I wasn't representing…' Her voice tailed off. Despite what her mother had said to her, she knew she had to tell him the truth and explain exactly who she was.

But Guy had other things on his mind and Chrissie abandoned any attempt to talk to him as he started to kiss her—again!

'You're late and you're lucky we kept you a table,' his sister told Guy severely over two hours later when they finally made it to the restaurant.

Standing at his side, Chrissie was blushingly conscious of just how she must look and of just how many of the subtle and not-so-subtle signs of *how* they had spent the past few hours must be clearly evident.

No amount of make-up could possibly cover the tell-tale glow warming her skin or the softness of her eyes, the bee-stung, kiss-swollen shape of her mouth, the sensual languor that still possessed her body. And she was conscious, too, of the discreet but very thorough inspection Guy's sister was giving her.

Like him, she, too, was dark-haired with arresting good looks. He had told Chrissie earlier when she had been unable to stop herself commenting with female appreciation on the powerful shape of his body and the dark golden warmth of his skin that he owed his physical appearance to the genes he had inherited from his Gypsy ancestor.

'Theirs was a relationship that caused quite a scandal at the time,' he had explained wryly and told her the story of how he came to have Gypsy blood in his veins and how, even now, as a family they were not always totally accepted by everyone locally.

'People in small towns have long memories and there was a time centuries ago when the description "gypsy" was synonymous with the word "thief", at least in some people's eyes. I want you to know exactly what you're getting,' he had added, watching her. 'Good *and* bad, because, make no mistake, my love, I mean to be a permanent part of your life, a *very* permanent part of your life.'

Chrissie had been too overwhelmed with emotion to make any coherent response or to tell him about her own family.

'He's definitely in love with her,' Frances exclaimed positively to her husband once she had shown them to their table and returned to the kitchen. 'You can tell just by the way he looks at her.'

'Of course you can,' her husband scoffed. 'Fran, Guy is damn near forty and to the best of my knowledge he's had any number of women running after him, yes and he's let a good few of them catch him as well and…'

'This is different,' his wife interrupted him firmly, tutting in disgust at his male lack of perception. She glanced at her watch and wondered if there was time to make a few phone calls. The rest of the family were going to be interested in what she had to tell them.

'You're going to have to stop looking at me like that or we'll have to leave,' Guy warned her.

'Looking at you like what?' Chrissie asked.

But of course she knew. It made her feel giddy, light-headed, light-years away from her real self, to know that she could barely take her gaze away from his mouth, his body…his… Her *real* self?

'Stop it,' she begged him huskily when he returned her look with an open sensuality that made her whole body go hot. 'We've got to be sensible,' she told him. 'We—'

'Sensible?' he queried ruefully. 'That's the last thing I feel like being, but I suppose you have a point. I don't even know how long you're going to be here or—'

'I don't know myself yet,' Chrissie told him. 'I've got an appointment with Jon Crighton tomorrow.'

'Jenny's husband,' he interjected, adding, 'Jenny Crighton is my partner in the antiques shop.'

Chrissie frowned. Something about the way he said the other woman's name and the way he looked struck a disconcerting warning note.

'Presumably you're acting for the Platt family. It's

hardly surprising that they didn't want to deal with things personally.'

'They can hardly be blamed for what…for what Charles did,' Chrissie protested defensively.

'No, but this is a small town and people have long memories and narrow minds, as my family has good cause to know. Charlie treated a lot of people very badly and rightly or wrongly anyone turning up here now and claiming to be related to him is bound to be treated with suspicion.'

'Is that what you would do?' Chrissie asked him a little stiffly.

Guy smiled at her as he reached across the table to take hold of her hand and shrugged. 'Does it matter? If I'm honest, I don't suppose I would be inclined to look charitably on another member of the Platt family, but right now neither Charlie Platt nor anyone else is of the remotest interest to me. In fact, right now, there is only one person on my mind….' He smiled into her eyes tenderly. 'Right now, the only person I want to think about or talk about is you….'

'There isn't anything to tell,' Chrissie fibbed uncomfortably. How *could* she tell him who she was after what he had just said? 'I'm here to represent the Platt family and I've got to see his solicitors and get the house put up for sale.'

'Well, Jon Crighton will help you do all that. His family have been the town's solicitors for heaven knows how many years now. In fact, the original Crighton connection with the law goes back even beyond that, to Chester, where Jon's ancestor actually came from.

'There are still Crightons practising as barristers and solicitors in Chester. And Jon and Jenny's elder son, Max, is presently a practising barrister in London. They're quite an extended clan, not quite so extensive as the Cookes, of course, but then, we have the advantage of our extremely prolific Gypsy genes to thank or blame for our colonisation of the town.'

Prolific! How prolific? Chrissie wondered uneasily, suddenly acutely conscious of something she had neglected to discuss with Guy in the fierce immediacy of their need for one another. Something she was now shamefully aware she *should* have mentioned, checked…insisted upon, out of practical considerations and health-conscious maturity, if nothing else. But she had been too overwhelmed, too hungry for the feel of Guy inside her to spare a thought for something so practical, and Guy, she suspected, must have felt exactly the same.

'Is something wrong?' she heard him asking her quietly.

Quickly she shook her head. The contraceptive pills she had been prescribed to regulate her monthly cycle would normally have protected her, but she was guiltily aware that her most recent prescription was still unfilled in her purse and she had taken her last pill a few days ago. First thing in the morning, she would make sure she went to the chemist's, she promised herself.

'Er…no…nothing,' she assured him, too distracted by the realisation that his sister was walking towards them to tell him what was bothering her.

'Is everything all right?' Frances asked Guy wryly, as she surveyed their barely touched, and now cold, food.

'Fine, but neither of us had much of an appetite,' Guy replied.

'Not for food,' Chrissie thought she heard the other woman murmur wryly as she gestured to a waitress to collect their plates.

'What time are you due to see Jon tomorrow?' Guy asked as soon as his sister had gone. 'Only I'm due to visit Lord Astlegh's estate manager in the morning to check over things for the Antiques Fair I'm organising there and I wondered if you'd like to come with me. It's quite an interesting house with some spectacular gardens.'

'I'd love to,' Chrissie told him warmly. 'My appointment isn't actually until three…'

'Wonderful, we can have lunch together, somewhere a little more private,' he added ruefully.

His sister had sharper eyes than he had given her credit for, he acknowledged inwardly, and she had certainly guessed exactly how he felt about Chrissie. He suspected she would lose no time in passing her discovery on to the rest of their family.

'If you don't want anything else we could leave and have coffee somewhere a little quieter…'

Chrissie looked at him knowing that everything she was feeling was in her eyes. 'Yes… I'd like that,' she told him a little breathlessly.

She wasn't totally surprised when she discovered that he was taking her to his home, but her heart was thumping heavily when he guided her up the narrow pathway to the immaculately painted front door of the handsome, brick-built, three-storey terraced house with its Georgian façade.

They entered a narrow but high-ceilinged hallway off which Guy opened a door, flicking on the lights to illuminate an elegantly furnished sitting room carpeted in a neutral sisal matting that showed off perfectly the room's antiques and at the same time blended with the two large, squashy, creamy damask-covered sofas that faced one another across the fireplace.

'Make yourself at home,' Guy invited her. ' I'll go and make some coffee.'

'I'll come with you,' Chrissie told him huskily, giving him a faintly tremulous smile as he extended his hand towards her and drew her down the hallway.

It was so unlike her to be like this, to be so up front and femininely demanding in her intense desire for him. Words, feelings and desires she simply could not contain seemed to have swept aside her normal caution and replaced it with emotions and needs so boldly brilliant that they filled her whole consciousness, blinding in that brilliance, in the same way that Guy's presence seemed to fill the unexpectedly large and well-planned kitchen he was now moving capably about, opening cupboards, removing mugs, filling a kettle.

Whilst he stood with his back to her, reaching up into the cupboard above him for a jar of coffee, Chrissie studied him openly, greedily absorbing the satisfying sight of his body. His shoulders were broad, tapering to a narrow waist, his legs long and lean, topped with neat buttocks. And as she had good cause to know, the flesh beneath his shirt would feel warm and smooth, sheer heaven both to touch and kiss. She was tempted to go over to him, wrap her arms round him, tease his shirt out from his belt and...

'What is it, what's wrong?' Guy asked her with concern, turning round just as the small yearning sound she had been trying to suppress escaped her lips.

'No, nothing,' she managed to tell him, but Guy continued to frown slightly at her as he spooned the coffee into their mugs.

'Coffee's almost ready,' he announced unnecessarily as the kettle boiled. But Chrissie's mind was made up. After spending these past few pulse-rate-inflating minutes standing in his kitchen, watching him, absorbing his every movement, wanting him, she knew exactly what she ached for and needed, and it certainly *wasn't* a cup of coffee.

'No…' Chrissie shook her head, caught off guard both by the trembling of her body and the surge of desire that possessed her. 'I…I don't want anything to drink,' she murmured, then admitted honestly, 'I…I just want you.'

'Oh God, what *have* I done to deserve you?' Guy groaned as he took her in his arms and showed her just how thoroughly her feelings, her needs, were returned. 'You don't *know* how much I ache for you right now,' he breathed into her mouth.

'Show me,' Chrissie invited him, shamelessly winding her arms round his neck and pressing her body close to his.

Somewhere on the edge of her consciousness was a vague memory of something she ought to tell him, but so many more pressing needs were demanding her attention, and right now all she could think of was just how good that unmistakable hardness she could feel in his body would be once it was inside hers.

She had never felt so completely overwhelmed by her own physical needs before or by the urge to express and share them. Swiftly she dismissed the unwanted jarring voice that dared to try to spoil the perfection of her new-found love.

The bedroom he took her to upstairs was furnished with the same sturdily constructed antique country furniture she had admired in the sitting room, the centrepiece a fine four-poster oak bed.

'I did at one time think of making a career in interior design,' Guy confessed when Chrissie commented on how much she liked the clever combination of heavy, natural, masculine-looking fabrics he had used. 'We're sometimes called in as consultants by clients.'

'You chose the décor for the restaurant, didn't you?' Chrissie guessed, recalling that despite her preoccupation with Guy she had still been aware of the comfortable and easy ambience of the restaurant.

'Yes,' Guy agreed. 'Frances and Roy are planning to extend and add on a conservatory area for summer dining and private parties, and with that in mind I felt that the Mediterranean colours we used in the main eating area would blend best with that kind of exterior and the outside eating area Frances and Roy hope will go with it.

'I spent a couple of years living and working in Italy and I have to confess that they have the art of alfresco dining to perfection.'

'Italy…mmm…I spent several months there myself during my gap year. I loved Florence.'

Her gap year. Guy grimaced inwardly. The idea of a

gap year either before or after university had been an unheard-of luxury when he had been that age. He had gone to Italy, driven by a restless urge to experience a different environment from the somewhat enclosed world he had grown up in, but he had had to work his way there—hard, dirty, manual work in the main. He had worked in Italy, too, harvesting potatoes, working in bars and kitchens, doing anything and everything he could to keep himself solvent.

Without her having to say, he already knew that Chrissie came from a very different background from his own; that she had grown up in a typical, comfortably affluent upper-middle-class household, where her father had no doubt been in one of the professions and her mother, if she had worked at all, had done voluntary work for a pet charity. Chrissie herself had probably gone to a private school.

He had sensed her reluctance to discuss her background and wondered if it was because she had guessed how very different it was from his own. Class differences in this modern age were supposed to be a thing of the past, dead and gone, but of course they were not.

His own parents, whilst thrifty and hard-working, had had a lifestyle a world away from that enjoyed by the upper middle classes.

His father had joined the navy after leaving school— there was a tradition in the Cooke family of its young men joining the armed services—and then after he had met and married Guy's mother, he had taken over the tenure of one of the town's public houses—another family tradition.

It had been the restlessness inherited from his Gypsy forebear that had spawned Guy's youthful travel bug. The years spent travelling and working on the continent had broadened his horizons, but there was a part of him that was aware that despite his financial success, or maybe even because of it, there was still a certain section of the town's population who treated him slightly warily.

'Tell me more about this antiques fair you're organising,' Chrissie commanded him sleepily as she snuggled deeper into his arms, her body relaxed and sated from their lovemaking.

'There isn't much to tell,' Guy protested, only half-truthfully.

As Jenny had remarked only the previous week, it had been an achievement in itself for him to have persuaded Lord Astlegh to agree to their using Fitzburgh Place as the venue for the fair, and of course it was that venue that attracted the very high quality of participators in the event.

Guy had been meticulous, too, in ensuring that only high-quality food outlets and caterers would be allowed to participate. The orchestra from a local music school had been engaged to play, along with a string quartet; traditional jugglers and other street acts in period costume would add a touch of liveliness and vibrant colour to the scene.

There had been a good deal of press interest both locally and nationally in the three-day event, which was to commence with a champagne reception hosted by the Lord Lieutenant of the county and held in the house itself.

'Organising the security for it must have been a real

nightmare,' Chrissie commented as she snuggled even deeper into his arms and remembered the problems her mother had had in getting adequate insurance and security cover for one of her charity events.

'It certainly was,' Guy agreed dryly.

He had lost count of the number of meetings he had had with the patient police inspector whose responsibility the event had become, and then there had been the additional headache of hiring security staff and even acquiring portable alarms.

'We can't provide for every eventuality,' he told Chrissie, 'and ultimately it's the responsibility of every participator to check the terms of their own insurance coverage and organise their own security if they feel it's necessary. One of our biggest headaches, in fact, has been getting the permission of insurers to hold the event.'

'I suppose Lord Astlegh must own a considerable amount of valuable antiques himself,' Chrissie commented.

'A very considerable amount,' Guy agreed. 'As well as an exceptionally fine art collection and a good deal of very rare porcelain.'

Chrissie, who had often helped her mother organise her charity events, smiled sympathetically as she leaned over to kiss him and then promptly forgot about the Antiques Fair and everything else as he kissed her back and proved to her own astonishment that she wasn't quite as sleepy as she had thought after all.

'Mmm…' Chrissie moved languorously against the teasingly explorative hand stroking her body.

'Wake up, sleepyhead,' Guy instructed her. 'It's gone nine o'clock in the morning.'

'What...?' Chrissie opened her eyes in disbelief. 'It can't be,' she protested.

'See for yourself,' Guy told her with a smile, showing her his watch. 'Nine o'clock,' he repeated, 'and you've been snoring your head off.'

'Snoring?' Chrissie repeated indignantly as she sat up in bed, her indignation giving way to laughter as she realised that Guy was teasing her.

Threateningly she reached for her pillow but before she could aim it at him, Guy started to wrestle it from her. Only somehow or other it was her naked body his hands were touching and her own laughter died as she recognised the look in Guy's eyes and felt herself responding to it.

In the end, it was gone eleven o'clock before they finally set off for Fitzburgh Place, calling *en route* at Charlie's house so that Chrissie could change her clothes.

'Lord Astlegh is very good about allowing both the house and the grounds to be used for a variety of local functions,' Guy told Chrissie as she made him stop his car so she could take a longer look at the spectacular vista revealed by a sharp turn in the drive leading to the house.

'Aarlston-Becker held a particularly spectacular masquerade ball here not so long ago,' Guy added, smiling at her awed excitement.

They both surveyed the man-made canal that bisected the grounds to the front of the house and the ornamental lake complete with island and 'Greek' temple that lay beyond it.

'The original design for the grounds dates from the time of Charles II,' Guy explained, 'with certain modifications incorporated during the reign of William and Mary, hence the Dutch influence. Fortunately, when the fashion for Capability Brown's "natural vistas" was at its height, the then-incumbent of the house was more dedicated to the gaming tables than redesigning his gardens and so they remained untouched.'

'They're beautiful,' Chrissie acknowledged, then asked, 'Where exactly will the fair be held?'

'To the rear of the house, in the mews area round the original stable yard, which is separated from the house and which Lord Astlegh has had converted into a series of workshops that are let to local craftspeople at very low rents. He also provides them with access to business advice, which ranges from help in preparing their books and accounts to guidance on the best market products.'

'He sounds very philanthropic,' Chrissie commented.

'Well, yes, he is,' Guy agreed. 'But it's a move that several big landowners are following, adopting a trend originally started by the likes of the Duke and Duchess of Devonshire.'

They were back in the car now, but instead of heading towards the main house, Guy took a narrow drive that angled out to the rear of the property and steered through a pair of stout wooden doors set in a high brick wall and into the cobbled stable yard that lay behind it. As Guy brought the car to a halt, Chrissie caught her breath.

What she assumed had originally been stables had been converted into small, double-storey units, each with its own window and smartly painted dark green door flanked by Versailles planters filled with an artistic profusion of summer bedding plants.

Several other cars were already parked in the large enclosed area, and as she studied her surroundings Chrissie could see how well it would adapt to a traditional market-place environment, right down to the smartly painted pump she noticed in the middle of the yard.

'The barn at the end there will be cleared out to house some of the exhibitors,' Guy was telling her as he indicated the large building forming one side of the rectangular area, 'while various empty units are going to be converted to shops selling a variety of traditional items. Stalls will be erected in the yard itself and the original tack rooms and the space above them will house a traditional market-place restaurant and bar.'

'It's going to be wonderful,' Chrissie enthused, genuinely impressed. 'The organisation must be causing you quite a few headaches, though,' she added.

'Just a few,' Guy agreed ruefully before bending his head to whisper to her, 'but I think I've discovered the perfect cure for them.'

Chrissie laughed.

'A headache is supposed to put you off sex,' she reproved him. 'Not—'

'What you and I have is a long, long way from mere sex,' Guy interrupted her seriously. 'A long, long way.'

The look he gave her made Chrissie feel weak at the knees.

Whilst Guy had his meeting with the estate manager, Chrissie elected to go for a walk in the grounds. The

Greek temple on its small island in the middle of the lake would make a very romantic venue for a wedding, she decided dreamily as she sat cross-legged on a grassy knoll overlooking the lake. So much had happened in such a very short space of time that she was still half-inclined to feel she ought to pinch herself just to make sure that she was fully awake. It was now totally impossible for her to contemplate a life for herself that did not include Guy—her relationship with him, and the love they shared, as the focal point of that life.

'This is Chrissie,' he had said, introducing her to his sister last night, and then he had looked at her in a way that showed more clearly than any verbal explanation ever could just how he really felt about her.

'I think your sister guessed about us,' Chrissie had told him later when they were in bed.

'Mmm…I suppose I did rather give the game away,' Guy had admitted as he nibbled delicately on her ear. 'She'll probably have told the whole Cooke clan by now. I hope,' he added teasingly, 'you don't have any skeletons tucked away in your closet because if you do, knowing the female side of my family, they won't take very long to dig them out.'

'None at all,' Chrissie had assured him lovingly, but of course, it hadn't quite been the truth, had it? She still hadn't told him about Uncle Charles, and she must do. She would do. Tonight, she promised herself as she glanced at her watch and realised that Guy's meeting would be over.

She got to her feet and started to walk back towards the stable yard. When she got there, another car had been parked next to Guy's, and as she crossed the yard she saw that Guy was talking with an elegantly dressed woman who looked slightly older than Guy himself.

Both of them were deeply engrossed in their conversation, and from the proximity of their bodies and the affectionate, almost intimate way Guy had his hand on her shoulder and the way she was responding by, if not actively nestling up against him, then certainly standing extremely close to him, Chrissie guessed that their relationship was a long-standing one.

Long-standing and… She bit her lip as she recognised that the feeling paralysing her, making her stay where she was a good ten feet away, unwilling to intrude on their closeness, was one of acute and very painful jealousy.

And then Guy turned his head and saw her.

Was it her imagination or had she, for the barest fleeting breath of time, seen a look in his eyes that suggested that her arrival, her presence, wasn't entirely welcome? If so, it was gone now and there was certainly nothing in the way he was smiling at her to suggest that he wasn't pleased to see her—far from it.

'Chrissie,' he exclaimed, 'come and meet Jenny.'

Jenny! So this was his partner…. Jenny Crighton, Jon Crighton's wife. A little hesitantly, Chrissie went forward.

The other woman wasn't beautiful in the obvious physical sense and she certainly wasn't young, but despite that, she had a warmth, a sweetness…a certain something about her that Chrissie could see would appeal very much to a certain type of red-blooded male. And although there was nothing in Jenny's manner to suggest it when she smiled warmly at Chrissie and shook her hand, Chrissie also somehow knew that Jenny's feelings for Guy were far deeper and more complex than those of one business partner for another.

Was the atmosphere she could sense between the two of them a legacy from some past relationship or the result of something that existed in the present? If so, how might it affect her own relationship with Guy? She wasn't a jealous person by nature but then she had never felt about another man the way she did about Guy, she recognised.

'Jenny and I were just discussing some of the arrangements for the fair,' Guy explained to Chrissie, adding to Jenny, 'Chrissie is dealing with Charlie Platt's estate. We met when I went round to check over the contents.'

As Jenny extended her hand towards her, Chrissie took it somewhat reluctantly. It wasn't like her to feel awkward or uncomfortable with a member of her own sex, but for some reason she discovered that she couldn't quite meet Jenny Crighton's eyes.

Because she was afraid of what Jenny might see in her own eyes or because she was afraid of what Jenny's might reveal to her?

'Will Louise and Katie be able to help out at the fair this year?' Guy asked Jenny, then turned to Chrissie to enlighten her. 'Katie and Louise are Jon and Jenny's twin daughters.'

'No, I'm afraid not. They're both studying hard for their exams,' Jenny informed him. 'So they won't have much spare time on their hands.'

'Louise is still determined that she and Katie are going to become Eurolawyers, I take it?' Guy smiled.

'Louise is, but I rather think that Katie has her own ideas about her future,' Jenny returned wryly. 'Jon and I had hoped to spend a few days visiting them this month, but the break-in has affected Ben quite badly and we're a bit reluctant to leave him. Ben is my husband's father,' Jenny explained for Chrissie's benefit. 'Queensmead, his home, was broken into recently and although Ben himself wasn't aware of what was going on—fortunately he was asleep in bed at the time and the burglars didn't disturb him—it has left him feeling very vulnerable.'

'Your father-in-law must have been terribly shocked,' Chrissie sympathised.

Despite her disturbing suspicions about the depth of intimacy that existed between Guy and Jenny, she had to acknowledge that there was a friendliness and warmth about Jenny, which in other circumstances would have had her wanting to get to know the older woman better. As it was...

Turning away, she frowned as Guy started to describe his meeting with the estate manager to Jenny, aware that, although she wasn't being deliberately excluded from their conversation, it involved a part of Guy's life about which she had very little knowledge and, in fact, revealed rather painfully to her just how wide the gulf was between her knowledge of him and Jenny's.

She *had* known him less than twenty-four hours, she reminded herself sternly. He and Jenny had quite obviously known one another for years, but she still was sharply conscious of the fact that Guy had made no move to reach out and draw her closer or even to touch her physically in any way, whilst Jenny was standing close enough to him for their bodies to be touching.

'It's been very nice meeting you,' Jenny told her with a smile, having glanced at her watch and exclaimed that she had things to do.

'We ought to be getting on, too,' Guy observed, adding, 'Chrissie has an appointment with Jon this afternoon to sort out the legal ramifications of Charlie Platt's estate.'

'Oh yes,' Jenny said, smiling at Chrissie. Jon had mentioned to her over breakfast that he had an appointment with the late Charlie Platt's niece concerning his affairs.

Jenny shook hands with her, but she and Guy hugged and kissed one another with obvious closeness and affection, Chrissie noticed before the older woman turned and hurried away, leaving them heading for Guy's car at a more leisurely pace.

'You and Jenny have obviously known one another a long time,' Chrissie remarked as Guy drove back to town, unable to resist bringing up the subject even though she felt a stab of jealousy.

'Yes, we have,' Guy agreed, the warmth in his voice and the way he was smiling fanning the flames of Chrissie's apprehensions into an unwanted positive belief that Jenny held a very special place in his life—and in his heart?

'How long have she and Jon been married?' she asked, unwilling to demand to know outright just what Jenny meant to him and yet increasingly anxious to dispel her growing fears.

'I'm not quite sure. Well over twenty-five years,'

Guy informed her. 'Max, their eldest child, must be in his late twenties, I should think.'

Over twenty-five years. Chrissie started to relax slightly. Well, at least that meant that there could have been no youthful relationship between Guy and Jenny, the embers continuing to smoulder throughout Jenny's marriage. But she still couldn't entirely relax.

'And they've always been happy together, have they?' she probed.

Guy frowned as he turned his head towards Chrissie. What on earth had made her ask that particular question and how the hell should he answer it?

The truth was that Jon and Jenny's marriage *had* gone through a bad patch at one time and he... His frown deepened.

The relationship between him and Jenny had never been anything other than that of business partners and good friends, but... But there had been a time when he had wanted it to be more, he acknowledged inwardly. There had, in fact, been a time when he had been ready and willing—more than willing, if he was being honest—to encourage Jenny to leave Jon...when he had actively wanted her to do so. Fortunately and wisely, Jenny had never allowed either of them to cross the fine line that divided the safety of friendship from the danger of...something else.

There was no logical reason why he couldn't tell Chrissie any of this. But how would she react to the knowledge that he had once come very close to wanting Jenny to break her marriage vows, to convincing himself that the emptiness he had been beginning to sense in his life at that time might be filled by her; that her vulnerability and need had aroused within him a protective and very masculine desire to shelter and take care of her and to convince both himself and her that those emotions could be transmuted into something they could both call love.

Surely it was sufficient for *him* to know that he had been wrong and that thankfully Jenny had known that and prevented them both from making what he now knew would have been a bad mistake.

He would eventually, of course, tell Chrissie about Jenny and about his own awareness of how emotionally vulnerable he had been at that time. And he could tell her then, too, how glad he was at the same time that she was the only woman he had ever and could ever want to make a formal lifelong commitment to. That now that there *was* love, that now that he *did* love, he could recognise the vast gulf, the huge difference, that existed between it and what he had believed he felt for Jenny.

Yes, he would tell Chrissie all of that later when their own relationship was far more firmly established. For now, he mentally crossed his fingers behind his back and assured himself that he was doing the right thing. Smiling at her, he replied, 'Yes, so far as I know, they've always been extremely happy together.'

She had the reassurance she needed, so why did she feel that Guy was keeping something from her? Withholding something from her? Chrissie wondered.

'We *can't* go on like this,' Guy was telling her groaningly less than an hour later as they lay together on his bed, Guy's hand resting possessively and tenderly on her body as he kissed her gently in the aftermath of their passionate lovemaking. 'I wanted to keep you to myself for just a little while longer before we went public but…'

'What are you trying to say?' Chrissie asked him, but from the excited way her heart was racing, she suspected she already knew.

'We could fly to Amsterdam tomorrow,' Guy told her softly. 'I know a dealer there who specialises in antique jewellery, or if you'd prefer something more modern…'

Chrissie's heart leaped into her throat. 'An engagement ring, do you mean?' she whispered.

'An engagement ring and, more importantly, a wedding ring,' Guy affirmed throatily as he bent his head to kiss her.

'We *can't* get married just like that,' Chrissie protested, but the look in her eyes as they met Guy's revealed just how much she would like to. 'My parents…' she began. Guy nodded regretfully and agreed.

'My family will be just as bad. If we don't have a big formal wedding, there'll be no end to the sulks and looks of disapproval.'

'Marriage,' Chrissie said wonderingly, her heart in her eyes as she asked him huskily, 'Are you sure that that's what you want…that I'm what you want?'

'More sure than I've ever been of any other thing in my whole life,' Guy told her solemnly and meant it.

'We can talk about it properly tonight,' Chrissie promised, then reminded him, 'If I don't leave now, I'm going to be late for my appointment with Jon Crighton.'

'Tonight,' Guy agreed. 'Tonight we'll make our real

vows to one another, our real promises…our real plans. It'll be our last chance before we're swamped with offers of bridesmaids and wedding cakes.'

Chrissie laughed, leaned forward and then smiled up into his eyes as he drew her closer to him for one last, lingering kiss. She would remember this moment for ever, she promised herself. Remember the smell and feel of him, his warmth, their shared closeness, the almost physical presence of their shared love as it engulfed and cocooned them.

Yes, she would remember it for ever.

CHAPTER FIVE

CHRISSIE saw that Jon Crighton was frowning when he got up from behind his desk and walked across the room to stand in front of the window as he listened to what she had to say.

Jenny's husband had turned out to be a tall, blond-haired man in his fifties whose slight shyness couldn't really conceal the natural warmth of his personality, and now that she had met him she felt oddly reassured that Guy had spoken the truth when he said that Jon and Jenny had a good marriage.

'My parents, my mother, would like to have a list of Uncle Charles's debts, especially the names of those people he personally owed money to,' Chrissie told Jon, watching as his frown deepened.

'There's no legal responsibility on her part to meet such debts,' Jon began, but Chrissie shook her head and interrupted him.

'My mother and her brother were never close. I barely knew him and there was a problem, a quarrel, within the family, which meant... But still my mother feels very strongly that she doesn't want other people to suffer financially because they...because they trusted her brother perhaps unwisely. She has a very strong sense of family,' Chrissie explained quietly to Jon. 'And an equally strong sense of moral responsibility.' She took another deep breath and plunged on. 'She knows, *we* know, that her brother was not always...honest in his dealings with other people.' She paused and looked at Jon.

'No,' Jon agreed calmly. 'He wasn't, and I have to be truthful, there are some people to whom he owed money who will not be repaid out of what there is left of an estate, who are financially in straitened circumstances themselves.' Jon paused, mentally reflecting on the wide differences that could exist between two members of the same family. He was no stranger to this state of affairs; he thought of his own brother David and himself. 'Your mother need have no fears that either she or her parents are remembered locally with anything other than very great fondness and respect,' he told Chrissie gently, adding, 'Your grandmother, in particular, was very well known locally for her generosity to a number of charities, both financially and through the voluntary work she did.'

'It's a family tradition my mother has continued,' Chrissie informed him, going on to explain to him a little of her parents' current way of life and the reasons why neither of them could be in Haslewich. 'To be truthful, I'm rather glad that my mother didn't come. The impression I've had from...from certain people is that my uncle wasn't particularly well liked.'

'No, I'm afraid he wasn't,' Jon agreed after a telling but brief moment of hesitation. 'He was a drinker and like all those who suffer from any kind of addiction, when he was in the grip of it, nothing and no one else mattered.'

'I understand what you're saying,' Chrissie returned quietly. 'And my mother...' She stopped and shook her head. It was obvious that Jon was well aware of what the situation was and she was thankful that there was no need for her to explain to him what manner of man her late uncle had been.

'There's no need for your mother to feel that her presence in Haslewich wouldn't be welcomed or that she will in any way be held responsible for her late brother's behaviour. There are very few families who can't count at least one black sheep amongst their number,' he added with a wry smile that warmed Chrissie's heart.

'I think my mother would *like* to come back. She often talks about the farm.'

Jon Crighton was an extremely likeable man, Chrissie reflected, all the more so because one could somehow sense that at heart he was basically a sincere and self-effacing person, one who would draw other people and their problems to him. He went on to tell her that he would do his best to expedite all the legal matters with regard to supplying her parents with a list of her late uncle's creditors.

'Although,' he added a touch hesitantly, 'from what I gather from my wife, it seems that you are not in any particular hurry to leave Haslewich.'

To her chagrin, Chrissie discovered that she was blushing as well as smiling as she made some inarticulate response to Jon's gentle teasing.

Half an hour later, their meeting concluded, Jon watched her as she walked across the town square. She was an attractive and pleasant self-possessed young woman and he could well understand why Guy Cooke should be 'smitten' with her as Jenny had claimed.

'Oh good, you're on your own.'

The sound of his wife's voice from the open doorway of his office had him turning round to welcome her. 'I thought when you phoned earlier you were going to be tied up for the day at Fitzburgh Place with the fair,' he commented.

'I was, but I decided to give myself a break, come home early and then perhaps go back later this evening. Is there any chance that you might be free to take me somewhere rather nice like the Grosvenor for afternoon tea?' she suggested.

'Mmm…' Jon pretended to give the matter some serious consideration before offering, 'I'm not so sure about the Grosvenor. We'd have to drive over to Chester and then back again, but there *is* this rather special little place I know where we could be all alone and where, if we're very lucky, we might be able to share rather more than afternoon tea.'

Jenny looked at her husband suspiciously. 'If you mean what I think you mean,' she began warningly, 'you're going to be out of luck. For one thing, I haven't been out shopping and we don't have a thing to eat other than last night's leftovers and for another…' She continued, overriding Jon's attempt to break in.

'I don't mind passing on the food,' he murmured.

'Jack and Joss will be at home.'

'Ah,' Jon sighed at this mention of the boys. Joss was his younger son and Jack was Jon's brother David's child. He had been living with Jon and Jenny since the breakup of his own parents' marriage.

Jack's married sister, Olivia, and her husband, Caspar, and their two young children lived close by and it had been Jack's own wish that he live with his aunt and uncle.

'Whom are you watching with such interest?' Jenny asked, walking over to the window to look through it. 'Ah…Guy's lady love. I'd forgotten she was coming to see you.'

'Mmm…she's nice. I liked her, and from what she's been telling me, her mother is nothing like her late brother. It seems that her mother and her uncle never really got on, but despite that, her parents apparently want to have a list of Charlie's main creditors so that they can pay off his debts.'

'That's very generous of them.'

'Very,' Jon agreed.

'But why has *she* come to Haslewich to deal with things and not her mother?'

'I rather suspect from what she didn't say that her mother, obviously knowing her late brother, feels that the residents of Haslewich might not make her very welcome, but as I pointed out to Chrissie, every family has its black sheep, and sometimes more than one of them, as we know all too well.'

Jenny looked up at him. 'I *do* wish David would get in touch with your father. It would mean so much to him, and apart from that card he sent at Christmas, he hasn't contacted Ben at all.'

'I know,' Jon agreed, placing his hand on his wife's shoulder and drawing her in against his body. 'Dad's Christmas card had a Spanish postmark, but David seems determined to keep his actual whereabouts a secret.'

'Perhaps it's for the best,' Jenny suggested, looking up at her husband. 'After all, if he *did* come back, what could he do? He couldn't come back to work here…not after…'

'No, he certainly couldn't do that,' Jon concurred sombrely.

'Do you still miss him?' Jenny asked gently. The brothers *were* twins, even if…

Jon shook his head. 'No, not really, not in a personal sense. But I do wish for Dad's sake that things could be different. He's been a changed man since David left.'

'He's getting old, Jon,' Jenny commiserated.

'Aren't we all?' Jon grimaced, thinking of the changes that the past few years had brought. Since that fateful night of the brothers' shared fiftieth birthday party and David's near fatal heart attack, both of them had become grandfathers, he through his son, Max, who was now married with two children and David through his daughter, Olivia, but whilst *he* saw his grandchildren regularly and enjoyed their company, he doubted that David even knew of his grandchildren's existence.

'Olivia was telling me the other day that Tiggy has decided that she wants to divorce David,' Jenny commented.

'Yes, I know,' Jon agreed. 'In fact, Olivia and I were discussing it only the other day. Tiggy's new man wants to marry her and he's pressing her to do something about ending her marriage to David.'

Jenny looked at her husband, unable to stop herself from asking, 'Do you…?' She bit her lip, wondering if it was wise to remind Jon that there had been a time when, if only fleetingly, *he* had been tempted to break his own marriage vows over his twin brother's wife, just as she had, oh so briefly, been tempted to respond to Guy's need for her.

But Jon, it seemed, had read her mind because he immediately shook his head and took hold of both her hands as he told her quietly, 'The only regret I have is that I was ever foolish enough to risk losing you,' he admitted truthfully.

'Oh, Jon,' Jenny whispered as she went into his arms and leaned her head against his chest. 'I do hope that everything works out for Guy with Chrissie. He's head over heels in love with her…'

'And she with him if the way she looked this afternoon when I mentioned his name is anything to go by,' Jon assured her.

'Well, she certainly looked as though she loved him when I saw them together, but…' Jenny nibbled at her bottom lip.

'But what?' Jon gave her a rueful look. 'Do I detect just a hint of the protective mother sheep anxious for her vulnerable little lamb there?' he asked her.

Jenny shook her head and grimaced. 'All right,' she agreed apologetically, 'perhaps I *am* being overly anxious and Guy is far too masculine to ever be called a lamb type but, well, they've known each other such a short time and if you'd seen the way Guy was looking at her…'

'You said yourself at Christmas that you'd like to see him married with children of his own.'

'Yes. I would, I do,' Jenny concurred. 'You're right.' She laughed. 'I admit it, I *am* being overprotective and Chrissie seems as head over heels in love with him as he is with her.'

She put her hand through Jon's and snuggled up to him, returning the loving look he was giving her as he looked down at her.

'Hello there…'

Chrissie gave a small start and then smiled as she realised that the woman addressing her in the street was Guy's sister.

She had another woman with her, some years younger than she was herself and who, Chrissie suspected from her rather strikingly handsome face and thick, dark curly hair, was probably another member of the family.

'I enjoyed meeting you last night,' Frances commented with another smile before turning to introduce her companion, explaining, 'Guy brought Chrissie over for dinner last night.' She looked at Chrissie. 'Natalie is another member of the Cooke clan.'

'Do you know Guy well?' Natalie asked abruptly, ignoring Chrissie's outstretched hand and frowning rather fiercely at her as she waited for a response.

Her glowering intensity made Chrissie feel uncomfortable and unsure of just how she ought to answer, but before she could say anything, Frances was replying for her, looking at Chrissie with teasing warmth as she informed Natalie, 'Not as well as Guy intends to make sure she *does* know him, if the way he was looking at her last night is anything to go by.'

'Oh, it's like that, is it?' Natalie responded disparagingly, flicking a disdainful and dismissive glance in Chrissie's direction. 'Well, Guy is always falling in love—and out of it even faster. He's a dreadful flirt.'

'Natalie,' Frances objected, frowning at her companion and giving Chrissie a rueful look.

'Well, it's the truth,' Natalie continued, ignoring the warning Frances was trying to give her. 'Guy's always been susceptible to a certain type of woman and, of course, we all know how he was over Jenny Crighton.'

'Natalie,' Frances protested rather more sharply.

'I'm not lying,' Natalie insisted with a scornful toss of her head. 'Guy can be a lovesick fool at times. Look, I've got to go,' she said, ignoring Chrissie completely as she bent to brush Frances's cheek with her lips and then turned on her heel to walk away.

'I'm sorry about that,' Frances apologised uncomfortably after she had gone. 'Natalie doesn't always realise…she's…' She glanced unhappily into Chrissie's pale, set face and sighed.

Natalie could be the limit at times. As a family, they were used to her disruptiveness and her acid remarks. She was and always had been the kind of person who enjoyed hurting and discomforting others. Frances tried to tell herself it was because at heart Natalie felt insecure herself rather than because she possessed a mean and spiteful nature, but sometimes Frances did wonder.

And, of course, it didn't help that the whole family

knew that Natalie had had a bit of a thing about Guy for years. Not that he had ever been remotely interested in her in that way. She simply wasn't his type. Guy had a distinctly chivalrous, protective side to his nature that instinctively drew him towards the kind of femininely gentle woman whom he could take under his wing and protect. Even if she had been his type physically, which she wasn't, Natalie's personality was far too brash and abrasive ever to appeal to Guy. But family loyalty and the sheer complexity of the situation prevented Frances from explaining things to Chrissie. She would, however, have to go and alert Guy as to what had happened as it was quite plain that Natalie's remarks had upset Chrissie.

'I'm not sure how long you're going to be staying in town,' she said gently to Chrissie now, 'but it's rather fortunate that I've bumped into you like this because I *was* planning to get in touch with you to ask you round for a meal. I don't know how much Guy has told you about our family, but it's rather a tradition for us that we all get together one Sunday in the month. Because so many of us work in the pub or catering trade in one way or another, getting time off together isn't always easy, so we take it in turns to host our monthly Sundays. It's my turn this month and we'd love it if you could join us.'

'Thank you, you're very kind,' Chrissie replied in a slightly stilted voice.

She wasn't so naïve as not to have been aware that Natalie had been slightly malicious in talking about Guy the way she had, but Chrissie had seen, too, how Frances had reacted to the other woman's comments and had sensed that there was just enough truth, specifically in what Natalie had said about Jenny Crighton, for Frances to feel uncomfortable.

Guy was bound to have had other relationships in his life, Chrissie realised, but *why* hadn't he been truthful and honest with her about his relationship with Jenny Crighton instead of concealing it from her? 'Guy is always falling in love—and out of—it,' Natalie had said scornfully.

Five minutes later, retracing her steps towards her late uncle's small house, she was forced to ask herself how much she really knew about Guy.

A stiff, chilly wind had risen whilst she was in Jon Crighton's office and several ominous grey clouds were now obscuring the sun, warning her that she had been too trusting and optimistic in coming out wearing just a thin cotton dress. Just as she had been too trusting in believing Guy?

Chrissie looked a little apprehensively at her watch. Another hour and Guy would be here. The bright, sunny promise of the morning had given way to a cold, wet evening. The cottage, without the benefit of central heating, felt cold and smelt damp, and for the first time since she had arrived in Haslewich she was conscious of a feeling of alienation and loneliness.

It didn't help that her parents would now be well on their way on the first leg of their trip to Mexico and that she was unable to even pick up the phone and hear the comforting sound of a familiar and loving voice.

But surely she had all the comfort and love she needed here with Guy. *Guy*, the man whom only this morning she'd been making plans to spend the rest of her life with. *Guy*, the man who suddenly in the space of a brief conversation had become almost a stranger to her.

She was being silly, she warned herself. There was bound to be a simple explanation for Guy's omission in telling her about Jenny Crighton. All she had to do was to ask him for it.

Guy was just leaving the local delicatessen with the purchases he had made for his supper with Chrissie when he saw Jon and Jenny crossing the square.

'Mmm…you've been in Lawfords,' Jenny commented enviously when she saw what he was carrying. 'Lucky you, their food is wonderful but a little bit pricey when you've got two hungry teenage boys to feed. No need for me to ask whom *you're* planning to share your feast with,' she added teasingly.

'No need at all,' Guy agreed dryly.

'Chrissie seems a lovely girl, Guy,' Jenny remarked warmly. 'But I can understand why she feels a little bit wary about going public with the fact that Charlie was her uncle. Of course, the family virtually disowned him years ago, we all know that. Oh, and by the way, you'll never guess what. The police apparently suspect that there may be a woman involved with the gang who've been doing the break-ins locally.'

Jenny saw the way Guy was frowning and shook her head.

'It sounds odd, I know, but it seems it's often easier for a woman to get inside a target house and check to see what's there that's worth stealing. She then passes this information on to the rest of the gang.

'Heavens, is that the time!' she exclaimed as the church clock chimed the hour. 'We'd better go. Enjoy your dinner party.'

Guy was still frowning as he watched Jon and Jenny walk away. Chrissie was Charlie Platt's *niece*? Then *why* hadn't she told him so? *Why* had she deliberately concealed the relationship from him and given him to believe that she was simply *acting* for the family, rather than being a closely related member of it?

He could remember quite vividly how, when he was a child, Charlie used to lie to him and pretend that he wanted to be his friend, that his malicious and cruel bullying of him had simply been a mistake. Guy could remember, too, how Charlie had taunted him when he had fallen for his lies and believed him. The wariness and cynicism, the hardness he had begun to develop as a means of protecting himself from the likes of Charlie Platt had stood him in good stead as an antiques dealer. It was a business where it paid to be cautious and a little bit suspicious at times, to thoroughly check the owner-ship of goods offered to him for sale rather than to au-tomatically assume that the would-be seller had the right to dispose of them, but it had simply never occurred to him to be suspicious or wary where *Chrissie* was concerned.

He had taken her completely on trust, believed her every word utterly, and he had never even thought of questioning or doubting her. His response to her had been so immediate, so intense, so emotional, that it had left no room for logic or rational thinking.

But she had obviously not felt the same, had she?

Otherwise it would never have occurred to her to withhold from him the fact that she was Charlie's niece.

To withhold from him. He grimaced to himself, his face suddenly bleak and cold.

Even now, he was *still* trying to make excuses for her. She hadn't simply *withheld* the truth from him; she had deliberately deceived him. There had been plenty of opportunity for her to tell him the truth, to explain to him just what her real relationship with Charlie was.

But her deceit seemed so out of character for her. One of the things that had struck him most forcibly about her had been her naturalness, her openness, her warmth, but quite plainly they were only illusory…manufactured.

As he crossed the square and headed for his own home, he tried to reason with himself that he was over-reacting, that he was judging her, condemning her, without allowing her a fair hearing. There could, after all, be some perfectly logical explanation of *why* she hadn't told him the truth.

Such as? the more cynical side of his nature demanded harshly.

A simple case of forgetfulness. Oh, by the way, I forgot. Charlie Platt was actually my uncle.

He shook his head, mentally deriding himself and in the fashion of his teenage nieces and nephews adding a sardonic *Not*.

By the time he had returned to his house, the shock of Jenny's unintentional revelation was beginning to subside enough for him to pause and respond politely to Ruth's comments about the attractive display of flowers in his small front garden.

Ruth lived a few doors away from him and he knew her both via her charity work and through her relationship with Jenny.

She was an elegantly attractive woman who still bloomed with the joy of rediscovering and marrying the man she had originally fallen in love with as a young girl. And if these days her life and her world was a rather more cosmopolitan one than that of a small Cheshire country town, with six months of the year spent in America with her new husband and their daughter and family and six months back home in Haslewich, she was still very much the extraordinarily warm and perceptive person she had always been.

'I can't take any credit for them,' Guy admitted in response to her comment about his garden. 'Unlike you, I'm afraid my fingers are not particularly green and I have to rely on Bernard to ensure my garden doesn't let the close down.'

Bernard Philips was yet another member of the extended Cooke clan, a second cousin of Guy's, who together with his two sons and his daughter had built up a local garden centre business—a business that Guy, in true entrepreneurial fashion, had yet another small investment in.

It was not for nothing that certain members of his family teasingly nicknamed him 'The Banker'.

He had a reputation amongst his family and friends, he knew, as a shrewd and astute businessman, and it had only been the previous Christmas that his sisters had been teasing him about the fact that he was too logical, too keen to weigh up the pros and cons to ever allow himself to fall deeply in love. And until he had met Chrissie, he had been inclined to share that belief.

Chrissie… Perhaps it would have been better if he had never met her, he decided savagely after he'd said goodbye to Ruth and let himself into his house.

Which was she really? The open, warm soul mate he had believed he had found, or someone very different?

Was *she* at fault for deceiving him or was *he* simply a fool for having deceived himself, for having credited her with virtues and attributes she simply didn't possess?

Had *he* imposed on her his own idealised version of her, lifting what was really merely an earthy lust into the realm of something more spiritual and divine?

Half an hour later, having abandoned his half-hearted preparations for their supper, he acknowledged that the only way he was going to discover the truth was by asking Chrissie outright why she had not told him about her relationship with Charlie Platt.

CHAPTER SIX

DESPITE the thorough cleaning she had given it, her late uncle's house still had that faintly musty smell she associated with neglect and decay, Chrissie acknowledged, wrinkling her nose slightly.

The old sheet she had thrown over the desk to protect it had slipped off, and as she went to replace it, she paused, studying the desk affectionately. She could well understand why her mother wanted to buy it from the estate.

It possessed a warmth and sturdiness that encouraged one to reach out and stroke the wood and Chrissie smiled a little to herself as she did so.

She was no expert but she doubted that the desk would prove to be very expensive. It would be her mother's birthday in two months' time and she was tempted to buy it herself and give it to her mother as a birthday present.

She was still smiling at the thought of her mother's pleasure when Guy knocked on the front door.

Quickly she went to let him in and was taken aback when she saw that he was frowning and that instead of moving to take her in his arms as she had been expecting, he actually seemed to move away from her as though he wanted to put some distance between them.

Natalie's contemptuous earlier comments ran through her brain and she hesitated uncertainly. Outside, the temperature had dropped and Chrissie felt a chill in the air inside the cottage. Shivering slightly, she turned to get her coat. The door to the small front sitting room was still open, and as she retrieved her coat from the hall chair where she had left it, she saw Guy freeze as he looked into the room.

'What is it…what's wrong?' she asked him anxiously.

'What's that desk doing here?' Guy demanded harshly.

Chrissie frowned as she heard the sharp accusatory note in his voice, her heart sinking.

'I'm waiting to get it valued. It belonged to…' She stopped and bit her lip. Guy was looking at her in a most peculiar way.

'Do go on,' he told her mock-gently. 'Or shall *I* say it for you? It belonged to Charlie Platt, better known locally as, at best, a con man and, at worst, a thief. A man who by no stretch of the imagination could ever legally or rightfully be the owner of *that* particular piece of furniture.'

'A con man!'

Chrissie went pale as she heard the pent-up fury in Guy's voice. She had known all along that he hadn't liked her uncle, had guessed it, sensed it, from all that he had not said about him rather than from what she'd heard, but the venom and bitterness she could now hear—see—in him seemed so totally out of character, so much the complete opposite from the tender, adoring lover who had left her only hours before that she could only stare at him in shocked bewilderment.

'But then, *you* probably know all this already, don't you, Chrissie? Which is why you've taken such good care to conceal this desk from me…just as you've also concealed from me the fact that Charlie Platt was your uncle.'

'No!' Chrissie protested.

'No? No what?' Guy demanded savagely. 'No, he wasn't your uncle?'

Chrissie bit her lip. She was in too much of a state of shock to speak or defend herself.

She had known, of course, that sooner or later she was going to have to tell Guy who she was. And if she was honest, she had perhaps put off telling him longer than she ought, but she had never dreamt he would react like this, *accuse* her like this. Look at her as though…as though he found her utterly and completely beneath his contempt, a creature so, so far beneath him that he could hardly even bear to look at her.

'I…I *was* going to tell you…I *wanted* to tell you,' she protested huskily, 'but—'

'Of course you did,' Guy interrupted with silky-smooth dislike.

'There hasn't been time…everything happened so quickly,' Chrissie told him doggedly, still trying to make him understand, to stop him before he ruined, destroyed, everything between them.

'Yes…too quickly for you to have time to get rid of this, I assume you mean,' Guy accused her grittily, giving a brief nod in the direction of the desk. 'I always knew Charlie wasn't too fussy about how he earned his drinking money, but I never realised he'd turned to fencing stolen property—'

'*Stolen*!' Chrissie exploded indignantly. 'That desk wasn't stolen. It belonged to my great-grandmother, my—'

'*That* desk,' Guy cut across her curtly, his mouth compressing as he carefully spaced out every word, 'was *stolen* less than a fortnight ago from Queensmead. I'd know it anywhere, even without having seen the description the police have circulated. I appraised it for Ben Crighton—not that it has much commercial value. It's a copy of the French original,' he told her coldly, 'and as a copy isn't worth a tenth of the original.'

'You're lying,' Chrissie declared, her own shock and anguish giving way to an anger intense enough to match his own.

Just what was he trying to accuse her of doing? Just *what* was he trying to imply? She had her mother's word that the desk had belonged to *her* grandmother and she would take her mother's word against anyone's— *anyone's*—any day of the week.

'*I'm* lying…?' For a moment, the rage she could see in Guy's taut face and clenched fists was such that Chrissie automatically took a step back from him, her face going scarlet with mortification as he told her icily, 'I don't hit women. Not even a woman like you.'

A woman like her!

'How much more stolen stuff did he have stashed here, I wonder, and where is it now? I'm sure that's a question the police would be very interested in hearing the answer to.'

The police! Chrissie's heart gave a frightened bound but she wasn't going to let him panic or terrorise her. Why *should* she? She had done nothing wrong and neither, in this instance, had her late uncle. The desk belonged to their family and Guy had simply mistaken it for the one stolen from Queensmead. He had to have done.

As they confronted one another across the narrow width of the small hallway, Chrissie found it hard to believe that just a matter of hours ago they had been lying in one another's arms promising eternal fidelity and love, discussing the future they hoped to share together.

She wasn't sure if she wanted to laugh or cry. Possibly both. How *could* she have been such a fool? It was obvious to her now that Guy was dangerously volatile and untrustworthy where his relationships were concerned. How many other women had he treated… deceived…the way he had done her? Had he come here this evening looking for an excuse to quarrel with her, blame *her* for the fact that he had fallen out of love with her?

Love! He didn't begin to know the meaning of the word. But she did. Oh yes, she did, because, despite the pain he was now causing her, she knew perfectly well that if he was to turn to her, take her in his arms, beg her forgiveness, say it was all a mistake and it was just the shock of discovering she was Charlie's niece that had made him behave so cruelly, react so badly, she would want to accept his apology.

But one look at his face told her that he was going to do no such thing and rather than risk losing face by allowing him to see how much he was hurting her, how difficult she was finding it to distance and detach herself from him and all that they had shared, she drew herself up to her full height and told him quietly, 'I think, in the circumstances, you had better leave.'

'Do you know something?' Guy responded sarcastically. '*I* think you could be right. My God,' he added, shaking his head as he turned back towards the front door, 'you really had me fooled, do you know that? If Jenny hadn't let it slip that you were Charlie's niece—'

'I would have told you about that,' Chrissie said proudly. 'In fact, it was only because you were so antagonistic towards him that I—'

'You *lied* to me,' Guy interrupted coldly.

'Just as *you* lied to me when I asked you about Jenny,' Chrissie challenged him.

She wasn't going to let him have things all his own way, she decided. Why should she?

'I met your sister in town this afternoon. She had one of your relatives with her. It seems that you've got rather a reputation as an unreliable and fickle lover,' she told him with a bitter little smile. 'Pity I didn't hear about it *before* we met.'

He looked so angry that Chrissie's courage almost failed her. But why *should* she let him be the one making all the accusations?

Yes, she had been wrong not to tell him about Uncle Charles but at least she had not concealed important facts about her sexual and emotional history from him.

No wonder he had been such…such an experienced lover, she decided, summoning all the mental cynicism and self-protection she could whilst fighting to suppress the aching weight of her inner anguish and heartbreak.

'I don't know what you've heard or from whom,' Guy returned bleakly, 'nor do I really care. What I felt for Jenny was a private and personal thing and at no time did Jenny reciprocate my feelings or waver from her love for Jon.'

'Well, you would say that, wouldn't you?' Chrissie sneered with deliberately calculated nastiness.

'You bitch!' Guy snarled as he wrenched open the front door and stormed through it.

The cottage was already more than damp enough without her adding to its mildewy atmosphere with her tears, Chrissie remonstrated with herself well over an hour later when the now-silent tears of loss and pain were still trickling hopelessly down her face to betray her each time she thought she had them under control.

Instead, to keep her hands if not her mind occupied, she had spent the evening rescrubbing every inch of the small, old-fashioned kitchen and so much so that her hands now felt as raw and tender as her emotions.

How *could* she ever have been such a fool as to believe Guy when he told her that he loved her? She must have been bemused, bedevilled, besotted. There was no other logical explanation for what had happened—no *logical* explanation at all.

Of course, he hadn't loved her. How could he? He didn't know her. He had probably just been using her to ease the pain of his—according to him, she decided darkly—unrequited love for Jenny. No, of course he hadn't loved her. Just as *she* hadn't loved him. So then, if she hadn't loved him, why on earth was she behaving like a tragedy queen, wringing her hands and crying, yes, *crying* foolish tears into a silent house? She ought to be feeling grateful that she had discovered so quickly just what he was.

All those unbelievable lies he had told her about wanting to take her to Amsterdam to buy her an engagement ring. Yes, she was far, far better off without him, she decided.

After he left Chrissie, Guy didn't go straight home. How could he? For the first time since he had left his young manhood behind him, he knew what it was to feel the need to expel his pent-up emotions via some act of physical violence, albeit not against another human being and not even against himself. However, he admitted grimly, right now he could see a lot of virtue in being able to hit some inanimate object very hard. Very, very hard.

He frowned as he suddenly realised that his fast-paced walk through the town had inadvertently brought him to his old junior school—the scene of his long-ago childhood fear of Charlie Platt and the bullying and attempted blackmail Charlie had inflicted on him there.

'I *was* going to tell you,' Chrissie had cried defensively when he had confronted her with the truth. But why should he believe her, how could he believe her, especially after he had seen that damned desk? And *she* had had the effrontery to pretend that it belonged to her family.

There had been a moment when he had seen the look in her eyes, that had made him doubt… wonder…but then she had thrown that accusation at him about his supposed reputation and followed it up with that even more contemptuous comment about Jenny.

He stared across the empty playground, mentally reliving their quarrel. His anger had gone now, leaving him feeling flat and drained, empty and disillusioned.

He should have listened to that small warning voice that had urged him to be more cautious instead of… But the damage was done now. His love for Jenny had been a slow-growing, gentle emotion that he had lived with for a long time and one that he had come to realise was undoubtedly the result of being too much alone and of recognising in Jenny the type of woman who couldn't help but nurture and support others.

His love for Chrissie had hit him like a bolt out of the blue. It had been an overwhelming force. It had possessed a passion, an intensity, a recklessness that had made him step so far outside his normal character, that at times, when he was with her, he had barely recognised himself. His love for her had…

Had? His mouth twisted with cynical self-mockery as he turned away from the school and started to walk home.

Just who did he think he was kidding? Love… The kind of emotion he had for Chrissie couldn't be wiped out by a mere act of will, no matter how much his pride and self-respect might demand that it was.

Half an hour later when he walked into his comfortable kitchen, the first thing he saw was the supper he had prepared for Chrissie. Grimly he picked up the dishes of mouth-wateringly delicious epicurean delicacies and thrust the whole lot into the garbage.

The vintage bottle of wine he had bought to go with their meal was still on the table. He picked it up, glanced at the garbage and then looked ruefully at the bottle. He couldn't do it. It was too sacrilegious. He had opened the bottle and left the wine to breathe before going out. Absently he poured himself a glass.

It was good, but not even its warm mellowness could ease the harsh, gritty pain he was feeling. He emptied the glass and poured himself another. He had always prided himself on being a good judge of character but tonight he had had proof of just how poor his judgement actually was. He had been utterly and completely taken in by Chrissie.

His wineglass was empty. He frowned as he refilled it. It was pointless now to curse the fate that had brought them together. Better to curse his own folly in being deceived by it and by her. He looked blearily at the wine bottle, now three-quarters empty. There was no point in wasting what was left. Picking up the bottle and his glass, he headed for the stairs.

Guy was dreaming, drawing Chrissie closer to him as he savoured the familiar warmth of her body, frowning as he felt her tense and look back over her shoulder to where another man was watching them.

'Why are you looking at *him*?' he demanded jealously as he watched Charlie Platt smirking at him from the shadow of the school gates. 'You know who he is, don't you?'

'I have to go to him,' Chrissie was protesting as she pulled away from his embrace. Then somehow Charlie was standing next to them, towering over him as he had done when Guy was a little boy, grinning tauntingly at Guy as he took hold of Chrissie's arm.

'You didn't really think it was *you* she wanted, did you?' Charlie challenged, then he and Chrissie were walking away from him and he heard Charlie laughing and saying gloatingly to her, 'Look what I've got for you,' as he showed her the desk that for some reason had manifested itself on the pavement.

'No. You mustn't touch it,' Guy heard himself protest, but Chrissie only laughed.

'Of course I can touch it,' she told Guy. 'It's mine. Charlie gave it to me.'

'No,' Guy denied, the sound of his own raw denial bringing him abruptly out of his dream to sit bolt upright in bed, blinking in the darkness as he tried to shake away the disturbing emotions aroused by his dream.

'Chrissie feels a little bit wary about going public with the fact that Charlie was her uncle,' Jenny had informed him innocently.

'That desk wasn't stolen. It belonged to my great-grandmother,' Chrissie had told him boldly.

'The police suspect that there may be a woman involved with the gang,' Jenny had said.

Guy groaned and rolled over in bed, punching his pillow. Of course Chrissie couldn't be connected with the gang who had broken into Queensmead. He was convinced of it. But twenty-four hours ago he had been equally convinced that she was incapable of any kind of deception or deceit, hadn't he?

Wide awake now, he lay on his back and stared up at

the ceiling. Ridiculously, given what he now knew about her, his body, and not just his body but his emotions, too, literally ached with yearning for her.

He had *never* felt like this about a woman before, no, not even about Jenny. He had been right, then, about one thing: Chrissie was destined to be the one woman he would love. But he had sadly deluded himself about so many others, such as the fact that she shared his feelings.

What was still a mystery to him was the way she had allowed a relationship to develop between them in the first place. Out of boredom? Simply as a means of passing the time whilst she was in Haslewich?

He would have staked his life on the slight hesitation and sexual inexperience she had revealed being genuine and on the belief that she simply wasn't the type to play sexual games.

His head ached from the wine he had drunk and his heart and his body ached even more from the bitter brew Chrissie had given him.

Grimly he closed his eyes, reminding himself that he was not a teenager and that he had responsibilities and duties. Savagely he asked himself if he wanted the whole county to know what a fool he had been.

Guy was just replacing the telephone receiver when he heard his front doorbell ring. Despite the paracetamol he had taken when he woke up, his head still ached appallingly, but that didn't stop his heart giving a short, savage jerk of expectation as he got up and went to open the door. Only, of course, it wasn't Chrissie standing on the other side of it. How could it have been?

That was over and if he had any sense at all he would be thankful that it had ended before he had had the chance to make even more of a fool of himself than he already had.

'Guy, are you all right?' Jenny asked in concern as he waved her in. 'You look dreadful.'

As he stood wincing in the bright sunlight, Guy suspected his expression gave her the answer.

'We've got a bit of a problem with one of the caterers for the fair,' Jenny explained as she followed him into the kitchen. 'I didn't want to disturb you too early. Is Chrissie…?'

'She's not here,' Guy told her abruptly, adding curtly as he kept his back to her, 'It's over between us.'

'Guy.' He could hear the shocked disbelief in Jenny's voice. 'Everyone quarrels,' she sympathized gently, 'and I'm sure—'

'This wasn't a lovers' spat, Jen,' he countered grimly. He turned round. 'Until you mentioned it yesterday, I had no idea that Chrissie was related to Charlie Platt. She'd led me to believe that she was simply acting for the family.'

Jenny frowned. 'Oh, Guy, I'm sorry. I shouldn't have said anything. I never meant…I just assumed you knew.'

'No. I *didn't* know,' Guy contradicted her heavily. 'She lied to me,' he burst out as he started to pace the kitchen, 'and she—'

'Guy, I can understand how shocked you must be…how hurt you must feel,' Jenny told him gently. 'I *know* you never particularly liked Charlie, but have you thought maybe that's *why* Chrissie felt that she couldn't tell you about the relationship?' she counselled him.

Guy looked out of the window. Would Jenny feel as charitably inclined towards Chrissie when she knew about the desk? Somehow he doubted it.

'It isn't just the fact that she kept me in the dark about her connection to Charlie,' he said stiffly. 'There's…there's something else….'

He paused whilst Jenny waited, obviously puzzled.

'Ben's desk is there,' he told Jenny, adding harshly, 'I saw it with my own eyes, Jen. There was no mistaking it. I valued the damn thing for Ben, for God's sake, and I told her so but she still kept claiming that it belonged to *her* family. She obviously knew it didn't belong to Charlie. She had to. For one thing…if you'd seen the rest of the junk he had and for another…'

'Perhaps she does genuinely believe it belonged to Charlie,' Jenny suggested uncertainly.

'*Why*…why *should* she think such a thing when I've already told her that it didn't! I've *told* her, moreover, just who it does belong to.'

'Oh dear,' Jenny commiserated. 'I'm so sorry, Guy. I just don't know what to say. She seemed so nice, so genuine. You two seemed so right for one another. Perhaps if you were to try to talk to her again?'

'What for?' Guy demanded harshly. 'So she could lie to me a *second* time.' He shook his head. 'Anyway, it's too late. I've rung the police to inform them about the desk. I had to, Jenny,' he added quietly when she said nothing. '*You* know that.'

'Yes. I know that,' Jenny agreed unhappily.

'They're calling round for me in half an hour. They want me to go with them to identify the desk.'

'Oh, Guy, I'm so sorry,' Jenny repeated.

'Nowhere near as sorry as I am,' he told her shortly.

They discussed the problem with the caterer and then Jenny announced that she had to leave.

'Jen, you'll keep it to Jon and yourself, won't you?' Guy asked her abruptly. 'What I said about the desk…? At least for now.'

'Yes, of course I will,' she promised him.

'It will all have to come out in the open soon enough. God knows what kind of fool I'm going to look, especially with the family.'

'There *could* be a rational explanation, Guy,' Jenny tried to comfort him, but Guy merely gave a harshly bitter laugh.

'Thanks, Jen. Nice try, but we both know the truth. There's no way that desk could ever have belonged to Chrissie's family. It's a one-off…unique. It was made to order, and while I don't want to be unkind, there is no way that a small-scale farmer like Chrissie's great-grandfather could have afforded, or I suspect, *wanted*, to commission a piece of furniture of that type.

'The only reason the Crightons had it made, according to Ben, was because *his* father felt he had been cheated of his rightful inheritance when the Chester branch of the family refused to hand over the original to him when his mother had promised him that on her death he should have it.'

'Mmm…well, Ben's memory *can* be rather selective when he wants it to be,' Jenny told Guy ruefully. 'As I understand it, there was never any question of Ben's father inheriting the original desk, which is actually one of a *pair* made in France for the twin daughters of the Chester family, and as far as I know, Ben's father had the desk copied more out of pique and a desire to thumb his nose at the Chester branch rather than because the desk should rightfully have been his.'

'A pair. That's interesting. Where are they now?'

'Well, Laurence has one and Henry has the other. They're very pretty…French and a world away from Ben's copy, although none of us would ever dare say as much to him.' Jenny laughed. 'You know how much rivalry Ben feels for the Chester side of the family, and in his eyes, of course, his father could do no wrong, even though from what Ruth's told me, her father was an extremely self-willed and autocratic man. Ben tends to see him through rather rose-tinted spectacles, though, I'm afraid.

'Give Chrissie another chance, Guy,' she advised him, touching his arm lightly.

'I can't, it's too late. Too much has been said and I doubt that she would even want me to. Much as I might be tempted, fool that I am,' he added with dry self-mockery.

Chrissie might not have imbibed the best part of a full bottle of red wine before going to bed, but she had slept just as badly as Guy and for much the same reasons.

It was too late now to regret not telling him the truth about her family connection with Charlie right from the very start. At least that way he could have rejected her there and then, she told herself miserably, instead of waiting until she had fallen deeply and irrevocably in love with him.

If he had *really* loved her, he would have *listened* to her, *let* her explain…*wanted* her to explain, but he hadn't, had he? It had seemed as though he was actually looking for an excuse to end their relationship. Was it because, as she had been warned, he had already fallen out of love with her?

As for his comments, his accusations, about her great-grandmother's desk…

She tensed as she heard the knock on the door, her hopes soaring against all logic and common sense and making it come as even more of a shock to see the police car parked outside the house and the stern-faced police officer standing on the doorstep with Guy standing equally cold-eyed to one side of him.

'Miss Oldham?' the police officer asked her, and when Chrissie nodded her head, he started to step forward, explaining, 'We understand that you have a desk here, which we have reason to believe could be stolen property.'

'Stolen property?' Chrissie darted a furiously indignant look at Guy, who was following the police officer into the hall. 'I do have a desk here,' she agreed with as much dignity as she could, 'but far from being stolen, it is…*was*, in fact, the property of my late great-grandmother.'

'I see. And do you have any proof of this ownership?' the policeman asked.

Of course she hadn't any proof apart from her mother's memories of the desk and her belief that her brother, Charles, had appropriated it at the time of their mother's death.

Unwilling for Guy to hear her being forced to admit

that she couldn't prove ownership of the desk, she lowered her voice as she turned her back on him and replied quietly, 'No, I'm afraid I don't. Only my mother's description of it and her belief that it belonged to her family.'

'I see, and where could we get in touch with your mother, please, miss?'

Chrissie bit her lip. 'I'm afraid you can't, not at the moment. She and my father are away on a business trip. That's why I'm here…because she…they couldn't come.'

'So what you're saying is that at the moment there's no one to corroborate your claim to ownership of the desk?'

'No, I'm afraid there isn't,' Chrissie agreed as evenly as possible. She could feel Guy's attention on her but there was no way she was going to turn round and give him the satisfaction of seeing the shame and despair she knew were in her eyes.

'And your mother…your parents…when will they be available?'

Chrissie bit her lip again. 'Not for quite some time.'

'And you, Mr Cooke, you believe this desk belongs to Mr Ben Crighton?'

'I *know* it belongs to him, Officer,' Guy corrected crisply. 'I valued it myself for him only a few months ago, and as you know, it *was* listed as one of the items stolen when the house was broken into.'

The way both men were looking at her was beginning to make Chrissie feel not just uncomfortable but actually guilty, as well. But she had *nothing* to feel guilty about. At the worst, the *very* worst, her mother had made a mistake and the desk was not the one she remembered, despite the fact that she had been so certain, so positive, in the way she had described it to Chrissie.

'My mother grew up with this desk,' Chrissie announced shakily, 'but if she…if there *has* been a mistake…'

'A mistake?' Guy derided, causing Chrissie to flash him a look of bitter contempt.

'A mistake,' she repeated firmly. 'Then I know she'll be the first to say so,' she told the policeman slowly. 'Until then, all I can do or say is…' She paused, appalled to discover her eyes were filling with tears. Fiercely she blinked them away. The last thing she wanted to do was to break down in front of Guy and let him see how much he had hurt her, how vulnerable he had made her feel.

'Well, I think the best thing we can do now is to have the desk removed until it can be properly identified,' the police officer said diplomatically.

Chrissie gave him a grave-eyed smile as he thanked her for her assistance and turned to leave. Her stomach muscles tensed when she realised that Guy was deliberately hanging back and that he wasn't going to leave with him.

'I had to inform the police about the desk,' he told her quietly once they were alone.

'Yes, I'm sure you did,' Chrissie agreed emotionlessly. And then, before she could stop herself, she burst out passionately, 'I know you think I'm lying, but I'm *not* and neither is my mother. That desk belongs in the family.'

'You weren't so sure of that ten minutes ago,' Guy reminded her pithily.

'My mother would *never* lie,' Chrissie asserted with quiet dignity, her face burning with hot colour as she saw the contemptuous look he was giving her. 'She wouldn't,' she protested heatedly. 'She's not…'

'She's not what?' Guy baited her. 'Not like you?'

Chrissie had had enough. Without thinking, she tried to lash out at him, but he reacted quickly, catching her wrist in mid-air and holding it pinioned behind her.

'My God, you really are a vixen, aren't you?' he breathed. 'Your Uncle Charlie would have been proud of you. Why didn't you tell the truth about him, Chrissie?'

For a moment she thought he genuinely wanted to know, but then just in time she recognised her own foolish weakness.

'If I *told* you, you wouldn't understand,' she informed him proudly.

'No, I dare say I wouldn't,' Guy agreed bitingly, 'but I *do* understand *this*.' Before she could stop him, he had pushed her back against the wall, and still holding her pinioned, he was plundering her mouth with a kiss of such raw savagery that its heat almost physically burned her mouth. Yet unbelievably she was actually responding to it *and* to him, letting him invade her mouth, her senses, her *self*, without even trying to raise the slightest pitiful defence against him. Where was her pride, her respect, her self-esteem and sense of self-preservation?

'I hate you,' she spat at him untruthfully when he finally released her. 'I *hate* you and I *never* want to see you again. *Never*. Do you understand?' But it was too late. Guy had already gone, loudly slamming the door behind him as he left so that the noise drowned out the protest she had made too late.

* * *

Outside in the street, Guy couldn't quite believe what he had done. He had never *ever* behaved towards a woman with such…such brutality before…or ever imagined that he might *want* to. Never guessed that he could want someone so much that he had to disguise and mask his need with the kind of macho display of faked anger that he had always despised.

He had *wanted* to kiss Chrissie…wanted to do far more than merely kiss her, he admitted with a groan. *Still* wanted to. Dear God, when was it all going to end…where was it all going to end?

CHAPTER SEVEN

'CHRISSIE…'

To her chagrin, Chrissie felt her eyes fill with tears she was unable to prevent from spilling over as she heard the gentle concern in Jon's voice.

It had been several weeks since her quarrel with Guy and the only comfort she could offer herself was that since she had now experienced the worst shock that life could possibly give her, things could only get better. But alas not yet. No, she was quite definitely not feeling anything like better yet.

She had arrived for her appointment with Jon ten minutes ago but had found it wholly impossible to concentrate on what he was saying to her about her late uncle's debts. Sorting through her uncle's possessions, finding a new valuer to assess them, and dealing with the assorted paperwork had taken longer than she, or her mother, had ever anticipated.

'I'm so sorry,' she apologised through her tears, accepting the box of tissues he proffered her. 'It's just…'

Jon, who had heard from Jenny what had happened, said nothing. Privately he found it extremely difficult to believe that Chrissie could have had anything to do with the theft.

'I suppose you've heard that the police are still investigating?' Chrissie commented when she had finally stemmed her tears. 'I'd thought about going back home to look in the family albums in the hope that there might be a photograph with the desk in it,' Chrissie admitted, giving a bitter little laugh. 'My mother was so sure,' she told Jon passionately. 'She said that her grandmother really treasured the desk, that she could remember watching her polishing it. She said she could actually remember her crying as she touched it, although she pretended she hadn't been when she saw my mother watching her.'

'Would it help if you were to return home?' Jon suggested gently. 'I could fax you with the details—'

'No,' Chrissie interrupted, shaking her head fiercely. 'If I did that, I would feel other people might think... I don't want anyone to think I'm trying to...escape or run away,' she finished quickly.

Jon gave her a small smile. 'I understand,' he told her simply.

When Chrissie left his office half an hour later, she was beginning to feel uncomfortably sick. She had skipped breakfast this morning and for the previous three mornings, as well, and now although she knew she ought to be hungry, for some reason the mere thought of food was beginning to make her feel extremely unwell. She felt light-headed, too, and oddly dizzy, so dizzy, in fact, that she had to stop walking and reach out to hold on to the railings separating the short cut she had taken through the environs of Haslewich's very grand Norman church from the graveyard that lay beyond it.

She felt most peculiar, Chrissie acknowledged, and she rather thought she ought to just stand where she was for a little while longer before trying to walk back to Uncle Charlie's house.

As she shook her head trying to clear the unfamiliar muzziness that seemed to have semi-paralysed the normally clear-thinking working of her brain, she realised to her consternation that she was standing only yards away from the elegant row of houses of which Guy's was one, but even *that* knowledge didn't give her the strength to move and, if anything, only made her feel worse. Hot tears began to press painfully on the back of her eyes as she fought to control the surge of painful emotions that overwhelmed her.

Ruth was feeling rather irritated with herself. She should have been in America with Grant right now. He had had to fly out there earlier in the week to attend some business meetings and she had planned to go with him, but almost at the last minute she had changed her mind, moved by guilt at the distressingly pathetic vulnerability Ben had displayed following the break-in at Queensmead.

'I *know* he can be stubborn and cantankerous,' she had explained to Grant as she snuggled up blissfully with him in bed. She was ruefully aware as she did so how very much out of character her delight in the physical proximity of her husband and her still-almost honeymoon enjoyment of the pleasures of simply knowing they were going to be sleeping together and that *she* was going to wake up with him there beside her in the morning might seem to those who had known her simply as the unmarried and rather strait-laced maiden aunt of the Crighton family. Indeed, she realised how disapproving some people might be of a woman her age actually enjoying herself in the physical, sexual and emotional sense by being as deeply in love with her husband as a young girl in her twenties. In truth, she herself sometimes wondered if her enjoyment of their new-found discovery of one another *was* quite appropriate in a woman of her mature years, but Grant assured her that it *was*, most certainly.

'But he is my brother,' she had emphasised firmly when Grant tried to kiss her. Then she added more seriously, 'I'm worried about him, Grant. He's aged so much since the break-in, become so vulnerable, and he's got this operation facing him, as well. *Would* you mind if I didn't come with you this time?'

'Of course I damn well mind,' Grant had responded gruffly, 'and of course I understand.'

Predictably, though, Ben was going through one of his awkward phases, refusing to see her or anyone else, so she might just as well have gone with Grant after all. She was missing him quite desperately already and he wasn't due back for another week. Ruth started to frown as something or *someone* on the other side of the walkway from her bedroom window caught her attention.

The poor girl, whoever she was, didn't look very well at all, she decided as she watched Chrissie cling to the railing for support. Concern etching her features, Ruth started to make her way downstairs.

'Hello there. I saw you from my upstairs window,' Ruth announced. 'You don't look very well. Why don't you come inside and sit down for a few minutes?'

Chrissie hadn't heard Ruth approach and so there was no way she could hide her tear-stained face from her. She tried to refuse her kind offer, but Ruth was already taking hold of her and gently but very firmly drawing her in the direction of her open front door.

Feeling too weak to argue or protest, Chrissie wanly allowed Ruth to direct her. She had always been very independent, stubbornly so, her mother had sometimes fondly protested. But, oddly, right now she was actually glad to have someone else taking control and making her decisions for her.

Ruth's house was a few doors down from Guy's, and like his, the hallway and the sitting room beyond it, which she ushered Chrissie into, was furnished with a happy mingling of old and new. Unlike Guy's, though, every polished surface held an obviously precious collection of photographs and family memorabilia. Chrissie tensed as she glanced at one and recognised Jenny and Jon Crighton standing side by side and laughing happily into the camera.

'My nephew, Jon, and his wife,' Ruth told Chrissie with a smile as she saw her looking at it.

'You're a Crighton?' Chrissie asked shakily.

'I was, but not any more,' Ruth answered. 'Do you know Jon and Jenny?'

Chrissie bit her lip. 'Sort of. Jon is acting for…for my mother in the estate of her late brother, Charles Platt,' she informed Ruth, defiantly lifting her head and looking her straight in the eye. 'I'm Chrissie Oldham,' she added with deliberate emphasis, 'and Charles Platt was my uncle. I appreciate that he didn't have a very good reputation locally and if you want me—'

Ruth didn't allow her to go any further.

'*All* of us have relatives, family members, who by choice we'd prefer not to have in our lives,' she told Chrissie calmly, guessing what was coming and unconsciously echoing Jon's comment to Jenny. 'Every family has its black sheep,' she said. 'I can certainly think of a few within my own,' she added cheerfully. But although her comment was deliberately casual, her discreet study of Chrissie's ashen face and tensely nervous fingers wasn't.

She was surely far more distressed than having Charlie Platt as an uncle would warrant. She didn't strike Ruth as a theatrically over-emotional type, but the bleakness Ruth could see in her eyes was beginning to worry her almost as much as her obvious physical vulnerability.

Quickly Ruth came to a decision.

'I'm going to make us both a cup of tea and then you can tell me all about it,' she informed Chrissie with kind firmness.

It had been a long time since anyone, never mind a stranger, had spoken to Chrissie with such determined authority. She was, after all, an adult woman and very much in charge of her own life, or rather she had been. The events of the past few weeks had shown her just how woefully inadequate she actually was when it came to dealing with emotional pain and trauma. She was still, for instance, actually dreaming that Guy had changed his mind; that he regretted the breakup, that he took back all his hurtful remarks and accusations. A dream indeed. But thinking about it was enough to bring a fresh glitter of tears to her eyes whilst Ruth had gone to make the tea.

'Right,' Ruth commanded ten minutes later, having poured them both a cup of fragrantly scented tea. 'Now, let's see. Where were we? Ah yes… You had just told me that Charles Platt was your uncle. He was a rather unsavoury character, I'm afraid,' she told Chrissie briskly. 'But I'm sure you already know that. I knew his mother and indeed his grandmother and your mother, too, although she left Haslewich some time ago, didn't she?'

'Yes,' Chrissie replied. 'She and my father are away travelling on business at the moment, which is why—'

'You are here on their behalf,' Ruth supplied for her.

'Partially,' Chrissie agreed cautiously.

She looked at Ruth and gave a small inner shrug. What was the point in not telling her the truth? Her mother, she knew, would understand, and it would be a relief to get the whole thing off her chest and unburden herself to someone. Painfully Chrissie started to speak.

'Oh dear,' Ruth sympathised when Chrissie eventually finished.

Ruth knew the desk Chrissie had referred to, of course. Her brother, Ben, was particularly attached to it because it had been one of the first pieces of furniture brought into their home by their father when he originally moved into Queensmead, but Ruth guessed that it wasn't so much the true ownership of a mere piece of wood, no matter how pretty, that was causing Chrissie so much distress.

'Have you tried to talk to Guy...explain?' she asked gently.

Chrissie shook her head. 'What's the point? He's already made his own judgement and anyway... They always say you should never put too much trust in passionately intense emotions, don't they, especially when...?' Chrissie took a sip of her tea and abruptly went pale. 'I'm sorry,' she gasped. 'I don't know what's wrong with me. It must be all the stress but I just keep feeling so sick. It can't be anything I've eaten because the mere thought of food makes me feel so horribly ill. I don't understand it. I'm normally so healthy.'

Ruth studied her thoughtfully. She had her own opinion of what could and could not make an otherwise patently healthy young woman unable to tolerate the thought of food and experience unfamiliar nausea. She had, after all, gone through the same experience herself, and as if that wasn't enough, the charity she had helped set up and still ran to provide emotional and practical support and care for single pregnant women had taught her to recognise perhaps earlier than most the tell-tale signs that suggested a woman might be pregnant.

'I don't want to interfere,' she began carefully, 'but...'

Ruth believed in plain speaking and being truthful and so she said quite simply, 'I may be way off course, but has it occurred to you that you might be pregnant?'

'No!' Chrissie gasped but even as she made the denial she knew that Ruth could well be right.

Was it really less than a couple of hours ago that she had been telling herself that she had faced the worst that life could possibly throw at her? Now, after listening to Ruth, she knew that she had been wrong. There could be worse. There *was* worse. Pregnant and with Guy's baby. How *could* this have happened to her?

Did she really need to ask herself that? After the passion and intensity with which she and Guy had made love, the wonder would have been in her not conceiving.

'I'm afraid I've given you a shock,' Ruth said gently, adding, 'I do know what it's like. I've been there myself.' She smiled as she saw Chrissie's disbelieving look. 'It was a long time ago, of course, and in a completely different climate. I felt I had to give my baby up for adoption.'

'Oh no, how awful,' Chrissie protested, unwittingly betraying to Ruth that already, even though *she* didn't know, Chrissie was going to be a fiercely protective and caring mother.

'Well, yes, it was, but I was lucky. Life gave me a second chance and my daughter…our daughter, is now very much a part of my and Grant's life,' she acknowledged. 'I know all this must be a shock for you, but you *are* going to have to tell Guy, you know.'

'No.' Chrissie's response was emphatic. 'It's nothing to do with him…and besides, he wouldn't want to know anyway.'

Ruth's eyebrows rose. 'Are you sure about that?' she queried. 'I *know* Guy, have known him ever since he was a little boy, and I think you'll find that he'll take his responsibilities towards his child *very* seriously.'

'But the baby wasn't planned. It was an *accident*,'

Chrissie started to tell her. 'I don't need his help…or his sense of responsibility. I can manage on my own. This is *my* baby.'

Ruth listened sympathetically. How well she recognised *that* stubborn female pride and how well she recognised, too, all the heartache that went with it, not just for Chrissie, but for her child, as well, but wisely she only advised Chrissie, saying, 'We have a very good medical centre here in town with a doctor who specialises in gynaecological matters. It might be wise to make an appointment.'

'Yes, thank you, I will,' Chrissie affirmed stiffly, accepting the slip of paper Ruth handed her once she had written the doctor's name and address down on it.

Half an hour later, having given in to Ruth's persuasion to eat some dry toast and have a fresh cup of tea, she stepped a little shakily through Ruth's front door and out into the street, having thanked her not just for her hospitality but for her kindness, as well. Pregnant with Guy's baby. She might not want to believe it, but instinctively she knew that it was true.

Now what was she going to do? What was she going to tell her parents who, although broad-minded and very loving, were bound to be a little disconcerted to discover that they were soon to be grandparents. Wearily Chrissie closed her eyes, reminding herself that other women with far less supportive parents and fewer earning skills than her somehow managed and so would she.

Guy had had an extremely frustrating day. Lord Astlegh's bailiff had apparently caught one of the catering staff for the fair wandering through a part of the house that was quite definitely off limits. She in turn had claimed that she had simply lost her way and had waxed highly indignant over the bailiff's treatment of her.

'Making out like I was some kind of thief,' she had complained to Guy. 'Just who does he think he is?'

With the fair officially opening in the morning, this kind of complication was the last thing Guy needed, especially when—

He braked hard as he suddenly saw Chrissie emerging from a side street into the road he was driving along. Her head was down and she looked tired and defeated. He had an overwhelming urge to get out of the car and rush over to her to take her in his arms. These few weeks when he had avoided seeing her had been the longest of his life. God, *why* had he had to see that damned desk?

If he hadn't… *Yes*, he had been angry…hurt in many ways, that she had omitted telling him that Charlie was her uncle, but as she had so promptly reminded him, *he* had kept things about his own life from her, as well. Now that he had calmed down, he could appreciate, as Jenny had pointed out to him, that Chrissie had not told him that she was related to Charlie simply because she had been reluctant to create any kind of barrier between them.

'Give Chrissie another chance, Guy,' Jenny had advised him several weeks before. Her words now echoed in his mind.

Head down, Chrissie turned the corner without having seen him. The lights changed. Guy drove through them and then on impulse indicated left to follow

Chrissie. He stopped the car, ignoring the yellow line he was parked on, and loped down the street after her.

As she heard the sound of someone running behind her, Chrissie instinctively came to a halt and turned round, her expression betraying her shock as she realised who it was.

'Guy,' she breathed, unable to stop herself from reacting to his presence.

'Chrissie, are you all right?' Guy asked, frowning as he saw how pale and fragile she was looking.

'Of course I'm all right,' she snapped, starting to turn away from him, suddenly mindful of the pitfalls of her situation, but as she moved away, Guy reached out towards her, accidentally jolting her arm so that she dropped the piece of paper Ruth had given her that she still was holding in her hand.

Immediately she bent down to retrieve it, but Guy moved faster, picking it up and frowning as he recognised the name and address of one of their local doctors.

'If you're not ill, then what are you doing with Dr Jardine's name and address?' he questioned her tersely. 'You certainly don't *look* well.'

'I said I'm perfectly all right,' Chrissie lied through gritted teeth, 'and if you would just give me that back…'

Dr Jardine. Guy's frown deepened. He knew she was one of the doctors at the local practice, and although she was not his own doctor, for some reason the name was starting to ring a bell. Dr Jardine…

He was just about to hand the slip of paper back to Chrissie when he suddenly realised just why the name was so familiar. Dr Jardine was the doctor one of his sisters had seen when she was first having trouble conceiving. Dr Jardine was the practice's gynaecological specialist. *Gynaecological* specialist... *Why* did Chrissie need to see a gynaecologist? What was wrong? She looked so pale, so drawn, so hunted and haunted almost, heartachingly proud at the same time, her hand crossed defensively across her body as though in protection of...

'You're pregnant!' He said the words almost instinctively, intuitively, without pausing to analyse his thoughts before giving voice to them, but he knew the moment he saw Chrissie's face that he was right.

A flash-flood of complex emotions swamped him—shock, pain, joy, anger, pride and love...most of all love.

Chrissie looked away from Guy, compressing her lips, her heart sinking.

'Chrissie,' she heard Guy demanding urgently.

'I don't have anything to say,' Chrissie responded with shaky hauteur.

'So you *are* pregnant,' Guy breathed, 'with *my* baby...*my* child....'

'No,' Chrissie denied vehemently, spurred into action by his words. '*This* baby, if there *is* a baby, has *nothing* whatsoever to do with *you*. This baby is *mine* and only *mine*.'

'I doubt a court of law would take that view,' Guy challenged her harshly, too caught up in emotion to be cautious. He had never had any particular cravings for children, fatherhood—even though he had always got on well enough with his nephews and nieces, so why did he have this intense and atavistic sense of pride, of involvement…of possession almost immediately he discovered that Chrissie was carrying his child?

Chrissie stared at him.

'A court of law?' she protested. 'But—'

'A father has rights,' Guy informed her.

A *father*. Chrissie opened her mouth and then closed it again before declaring bitterly, 'I doubt fatherhood was very much on your mind when you…when I… when we…'

'Was motherhood on yours?' Guy challenged her.

There wasn't anything that Chrissie could say.

'We need to talk,' Guy said tersely, but Chrissie shook her head.

'Leave me alone, Guy,' she told him bitingly, turning her back on him and starting to walk swiftly down the street.

Angrily Guy began to follow her, catching up with her and taking hold of her arm to pull her round to face him.

'Let go of me,' Chrissie demanded furiously.

'Not so long ago you were begging me never to let you go,' Guy reminded her mercilessly.

Chrissie flushed hotly but managed to fight back, telling him cuttingly, 'And you were telling me that you loved me, but we both know…'

She paused and she could feel Guy's grip on her arm tighten slightly as he grated, 'We both know what, Chrissie?'

Chrissie shook her head. She felt tired and weak and cross with herself for wasting her fragile strength on arguing with Guy when her baby needed it so much more.

'My car's just round the corner. I'll take you home,'

Guy commanded grimly. 'Don't argue with me, Chrissie. You look as though you're about to collapse.'

She *felt* it, too, Chrissie acknowledged whilst she mentally berated herself for her weakness in allowing him to dictate her actions to her.

'When did you find out…about the baby?' Guy asked curtly once they were in the car.

'Does it matter?' Chrissie responded wearily, unwilling to tell him that she would probably still be in ignorance about her impending motherhood even now if Ruth hadn't enlightened her.

She closed her eyes. She really did feel quite unwell, and then she opened them again abruptly. This wasn't the way to her uncle's cottage. It wasn't the way to anywhere *she* knew at all.

'Where are you going? Stop the car at once. I want to get out,' she demanded furiously, reaching for the door handle only to discover that Guy had activated the central locking system.

'What are you doing? You have no right to do this!' she cried out. 'You—'

'I have my right as a father to protect the health of my unborn child,' Guy returned determinedly.

Chrissie couldn't find the words to respond. *His* right as a *father*.

She really did feel unwell; the motion of the car wasn't agreeing with her at all.

'Guy, I think I'm going to be sick,' she announced in a small voice.

'Right now?'

Chrissie nodded her head slowly.

Guy showed commendable promptitude and dexterity in stopping the car so swiftly and in refusing to display any male annoyance or distaste she might have expected in her nauseous condition, she decided ten minutes later when she was beginning to feel a little better.

'I want to go home,' she told him plaintively.

'You *need* to go somewhere where you can be looked after,' Guy responded dryly, 'and *that* is exactly where I am taking you. Come on….'

As he led her back to the car, Chrissie told herself that she was a fool for not taking her chance to escape from him whilst she had it, not, she suspected, that he would have let her get very far and she certainly didn't feel well enough physically to even *try* to outrun him.

As they got back in the car and he started the engine, she realised that he was driving away from the town. 'Where are we going?' she demanded again, uncertainly.

'I've just told you,' Guy responded calmly. 'Somewhere you and *our* baby will be looked after.'

Our baby… She wanted to protest that *her* baby had nothing whatsoever to do with him but she was too drained to make the effort. They were in the country now, driving down narrow lanes bounded by high hedges, and then Guy was turning off the main road and into a narrow dirt track, through a farm gate and towards the farm itself.

Chrissie's eyes widened as she saw it. Unable to stop herself, she turned to Guy and exclaimed feebly, 'This was my grandparents' farm….'

'Yes,' Guy affirmed. 'My sister and her husband bought it last year,' he went on to explain. 'It isn't a working farm any more. All the land had been sold off and all that was left was a couple of paddocks. My sister teaches disabled children to ride and so they needed the land for the ponies.'

'Your sister... How many have you got?' she asked him faintly.

'Five,' Guy told her dryly.

'Five!'

'You'll like her.'

'But you can't drive up and expect her... She won't—'

'She can and she will,' Guy corrected her, refraining from adding that he had helped his sister and her husband buy the house with an interest-free loan or that even apart from that act of generosity he knew that his sister with her generous heart would never turn away someone in need.

'Is that her?' Chrissie asked nervously as she saw the tall, dark-haired woman emerging from the front door of the farmhouse as they drove up.

'That's her,' Guy confirmed laconically.

As Guy stopped the car, she came running towards it and immediately Chrissie could see the family re-semblance between them. They shared the same strong bone structure and dark hair, and despite the fact that she was obviously in her early fifties, Guy's sister still had an enviably slim and fit-looking body.

'Guy,' she exclaimed fondly as he opened the car door. 'What a lovely surprise. Oh, and you've brought someone with you, as well. You must be Chrissie.' She smiled as Chrissie looked uncertainly at her. 'I've heard about you from Frances.'

'Mmm…well, there's something that Frances *won't* have told you,' Guy began, but Chrissie placed her hand on his arm, pleading with her eyes for him not to say any more.

'Chrissie and I are not exactly the best of friends at the moment,' he told his sister calmly, 'as I'm sure she'll lose no time in telling you. But right now, she isn't feeling very well. She's been living in that wretched hovel of a cottage that Charlie Platt used to own. The walls are running with damp and I've never been convinced that the old cesspit those cottages were built over was ever sealed off properly.'

'Mmm…it always used to smell rather odd down there on hot summer days,' his sister mused whilst Chrissie listened to them in growing anxiety.

The cottages were old enough to have been built in the days when jerry-builders had thrown up houses as cheaply as they could and she herself had been aware of an unpleasant mustiness about the air in the cottage, which she had previously put down to the damp. But supposing it was not. Supposing it was something more sinister…more dangerous and potentially harmful not just for her but for her baby, as well.

'You *do* look pale,' Guy's sister sympathised. 'Come inside and sit down. My name is Laura, by the way. Rick, my husband, is away at the moment trying to buy more ponies.'

'Guy said you taught disabled children to ride,' Chrissie commented as she walked to the house, flanked on one side by Laura and on the other by Guy.

'Yes, I do, and we desperately need some more, but it isn't easy to find the right kind of mount.'

As Laura opened the front door, Chrissie hesitated, looking round at her surroundings.

'Chrissie's grandparents used to own the farm,' Guy explained to his sister.

'Oh…' Laura frowned and then exclaimed, 'But that means—'

'That I'm a Platt,' Chrissie supplied with a tight smile. 'Well, yes, actually my mother *was* a Platt. Charlie was her brother,' she added, holding her head up high, her chin jutting out firmly as she dared either of them to make a critical comment.

'Oh yes,' Laura remarked, but instead of looking disapproving, Laura's face lightened in a warm smile.

'Yes, of course,' she agreed. 'I remember your mother from school. She was completely different from Charlie, very quiet and studious.'

'Yes, she was, she still is,' Chrissie acknowledged, quietly refusing to give in to the temptation to look at Guy to see how he was reacting to this confirmation of her mother's character.

'Look after her for me,' Guy told his sister half an hour later when she saw him out to his car, leaving Chrissie in the house.

She raised a querying eyebrow, but when Guy simply shook his head, she knew better than to press for an explanation.

It was obvious that they had quarrelled and equally obvious, too, that Chrissie was both unwell and unhappy, and Laura was simply not the kind to pry into other people's unhappiness or to demand confidences, but the white-faced, hollow-eyed young woman who had accompanied her equally grim-faced brother this afternoon bore no resemblance whatsoever to the couple Frances had described as being practically incandescent with love for one another.

As Guy drove away, she retraced her steps to the farmhouse. She found her visitor where she had left her, staring out of the sitting-room window at the farm land beyond.

'I'm sorry that Guy has dumped me on you like this,' Chrissie apologised awkwardly to Laura. 'If I could just call a taxi, I'll take myself off your hands.'

'It's more than my life's worth to let you do such a thing,' Laura countered humorously, adding more seriously, 'and besides, no matter how much we as women might quarrel with Guy's absurdly male high-handed behaviour, it *is* rather obvious that you aren't very well. We have plenty of room here, and in all honesty, I get lonely when my husband is away. You would be doing me a favour if you did stay for a few days. Guy's right about there being something polluted in the atmosphere in those cottages,' she remarked, shaking her head. 'I had a friend who lived in one and she was always ill.'

'I'm not ill,' Chrissie told her quietly. 'I think I'm pregnant. You must be shocked,' she added when Laura made no comment. 'I hadn't intended to tell you, but—'

'No, I'm not shocked,' Laura interrupted her, 'just rather envious. Rick and I have never been able to have children,' she explained, 'Of course, I'm too old now and well past the sharp unbearableness of the pain it used to cause me. My work has helped me with that and time…. Is the baby the cause of the problem you and Guy…?'

'No…not as such,' Chrissie replied, shaking her head. 'Although…' She stopped. Perhaps now was not the time to tell Guy's sister that she suspected it could be a problem later if Guy insisted on claiming his rights as a father as he had already threatened he would. 'No, the problem is that…' She took a deep breath before continuing. 'The problem is that we both rushed into a relationship without knowing enough about one another,' she said sadly.

'And now that you do, what you thought was love has turned out to be…not love…?' Laura guessed.

Chrissie gave her a painful smile and told her wryly, 'I *wish*. I'd rather not talk about it if you don't mind,' she said tiredly.

'*I* don't mind in the least,' Laura assured her. 'I'll take you upstairs and show you where everything is, and then perhaps later when you're feeling a little more rested, we can drive into town and collect your things.'

CHAPTER EIGHT

'I THOUGHT if you were feeling up to it, we might drive over to Fitzburgh Place this morning,' Laura commented.

'Why?' Chrissie demanded suspiciously.

'It was the official opening of the Antiques Fair yesterday, and I rather thought it might be fun to rifle through a few bric-a-brac stalls,' Laura said encouragingly.

'Yes, it would,' Chrissie replied truthfully.

She had been staying with Laura for two days now and had to admit that she couldn't have had a better hostess. They were both on the same wavelength, sharing a rather dry sense of humour. Laura supplied the relaxed and unselfconscious mothering that Chrissie knew she needed at the moment and in other circumstances she recognised that in Laura she would have found a friend she would want to keep for life. But Laura was Guy's sister.

'No ulterior motives,' she challenged her.

'Not a single one,' Laura promised, adding, 'Guy *will* be there, of course, and if you feel you'd rather not go…'

Chrissie glanced through the kitchen window. It was a bright, sunny morning. She had woken up today without feeling sick and why should she deny herself and Laura a treat just because Guy was going to be there? Jon had almost completed the work on her late uncle's estate. It wouldn't be long before she would be able to return to her own life and, once there, she need never have to see Guy again.

'No, it'll be a nice outing,' she agreed, 'but if you're harbouring any plans for staging a reconciliation…' she warned darkly.

'You're adults, not children,' Laura responded calmly as Chrissie got up and started to clear away their breakfast dishes.

'Yes, we are.' Chrissie wondered as she watched Laura start loading the dishes into the dishwasher why the knowledge that Laura *wasn't* planning to try to bring her and Guy back together should leave her feeling so flat.

Surely she didn't *want* him back? After what he had said…after the accusations he had made? He had proved only too clearly that she was really better off without him in her life…in *their* lives.

But he *was* her baby's father. Comfortingly she touched her still-flat stomach as though to reassure the life growing within it that *she* would give it all the parenting it needed; that *she* would give it all the love it needed.

'Are you all right?' Laura asked her, frowning.

'Yes, yes, I'm fine,' Chrissie responded.

The previous day, she had seen the doctor who had cheerfully announced that so far as she could see, Chrissie was a perfectly healthy mother-to-be, if a somewhat nauseously inclined one.

'We generally find it stops around three to four

months,' she had consoled Chrissie, laughing when Chrissie's face had dropped.

'Four months...?' she had wailed.

'I prefer not to prescribe antinausea drugs,' the doctor had added, 'unless the mother-to-be is so ill that it is beginning to affect the baby's growth. Have you tried a couple of dry biscuits in the morning when you wake up?'

Laura, too, had recommended the same remedy, explaining that although she had no personal experience of its efficacy, both her sisters who had suffered from the same problem had sworn by it.

'We could take a picnic lunch,' Laura was telling her now. 'As you'll have already seen the grounds are really something special, but I suspect Guy won't be too pleased with me if he learns that I've dragged you all round them.'

'Guy has absolutely no input into what I choose to do,' Chrissie informed her determinedly but either Laura hadn't heard her or she was choosing not to hear her, Chrissie recognised as the other woman busily wiped down the worktop before setting the dishwasher in motion.

'Guy *is* concerned about you,' she told Chrissie half an hour later as she drove them both to their destination. 'He telephones at least twice a day asking how you are.'

Chrissie averted her face before saying brusquely, 'He's not concerned about me. It's the baby he's worrying about. This is my baby, Laura,' she declared fiercely. 'It has nothing to do with Guy.'

'Apart from the fact that he is its father,' Laura reminded her.

Chrissie sighed. They had been over this argument

several times during the past couple of days, and whilst Laura had in no way attempted to press Guy's claim, neither had she offered Chrissie the comfort of taking her side.

'Most men in his position would be only too glad to be told they had no responsibility,' Chrissie fretted.

'Some would, I agree,' Laura replied. 'But Guy simply isn't like that. He's always been extremely responsible.'

'But not responsible enough to check before he told me that he'd fallen in love with me that he really meant it,' Chrissie couldn't help retorting.

She bit her lip when Laura made no response. She hadn't intended to say what she had but sometimes the hurt of what Guy had done to her was just too much for her to bear.

'In fact, given his reputation, I'm only surprised that this hasn't happened to him before,' she muttered bitterly.

Now she had got Laura's attention and she could see the frowning lack of comprehension in the other woman's eyes as she unexpectedly brought the car to a halt at the side of the country lane they were travelling and demanded shortly, 'What on earth are you talking about, Chrissie? *What* reputation?'

Chrissie swallowed, dismayed to see the unexpectedly stern expression on Laura's face. It made her look disconcertingly similar to the way Chrissie could remember her mother looking at her over some childhood misdemeanour.

'I…er…Natalie mentioned it…' She found herself almost stammering as Laura continued to regard her with frowning concentration.

'Natalie,' Laura scoffed dismissively. 'That woman is a troublemaker who wouldn't recognise the truth if it walked past her in the street. Besides which Natalie has always been rather...possessive where Guy is concerned, completely without reason, and over the years I suspect she's been rather clever at manipulating certain situations to her own advantage. I can assure you, Chrissie, that Guy has *never* had the kind of reputation you're talking about. He has had women...friends, of course, relationships, but...'

She paused, shaking her head. 'This is an issue you should really be discussing with Guy, not me. I must confess I'm rather surprised at you, though, Chrissie,' she added, much to Chrissie's discomfort. 'I had thought you far too sensible and intelligent to be taken in by the spiteful comments of an obviously jealous woman.'

Chrissie gave a small shrug. 'It isn't important anyway,' she fibbed.

'Have the police been back to you yet regarding ownership of the desk?' Laura enquired as she restarted the car, changing the subject.

Chrissie shook her head. 'No, they say they want to wait until my parents return so that they can interview my mother. After all, she hasn't actually seen it yet and until she does...'

'When she and your father come to Haslewich, they'd be more than welcome to stay at the farm,' Laura told her. 'As you know, we've got the space and since this *was* your mother's childhood home...'

Chrissie was touched by the generous offer.

'I'll pass your invitation on to her,' she assured Laura.

'I know she'll be worried about coming.' She hesitated. 'She's also very sensitive about the reputation that her brother had in the town and—'

'Good heavens, no one will hold that against her, or judge her because of it,' Laura informed Chrissie firmly.

Chrissie bit her lip but couldn't prevent herself from saying quietly, 'Guy held it against me.' She heard Laura sigh.

'I don't know if I should tell you this,' Laura began quietly, 'but Guy had a very specific reason for not liking your uncle.'

Chrissie listened, horrified, as Laura went on to tell her about Charles's bullying of the not-so-robust little boy that Guy once was.

'That kind of thing can leave scars, especially for a man like Guy. He would never use his own physical strength against anyone else, he simply isn't like that. But I suspect that there's a macho instinct in every man that makes it hard for him to admit that another male has caused them to feel fear or physical pain. In their eyes it demeans them as a man. Guy was always scrupulous about not doing anything to take revenge for the way Charlie treated him when he was young. However, deep down inside himself, I think a part of him still carries what he sees as the humiliation of allowing Charlie to bully him, of not being able to stand up for himself and defend himself. Am I making any sense?' she asked Chrissie quietly. 'Or…'

'Yes,' Chrissie told her huskily, her eyes filling with tears. She could hardly bear the mental images Laura had so poignantly drawn for her and in her mind's eye she could clearly see the small, pale, perhaps even fragile-looking boy being tormented by his much bulkier and bigger tormentor and, yes, she could understand, too, what Laura meant when she said that Guy might still carry a sense of humiliation because of what had happened. 'Why didn't he *tell* me…say something?' she asked Laura.

Laura's eyebrows rose. 'Do you really need to ask?' she returned dryly. 'He's a man.'

Chrissie sighed in acknowledgement of her comment.

Although Guy had shown Chrissie round the site of the Antiques Fair, what she had seen then had not prepared her for the scene that met her eyes when, after parking the car, she and Laura turned the corner into the stable yard.

It was like being transported back to an earlier and more robust century, Chrissie recognised, as all her senses were assailed by the sights, sounds and smells of a Victorian fair in progress.

Street musicians in costume played cheerful tunes; acrobats and a clever pickpocket were entertaining the crowd with their antics; on a stage elevated safely above the visitors, a fire-eater performed feats of daring. A pieman sang out his wares whilst a very convincing Gypsy woman with two highly enthusiastic children at her side, all in traditional costume and all, Chrissie suspected from their features, members of Guy's extended family, 'hawked' lucky pieces of heather, which Chrissie realised they were actually giving away.

Everything that could be done to create the authentic flavour of a bygone age *had* been done and Chrissie

could only stand and marvel at the colourful and pictu-
resque sight in front. 'Is *Guy* responsible for all of
this…?' she asked Laura wonderingly.

'I'm afraid so,' Laura responded dryly. 'He loves it,
you know. Oh, he pretends not to…claiming that all
these extras are necessary if you want to pull the crowds
in, but secretly…' She shook her head and laughed. 'At
Christmas he always organises a family event. I don't
really know what to call it. It's a sort of play, only
everyone gets involved and we all have to get dressed
up and there's no audience, only every one of us
hamming it up and acting out the roles Guy's given us.'

'It sounds wonderful,' Chrissie told her and meant it.
Suddenly the light went out of her eyes when she
realised that *her* child would never be able to take part
in such festivities, that *her* child would never know the
fun and pleasure that went with being part of such a
large and extended family group.

As she looked round, a stall selling art deco jewellery caught her eye. It was one of her mother's passions
and instinctively Chrissie began to walk towards it.

Across from the stall, a flat waggon pulled by a large
shire-horse was having beer barrels unloaded from it.
Chrissie heard the warning shout but didn't realise what
had happened until a child screamed and she saw the
heavy barrel that had broken free from the load was
rolling straight towards her.

For some reason, instead of moving she discovered
she could only stand there transfixed, paralysed, her heart
pounding with fear, the ominous rumble of the barrel accentuated by the dull roaring she could hear in her ears.

'Chrissie!' She heard Guy's voice and turned instinctively to look for him, only to see him running through the crowd towards her, his face set with tension.

'Guy,' she whispered, then her knees suddenly started to buckle beneath her and the whole world turned dark.

Groggily Chrissie opened her eyes. She was lying on something soft and warm. Warily she turned her head. A man's jacket…a man's jacket that smelled disturbingly familiar.

'Guy…' She tried to sit up and was instantly, gently, restrained.

'It's all right…everything's all right,' she heard Guy saying quietly. 'You fainted.'

'What happened…?' Dizzily Chrissie put her hand to her head. She had a vivid memory of a child screaming and a barrel… She started to shudder and cried out, 'My baby!'

'Your baby's fine,' she heard a different voice telling her.

'This is Dr Miles,' Guy informed her, introducing the fair-haired young man kneeling on the grass beside her. They were outside the stable yard in what looked very much like a private garden, Chrissie recognised as she tried to study her surroundings—not a particularly easy task from a supine position.

'The barrel…?' she questioned fearfully. But the doctor was shaking his head firmly.

'Guy reached you before it did—fortunately,' he assured her. 'Either the shock of seeing it, or the heat, combined with your pregnancy, caused you to faint, but from what I can tell both you and your baby are perfectly well, although it might be an idea to make an appointment to see your own doctor, especially if you're going to make a habit of passing out,' he teased her.

'Where's Laura?' Chrissie asked, still not fully able to take in everything that had happened.

'She's gone to get us all a cup of tea,' the doctor told her matter-of-factly, turning away from Chrissie after warning her to take her time before she tried to sit up. 'Now I'd better take a look at that arm,' he said quietly to Guy. 'Your tetanus injections *are* up to date, I hope?'

'As luck would have it, yes, they are,' Chrissie heard Guy affirming ruefully.

Because the doctor had moved in between her and Guy, she was unable to see just exactly what was wrong with Guy's arm, but she could hear him wince and draw his breath as the doctor examined him.

'Mmm…it's quite a deep gash and it's going to need stitching,' she heard him say. 'I'll clean it up as best I can and put a dressing on it but I'd like you to pop into the out-patients' department as soon as you can so they can check it over properly and stitch it for you.'

'Easier said than done,' Guy responded, shaking his head. 'I simply can't leave here until we close the fair down for the day, which won't be until this evening. I have a moral obligation to the exhibitors to be here and a legal one to Lord Astlegh who, as you very well know, only agreed to allow us to have the fair here on the understanding that I would take personal responsibility for its good conduct.'

'Oh yes, and I'm sure he'd want you to die of

gangrene rather than break your word,' Laura said sarcastically, having just returned with the tea.

'Gangrene…' Only Chrissie could hear the wobble of fear in her voice as she repeated the word under her breath.

Wearily Chrissie closed her eyes. Her head was aching and she felt very queasy, but for once not because of her pregnancy. No, this time her nausea had a rather different cause.

Guy had saved her from being hit by the runaway barrel and in doing so had sustained injuries himself.

'Look, I'm sure Jenny won't mind standing in for you so that you can go to hospital,' Laura was saying to Guy. 'You could ring her now and then I can drive you both there. 'Where is your mobile?'

'I left it at the unit,' Guy told Laura. 'I'll go and get it.'

'You're not going anywhere,' she retorted. '*I* shall go and get it. You stay here with Chrissie.'

'I'd better get back to the first-aid station,' the doctor was saying as he repacked and then closed his medical case.

Chrissie waited until they had both gone before telling Guy in a low voice, 'I haven't thanked you yet for…for what you did. That barrel…'

'I didn't do anything that any other man wouldn't have done,' Guy told her tersely. 'And if it *had* hit you, it would have been my fault. After all, *I'm* responsible for the safety aspects of the fair.'

'It was an accident,' Chrissie told him quietly, but even though she knew it was the truth, she couldn't help shuddering as she realised what could have happened if the barrel had hit her. Instinctively she wrapped her arms protectively around her stomach, causing Guy to go even paler than he already was.

'My God, what if it…where's the doctor…are you…?' he demanded hoarsely.

'I'm fine…I'm fine, Guy.' She reached out to restrain him when she saw him turning away as though he intended to go after the young doctor and drag him back by force if necessary. 'Really,' she insisted.

'I was only thinking about what might have happened if I…if you… It's funny, isn't it? A few days ago the thought of being pregnant, of having a child, was the furthest thing from my mind. Yet now the thought of *anything* happening to the baby…' She bit her lip, unable to go on.

'Don't you think *I* feel exactly the same way?'

The harshness in Guy's voice startled her.

'It isn't the same for a man,' she denied, trying to ignore the unwary response of her emotions to his words.

'No…? That's all *you* know,' he returned bitterly, adding in a low growl, 'Just what the hell do you think it does to me, knowing that you and our child could have been hurt and that I couldn't have done a damn thing to protect the both of you?'

'But you did,' Chrissie reminded him rather breathlessly, desperately wanting to change the subject to something less emotive before he realised the effect his words were having on her.

It was completely ridiculous for her to feel so…for her to wish…for her to *want* to reach out and touch him comfortingly. After all, why should she care about his pain? Why should *she* care about *him*?

She turned her head to look at him, then froze as she saw the huge livid bruise on his forehead and the dark bloodstain on the ripped sleeve of his shirt.

The sight of Guy's blood and the knowledge that it had been spilled in saving her produced a startling combination of fear, shock, pain and, yes, even anger that he should dare risk himself when she and their baby needed him so much. It was such a strong feeling and one she hadn't ever experienced before.

Chrissie glanced at the hospital waiting-room clock. She had been given the all-clear and was now waiting for the doctor to finish stitching up Guy's wound. Laura had disappeared to chat with an old friend whom she'd caught sight of in the corridor.

The waiting-room door opened and Chrissie could feel her face starting to burn with hot colour as Guy walked in.

'Is everything...are you all right?' she asked him awkwardly.

'It seems so. They fished a couple of splinters out of my arm but they seem pretty sure there aren't any more,' he told her cheerfully. 'Chrissie,' he announced in a very different and far more serious voice whilst Chrissie tensed, wondering what he was about to say. 'Couldn't we try again...start again?' she heard Guy asking her in a husky voice. He waved his good arm in her direction and added rawly, 'Today earlier...thinking, fearing... Don't we owe it to our child, son or daughter, to at least show him we cared enough for us both to be there for him?'

'Yes, I suppose we do,' Chrissie agreed in a small voice.

'We both had the advantage of growing up with two loving parents, as part of a family,' Guy continued, pressing home his advantage. 'I'm not saying that a single parent can't do a damn fine job of raising a child but...'

'I understand what you're saying,' Chrissie breathed, trying hard to swallow the lump of emotion threatening to choke her voice with the tears she dared not let him see her shed.

'But a child...two parents who love one another... who...who respect and value one another and not...'

'I'm sorry I didn't tell you the truth about Charles,' she told him with quiet dignity. 'I should have done. I *had* intended to tell you but...' She gave a small, despairing shrug, willing herself not to give in and grab hold of the emotional lifeline he was throwing her and not just for their baby's sake, either.

This afternoon, lying on the grass listening to the doctor explaining to him that he should have his gashed arm properly attended to, she had known just how deeply and permanently she loved him, but she couldn't allow herself to be swayed by her own emotions, not when she knew... Guy loved Jenny and even if he didn't, there was still the issue of the desk.

'We *could* make it work,' Guy was telling her.

'Maybe for a while,' she agreed, then forced herself to look him in the eye as she asked him, 'But what if the baby...our baby should look like Uncle Charles? Would you still want the baby then?' she asked him painfully.

Guy had gone white.

'Would *you* love him if he looked like me?' he countered.

Chrissie closed her eyes. Of course she would…of *course* she would.

'It wouldn't work, Guy,' she told him wearily. 'There'd always be the issue of the desk between us and the fact that Charlie was my uncle and then…'

She paused and gave a small shrug. 'And I'd always know that I was just a substitute for the woman you really love and that you'd only married me for the sake of our child. I suppose as far as you're concerned, if you can't have Jenny, then anyone…'

She broke off, unable to continue as emotion threatened to silence her voice completely.

'If I can't *what*? Chrissie!' Guy started to expostulate, but the waiting-room door opened at that moment to admit Laura.

Oblivious to the tense atmosphere between them and the look of extreme irritation on Guy's face, she exclaimed, 'Good, you're both ready to leave. If you like, we can drop you off at your house on the way, Guy.'

Cursing under his breath, Guy switched on the bedside light and reached for the bottle of painkillers the doctor had given him. His arm was throbbing like the devil just as he had been warned it would, but it was not that that had woken him from his shallow sleep.

He had been dreaming about Chrissie and seeing her standing there directly in the path of that damn barrel. It had taken him three seconds of frozen disbelief before he had leaped into action.

He could feel the sweat springing up all over his

body. Tiredly he pushed his hand into his hair. The bruise on his temple felt raw and painful and his head ached.

After he had carried Chrissie out of the stable yard, calling to Laura to get the medical officer and whilst he waited to hear how she was…how *she* was, and not just their baby, he had known that he really didn't care any more that she hadn't told him the truth about Charlie Platt and he didn't even damn well care about the desk, either. In fact, if he could, he'd probably very likely destroy it himself, then there would be no issue over its rightful ownership.

The only *thing* that made any kind of sense to him right now—that *mattered* to him right now—was that he loved her and that he would go on loving her for the rest of his life. Somehow or other he had to find a way of convincing her of that fact. Because he was pretty sure that she loved him. No woman could fake the reaction he had seen on her face this afternoon when she realised he had been hurt. No woman would strive so hard to hide her strong emotions the way Chrissie had done at the hospital if she *didn't* love the perpetrator of them so very deeply. And as for that comment she had made about him loving Jenny!

Tomorrow he would sort it all out. Tomorrow. Now where were those painkillers? He groaned as he reached out for the bottle and in doing so knocked over the bottle of antibiotics the doctor had also given him. Well, he certainly wasn't going to pick them up now. They could stay where they were until morning.

CHAPTER NINE

ONLY by morning Guy was in no state…no state at all to do any such thing.

By morning Guy was both unconscious and feverish, tossing uncomfortably in his bed, muttering into the silence of the room, his hair and body soaked with perspiration whilst under the dressing the hospital had put on his wound his arm had swollen to almost twice its original size and was pulsing with the pain generated by the poison that was slowly spreading in a dark red line up his arm towards his armpit.

'Hello, Jon, you look a bit frazzled,' Ruth greeted her nephew with a smile as their paths crossed in the square.

'Mmm…just a bit,' Jon agreed. 'I had to do the school run this morning because Jenny had to go to Fitzburgh Place to stand in for Guy again. He was supposed to be there at eight apparently, but he hasn't turned up and Jen couldn't raise him on the phone. Maybe they kept him in hospital overnight.'

'Hospital?' Ruth queried.

'Mmm... There was a bit of an accident at the Antiques Fair yesterday. It seems a barrel broke free from a dray and if Guy hadn't intervened, young Chrissie could have been very seriously injured.'

'Oh dear. Well, I don't think Guy *is* in hospital,' Ruth informed him. 'I certainly saw Laura dropping him off at home yesterday. She had Chrissie in the car with her, too. Is there a reconciliation on the cards there, do you think?' Ruth asked her nephew.

Jon looked grave. 'It would be nice to think so but...'

'Lovers *do* quarrel and make up,' Ruth pointed out.

'Well, yes, and if it was merely a lovers' quarrel, I would agree with you, but there's also the side issue of this desk—Ben's desk according to Guy, but her family's according to Chrissie.'

'Yes, I can see what you mean,' Ruth agreed.

'Look, I'm sorry to have to dash off,' Jon apologised, bending his head to kiss her, 'but I really must go. I've got a client due in ten minutes.'

As she watched him walk away before she had a chance to reply, Ruth hoped that his secretary, a nice woman, would notice that he had a piece of toast sticking out of his jacket pocket.

It was a lovely morning, but as she retraced her steps Ruth's mind wasn't really on the weather. It was such a shame that something so silly as a mere desk—not even a particularly valuable desk at that—should be keeping two people, so plainly meant to be together as Guy and Chrissie, apart...three people if you counted their baby and Ruth certainly did.

But unfortunately she wasn't Solomon and this

problem couldn't be solved by offering, *threatening*, to cut the desk in two.

In two… Ruth frowned. Something had been tugging irritatingly at the corner of her mind ever since the whole issue of the desk had come up.

'What are you doing here?' Ben demanded tetchily when he saw Ruth.

'I thought I'd come and see how you are,' Ruth informed him, ignoring his scowl. 'Oh, and while I'm here there's something I want to check up on in the library,' she added.

'Oh, and what might that be?' Ben demanded.

'Nothing that would interest you,' Ruth informed him with deliberate vagueness. 'By the way, I've asked Mrs Brookes to bring us a tray of tea.'

'Tea. Bah…can't stand the stuff. It makes my rheumatism worse,' Ben complained grumpily.

'Really, *I've* never heard of it having that effect on anyone before,' Ruth replied straight-faced, managing not to point out that the heavy port that Ben enjoyed after his evening meal was far more likely to be the culprit.

However, she noticed that when Mrs Brookes had brought the tea, Ben seemed to enjoy his well enough, although she could tell by the way he moved that he was suffering a great deal of discomfort.

Hopefully once he had had his operation he would be able to move about more easily and he should certainly have less pain, but since she knew he hated to be reminded of it, she wisely said nothing, waiting until they had both had a second cup of tea before announcing that she would just pop into the library before she left.

She knew exactly what she was looking for. Quickly closing the door, she went immediately to the cupboard housing the meticulous account books that went back to her father's time.

It took her rather longer than she had hoped to find what she was looking for, mainly because she hadn't known which year she needed to look under and consequently had had to search through several before finding the item or rather items she had been searching for. When she did, she couldn't help giving a small, triumphant yelp of exultation as she read the entry she had turned up.

There it was as clear as day, in her father's elegant copperplate hand.

Account…To Thomas Berry, woodcarver, £2 10s 6d. each for the construction of a pair of matching desks in yew tree wood.

Two…a pair! So she had been *right*. She *knew* there just couldn't have been one. It would have been completely out of character for her father, a perfectionist in everything he did, to go to the trouble of having the Chester family's heirloom desks copied and only having *one* made instead of the matching pair *they* possessed.

So at least she knew there *had* been two desks, which meant that both Guy and Chrissie *could be* right in claiming different ownership, but what still rather intrigued her was the matter of how one of the desks came to be in the possession of Chrissie's family in the first place.

She heard the study door rattle and was just closing the account book when Ben limped in.

'Still here?' he grumbled, then tensed as he saw what she was holding. 'What are you doing with that?' he demanded harshly.

'I was just checking something in it,' Ruth responded calmly.

'You…you had no right,' he began to bluster. 'You—'

'Ben, I'm your *sister*,' Ruth reminded him firmly. 'You can't bully or frighten me. I have *every* right. Now there's something I want to ask you…about the missing desk…or rather the two missing desks.'

She watched as he sat down very heavily.

'I don't know what you're talking about,' he declared with patent untruth.

'Oh, yes, you do,' Ruth argued cheerfully. 'You know very well what I mean. You really are naughty, Ben,' she chided him. 'You should at least have told the police that there were originally two desks.'

'No, I shouldn't.' Ben glowered at her. 'I gave my father my word it would never be mentioned…*our* secret.'

'Well, I certainly didn't make him any such promise,' Ruth told him crisply, 'and I have every intention of telling them. Good heavens, Ben, what does it matter? So there were two desks. Anyone with a logical brain can work out for themselves that there had to be, especially once Rose Oldham can prove the identity of the one the police are holding. So come on…tell me…what happened?'

Ben scowled even more deeply.

'I mean to have the truth, Ben,' Ruth warned him, 'and I'm quite prepared to stay here until I get it. Our father commissioned a pair of matching desks, copies of the ones owned by the Chester family. I know that much. At some point or other, one of the desks became the property of the Platt family. How?'

Ben frowned and shifted uncomfortably from one foot to the other before telling Ruth hesitantly, 'Father gave it to the Platt girl as a dowry...a wedding gift. She was working here as a nursemaid.'

'Our *father* gave a nursemaid one of a pair of desks he had specifically commissioned as a wedding gift?' Ruth snorted. 'I'm not saying that he was a mean man, Ben, but I *know* he would never have done anything like that...not unless he had some definite reason.'

'I don't know how she came by it,' Ben grumbled. 'Perhaps she stole it...or...'

'Ben,' Ruth warned before adding thoughtfully, 'Of course, we can always wait until Chrissie's mother arrives. She probably knows how it came into her family.'

'No, she doesn't,' Ben returned swiftly. 'The girl knew what side her bread was buttered on. And old Platt, well, he would have kept quiet about it, as well. Yes, and would most likely have taken it to the grave with him.'

'Ben...I'm sorry. I'm just not following you,' Ruth interrupted him, frowning.

'Told you plainly enough, haven't I?' Ben har-rumphed. 'The nursemaid got herself in the family way and had to be married off. Old Platt had already lost one wife and there were no children, so he was glad enough to take her on, but she insisted that she deserved something and threatened to kick up such a fuss that Father was forced to let her take the desk, otherwise…'

'You mean that the nursemaid, Chrissie's great-grandmother, was pregnant with our father's child?' Ruth demanded. 'And that *he* married her off to Archie Platt…paid her off with a *desk*?'

'It was what she wanted,' Ben defended, 'and damn lucky to get it, too, yes, and a husband.'

'A *nursemaid*, Ben,' Ruth protested. 'She wouldn't have been much more than a child…seventeen or eighteen at the most. Oh, the poor girl, and she probably loved him, I imagine.'

'Who? Archie Platt? I doubt it. He must have been twice her age and—'

'No. Father,' Ruth corrected him. 'The poor girl. So Chrissie isn't just a Platt. She's part Crighton, as well.' Ruth smiled.

'Now don't you go telling anyone that,' Ben urged. 'I gave my word.'

'I doubt it's a relationship *she* will particularly want to lay claim to herself,' Ruth informed him tartly, mentally reflecting that she could guess now where Charlie Platt had got his less attractive characteristics from. There was a certain very selfish and greedy streak that notoriously manifested itself every now and again in the male Crighton line.

Jon's twin brother, David, had it. Jon's own elder son, Max, most certainly had it. Her own father, she suspected, had had it, too, and from the sound of it, Charlie Platt had inherited it in full measure, but of course, *that* was simply a *private* opinion and could never be proved.

Chrissie and Guy would both have to be told and so would the authorities—the police. Ruth doubted that Ben would react well to this news. She frowned a little.

Whilst there was now a logical explanation for Chrissie and Guy believing that they knew the rightful ownership of the desk, Ruth was too wise and knew too much about life to believe that this knowledge could instantly make everything right between them.

No, the reasons for them both doubting one another, for them *both* perhaps subconsciously *wanting* to doubt one another went far deeper than the issue of the desk.

Mutual fear of commitment would perhaps be the fashionable media explanation; a mutual fear of allowing themselves to truly trust another person was, in Ruth's view, closer to the truth. But then, who was she to blame them for that?

For the sake of their unborn child, she hoped their differences could be resolved, but with love rather than by necessity. A sterile relationship without trust was no relationship in which to bring up a young life, no relationship at all, but she was perhaps old-fashioned in her outlook, Ruth acknowledged, and of course, *she* had the benefit of her own mistakes, her own wrong judgements, to guide her.

CHAPTER TEN

CHRISSIE wakened abruptly, sitting up in bed, her hand on her stomach, her heart beating fast, not knowing what had brought her so immediately out of her deep sleep, only relieved to discover as she came fully awake that the anxiety that had tugged at her subconscious forcing her to wake up had nothing to do with the new life all her maternal instincts told her was perfectly comfortable and happy in its protected environment.

So what then had made her wake up feeling so fearful and anxious? Even through the curtains and as early as it was, she could see that the sun was already shining, the ambience within Laura's comfortable guest room was as relaxed and welcoming as it always was, and so far as she could tell, yesterday's unpleasant experience had left her remarkably physically unscathed. In fact, she suspected, of the two of them, that Guy…

Guy… Her heart suddenly lurched so heavily against her chest wall that she could feel the physical shock of it. By the corresponding tightness within it, the struggle she had to catch her breath and without even knowing how, she knew immediately that something was wrong with Guy, knew it so overwhelmingly and intensely that she was already out of bed, hurrying into Laura's bedroom to shake her awake.

'Chrissie…what is it, what's wrong? The baby…?' Laura mumbled as she opened her eyes and saw Chrissie bending anxiously over her.

'No, not me. I'm fine,' Chrissie assured her. 'It's Guy.'

'Guy…?' Frowning, Laura started to sit up. 'Why… what…has he…?'

'I'm not sure. I can't explain it. I just *know* something is wrong,' Chrissie told her urgently. 'Laura, something *is* wrong…I know it. I…I feel it.'

'What makes you think so?' Laura asked her doubtfully, fully awake now. 'I know what happened yesterday must have given you a bad shock, and a woman in your condition…'

Her *condition*! Chrissie grimaced. In a way, Laura was right; it *was* her condition that was responsible for making her feel so concerned. But the condition making her feel so anxious, so sure that something was wrong, was not the fact that she was carrying Guy's child as Laura seemed to think, but the fact that she loved him. Her *love* for him was the condition that was giving her this feeling. This knowing…

'Laura, please,' Chrissie pleaded, glancing at the telephone beside the bed. 'Just ring him.'

'All right,' Laura agreed, 'but I doubt he's going to be very pleased at being woken up at six o'clock in the morning.'

Chrissie didn't care; she was being driven by a knowledge, an instinct, that simply couldn't be ignored.

She watched as Laura dialled Guy's number, then waited as she heard the telephone ring and ring and ring…

'He's probably so drugged by the stuff the hospital gave him that he can't hear the phone,' Laura reassured her. 'I know you're worried about him,' she told Chrissie gently as she finally replaced the receiver. 'But you heard what they said at the hospital…he's fine.'

'Laura…please…please,' Chrissie pleaded again, her voice quivering with the intensity of her emotion. 'I know there's something wrong.'

As she turned away and started to head for the door, Laura asked her tiredly, 'Where are you going?'

'I'm going to get dressed and drive round to Guy's,' Chrissie informed her determinedly.

Behind her, she could hear Laura sighing.

'All right…wait…I'll come with you,' Laura conceded, 'but I warn you now, I doubt he's going to welcome us with open arms or thank us for disturbing him.'

It was an unfamiliar sensation to be out and abroad when the day was so young and fresh. In other circumstances, Chrissie acknowledged she would have enjoyed the breathlessly clean newness of the day and the sense of being in tune with nature and the world around her, but much as it gave her pleasure to watch a pair of geese taking off from a small lake as they drove past it, that pleasure was only fleeting and marred by the dark current of her underlying concern for Guy.

'For someone who claims not to love him, you're certainly showing an awful lot of anxiety over Guy,' Laura remarked dryly as they drove into the empty streets of Haslewich.

'I…I do love him,' Chrissie admitted huskily. 'But I can't have a relationship with a man who doesn't trust or respect me and who…' She stopped abruptly, unable to go on, shaking her head slightly.

'I'm sorry, I didn't mean to upset you,' Laura apologised gently.

'You didn't,' Chrissie returned ruefully. 'I upset myself.'

'We'll have to park here,' Laura told her.

The church walk was empty and quiet as they entered it. Chrissie looked anxiously towards the house; the upstairs curtains were closed but those downstairs were open.

Laura knocked briskly on the door and then rang the bell, wincing as it pealed loudly through the house. 'Well, that should wake him,' she commented wryly, but although they waited for several minutes, there were still no sounds from within.

'Perhaps we should ring again,' Chrissie urged her, but Laura shook her head.

'I've got a better idea,' she declared firmly, rooting in her handbag and producing a small bunch of keys. She rummaged through them and, with a pleased smile, selected one.

'Guy gave me a key so that I could keep a check on things when he goes away,' she explained. 'Come on,' she instructed Chrissie briskly as she inserted it in the lock and turned the handle.

As she followed Laura, Chrissie shivered. The house felt so quiet, deathly quiet.

Laura began to climb the stairs, Chrissie close behind her. The door to Guy's bedroom was closed. Calling out his name, Laura turned the handle and went in, the somewhat irritated scepticism she had been exhibiting from the moment Chrissie had woken her up suddenly abandoned as she reached the bed and exclaimed in a shocked voice, 'Oh my God!'

'Laura, what is it…what's wrong?' Chrissie asked anxiously as Laura's body blocked her view of the bed and of Guy.

'I'm not sure, but it looks like blood poisoning,' Laura answered faintly, moving to one side so that Chrissie could now see Guy's arm.

Even in the shadowed light of the curtained room, Chrissie could see quite plainly how swollen and inflamed the arm was. She could also see the tell-tale red line running towards his armpit.

'Guy. Guy,' Laura called, shaking her brother gently by the shoulder, but although he muttered and frowned, moving uncomfortably beneath her touch, he didn't open his eyes.

Thank God she'd followed her instincts, Chrissie fervently thought ten minutes later as a grim-faced ambulance man confirmed that Guy needed immediate hospital treatment.

Four hours of waiting while Guy went into surgery to have a sliver of wood removed had taken their toll on Chrissie, and if Laura had entertained any doubts about the strength of Chrissie's feelings for Guy, these past hours would have determinedly routed them.

If ever she had witnessed a woman deeply in love, then Chrissie was that woman, and Laura hadn't forgotten that if it hadn't been for Chrissie's insistence, Guy could have been even more seriously ill than he already was.

Outside the door of his room, Chrissie hung back, telling Laura huskily, 'You go first.'

Wisely Laura didn't argue. As she opened the door, she saw the way Guy's eyes lit up with hope and expectation, which quickly faded when he saw her.

'I hope you're up to having more than one visitor,' she told Guy cryptically as she beckoned Chrissie into the room. This time, she noted with satisfaction, the intense emotion in Guy's eyes didn't fade as he watched Chrissie walk uncertainly towards his bed.

'How…how are you feeling?' Chrissie asked him tritely, her throat so dry with tension and the aftermath of her fear for him that she could hardly get the words out.

'Sore and apparently fortunate to be here,' he commented wryly.

'Well, you've got Chrissie to thank for the fact that you are,' Laura informed him matter-of-factly, ignoring the warning glance Chrissie was giving her. 'I must admit, when she woke me at six o'clock this morning claiming you were ill, I took an awful lot of persuading that she was right. It's just as well she's so tenacious, otherwise…'

She had her reward in the look Guy gave Chrissie as he whispered, 'You knew…but…'

'Chrissie, I really think you should sit down,' Laura insisted firmly. She turned her attention back to Guy. 'She's been pacing the waiting-room floor for the past four hours,' she explained. 'I felt exhausted just watching her, which reminds me, there's a phone call I have to make. If you two will just excuse me…'

She was gone before Chrissie could open her mouth to protest. Her heart started to thump very heavily and she turned uncertainly towards the door.

As though he sensed what she was feeling, Guy held out his good arm to her and pleaded, 'Don't go, Chrissie. Please…'

When she turned back in response, he told her quietly, 'The surgeon tells me I'm lucky to be alive. Another few hours and the septicaemia could have been so bad it would have meant amputation at best and at worst…'

The look in Chrissie's eyes and the small sound she made in her throat told him all he wanted to know.

'Oh God, Chrissie,' he said roughly. 'What have we *done* to each other? *Why* have we made such a mess of things? I can remember thinking last night just before the fever made it impossible for me to think, that if anything happened…you'd never know just how much I love you…just how much I wish this whole sorry business of that damned desk had never come between us, or how much I wish I'd never let my idiotic prejudice against your uncle—'

'Laura told me what he did to you when you were a child,' Chrissie interrupted him huskily, 'how he bullied you. He did the same to my mother even though she was much older than Charlie. She…she told me once that she used to feel so guilty because she hated him so much.'

'Yes, it must have been hard for her,' Guy agreed quietly, 'but not as hard as I've made things for you.'

Somehow or other without Chrissie being aware of how it happened, they were holding hands, their fingers entwined, their body language giving away all the things that logic and suspicion had urged them to suppress.

'You're having my baby,' Guy whispered rawly. 'When the surgeon told me how close I'd been to... I couldn't bear to think that our child would come into the world without my knowing...without my being there to share the miracle we've created between us. Without my being there to look after and protect the both of you the way... I *want* to be there, Chrissie, not just for our baby, but for you, as well.'

'I want you to be there, too,' Chrissie heard herself admitting as her tears started to fall. Guy, ignoring her protests, heaved himself up in the bed and, using his good arm, drew her down against him, gently kissing her head and trying to comfort her.

'I *know* there are still problems,' he admitted when she finally lifted her head from his chest. He smiled lovingly down at her and smoothed her damp hair back off her face. 'But somehow we'll find a way to work them out.'

'I never meant to keep the truth from you,' Chrissie murmured sadly.

'Shush,' Guy ordered her firmly and she gave him a painful smile. 'It wasn't so much the fact that you were Charlie's niece that bothered me,' Guy explained. 'It was knowing that you didn't trust me enough to tell me...and that hurt. Stupidly because I was hurt...I lashed out unforgivably. Instead of admitting that I *was* hurt and behaving like an adult, I reacted like a child, accusing and blaming you.'

'The reason I didn't tell you was because I loved you too much,' Chrissie responded shakily. 'I was too afraid of losing you and then my mother suggested that I should keep quiet about being related to Charlie and I knew how you felt about him…' She shook her head, then went on quietly, 'I was hurt, too, you know, when you weren't honest with me about your…your relationship with Jenny.'

She paused and waited painfully to see how he would respond.

'Yes,' Guy agreed after a small pause. 'I wasn't entirely honest with you about that, I know—'

'Because you didn't want me to know how much you loved her,' Chrissie interjected sadly.

'No!' Guy denied her assertion so forcefully that he winced as he tried to catch hold of her and jarred his bandaged arm.

'No,' he reiterated more gently whilst Chrissie fussed over his pain. 'No, the reason I didn't tell you about her was because I was ashamed of myself for…for being weak enough at that particular time in my life to believe that the answer to all my problems lay in forming a relationship with another man's wife, a woman who I already knew in my heart of hearts was quite simply not available to me. I was at an age where I *wanted* to fall in love, to settle down and have a family, but because it wasn't happening, because there was no one around who appealed to me in that way, I convinced myself that I was in love with Jenny, a woman who already had her family and who was so much in love with her own husband that there was absolutely no possibility of her ever falling in love with me.

'I never really loved Jenny at all, Chrissie, and she was wise enough to know as much and that was why I was so reluctant to discuss what happened with you. I didn't want to expose myself to you as a flawed human being. The truth is that I didn't have a clue what real love was until I met you…until I saw you, and then when I had, when I did, the truth was so illuminating, so blinding, that…' He paused and shook his head. 'I'm very fond of Jenny and I always will be, but *you* are the woman I love. You will *always* be the woman I love.'

'Even though you think I'm lying about the desk?' Chrissie asked him quietly.

Guy sighed. 'I don't know what to say. I only know the evidence of my eyes.'

'I understand,' Chrissie agreed quietly, disentangling herself from his embrace and walking slowly towards the door.

She was just about to open it when she heard Guy calling her name. Thinking that something was wrong with his arm, she reacted instinctively, turning round and running back to his side.

'Guy, what is it?' she demanded. 'What's wrong… your arm…?'

'My arm's fine,' he replied in a muffled voice. 'But I'm not. Oh God, Chrissie, I don't give a damn about the wretched desk. You're what matters to me…all that matters to me. I can sell my share in the business, we can move, go and make a fresh start somewhere where no one…'

Chrissie stared at him. 'You'd do *that* for me?' she whispered. 'Even though…'

'I'd do *anything* for you,' Guy groaned as he reached for her, pulling her down onto the bed beside him.

'Anything and *everything*. I *love* you, Chrissie, and that's *all* that matters, and just as soon as I get out of this damned hospital, you and I are going to sit down together and make plans...not just for our own future but for our child's, as well,' he promised her firmly as he started to kiss her.

Laura opened the door, saw the couple on the bed, Guy's good arm locking Chrissie to him as he kissed her, and discreetly closed the door again.

'We're going to be so happy together, the three of us,' Guy declared when he finally released her, but although she smiled at him, Chrissie wondered.

It was all very well for Guy to talk of leaving Haslewich and making a new start, but the issue of her family's trustworthiness would always be there between them, no matter how deeply they tried to bury it.

'We've had an official invitation to go round and have tea with Ruth Reynolds, one of my neighbours,' Guy announced as Chrissie walked into his sitting room.

He had been allowed home from the hospital the previous day but only with the proviso that there was someone to look after him.

There was no way *she* could take on the task, Laura had insisted determinedly. Not with her own husband due home in the next twenty-four hours, and the horses to look after, so of course Chrissie had really no option other than to take on the role in her stead.

'Oh, when does she want us to go?' Chrissie asked him.

* * *

'Come in, both of you,' Ruth invited warmly as she answered the door to Guy and Chrissie's ring. 'I've invited Jon to join us,' she added unexpectedly as she led the way to her pretty drawing room. 'I feel it's important that he should be here, if only as an informal recorder and, of course, to give corroboration to what I have to say, just in case. But I'm rather jumping the gun. How are you feeling, Guy?' she enquired solicitously.

'Much better than I was,' Guy told her wryly. 'Much better than I might have been if it hadn't been for Chrissie,' he added as he turned towards her and smiled tenderly.

Ruth had, of course, heard about their reconciliation, and as Jenny had said, it was lovely to hear that they had resolved their differences and that their love for one another had proved to be strong enough to overcome them.

'I'm so glad for them both,' Jenny had continued. 'They are so obviously right for one another.'

'Come in and sit down,' Ruth invited. 'Chrissie, if you wouldn't mind pouring the tea, I have a rather interesting story to tell you both.'

She smiled at Chrissie's slightly surprised look as the younger woman dutifully went over to the table and started to pour the tea.

'I've been rather puzzled and concerned,' Ruth began, 'about this problem concerning the true ownership of the desk that was found in Charlie Platt's house. So I've been doing a little bit of investigating. As Jon is aware, my father had rather a thing about his relatives in Chester, and since he knew that the desk he had copied was one of a pair made as birthday gifts for twin daughters in the Chester family, it seemed to me that it didn't make sense that he should only have had the *one* desk made. That's why I decided to do some research....'

She paused before reaching for the heavy book that lay on the floor at her feet.

'This is the account book for the year when the desk was commissioned, or should I say when the *desks* were commissioned?'

It took some time for her wry words to sink in, but once they had, Guy exclaimed, 'You mean there were *two* desks, but—'

'Yes, there were two desks,' Ruth interjected calmly. 'Two identical desks, just like the pair made for the Chester family.'

'But that still doesn't explain how one of them came into the possession of my family,' Chrissie observed.

'That it doesn't,' Ruth agreed quietly. 'Accounts are simply statements of funds paid out and gathered in.'

'Surely my great-grandfather didn't *buy* one of the desks?' Chrissie questioned doubtfully. 'That would—'

'No, Chrissie, he didn't,' Ruth returned gently before looking at Jon. 'Our father, Ben's and mine, was married twice. Our mother died shortly after my birth and a young girl was hired to help out in the nursery.' Ruth paused and then continued.

'That girl was your great-grandmother, Chrissie. A relationship developed between her and my father, and when she became pregnant he apparently persuaded her to marry one of his tenant farmers, who was himself a widower with no children.

'It was agreed between the two men that the baby, a son, would be brought up as the farmer's child. He, it seems, was already middle-aged and desperate for an heir. A sum of money also changed hands.' Ruth grimaced slightly. 'That poor girl. I suspect she must have loved my father very much, so much so it seems that she pleaded with him to be allowed to take with her to her new home some memento of what they had shared. He agreed and she chose the desk,' Ruth concluded simply.

Chrissie stared at her in shock before demanding huskily, 'Is this really true? It seems so…'

'Yes, it's really true, Chrissie,' Jon confirmed with quiet authority.

'But *why* hasn't my mother ever said? Why…?'

'I doubt very much that she knew,' Ruth told her. 'I certainly knew nothing about it myself and Ben, my brother, only found out when our father was dying. According to Ben, it was confided to him as a secret that he was sworn to keep. It was only when I challenged him about the fact that there were two desks and threatened to inform the police that he finally admitted the truth to me.'

'I still can't quite take it all in,' Chrissie whispered, tears filling her eyes as she turned to Ruth and confided emotionally, 'You can't know how much I've been dreading having my mother identify the desk. How much…'

'I think I can,' Ruth corrected her gently.

Guy still hadn't said anything, but his expression gave him away. 'Two desks,' he announced grimly, standing up now and pacing the floor. 'Of course. *Why* didn't *I* guess that for myself? I *knew* there were two originals.'

'There was really no reason why you should have done,' Ruth soothed him. 'You had, after all, only seen the one and no one had ever suggested to you that there might originally have been two.'

'Maybe not, but I should have thought...*questioned*... Chrissie!'

'It's all right,' Chrissie reassured him unsteadily as she reached for his hand. 'Ruth's right. You really couldn't have known and,' she added with heart-warming honesty, 'in your shoes, I would probably have reacted just as you did.'

The look Guy gave her made Ruth bite her lip and look away. Some feelings, some emotions, were just too intense, too passionate, too raw, to be witnessed by any outsiders.

'You're a liar,' she heard Guy saying huskily, 'and a very generous one.'

Chrissie shook her head. She was still feeling too overwhelmed by Ruth's astonishing revelations. 'I can't believe this is happening,' she told Ruth and Jon shakily. 'It seems so...well, it's so unexpected.'

'Well, it certainly helps to explain where Charlie got his rogue genes from,' Ruth commented humorously, explaining wryly to Chrissie, 'Unfortunately there is a certain inherited characteristic in the Crighton ancestry that tends to produce the odd individual who is not only monumentally selfish, but totally lacking in what the rest of us might describe as moral responsibility, as well, which reminds me...'

She stood up, then walked over to Chrissie and embraced her warmly.

'Welcome to the Crighton family, my dear.'

The *Crighton* family. Chrissie opened her mouth and then closed it again.

'It's all right,' Ruth told her in a kind voice. 'We'll all understand if you choose not to acknowledge us as part of your family.'

'I just don't know what my mother is going to say about all this,' Chrissie exclaimed weakly.

'I expect you and Guy would like some time on your own now to talk over…everything,' Ruth said, gently touching Chrissie lightly on the wrist and then giving her another warm hug as Chrissie stood up to leave.

Jon, too, hugged her before she left, and as she said afterwards to Guy when they were on their own in his home, 'They were both just so warm and welcoming.' She started to cry and Guy who had been getting them both a drink walked across the kitchen to catch hold of her and demanded gruffly, 'What is it…what's wrong?'

'Nothing,' Chrissie hiccupped into his shoulder. 'I'm just so glad that it's all over. I was so afraid that this would always haunt us, that it would always come between us…that you'd never be able to completely trust me.'

'*Me* trust *you*?' As he bent his head to kiss her, the apology he was starting to make was muffled by the warm pressure of Chrissie's mouth against his, soothing the pain of his guilt and remorse. 'First thing tomorrow morning we're flying to Amsterdam,' Guy informed her huskily once she had released his mouth, 'and it won't just be an engagement ring I shall be buying you. And while we're there we might as well add an eternity ring, as well,' he added, as he gently stroked her finger, 'because this time, my love, it is for eternity.'

'Yes, it is,' Chrissie concurred softly.

'May I see your rings? Oh yes, they are beautiful,' Ruth's granddaughter, Bobbie, admired as Chrissie ignored the shower of rose petals one of the wedding guests was throwing over both her and Guy to step forward and extend her hand.

Chrissie had surprised herself by choosing not an antique ring as she had first intended, but a modern trio of rings, especially designed for her by one of Amsterdam's top jewellers. The heart-shaped diamond of her engagement ring had been chosen by Guy, and Chrissie had gasped over its breathtaking magnificence.

It only stopped short of being vulgar by just a heart-beat, she had told him at the time, but both the jeweller and Guy had argued and assured her that in comparison with some of the solitaires they sold, it was, in fact, rather modest. The simple band it was set into had been specially made to interlink with both the diamond-studded, entwined-rope design of her white-and-gold wedding and eternity rings, whilst around the centre of the eternity ring ran an additional ring of perfect but more modestly sized individual diamonds.

'They all interlock and belong together, like the three of us,' Guy had told Chrissie tenderly when they had chosen the design. The three of them.

Her wedding outfit had been made in Chester, its simple cut and the richness of the heavy cream satin discreetly masking her growing pregnancy. That was why Chrissie had decided against a traditional wedding gown and opted instead for a full-length plainly cut dress and a matching full-length satin coat over it with a small train at the back.

'I'm not ashamed of the fact that I'm carrying our child,' she had told her mother proudly. 'But we *are* having a church wedding and I just don't feel that a traditional dress would be appropriate.'

'You'll look lovely, darling,' her mother had assured her as they studied the design Chrissie had chosen.

And of course she did.

More than lovely as Guy had already told her.

She smiled at him now, touching his arm to draw his attention to where her mother was standing with his sister, Laura, the two of them deep in conversation.

The fact that Laura and her mother had struck up such an immediate bond had been an additional bonus so far as Chrissie was concerned. It had been Laura who had taken charge when her parents had travelled south, insisting that they stay with her and her husband and very firmly dealing with her mother's reservations about how she might be judged.

'You are *not* your brother. You are yourself and people will judge you accordingly,' Laura had told her forthrightly.

And so it had proved to be. Several women who had been at school with her mother had made very warm overtures to her. Chrissie might suspect that Laura had had a hand in their warm welcome, but she certainly wasn't going to spoil her mother's pleasure in being remembered by saying so. And both Guy's family and the Crightons, as well, had made it plain that they considered them very welcome additions to their family circles.

Only Natalie had held herself rather aloof, and Chrissie hadn't been upset at all to learn that she had decided to move to London.

Her mother had received the news about their connection with the Crightons with the same astonishment as Chrissie, but what had touched Chrissie most of all was to overhear her mother remarking to Jenny the day before the wedding that she and Chrissie's father were definitely thinking of moving South when they retired.

'After all,' she had said to Jenny, 'it won't just be our daughter and son-in-law who are living here, but our grandchildren, as well.'

'If I didn't know better,' Guy teased her as they watched one of his teenage nieces flirting outrageously with a gangly-looking boy who seemed more embarrassed than flattered by her attention, 'I almost suspect that you'd rather stay here than go to Barbados with me.'

'Only almost?' Chrissie teased him back. 'It's so wonderful to be part of a big family, Guy, to know that our child, our children, will be growing up with that advantage, but it's nowhere near as wonderful as knowing you love me,' she whispered huskily in his ear. 'And as for Barbados…'

'Barbados. Why the hell didn't I just book us a suite at the Grosvenor in Chester?' Guy groaned against her mouth as he bent his head to kiss her. 'Do you know how long that flight is?'

'We've still got the reception to get through yet,' Chrissie reminded him demurely.

'Just you wait until I get you on my own,' Guy warned her.

'On my own?' Chrissie raised an eyebrow and patted her gently rounding body teasingly. 'I don't think so,' she reminded him archly. 'By the way, I'm glad they've caught the gang responsible for those break-ins.'

'So am I,' Guy agreed, giving her a sombre look. 'I can't believe that I even thought in my dreams that you were remotely involved.'

'Shush.' Chrissie placed her fingers over his lips. 'It did all seem to fit into place and the gang did have a female member.'

'I don't deserve you,' Guy whispered tenderly.

Across the churchyard, Madeleine Crighton saw them laughing and witnessed the look they exchanged, the love they so obviously shared so palpable you could almost reach out and touch it.

Tiredly she looked away.

When she had been pregnant with both their children, Max had treated her not with tenderness and love but with acidic fury, reminding her that he had not wanted children, just as he had not really wanted her.

She started to make her way quickly through the crowd to where Jenny, Max's mother, was standing with the children.

Thinking about Max and their marriage was something Maddy tried very hard not to do these days. Their marriage… What marriage? It was simply a worthless piece of paper, a legal document. Max didn't love her and she was beginning to question if he had ever loved her. He made her feel so worthless, so useless. In his eyes she felt unwanted, undesirable, and she was almost glad of the physical distance between them, the 'business' that had taken him to Spain.

Almost… A part of her still remembered how it had once been…how they had once been…just…

'Mmm…this is pure heaven,' Guy exclaimed contentedly as they lay on the bed of their holiday villa, the fan whirring soporifically above them as it cooled the hot Barbadian night air.

'Was it worth waiting for?' Chrissie teased him tongue-in-cheek as he raised himself up on one elbow. He leaned over her, tracing the shape of her mouth with one fingertip, then lazily bending his head to kiss her naked breast.

'Oh, well worth waiting for,' Guy purred with the sheer satisfaction of a sensually satiated male animal.

And he was very much a male animal, Chrissie acknowledged as she watched him leave their bed and walk across the bedroom, his naked body gleaming in the soft, shadowy light. The combined warmth of the air and the heat of their passionately intense lovemaking had left a fine oiled sheen on his skin highlighting its taut muscle structure. A feeling she was fast coming to recognise began stirring wantonly deep within her body.

'We never had time for this earlier,' Guy announced as he picked up the bottle of champagne. It was still in its ice bucket and he'd intended to share it before he took

Chrissie to bed and they consummated physically the vows they had made verbally and emotionally to one another earlier.

Chrissie watched as he opened the bottle and poured them both a glass. She could watch him for ever, she decided contentedly. He had such masculine grace, such unconscious male arrogance and authority. He turned his head and saw her looking at him and she watched his eyes darken as he subjected her naked body to a far less inhibited and smoulderingly sensuous scrutiny than she had been giving him.

So much so that she could actually feel the colour starting to rise up under her skin. But she was pleased to note she was not the only one to be affected by the small exchange, because Guy's hand trembled slightly as he came back to the bed and handed her a brimming glass of champagne. A few drops of the golden liquid splashed onto her naked body but as she moved to wipe them away, Guy stopped her, caught hold of her free hand and then bent his head to lick away the champagne, his tongue tip doing impossibly erotic things to her nervous system as he teasingly inched closer and closer to her now very erect nipples.

'Mmm…' he murmured pleasurably, then put his glass down, cupped the side of her breast and started to gently suck on the tight nub of flesh he had been tormenting.

Chrissie could feel the excitement pulsing through her body as she tried to stifle her soft groan of pleasure, but Guy had obviously heard it because his caresses became more intense, more purposeful, and no longer merely playful.

She wanted him…oh, how she wanted him, but he deserved a little bit of punishment himself for the way he had teased her, Chrissie decided, laughter sparkling in her eyes as she deliberately tipped some of her champagne onto his body.

'What the…' Guy exclaimed, momentarily releasing her whilst she calmly put down her glass.

Firmly pushing him onto the bed, Chrissie informed him firmly, 'If you can't take the heat, then stay out of the kitchen,' before bending her own head and slowly and deliberately following the trickle of golden liquid arrowing its way along the valley that conveniently provided a pathway down the centre of his body, lazily lapping at it with her tongue whilst at the same time deliberately encouraging it to run faster and farther.

It gave her immense satisfaction to hear Guy groaning in much the same way as she had done herself as she forced him to endure her teasing love play. Later she decided that it was the leisurely lap of honour with which she had triumphantly circled his navel, first with tiny kisses and then with the moist tip of her tongue, which had been her undoing, because it was after that and whilst she was in pursuit of the errant drop of champagne still making its way down his body that she lost control of the game. Not that she minded. Who cared about victory when being defeated, overwhelmed, by their mutual passion and then mutual love could be so hotly and sweetly satisfactory?

Dawn was just beginning to pearl the sky with its translucent light when Guy finally drew Chrissie down against his body and groaned, 'Just think… another three weeks of this. How on earth will we stand it?'

Both of them were still smiling when they finally fell asleep.

The Perfect Lover

CHAPTER ONE

'MY GOODNESS, we *are* honoured, aren't we? It isn't very often these days that you manage to tear yourself away from the bureaucratic delights of Brussels.'

Louise tensed as she heard the sarcastic voice of her elder brother, Max. They had never got on particularly well, even as children, and in her view maturity had done nothing to improve either their relationship or her brother.

'It was commented at Christmas that you weren't around,' Max continued jibingly. 'But, of course, we all know Saul was really the reason for that, don't we?'

Louise gave him an angry look before retorting, 'Perhaps if you spent more time thinking about your own relationships and less talking about other people's you might learn something genuinely worthwhile, but then you never were much good at appreciating what's really of value in this life, were you, Max?'

Without giving him any opportunity to retaliate, Louise turned on her heel and walked quickly away from him.

She had promised herself that on this, her first visit home since she had started working in Brussels over twelve months ago, she would prove to her family just how much she had changed…matured…and just how different, distant almost, she was from the girl who…

Out of the corner of her eye she caught sight of Saul, her father's cousin, who was standing with his wife, Tullah, and the three children from his first marriage. Tullah had her arm around Megan, Saul's daughter, while Saul held the little boy they had had together.

The large drawing room of her grandfather's house seemed to be filled by the presence of her peers, proudly showing off their growing families.

Clustered around the fireplace were her cousin Olivia, with her husband and their two children, talking animatedly with Luke, from the Chester branch of the family, and his American wife Bobbie and their little girl, while Maddy, her brother Max's wife, kept a discreet eye on Gramps, who was becoming increasingly irascible.

According to her mother, Maddy was close to a saint for humouring him the way she did. When Jenny Crighton had made this comment this morning, over breakfast, Louise had immediately pointed out that if Maddy could put up with being married to Max, then her grandfather must come as a form of light relief.

'Louise,' her mother had protested, but Louise had remained unrepentant.

It was no secret in the family that Max was not a good or kind husband to Maddy, and privately Louise couldn't understand why on earth Maddy stayed with him.

'You're looking very cross.'

Louise grimaced as she saw her twin sister. Twins were a feature of the Crighton family, in the same way that poppies were a feature of a field of corn—they sprang up all over the place, although as yet there were no sets in the current new generation.

'They'll come,' her father's aunt Ruth had predicted.

'I've just been receiving the benefit of Max's brotherly conversation,' Louise informed her grimly. 'He doesn't change…'

'No…' Katie looked at her twin. 'You know, in a lot of ways I feel quite sorry for him. He—'

'*Sorry* for *Max*?' Louise exploded. 'What on earth for? He's got everything he's ever wanted—a cushy place in one of the country's leading sets of chambers, with his pick of all the best briefs—and all he's had to do to get it is to persuade poor Maddy to marry him.'

'Yes, I know what he's got in the material sense, Lou, but is he happy?' Katie persisted.   'I think he feels what happened with Uncle David far, far more than he's ever shown. After all, they—'

'They were both made in the same mould. Yes, I know,' Louise cut in. 'If you want my opinion, it would be a good thing for this family if Uncle David *never* surfaced again. Olivia as good as told me that her father had been guilty of serious malpractice when he and Dad were partners, and that if he hadn't disappeared when he did…'

Both of them were silent for a moment as they remembered David Crighton, their father's twin brother and Olivia's father, and the near disaster he had plunged the family into prior to his disappearance some years earlier.

'That's all in the past now,' Katie reminded her gently. 'Dad and Olivia have managed to sort out all the problems they had been having with the practice—and in fact they've built up the business so much that they've decided they need to think about taking on an extra qualified solicitor to cope with the increased workload. But Gramps still misses David, you know. He was always—'

'The favourite. Yes, I know. Poor Gramps. He never has had very good judgement, has he? First he makes David the favourite, ahead of Dad, and now it's Max.'

'Mum's really glad that you were able to make it home for Gramps's birthday,' Katie told her sister quietly. 'She was…upset at Christmas when you didn't come home…'

'When I *couldn't* come home,' Louise corrected her sharply. 'I told you at the time. My boss put me under pressure to put together a report on the legal aspects of a new community law she thought might be passed, and I had no option but to agree. It wouldn't have been worth coming home for what would have amounted to just about forty-eight hours, even if I could have got the flights.'

Three months after leaving university, and not wanting to take the next stage in her training to become a barrister immediately, Louise had taken a temporary post working for a newly appointed Euro MP who'd wanted someone to work for her as a legal researcher.

Six months ago the temporary post had become a permanent one, and while the hours were long and the work extraordinarily demanding, Louise had thrown herself into it with determination, knowing that the contacts she was making in Brussels would ultimately equip her to make a change of career should she want to do so.

Their choice of careers couldn't have been more different, Katie acknowledged as she silently and sympathetically studied her twin. While Louise, true to her nature, had chosen to fling herself head-first into the maelstrom of politics and intrigues in the hot-house melting-pot atmosphere of Europe's bureaucratic

capital, she had opted to join a still very youthful and
emergent new charity which had been set up to help
young children across the world who had been made
orphans and refugees by war.

'Have you spoken to Saul and Tullah yet?' Kate asked
her sister softly.

Louise reacted sharply to her question, tensing and
almost physically backing off from her as she replied
angrily, 'No, I haven't…Why should I? For God's
sake, *when* is everyone in this wretched family going
to stop behaving as though…?' She stopped, and took
a deep breath.

'Look, for the last time, Saul means nothing to me
now. I had a silly, stupid crush on him, yes. I made a total
and complete fool of myself over him, yes. But…' She
stopped again, and shook her head.

'It's over, Katie. Over.'

'Mum thought when you didn't come home at
Christmas—' Katie began.

Louise wouldn't let her finish, breaking in bitterly,
'That what? That I couldn't bear the thought of seeing
Saul? Or, worse, that I might—'

'She thought that perhaps you'd met someone in
Brussels.' Katie overrode her with quiet insistence. 'And
that you weren't coming home because you wanted to
be with him…'

Interestingly, a soft tide of warm colour started to
tinge her sister's skin, and, even more interestingly, for
once in her life she seemed almost lost for words as she
turned her head and looked down at the carpet before
saying quickly, 'No. No, there isn't anyone…at least not
like that. I…'

It wasn't totally true—there was someone, of sorts—

but she knew perfectly well that the relationship Jean Claude wanted with her was one based on sex only.

Jean Claude was twelve years older than her, and moved in the higher echelons of Brussels' diplomatic circles. He was, as he himself had told Louise, a career diplomat, who currently held a post connected with the French fishing industry.

Louise wasn't quite sure as yet how she felt about him. He had a suave, dry sense of humour, and the kind of Gallic good looks that fell just short enough of outrageously handsome to ensure that he was very attractive to the female sex. Politics and the law, as Jean Claude had already teasingly commented to her, could make very exciting bedfellows.

'Brazen, I think you mean,' Louise had corrected him firmly.

'Be careful if you're looking for commitment,' a colleague had already warned Louise. 'He's got a reputation for liking variety.'

Louise had shrugged away the other woman's comments. Commitment was the last thing on her mind at the moment, and would be for a very long time to come. She might be over Saul in the sense that she was no longer suffering from the massive crush which had caused her to make such an idiotic fool of herself, but she was certainly far from over the feelings of humiliation and searing self-disgust—self-dislike—which had resulted from the sharp realisation of just how dangerously and potentially destructively out of control her feelings for Saul had threatened to become.

She would certainly never make that mistake again. *Never* allow herself to become such a victim, such a slave to her emotions ever again—she didn't really understand how it had happened in the first place. Right from her early teens she had set her sights firmly on aiming for a career. Marriage, babies, emotions, although she'd once have openly welcomed them with Saul, were more Katie's forte than her own. The terrifying force of her feelings for Saul had been an abberation, and the behaviour they had resulted in so totally abhorrent and repugnant to her that even now, nearly three years later, she could scarcely bear to think about it.

Yes, it was possible now for her to look at Saul with Tullah and the children without suffering even the smallest flicker of the emotion which had torn her apart and threatened every aspect of her normal life during those months when it had held its strangulating, choking grip on her life. But what *wasn't* possible, what she suspected might *never* be possible, was for her to forget just how traumatic that time, those *feelings* had been.

Louise frowned, her thoughts switching from the past to the present as she recognised the suspiciously furtive way her younger brother Joss and their cousin Jack were edging their way towards the French windows.

Discreetly following them, she waited until Joss was on the point of unlatching the door before demanding sternly, 'And just where do the pair of you think you are going?'

'Lou…'

Considerably startled, her brother released his hold on the door handle and spun round to face her.

'We were just going down to the greenhouse,' Jack told her with virtuous innocence. 'Aunt Ruth is growing some special seeds there and…'

'The greenhouse?' Louise questioned loftily. 'This

compelling expedition to view Aunt Ruth's seedlings wouldn't have been taken via the TV room, would it?'

The look of contrived injured innocence her brother gave her made Louise's lips twitch slightly, but Jack wasn't quite such a good actor, and his fair skin was already starting to flush with guilt. Both boys were ardent rugby fans, and Louise had overheard them pleading with her mother, without success, earlier in the day to be allowed to sneak away from the family party in order to watch their favourite game.

'The All Blacks are playing,' Joss told her pleadingly.

'You'll be all black, or rather your good behaviour record will be, if Mum catches on to what you're up to,' Louise warned him.

'If we go now, we can just about catch the last half,' Joss told her winningly. 'And Mum won't even notice. We'll be back before she knows we're gone.'

'I don't think…' Louise began, but Joss was already reaching up to give her a fervent hug.

'Thanks Lou, you're the best,' he announced. 'And if Mum should ask…'

Louise shook her head firmly.

'Oh, no…don't drag me in. If you get found out, you're on your own, the pair of you.' But she was smiling affectionately as she returned her brother's warm hug. After all, it wasn't such a very long time ago that she herself had found such family gatherings rather dull, and had, like Joss and Jack, made her escape from them just as quickly as she could.

'Bet you wish you could come with us,' Joss whispered to her with an engaging grin before quickly sliding through the French window.

'To watch the All Blacks? No, thanks,' Louise retorted with a small female shudder, but she was smiling as she discreetly closed the French windows behind the two boys.

On the other side of the room Tullah, who had been watching the scene, touched Saul on the arm.

As he turned to look at her she took their son out of his arms and told him, 'I'm just going to have a word with Louise.'

Frowning slightly, Saul watched her. She had totally transformed his life, and the lives of his three children from his first marriage.

Louise stiffened as she saw Tullah making her way towards her. She looked quickly over her shoulder, but the door from the drawing room was blocked by her father and Aunt Ruth, who were deep in conversation. Katie, whom she might have expected to be her ally, had somehow or other managed to melt away, and now there was no escape for her. Tullah was already at her side.

'Hello, Louise…'

'Tullah.'

'You've had your hair cut. I like it. It suits you…'

'Thank you.'

Automatically Louise touched one of the short feathery curls of her newly shorn hair. She had had her hair cut on impulse the day before she had flown home, and the feminine cut showed off the delicacy of her bone structure and emphasised the shape and colour of her dark eyes. The weight she had lost while away at university had never totally been replaced. She looked, Tullah acknowledged inwardly, almost a little too fine-boned and fragile, and she could well understand, as a mother herself, why Jenny should be a little bit anxious over her well-being.

As the silence between them stretched Louise was acutely conscious of the fact that virtually everyone else in the room was probably watching them and remembering…

As she turned to move away from Tullah, baby Scott reached out and, grinning winsomely at Louise, patted her cheek with one fat baby hand, pronouncing solemnly, 'Pretty.'

Over his downy head Tullah's sympathetic eyes met Louise's wary, startled ones.

'Oh, dear. I think I'm going to sneeze.' Tullah told Louise. 'Could you take him for me?'

Before Louise could protest she found herself holding a solid armful of gurgling, beaming baby, whilst Tullah dived into her jacket pocket for a tissue.

'No. No, it's gone…' Tullah announced when the threatened sneeze was not forthcoming, but she made no attempt to take her son back from Louise as she commented, 'It's so nice to see virtually all the family here. I know your grandfather isn't always the easiest person to get along with…'

'You can say that again,' Louise agreed wryly, gently detaching the baby's clutching fingers from the gold chain she was wearing around her neck. 'He's got your colouring but Saul's eyes,' she told Tullah. 'How have the other three…?'

'So far, so good,' Tullah told her, showing her her crossed fingers. 'It's probably been easier for them, and for us in one way, because they live with us full time. So there's no question of them feeling that Scott, here, gets to see more of their father than they do.'

Scott, for some reason, had quite obviously taken an immediate liking to Louise, and much to her own astonishment, and Tullah's patent amusement, he started to press loud juicy kisses against her face.

Louise, despite her determination to focus on her career, had always liked children and enjoyed their company. As a teenager she had often babysat for Saul, and had formed quite a close bond with his three, and now, to her chagrin, she suddenly felt her eyes filling with emotional feminine tears as Scott's baby kisses touched her skin.

Quickly she handed him back to Tullah, telling her chokingly, 'Tullah, I'm sorry…'

And both of them knew that it wasn't what was happening now that she was apologising for.

Very gently Tullah touched her arm.

'It's over, Lou,' she told her softly. 'Forget it. We have. You were missed at Christmas—by all of us…' As she turned to return to Saul and the children, she paused and dropped a light kiss on Louise's cheek.

'Forget it', Tullah had said. Louise closed her eyes as Tullah walked away. If only she could. Tullah and Saul might have forgiven her, but she doubted that she would ever be able to forgive herself…

'Is everything all right, darling?'

Louise forced a determined smile as she read the concern in her mother's eyes.

'Fine,' she assured her. A quick look around her grandfather's drawing room reassured her that she was no longer the object of everyone's discreet attention. Taking a deep breath, Louise commented as steadily as she could, 'I was just saying to Tullah that Scott has Saul's eyes but her colouring…'

'Yes, he has, hasn't he?' Jenny Crighton agreed gratefully, relief leaking through the anxiety that had gripped her.

In one sense it had been a relief when Louise had finally agreed to come home for her grandfather's birthday, but in another...

Louise was her daughter, and she loved her, worried over her—how could she not do so?—but she had to admit that she had been anxious.

Louise had a quick temper coupled with a very easily bruised sense of pride. Watching Max talking with his sister earlier had made Jenny pray that Max wouldn't do or say something to upset his sister and put her on the defensive.

Tullah and Olivia—Jenny's niece and Louise's cousin—had both tried to reassure Jenny that everything would be all right, that teenage crushes were something that happened to everyone, and that it was just Louise's misfortune that hers had happened to be conducted under such a public glare of family attention, and that the object of her untrammelled teenage passion had been a member of her own family.

'She behaved so very badly,' Jenny had reminded them sorrowfully.

'Things did get a little out of hand,' Tullah had agreed. 'But since Louise's behaviour resulted in Saul and I getting together, and recognising how we really felt about one another far more quickly than we might otherwise have done, I have to admit that I feel more inclined to be grateful to her than anything else.'

'Louise made a mistake,' Olivia had added. 'Making mistakes is something we all do, and personally I think she'll end up a better, more well-rounded person for having had it brought home to her that she is fallible and human. She *was* rather inclined to think herself above everyone else,' she had reminded Jenny ruefully. 'A combination, perhaps, of a certain Crighton gene plus a very, very shrewd brain. What happened has softened her, made her realise that she's a human being and that there are some things she can't programme herself to achieve…'

'Have you had anything to eat yet?' Jenny pressed now. Jon, her husband, kept reminding her that Louise was now an adult woman, living her own life and holding down a very high-pressured job, but to Jenny she was still very much one of her babies, and to a mother's concerned eye Louise looked just that little bit too slender.

'I was just going to get myself something,' Louise fibbed. She was well aware of just how generous Tullah had been in coming over to her like that, but despite that generosity there was still a small knot of anxiety in Louise's stomach which made her feel that it would be unwise trying to eat.

'I was just on my way to wish Gramps a happy birthday,' she told her mother, and hopefully, once she had done so, she would be able to leave without the others thinking that…that what? That she was running away?

Running away. No, she wasn't doing that, had *never* done that, despite what some people chose to think!

'European Parliament…bunch of committee-making bureaucrats who are far too removed from what's going on in the real world…'

Louise gritted her teeth as she listened to Ben Crighton, her grandfather and family patriarch, a few minutes later. As she was perfectly well aware, so far as *he* was concerned the only real way, the only worthwhile way, to practise the law was from a barrister's chambers.

Excusing herself before she allowed him to provoke her into an argument, Louise couldn't help feeling sorry for Maddy, who had moved into the old man's large country house following an operation on his hip the year before.

The move, at first merely a temporary one to ensure that he had someone to care for him in the short term, had turned into a more permanent arrangement, with Maddy and the children living full time in Haslewich with Max's grandfather while Max spent most of his time living and working in London.

Louise couldn't understand how or why Maddy put up with Max's blatant selfishness—and his equally blatant infidelities. She certainly would never have done so, but then she would never have married a man like her brother in a thousand lifetimes. She knew how much it distressed her parents that he had turned out the way he had. Max was as unprincipled and selfish in other areas of his life as he was in his role as a husband.

Unlike their uncle David, Olivia's father and her own father's twin brother, Max might never have actually broken the law, but Louise suspected that he was perfectly capable if not of doing so, then certainly of bending it to suit his own purposes.

'He doesn't change, does he?' The rueful, familiar tones of Saul's voice coming from behind her caused Louise to whirl round, her face a stiff mask of wariness as she watched him.

The last time she and Saul had spoken to each other had been when he had consigned her to Olivia's charge, having just made it clear to her that, far from returning her feelings for him, he would really prefer never to have to set eyes on her again.

Words spoken in the heat of the moment, perhaps, but they had left their mark, their scar upon her, not least because she knew how richly deserved his fury and rejection of her had been.

'I suppose at his age…' Louise began, and then shook her head and agreed huskily, 'No. No, he doesn't.'

Ridiculous for her, at twenty-two, to feel as uncomfortable and ill at ease as a guilty child, but nevertheless she did.

Whatever malign fate had decided to make Saul the object of her teenage fantasies and longings had long since upped sticks and decamped from her emotions. The man she saw standing in front of her might not have changed but she certainly had. The Saul she saw standing before her now was once again, thankfully, nothing more to her than another member of her family.

'Your mother says you're only paying a flying visit home this time.'

'Yes. Yes, that's right,' Louise agreed. 'Pam Carlisle, my boss, has been asked to sit on a new committee being set up to look into the problems caused by potential over-fishing in the seas off the Arctic. Obviously from the legal angle there's going to be a lot of research work involved, which I'll be involved in.'

'Mmm…sounds like a good breeding ground for potential future Euro politicians in the Crighton family,' Saul teased, but Louise shook her head.

'No. Definitely not,' she denied firmly. 'Politics isn't for me. I'm afraid I'm far too outspoken for a start,' she told him ruefully. 'And politics requires a great deal more finesse than I'll ever possess.'

'You're too hard on yourself,' Saul told her. 'In more ways than one,' he added meaningfully, forcing her to hold his gaze as he added quietly, 'It's time for us to make a fresh start, Lou. What happened happened, but it's in the past now…'

Before she could say anything he added, 'Tullah and I will be coming over to Brussels some time in the next few months on company business. It would be nice if we could meet up…go out for dinner together…'

Saul worked for Aarlston-Becker, a large multinational company whose European head office was based just outside Haslewich. He and Tullah had met when she had gone to work in the company's legal department under Saul.

Unable to do anything other than simply nod her head, Louise was stunned when Saul suddenly reached out and took her in his arms, holding her tightly in a cousinly hug as he told her gruffly, 'Friends again, Lou.'

'Friends,' she managed to agree chokily, fiercely blinking back her tears.

'And don't forget…write to me…'

Louise grimaced as she listened to Katie's firm command. 'Why on earth did you have to go and get yourself involved with some wretched charity outfit that can't even run to the expense of a fax machine?' she groaned.

'*You* tell *me*…but I do enjoy my job,' Katie pointed out.

They were saying goodbye at the airport, their mother having dropped them off on her way to a meeting of the charity she and their great-aunt Ruth had set up in their home town some years earlier.

'Sorry I can't see you off properly,' she had apologised as they climbed out of her small car.

'Don't worry about it, Mum; we understand,' Louise had consoled her.

'You could always come over to Brussels to see me, you know,' Louise told her twin abruptly now. 'I'll pay for the ticket, if that would help.'

Katie gave her a brief hug. She knew how difficult it was for her sister to admit that there were any chinks in her emotional armour, even to her twin. To the world at large, Louise always came across as the more independent one of the two of them, the leader. But in reality Katie believed that *she* was the one with the less sensitively acute emotions, even though she knew that Louise would have sharply denied such an allegation. Louise had always taken upon herself the role of the bigger, braver sister, but Katie knew that inside Louise was nowhere near as confident or as determinedly independent as others seemed to think.

Even their parents seemed to have been deceived by Louise's outward assumption of sturdy bravado, and consequently *she* was the one who was always treated that little bit more gently, the one for whom extra allowances were always made, Katie acknowledged. A fact which made her oddly protective of her sister.

'Oh, by the way, did you know that Professor Simmonds has been seconded to Brussels? Apparently he's been asked to head some committee on fishing rights in the North Sea,' Katie told her vaguely.

'What? No, I *didn't* know,' Louise responded, her face paling.

'No? I thought that perhaps you may have bumped into him,' Katie told her innocently.

'No, I haven't!' But if what Katie had just told her was true, Louise suspected that she was certainly going to do so. The committee Katie was talking about had to be the same one that Louise's boss had just been co-opted onto. Of all the unwanted coincidences!

Louise's thoughts rioted frantically, her stomach churning, but she dared not let Katie see how shocked and disturbed she was.

'I know you don't *like* him,' Katie was saying quietly.

'No. I don't,' Louise agreed curtly. 'After all, he cost me my first, and—'

'Louise, that's not fair,' Katie objected gently.

Louise looked away from her. There was so much that Katie didn't know, that she *couldn't* tell her.

Gareth Simmonds had been her tutor at Oxford at a particularly traumatic time in her life, and he had been a witness not just to that trauma, and the way she had made a complete and utter fool of herself, but he had also…

Louise bit her lip. The feeling of panic churning her stomach was increasing instead of easing.

'That's the final call for my flight,' she told Katie thankfully, giving her twin a swift hug before grabbing hold of her flight bag and heading for her gateway.

Gareth Simmonds in Brussels!

That was all she needed!

CHAPTER TWO

GARETH SIMMONDS in Brussels! Louise gave a small groan and closed her eyes, shaking her head in refusal of the stewardess's offer of a drink.

Trust Katie to wait to drop *that* bombshell on her until the last minute. Still, at least she *had* warned her, and forewarned was, as they say, forearmed.

Gareth Simmonds. She ground her teeth in impotent fury. She had been halfway through her first year when he had stepped into the shoes of her previous tutor, who'd had to retire unexpectedly on the grounds of ill health, and he and Louise had clashed right from the start.

She had resented the far more pro-active role he had made it plain he intended to play as her tutor. She had been used to his elderly and ailing predecessor, who had, in the main, been content to leave her to her own devices—something which had suited Louise down to the ground, giving her, as it had, ample opportunity to give the minimum amount of attention to her studies whilst she concentrated on what had become the far more important matter of making Saul fall in love with her.

The situation would have been bad enough if Gareth Simmonds had merely concerned himself with his official role as her tutor, but, no, that hadn't been enough for him. He had had the gall…the cheek… the…the effrontery to take it upon himself to interfere in her personal life as well.

Louise's tense shoulders twitched angrily. The last thing she needed right now—just when she was beginning to feel she was getting her life back on an even keel again, just when the events of the weekend had made her feel that at last, *finally*, she had begun to reclaim her sense of self-respect—was to have the whole ugly mess of her past dragged up again in the person of Gareth Simmonds.

He was going to Brussels to head a committee, Katie had said, when repeating to her the information she had garnered at an informal reunion of her old university classmates, and not just any committee either. Louise could feel her body starting to tense defensively. The thought that she might have to have any kind of contact with Gareth Simmonds was unacceptable, untenable. Anger, pride and panic started to well up inside her, causing her throat to tighten as though her own despairing emotions were threatening to choke her.

Gareth Simmonds. They had clashed straight away, something about him sending sharp, prickling, atavistic feelings of dislike and apprehension quivering through her body, and that had been *before* that disastrous confrontation between them at the end of her first year at Oxford, when he had sent for her and warned her of the potentially dire consequences of her not giving more time and attention to her work.

She had been far more headstrong and self-willed in those days, and the fact that he had had the gall to challenge her over anything, never mind the torment of her love for Saul, had driven her to retaliate. But he had been too quick for her, too subtle…too…

She had hated him with much the same intensity with which she had loved Saul, and with just as little effect, and the last thing she wanted or needed at this stage in her life was to be confronted with the physical evidence of her own youthful stupidity.

She could still remember…

There had been a good deal of giggling and gossip when he had first arrived at Oxford—the youngest Chair they had ever had, and the sexiest, according to his female students. Louise had shrugged her shoulders in disdain. *However* sexy *others* might find him, *she* was not interested. In her eyes he could never match up to Saul. No man could.

True, he might be over six feet with the kind of Celtic colouring that produced a lethal combination of thick dark hair and incredibly brilliant dark blue eyes, but for all Louise cared he could have modelled for the hunchback of Notre Dame.

'Have you *heard* his voice,' one besotted student had breathed, wild-eyed. 'I could orgasm just listening to him.'

Louise had looked witheringly at her. *Saul's* voice made her go weak at the knees, and Gareth Simmonds sounded nothing like him. In fact, the only things they did have in common were that they were both in their thirties—although Gareth Simmonds was a good seven years younger than Saul—and they could both display a decidedly brutal verbal toughness when they so chose. From Saul, the merest hint of a sharp word could reduce her to choking black misery. From Gareth Simmonds it tended to provoke a fierce desire to retaliate in kind.

He *might* have been her tutor, but that hadn't given him the right to interfere in her life in the way he had done—and besides… But, no, she must not think about that—not now.

Abruptly Louise realised that the plane had landed.

Automatically she stood up and reached to retrieve her bag from the overhead locker, and then froze as the man occupying the seat behind her also stood up to do the same thing.

'You!' she whispered as she came face to face with the very man who had just been occupying her thoughts and exercising her temper.

'Hello, Louise.' Gareth Simmonds acknowledged her calmly. Shakily Louise grabbed her bag and turned her back on him. What an appalling coincidence that *he* should be on the same flight as her!

Determinedly keeping her back towards him, Louise edged her way into the aisle and headed for the exit.

A sharp wind whipped across the tarmac as they left the plane, and as she hurried towards the arrivals lounge Louise reassured herself that her quickened pace was caused by the chilly evening air, and certainly not by any fear of coming face to face with Gareth Simmonds a second time.

Once through Customs Louise headed for the taxi rank, giving the cab driver her address at the large block of apartments where she lived. The apartment she rented was small, and fearsomely expensive, but at least she lived on her own, she comforted herself as she paid off the taxi driver and walked into the apartment block foyer.

While she filled the kettle, Louise ran her answering machine tape. A small rueful smile curled her mouth as she heard Jean Claude's familiar, sexy, smoky French accent. She had dated the Frenchman casually a few times, but was well aware of his reputation as an incorrigible flirt.

He was telephoning to ask if she was free for dinner during the week. Louise went to pick up and open her diary. She was due to accompany her boss to an inaugural meeting of the new committee in the morning. She suspected it might possibly run on until after lunch, and then at night there was an official dinner.

'The French contingent especially are going to be asking some tricky questions,' Pam Carlisle had warned Louise. 'They're none too happy about the fact that the Chair appointed is British. It's only the fact that he's known to be pro-European that's persuaded them to give their grudging acceptance of his appointment. The disputed waters are, after all, still officially British.'

'But they want to change that…' Louise had guessed.

'Well, they certainly want to get their own legal right to fish the waters.'

They had gone on to discuss the legal ramifications of the situation, and Louise had never thought to ask her boss the identity of the committee's Chair. Why should she have done? It had never even crossed her mind that the new appointee could possibly be her ex-tutor and protagonist Gareth Simmonds. Hadn't his prestigious lectureship coupled with the doting adoration of half the female student population been enough for him? Louise wondered bitterly.

'I'll bet he's absolutely heaven in bed,' she could remember one of her co-students breathing excitedly. 'And he's not married.'

'Heaven in bed'. Louise tensed abruptly. He had certainly been hell out of it! To her at least.

'He's rumbled us,' Katie had warned her. 'He's guessed that I've been sitting in at lectures to cover for you. He actually *called* me Katherine yesterday…'

'So…?' Louise had said grittily. 'That *is* your name, isn't it?'

'It's *my* name,' Katie had agreed. 'But at the time I was attending one of his lectures pretending to be *you*.'

'He probably made a genuine mistake,' Louise had told her irritably. She had gone home to Haslewich, on the pretext of having left some of her books behind on her last visit home, but in reality so that she could see Saul. To her chagrin, though, Saul had been away on business, and the whole exercise had proved to be a complete waste of time.

In those days she had not always treated her twin as considerately as she might have, Louise acknowledged now, as the boiling kettle disturbed her reverie, and in fact it was probably very true to say she had often been guilty of bullying and browbeating Katie into doing as *she* wanted.

Things were different now, of course. She had done what she could to make amends, and, as she was the first to acknowledge, there were areas in which her twin had shown considerably more strength of purpose and determination than she could ever have exhibited herself.

She had been in her late teens then, though, and so totally obsessed with Saul that nothing else, *no one* else, had been important.

Briefly she closed her eyes. This afternoon, when Saul had put his arms round her to give her that firm fraternal hug, initially her body had totally recoiled from his touch—not out of rejection but out of fear, a deep-rooted, instinctive, self-protective fear that there might be some hidden part of her that was still susceptible to her old romantic dreams. But to her relief what she had actually felt, *all* she had actually felt, had been a warm and very reassuring sense of peace and release, coupled with the knowledge that there was nothing, after all, for her to fear. Being hugged by Saul, being held in his arms, had meant no more to her than if he had been Olivia's husband Caspar, or one of the Chester cousins, or indeed any other man of whom she had reason to be fond in a totally non-sexual and uncomplicated way.

She had *known* then that she was truly and totally free of the past, at least where *Saul* was concerned.

Frowningly she stirred her coffee.

She had behaved foolishly when she had been at university, there was no getting away from that fact, but she wasn't alone in having done that—many other students had done the same.

She picked up her coffee mug too quickly and some of the hot liquid spilled onto her hand. She cursed angrily under her breath.

Damn Gareth Simmonds. *Why* on earth couldn't he have stayed safely where he was in Oxford—and in her past?

The *last* thing she needed right now was having him around studying her…watching her with those too perceptive, too knowing evening-sky-blue eyes of his…judging her…just *waiting* for her to make a mistake…

Louise started to grind her teeth.

Well, she'd got news for him. She wasn't the Louise she had been at Oxford any longer. She was a *woman* now, an adult, holding down a highly responsible and demanding job, proving that she could control and run her *own* life, that she didn't need the constant back-up and support of her twin sister to be there at her side all the time, to do her bidding, to make her feel whole and complete. God, but she had hated him for throwing that accusation at her—just one of the scathing criticisms he had made of her!

It should have been *Saul's* denouncement of her, after she had so dangerously tricked Tullah into following her into the maze and left her there at the masked ball, that should have remained like a scar on her consciousness, a dialogue that ran for ever through her head as she tried to argue her way out of it, but oddly it wasn't. It was her arguments, her confrontations with her tutor about which she *still* had bad dreams, and still, in times of stress, played over and over again through her memory.

Oxford, the time after she had finally been forced to realise that Saul would never love her, that in fact he loved someone else. Oxford and Gareth Simmonds. Oxford, Italy—and Gareth Simmonds. *Italy* and Gareth Simmonds.

Picking up her coffee, Louise walked into her small sitting room and curled up on the sofa, closing her eyes. She didn't *want* to relive those memories, but she could feel the weight of them pressing down on her, pushing their way into her consciousness just as Gareth Simmonds seemed to be pushing his way into the new life she had made for herself.

As though the debacle of the masquerade ball had not been punishment enough for her to contend with, that following week she had received a letter from Gareth

Simmonds. A curt letter informing her that he wished to see her as there were certain matters concerning her work which he wished to discuss with her.

Her parents knew she had received the letter, and there had been no way she had been able to keep its contents a secret from them—although Katie had been sworn to secrecy over the worst of her excesses in skipping tutorials. If her mother and father had not actually stood over her while she went through the humiliation of telephoning Gareth Simmonds and making an appointment to see him, they had certainly left her in no doubt about their feelings of shock and disappointment at the way she had been abusing both her intelligence and the opportunity that going to Oxford had given her.

Furiously she had blamed Gareth Simmonds for adding to her problems, while having to give way to her parents' firm insistence that they would drive her to Oxford for the interview, where she planned to stay for a few days in order to try to catch up with her work.

They had set out after breakfast, her mother patently unhappy and trying to control her tears and her father unexpectedly grim-faced and distant, and Louise had known what was going through both their minds. Was *she*, like her elder brother Max, going to turn out to be one of those Crightons who had inherited the same genes as her uncle David—the 'S' gene, as she and Katie had nicknamed it as teenagers. The 'S' standing for selfish, stupid and self-destructive.

She had *wanted* to reassure them, to tell them that there was nothing for them to worry about, but she had still been deep in shock herself, still traumatised not just by *what* she had done but by the frightening emotions which had given rise to her dangerous behaviour.

'I can't believe you could behave so appallingly,' her father had told her grimly, his voice shaking slightly with emotion as he'd confronted her with the full enormity of what she had done after the ball.

'What were you going to *do*? Leave Tullah in the maze until—'

'No… No… I just…' Tears streaming down her face, Louise had turned her head away from him, not able to bring herself to admit that she had been so obsessed by her need to make Saul see her as a woman, to make him *love* her as a woman, that she had simply seen Tullah as a hindrance who was standing in her way. Someone who was preventing Saul from seeing her, Louise, properly, and recognising that they were meant to be together.

Katie had travelled to Oxford with them to give her some moral support. She was also going to use the time to see friends who'd stayed up in Oxford to earn some money waiting at the local bars and restaurant. While her mother had fussed around her rooms, tidying up Louise's discarded clothes and books, Katie had simply taken hold of her hand and gripped it tightly in a gesture of sisterly solidarity and love.

It was only when her mother had gone to shake her duvet and straighten up her untidy bed that Louise had finally moved, pushing her away and telling her fiercely, 'I can do that…'

What had already happened was shameful enough. To have her mother move her pillow and discover that she slept with Saul's purloined shirt beneath it would have been the ultimate humiliation.

When they were on their own Katie asked her awkwardly, 'Do you…do you want to talk about it…?'

Angrily Louise shook her head.

'Oh, Lou,' Katie whispered sombrely, her voice full of pain and despair at what her twin had done, and love and pity for Louise herself.

'Stop fussing,' Louise commanded her.

'I'm sure Professor Simmonds knows what we've been doing,' Katie warned. 'I didn't want to say anything in front of the parents, but, as I told you, he's definitely rumbled the fact that I've been standing in at his lectures for you,' she went on. 'Have you got the notes I did for you?'

'Yes,' Louise acknowledged shortly. 'But how could he know of our switch? We've played tricks on our friends before now, and they've never realized.'

Katie waited several seconds before responding quietly, 'It's different with Professor Simmonds. He just seems to know. It's almost as though he's got some kind of sixth sense which allows him to tell the difference between us.'

'Some sixth sense?' Louise derided, scoffing. 'He's a professor of law, not a magician.' But even so she was left feeling uneasy and on edge. Something about Gareth Simmonds challenged her to defy him and to get the better of him, and it infuriated her that so far all her attempts to do so had ended up in her ignominious defeat.

'He called me Katherine,' Katie reminded her. 'Even though I was wearing your clothes and the others all believed I was you.'

'Arrogant, self-assured pig,' Louise muttered aggressively. 'I *loathe* him.'

But nowhere near so much as she loathed herself.

After Katie had left to let her sister draw her thoughts together—they had made the decision that, although they both wanted to go up to Oxford, they did not want to live together, nor to be thought of as an inseparable pair, and so were taking different courses and rented separate accommodation—Louise picked up the course notes her twin had left for her. But although her eyes skimmed over their contents her brain was simply not capable of taking in their meaning. How *could* it, when it, like her emotions, was still struggling to come to terms with the death blow that events had dealt her?

She had been in love with Saul and had dreamed of him returning her feelings for as long as she had been capable of knowing what being in love meant, and it had simply never occurred to her that she would not ultimately win him. Why should it? Every other goal she had ever set herself she had reached, and it had never entered her head that securing Saul's love would be any different.

Katie's writing started to blur in front of her eyes. Shakily she flung the papers down, wrapping her arms around her body. She felt so cold inside, so empty, and yet at the same time filled with such an enormous weight of fear and pain.

Automatically she went over to her bed and felt beneath the pillow for Saul's shirt, hugging it to her, closing her eyes and breathing in the warm Saul smell of him which still clung to it. But for once his faint but oh, so evocative scent failed to comfort her.

It wasn't his shirt she wanted to hold, she acknowledged as she threw it away from her with a wrenching shudder. It was the man himself. *Saul* himself. But he had made it cruelly plain to her that *that* was never going to happen.

'Saul, Saul, Saul…' Helplessly she cried out his name, whispering it over and over again inside her head as the tears started to flow.

Worn out by the intensity of her emotions, she finally fell asleep, only to wake up in the early hours, cold and shivering, her eyes sore and hot.

She was still fully dressed. She hadn't eaten, but she knew that the very thought of food was totally repugnant to her. As she got up she caught sight of the discarded notes that Katie had given her, and her heart gave a small, anxious thud.

Gareth Simmonds wasn't like old Professor Lewis. There was no way she would be able to sweet-talk him into overlooking the falling standard of her work—and Louise knew that it *had* been falling—but how could she be expected to concentrate on her studies when her thoughts, her heart, her whole self had been focused so totally on Saul?

'Ah, Louise. Good. Thank you for returning to Oxford at short notice. Did *your sister* come with you?'

Despite the calm and apparently friendly tone of his voice as he invited her into his study, Louise was not deceived by her tutor's apparent affability, nor by the way he'd emphasised the words 'your sister'.

Her plan of action, before her arrival here in Gareth Simmonds' study, had been to attempt to bluff things out, and to stick determinedly to the fiction that she had attended all his lectures and that *he* was at fault in mistaking her for Katie. But one look at his face, one brief clash between her own still sore and aching dark beautiful eyes and his far too clear and penetrative navy blue gaze, had been enough to alert her to the disastrous potential of such an unwise course of action.

'Sit down,' he instructed her when she failed to make any response—a first for Louise. She was not normally short of quick, sassy answers to even the most awkward questions.

It was a new experience for her to feel unnerved enough to hold her tongue and apprehensively await events. She could see a mixture of pity and irritation on his face that hurt her pride. How dared he pity her?

To her chagrin, she could feel her eyes starting to burn with the betraying sting of her emotions. Quickly she ducked her head. The last thing she wanted was for the urbane, controlled and hatefully superior man seated in front of her to guess that she wasn't feeling anywhere near as sure of herself as she was trying to pretend, and that in fact, far from not giving a damn about what he was saying to her—as she was desperately trying to show—she was feeling thoroughly and frighteningly vulnerable, and shocked by the situation she had got herself into.

Blinking furiously to banish her tears, she was unaware of the fact that Gareth Simmonds had got up from behind his desk until she suddenly realised that he was standing beside her, the muscled bulk of his body casting not just a heavy shadow but inexplicably causing the air around her suddenly to feel much warmer.

'Louise. The last thing I want to do is to make things hard for you. I know things haven't been…easy for you and that emotionally…If there's a problem that I…'

Immediately Louise stiffened. It had been bad enough having to cope with the mingled anger and pity of her family, but to have Gareth Simmonds offering her his lofty, condescending 'understanding' was more than she could bear.

'The only problem I have right now is you,' she told him aggressively, relieved to be able to stir up her own anger and use it to keep the humiliating threat of her tears at bay.

She thought she heard him catch a swiftly indrawn breath, and waited for his retaliation, but instead he simply said humorously, 'I know that legally you're an adult, Louise, but right now you remind me more of my six-year-old niece. I'm not your enemy, you know. I'm simply trying to help you.'

'Don't you dare patronise me. I am not your niece,' Louise retaliated, standing up, her cheeks flushed with temper, fully intending to storm out of his office.

But before she could do so he stopped her, taking hold of her wrist and gently but determinedly pushing her back down into her chair. And then, before she could voice her anger, to her consternation he knelt down beside her chair, so that their eyes were level as he told her, 'Stop making things so hard for yourself. You've got a first-class brain but it won't do you any good whatsoever unless you stop letting it be overruled by that stiff-necked pride of yours. We all go through times in our lives when we need other people's help, you know, Louise—'

'Well, I don't,' Louise interrupted him rudely, adding fiercely, 'And even if I did, the last person I would turn to for it would be you.'

There was a long pause before he finally said softly, 'That's a very interesting statement, Louise, and if I may say so, a rather dangerously challenging one.'

He was, Louise recognised with a sharp thrill of awareness, looking not into her eyes any more but at her mouth.

'He is just so sexy,' she remembered her fellow female students saying when they talked about him, and now, like someone hurtling recklessly into unexpected danger, she knew exactly what they meant.

As immediate as that recognition, and twice as powerful, was her panicky, virginal rejection of it. She didn't want to see Gareth Simmonds as a sexually compelling and desirable man. She was only allowed to have that kind of reaction to Saul.

'I want to go,' she told him unsteadily. 'I…'

'Not yet. I haven't finished talking to you,' he had countered calmly. But he stepped back from her, as though somehow he had guessed just what she was feeling and wanted to make things just that little bit easier for her—which was totally impossible, of course. Louise knew that he disliked her every bit as much as she did him, and that he enjoyed making life difficult and unpleasant for her.

Holding her gaze, he said, 'Very well, Louise, if you want to do this the hard way then that's your choice. I do know what's been going on, Louise, so don't bother to waste my time or your own apparently failing brain power in trying to lie to me. In your shoes it would be pointless wasting the energy and intelligence you very obviously need for your studies on dreaming up unrealistic scenarios.

'In *my* experience there are generally two reasons why a student suddenly fails to live up to his or her forecast academic expectations. One of those is that quite simply, and unfortunately for them, they can't. By some fluke of fate and the examination board they've managed to get themselves onto a degree course they are in no way intellectually equipped to handle. The other…'

He paused and looked calmly at her. 'The other is that for reasons of their own they have decided that they don't want to, that there are other and no doubt more important matters to claim their attention. The solution in both cases is, however, the same. For those who don't have the ability to continue with their course, to bring it to a swift end is, I think, the kindest way to end their misery. To those who have the ability, but who don't wish to use it… It isn't so much *their* misery one wants to bring to an end, but one's own, and that of their fellow students…'

Louise stared at him in furious disbelief.

'You're threatening to have me sent down. You *can't* do that,' she told him flatly.

Gareth Simmond's dark eyebrows had risen.

'No? I rather think you'll find that I can. But forgive me, Louise, I assumed that this must be what you wanted. After all…' he picked up her course work and threw it disdainfully across his desk towards her '…to judge from this, continuing with your course is the last thing you really want to do.

'Look,' he went on, when Louise continued to glare at him. 'If I've got it wrong, and the problem is that the work is too taxing for you, please tell me and I'll try my best to get you transferred onto a less… demanding course. There *are* university standards,' he reminded her, with deceptive gentleness, 'and I'm afraid that we do still strive for excellence rather than the mere pedestrian. If you feel that you're not up to the work—'

'Of course I'm up to it,' Louise snapped angrily at him, her eyes flashing. How dared he stand there and suggest that she wasn't up to the work? His predecessor had told her on more than one occasion, albeit perhaps in a roundabout way, that he considered her to be one of his most promising students. His predecessor… Louise clenched her fists.

'When a student's grades suddenly start to fall, *some* people believe that it's more the teaching that's at fault, rather than the pupil,' she challenged him feistily.

Gareth eyed her thoughtfully.

'Some people might,' he agreed coolly. 'But others might more intelligently suspect that the pupil's non-appearance at nearly half her lectures and tutorials might have something to do with the situation. Wouldn't you agree? I'm not a fool, Louise,' he said, at her look of surprise. 'I know very well that your sister has been standing in for you at my lectures.

'Look,' he continued, when Louise made no reply, 'we could argue about this all day. The fact is, Louise, that you've been skipping lectures and missing out on vital course work. And you've lost weight,' he told her abruptly, causing Louise to stare at him in astonishment. How on earth could he tell? Not even her twin or her mother had commented or appeared to notice—and with good reason, since she had taken to wearing loose baggy tops over her regulation jeans, knowing how much her mother would start to fuss if she thought for one moment that she wasn't eating properly.

Olivia's mother, although only a Crighton by marriage, had suffered from bulimia for many years, and her behaviour during the years of her marriage to David, her father's brother, had left its scars on the family. Her own mother was fervently keen on healthy, sensible eating—mealtimes, until Louise had left home, had been old-fashioned family affairs, with everyone seated around the same table. Not that Louise had any problem with that—at least, not usually. She liked her food, and had a good healthy appetite, but just recently she had found herself unable to eat, too sick with longing and need, too hungry for Saul's love to satisfy her appetite with anything else.

'I appreciate that you're having personal problems...' Gareth said now.

But before he could finish, and suggest that she might benefit from talking them over with someone, she jumped in, demanding aggressively, 'Who told you that? They—'

'You did,' Gareth interrupted her levelly as he studied her mutinous face. 'You've lost weight. You're obviously not sleeping and you're certainly not working,' he reminded her quietly. 'The facts speak for themselves. I don't need a degree in psychology to interpret them.

'Professor Lewis told me that he confidently expected you to get a double first. On the basis of your current course work I'd say you'd be lucky to make a third. It's up to you, Louise. Either start giving your work some serious attention or...'

'You'll have me thrown out,' Louise guessed bitterly.

Without giving him the opportunity to say any more, she snatched up her papers and stormed angrily out of his room.

God, but she hated him. *Hated* him!

'Well, how did it go?' Katie demanded. She had been waiting anxiously for Louise to return from her interview and now, as she came hurtling out into the quadrangle, almost running, Katie had trouble keeping up with her.

'Slow down,' she begged her, catching hold of her arm, 'and tell me what he said.'

'He *said*... He *threatened* to have me sent down,' Louise told her flatly.

'What? Oh, Lou, no! Did you tell him, explain…? Did you…?'

'Tell him what?' Louise asked bitterly.

'About…about Saul… Did you explain? Did you—?'

Abruptly Louise stopped moving and turned round to face her twin.

'Are you *mad*?' she asked her grimly. 'Tell *Gareth Simmonds* about Saul?' She closed her eyes as she remembered the revolting pity she had seen in his eyes. How *dared* he pity her? How *dared* anyone?

'He's given me until Christmas to catch up…'

'Well, that shouldn't be too difficult.' Katie tried to comfort her. 'We've got the rest of the summer vac. And I can help you.'

'I don't *want* your help. I just want—' Louise began angrily, and then stopped.

The force, the futility of her own feelings frightened her. She felt oddly sick and light-headed.

'Why don't we spend the evening together?' she suggested to Katie, trying to make amends for her earlier bad temper. 'We could have supper and share a bottle of wine. I've still got that case in my room that Aunt Ruth gave us at the beginning of term. She said it would come in useful for student parties…'

'I'd love to but I'm afraid I can't,' Katie told her regretfully, shaking her head before explaining blushingly, 'I…I've got a date and…'

'A date? Who with?' Louise questioned her sister.

But Katie shook her head and told her awkwardly, 'Oh, it's no one you know… Oh, Lou,' she pleaded as she turned to give her twin a fierce hug, 'I do understand how you must feel, but please, please try to forget about Saul.'

'I wish to God I could,' Louise told her chokily. 'But

I'm not to get the chance, am I? Not if I get sent down
and I have to go back to Haslewich. Oh, Katie…' It was
on the tip of her tongue to plead with her twin to cancel her date and spend the evening with her, but then
she remembered the look she had seen in Gareth
Simmonds' eyes when he had told her that he knew she
had been using Katie to stand in at his lectures for her,
and she resisted the impulse.

She was not, she assured herself fiercely, the selfish,
thoughtless, self-absorbed person his look had implied.
She would have done the same thing for Katie…if
Katie had asked…

But Katie would not have asked, a small inner voice
told her.

The summer afternoon had given way to evening.
Louise stared tiredly around her room. Papers and text-
books covered every surface, and her head was swimming with facts she couldn't assimilate; they floated in
her brain like congealing fat on top of her mother's
home-made stock, coagulating and clogging.

Saul. Where was he now…? What was he doing…?
She got up and walked into her small kitchenette. She
couldn't remember the last time she had eaten, but the
mere thought of food made her feel sick.

Out of the corner of her eye she caught sight of
Aunt Ruth's wine stacked in a dusty corner. Dizzily she
went and removed a bottle.

Aunt Ruth had quaintly old-fashioned ideas about
how Oxford's modern-day undergraduates lived. The
wine she had chosen for her great-nieces had been carefully selected for its full-bodied richness. Ruth had
imagined it would be drunk at the kind of undergrad

gathering that featured in expensive TV dramas—adaptations of books set in a glittering gilded era.

Louise opened one of the bottles and poured herself a glass. She was not normally a drinker. Oh, she enjoyed a decent glass of wine with good food, and she had gone through the normal student ritual of drinking at the bar in the students' union during the first few weeks at university, but that had simply been a rite of passage, something to be endured rather than enjoyed.

The red wine was rich and fruity, warming her throat and heating her cold, empty stomach.

Louise sank down onto the floor, owlishly studying the mass of paper she had spread all around her. Katie's handwriting danced dizzily before her eyes. Frowningly she blinked as she tried to focus and concentrate, quickly finishing off her glass of wine.

It was making her feel distinctly better—lighter, number. It was even making it possible for her to think about Saul without that wrenching, tearing pain deep inside her, threatening to destroy her.

Saul…

As she walked erratically back from the kitchenette, having refilled her glass, Louise tried to summon up Saul's beloved mental image and found, to her consternation, that she couldn't—that for some reason his beloved, adored features had become amorphous and vague, sliding away before she could crystallise them into a hard image. Even more infuriatingly, the harder she tried to visualise him, the more impossible it became. Instead, the male image that came most easily to her mind's eye was that of Gareth Simmonds.

Frantically Louise took a deep gulp of her wine, keeping a firm grip on it as she searched feverishly through her diary for the photograph of Saul which she always, always kept there.

Louise was clutching the photograph when she heard someone knocking on her door.

Katie… Her sister had changed her mind, cancelled her date realising just how much she needed someone to be with her. Tipsily, Louise lurched towards the door, yanking it open as she cried out, 'Oh, Katie, thank goodness you're here. I…'

Her voice faded away as her visitor stepped grimly over the threshold, firmly closing the door behind him.

'You!' she said shakily as she looked up into the merciless gaze with which her tutor had swept the room before finally coming to rest on her tear-stained face. 'What do you want…?'

'I came to bring you these,' Gareth Simmonds told her, and held some papers. 'You left them on my desk this morning…'

'Oh… I…' Awkwardly Louise reached out to take them from him, forgetting that she was still holding not just Saul's photograph but also a half-full glass of wine.

As she reached for the papers Saul's photograph slipped from her fingers. Immediately Louise tried to retrieve it, accidentally bumping into Gareth Simmonds as she did so, wine slopping from her glass onto both his wrist and her own arm.

Before she could stop him Gareth Simmonds was bending down to pick up Saul's photograph.

'No. Don't…' she began, but it was too late.

As he picked it up he paused, studying Saul's features thoughtfully and then looking from the photograph to her face before declaring ironically, 'He's a very good-looking man, Louise, I'll grant you that. But is he really worth messing up the whole of your future over? He's too old for you, anyway,' he added dismissively.

Louise's temper, rubbed raw during her earlier dressing down at his hands, burst into crazy pain.

'No, he's not…he's…' To her consternation she felt fiery tears beginning to burn the backs of her eyes. Pouring the rest of the contents of her glass down her throat, she gulped rebelliously, 'I'm not a child, you know. I'm a woman…'

The derisive look in his eyes demolished the last of her precarious hold on her temper and pushed her over the edge of caution into reckless fury.

'What is it?' she demanded. 'Don't you believe me? Well, I am, and I'll prove it to you… Saul *would* have wanted me if she—Tullah—hadn't come along…'

'How much of that stuff have you had to drink?' she heard him demanding as he ignored her furious statement and removed from her hand the glass she was still holding to sniff it with an irritated frown.

'Not enough,' she told him forlornly, adding aggressively. 'And give me back my glass. I *need* another drink…'

'No way. You've already had more than enough.'

'No, I haven't…' Angrily Louise reached out towards him, trying to snatch back her glass, but he was holding onto it too tightly, and as he lifted his arm to remove it even further from her reach she lost her balance and staggered heavily into him. His body had all the unyielding hardness of solid rock, only it felt much warmer… warmer and…

Louise blinked as she realised that the heavy thud she could feel beneath her hand was the beat of his heart.

It felt oddly reassuring…*comforting*… Dizzily she

started to frown as her alcohol-confused brain tried to assimilate this unacceptable information. She had the most peculiar desire to put her head against his chest, just where her hand was resting, and close her eyes, to let herself be comforted by that steady, sure heartbeat, like a child being soothed by the comfort of its parent.

Experimentally her fingers flexed and relaxed. She could feel the springiness of his body hair beneath the fabric of his shirt. Her eyes widened as she took in this additional information. Louise instinctively let her body start to relax against the warmth of his.

The arm he had raised to steady her when she had first fallen against him was still there, holding her, supporting her. She wriggled closer to his body and closed her eyes. She could smell the man-scent of him—so much stronger than the elusive, hard-to-reach scent that clung to Saul's shirt. This was the real thing, a *real* man. Louise breathed in deeply and appreciatively. His hand had moved to her hip, hard and warm through her clothes. She *liked* the feel of it there.

'Louise.'

The sharp warning note in his voice made her open her eyes and focus dizzily on him.

'No, don't go,' she whispered drunkenly. 'Don't go… I want you to stay with me… I want…'

He started to withdraw from her, and she read the stern message in his eyes. She quickly closed her own eyes and reached up with one hand to cup his face. She lifted her head and opened her mouth against his, using her other hand to take his hand from her hip to her breast.

As she felt the hard male warmth of his palm against her breast her body stiffened, quivering in excited expectation. The deep, tremulous breath she took lifted her breast against his hand. She felt his fingers curve into the shape of her body and his touch become a caress. The pad of his thumb stroked her nipple gently, and a quiver of sensual delight ran through her. This was what she had ached for, *yearned* for. Her tongue-tip stroked his lips, urgently demanding entrance, her breathing quickening in passionate arousal.

She had waited so long to be with him like this. Her teeth tugged pleadingly at his bottom lip as desire flooded through her. She could feel his lips starting to part as he gave in to her feminine aggression.

She had been *so* hungry for him to kiss her like this, she acknowledged dizzily as his mouth started to move over hers. She adjusted her body to get closer to him, and felt him shift his weight to accommodate her. A jolt of sensations rocketed through her, her inhibitions obliterated by the powerful force of the rich wine she had consumed. She felt as though she was floating on a high tide of incredible sensation. Her tongue darted wantonly into his mouth. She *wanted* him to touch her without her clothes, to feel his hands on her bare body. She *wanted* to touch him the same way—to absorb every last essence of him.

This was what she had been crying out for, starving for. *Dying for!* This, and *him*.

Against his mouth she cried his name…

'Saul. Saul… Saul…'

Abruptly Louise found herself being set free, *pushed* away from the intimacy of the male body her own craved so badly. Only his hands still held her, manacling her wrists as he shook her.

'Saul,' she protested.

'Open your eyes, Louise,' she heard a harsh and

shockingly familiar male voice demanding bitingly. 'I am *not* your precious Saul, whoever he might be...'

Her tutor! She wasn't... This wasn't Saul at all. It was...

Abruptly she opened her eyes, gagging nauseously on the combination of too much wine, too little food and too much man—much too much man, her body told her as she reeled with shock. It was a lethal combination of strong wine mixed with strong emotion.

'I feel sick,' she wailed piteously.

'Oh, God,' she heard Gareth breathe irately, and then the next thing she knew was that he had picked her up and was half carrying her, half dragging her into her small bathroom, where he pushed her down in front of the lavatory—*and* only just in time, Louise realised as her stomach heaved and she started to retch.

It seemed like a lifetime before her stomach had disgorged its unwanted contents, but logically she knew it could only have been minutes.

Cold and shaking, she stood up, clinging onto the edge of the basin, running the tap and reaching automatically for some mouthwash.

She still felt dizzy, confused, not really sure just what was happening. Clumsily she headed for the bathroom door, only to find herself being taken hold of very firmly and marched into the living room.

'Sit down and eat this,' she heard herself being told, and she was pushed unceremoniously into a chair and handed a plate of hot toast.

'I'm not hungry...' Apathetically she started to turn her head away.

'Eat it,' he ordered. 'My God, what's the *matter* with you? What the hell are you trying to do to yourself...?'

Louise felt her head starting to ache.

'Why don't you go away?' she demanded shakily.

'Not until you've eaten this,' she was told implacably.

Louise looked at the toast. Her stomach started to heave again.

'I don't want it,' she told him stubbornly. 'I just want—'

'Saul…' he interrupted her savagely. 'Yes. I *know*. You've already told me that…remember…?'

Louise blanched as she realised just what he meant. The alcoholic fog clouding her brain was beginning to clear with unwelcome speed. She looked at his mouth. Had she actually…? She could see a small swollen bruise marking his bottom lip, where she had… Quickly she looked away.

'I don't feel well. I…I want to go to bed…'

'Why? So that you can fantasise over your precious Saul?' he derided unkindly.

Louise closed her eyes. She could feel another wave of dizziness surging over her. She tried to stand up and the dizziness increased. She could feel herself starting to black out. She tried to fight it, and then stopped. What was the point? What was the point in *anything* in a life that didn't have Saul in it.

Defeatedly she let herself slide down into the darkness.

When she woke up she was lying, still dressed, in bed, and Katie was sitting on a chair next to it, watching her. Her room had been tidied up and the air smelled fresh with polish and coffee. It was light outside, she recognised.

'What are *you* doing here?' she asked her sister

groggily. Her throat felt sore and her head ached dreadfully.

'Professor Simmonds came looking for me. He said you weren't very well,' Katie told her carefully, avoiding looking directly at her.

Professor Simmonds. Louise closed her eyes, her body starting to shake as she remembered what she had done. With appalling clarity and total recall, behind her closed eyelids she could not only *see* the expression on Gareth Simmonds' face, she could even more demeaningly actually *feel* every sensation she had felt when she had…when *she* had…

Groaning, she rolled over, burying her face in her pillow.

'What is it? Aren't you feeling well? Do you want to be sick?' Katie asked anxiously.

'I… I… What did Professor Simmonds say to you about…about me?' she demanded frantically.

'Er…nothing… Well…he just said that you weren't well,' Katie told her, adding hurriedly, 'There's some kind of bug going round. Loads of people have gone down with it. He *did* say that if you wanted to go home immediately, without spending those few days sorting yourself out, starting the job of catching up…'

'No. No, I can't.' Louise panicked. 'Saul…'

'Saul has taken Tullah down to see his parents,' Katie explained quietly.

'I don't want to go home,' she told her twin angrily, stopping to frown as she saw the way that Katie was avoiding meeting her eyes as she fidgeted with the pile of books she had just straightened.

'What is it? What have you done?' she demanded, with that intuition which was so strong between them, knowing immediately that there was something Katie was hiding from her, something she didn't want her to know.

Immediately Katie flushed.

'Tell me…' Louise ordered bossily. 'Tell me, Katie…'

'Uh…Professor Simmonds, when he came to look for me to tell me that you weren't very well, he said…he asked me about Saul…'

'He *what*? And *what* did you tell him?' Louise demanded, her eyes blazing furiously with temper and dread.

'I…I tried not to tell him, Lou,' Katie told her, begging her, 'Please try to understand… He was… I *thought*, from the way he was talking about Saul, that *you* must have told him—that *you* had said…'

'*What* did you tell him, Katie?' Louise demanded inexorably, ignoring her twin's attempts to sideline her.

'I told him what Saul meant to you… I told him… I told him that you love Saul, but that he…' Katie stopped and looked away from her.

'I'm sorry, Lou, but he was so insistent, and I…' She shook her head. 'He said you were ill, and I was just so worried about you that—'

'You told him about my emotions for Saul, matters personal to me. *You betrayed me*…' Louise cut her off in a flat, toneless voice that hurt Katie far, far more than if her sister had lost her temper and shouted and stormed at her.

'I thought he knew… He seemed to know. It was only afterwards that I realised…guessed… Lou, where are you *going*?' Katie demanded anxiously as Louise pushed her way past her and headed for her door.

But Louise didn't answer her. At least not directly, waiting until she had opened the door and was on the point of leaving before turning to Katie and telling her emotionlessly, 'When I come back, I don't want to find you here. Do you understand?'

It was the most serious falling-out they had had in all their lives.

Louise didn't turn back to look at her twin. She couldn't have seen her even if she had; her eyes were too blurred with tears.

How *could* Katie have betrayed her like that? How could she have told someone else something so personal about her? *Anyone* else, never mind Gareth Simmonds.

Gareth Simmonds. For a moment Louise was tempted to march round to her tutor's rooms and tell him just what she thought of him, but already the cool, fresh outdoor air was making her shiver, as her head spun with a weakening mixture of nauseating emotion and lack of food.

CHAPTER THREE

ABRUPTLY shaking her head to dispel her thoughts, Louise came back to the present. Her coffee had grown cold while she had been lost in her painful thoughts of the past and she would have to make a fresh cup. As she refilled the kettle and waited for it to boil she picked up one of the collection of smooth polished stones which decorated the open shelves, holding it cupped in her palm and smoothing her fingertips over its cool surface.

It had been a gift to her from her brother Joss. It was one of his most special stones, he had told her solemnly when he had given it to her, and holding it and stroking it would make her feel calm.

He had found it on one of his regular walks with Great-Aunt Ruth, with whom he shared an affinity for the countryside.

Louise smiled ruefully now as she closed her fingers around its comforting strength. It had galled her a little at the time, even though she had refused to acknowledge it, that someone as young as Joss had been so easily able to identify that part of her personality which she herself least liked.

The turbulence of her own nature offended her pride.

She liked to think of herself as someone who was totally in control of herself, *and* her reactions. Perhaps because she needed to feel that they *were* under her control, because that was the only way she could reassure herself that the way she had behaved under the influence of her intense adolescent crush on Saul and the things she had done would never, ever happen again.

Joss. Her smile deepened as she thought affection- ately of her brother. He had all the virtues that Max, the eldest of them, lacked. She had never met anyone as well rounded, as complete within themselves, as her younger brother. Even as a young child he had exhib- ited an extraordinary degree not just of sensitivity and awareness of the emotions of those around him, but also a compassion and a wisdom which Louise had always secretly rather envied.

As she replaced the stone her eye was caught by the small print that hung on the wall close to the shelves. It was a sketch of the Tuscany countryside which she had drawn herself while on holiday there with her family. That had been the summer— Biting her lip, she turned away abruptly.

After she and Katie had made up their quarrel over what she, Louise, had seen as Katie's betrayal of her in telling Gareth Simmonds about her crush on Saul, that should have been the end of the matter—and of Gareth Simmonds' involvement in her personal life. But it hadn't been.

Briefly Louise closed her eyes. She had never been back to Tuscany since that summer, although she had spent time in other parts of Italy. Her parents thought it was because she had outgrown the simple pleasures of the family holidays they had spent there, in the large rambling villa which they rented every summer just outside the small, unpretentious little village where they, as regular summer visitors, were on first-name terms with all the inhabitants. But her refusal to return had nothing to do with thinking herself too sophisticated and grown-up for the company of her family.

Tuscany... Even now she could smell the warm, rich scent of the earth, feel the warmth of the sun.

By the time they had arrived at the villa that summer she and Katie had been talking again—*just*—and by a common but unspoken agreement nothing had been said or shown by either of them to their parents, nor the other members of the family holidaying together, to reveal that they had ever fallen out.

If, for the first time since their birth, apart from their choice of university courses, they were opting to do things separately, spend more time apart, then it had been put down to the fact that they were growing up and wanting to become individuals.

While Katie had stayed close to the villa, spending hours in the kitchen with Maria—the second cousin of the family who owned the villa, and who spent her widowhood looking after the villa's visitors—going with her to shop at the local markets and indulging her passion for cooking, Louise had set off in an ancient borrowed Fiat with her sketchpad to explore the neighbourhood.

It had perhaps been inevitable that the Fiat, unloved by the family who owned it and, perhaps more importantly, also unserviced by them, should have decided to stage a protest in the form of refusing to start one hot dusty afternoon, when Louise had returned to it having spent the morning sketching a small shrine she had seen at the roadside.

Recognising defeat when the Fiat had stubbornly refused to start after several attempts, Louise had looked up and down the empty road along which only one single, solitary car had passed that morning.

There was nothing else for it. She would have to walk to the red-roofed villa she could see set in the midst of an ancient grove of poplars lower down the hill.

The walk had taken her longer than she had anticipated, the road winding its way steadily downwards. The villa's wrought-iron gates had been closed, but she'd been able to see a car parked in the driveway. As she'd opened the gates she'd realised that the car had British plates which was a relief, although the thought of appealing to an Italian family for help hadn't particularly worried her. She was fluent in the language after so many holidays spent there.

She'd been perspiring stickily from her walk, and ruefully conscious of her dusty bare legs and sunburned nose as she'd approached the villa.

When no one had answered her knock on the villa's front door she'd walked a little warily round the side of the house, and then stopped.

In front of her had been a sparkling, simple-shaped swimming pool, surrounded by an elegant paved area set out with sun loungers and decorated with huge tubs of cascading flowers.

Someone was using the pool, cutting through the water with an impressively fast crawl, brown arms neatly cleaving the water.

As she'd studied the seal-dark male head turned away from her an odd sensation had gathered in the pit of Louise's stomach, tiny quivers of unmistakable female appreciation running like quicksilver along her veins.

Irritated with herself, she'd turned away, her face suddenly warm with a heat that had *nothing* to do with the sun. The swimmer had obviously seen her, she'd recognised, because she could hear him heaving himself out of the water.

Warily she'd turned to face him, hoping her expression wouldn't betray what she had just been feeling.

'Louise! What…?'

Through the shock of recognising Gareth Simmonds' voice, two startling but totally unrelated facts hit Louise. The first was that he had instantly and immediately recognised who *she* was, even though he could quite easily have been confused as to which twin she might actually be. The second was that now, confronted with him, advancing towards her and sending droplets of pool water showering to the floor, and wearing a pair of black swimming shorts which she was breath-gulpingly sure ought only to have ever been on sale with a stern warning of the effect they might have on a vulnerable female, she knew that odd earlier frisson of awareness had *not* been a mere trick of her imagination. Dizzily she discovered that she was focusing on the exact point where the dark wet arrowing of body hair disappeared beneath the waistband of his shorts.

'My car's broken down. It won't start,' she told him breathlessly. 'I didn't…'

Quickly she fought to get control of herself, demanding aggressively, 'What are *you* doing *here*…?'

The look he gave her made her glower even more ferociously at him.

'What's wrong?' he asked her dryly. 'There isn't, so far as I know, any law that says holidaying professors aren't allowed to inhabit the same turf as their students.

And I could, of course, ask you the same question. As it happens, my family own this villa. They bought it about ten years ago, when they were holidaying here and fell in love with the area. Normally the whole family would be here, but unfortunately this year…'

'The *whole* family?' Louise questioned him, unable to stop herself.

'Mmm… I *do* have one, you know.'

'But they aren't here now…?'

'No,' he agreed.

'Have you got a large family?' Louise asked him, without knowing why she had done so. After all, why should she care?

'Mmm…sort of… I've got three sisters, all older than me and all married with children; they, along with my parents, normally descend on the villa for at least a month during the school holidays, but this year my eldest sister and her husband have taken their three children to New Zealand to see her husband's family.

My second sister and *her* husband and two boys are sailing with friends off the Greek Islands and my youngest sister and *her* husband, who, like my father, is a surgeon—there's a tradition of going into medicine in the family, and in fact I've rather broken with that tradition in electing to go into teaching rather than following my father and sisters into medicine—have gone with my parents to India. My mother is involved with UNICEF in a fund-raising capacity, and they've gone to see some of the work that's being done with the money they've raised.'

He spread out his hands in a dismissive gesture and told her dryly, 'So there you have it, a short, potted history of the Simmonds family. Oh, and I forgot, there's also my grandmother, who is very much in the tradition of a grand matriarch—though not exactly in the Italian style. My grandmother's forte lay in bringing up her three sons single-handedly after she was widowed, and in feeding their appetite for education rather than pasta—she's a Scot, so that's perhaps where *that* comes from.'

As he spoke he was reaching for a towel from one of the sun loungers, and briskly began to rub himself dry.

He had a surprisingly muscular-looking body for a university professor. Louise could have sworn that beneath his tutorial 'uniform' of soft Tattersall check shirt and well-worn cord trousers lay a body as misshapen as the old-fashioned knitted cardigans favoured by many of his older colleagues, but quite obviously she had been wrong.

He had stopped speaking briefly, and as she turned her head towards him she drew in a small, surprised gulp of air. He was rubbing his wet hair dry with the towel, his stance revealing the hard firmness of his belly and the strength of his upper arms.

Louise had no idea how long he'd been in Tuscany, but it had certainly been long enough to give his skin an undeniably warm golden tan.

'You're not feeling faint or anything, are you?'

His sharp frowning question made Louise's face burn, and she hurriedly averted her gaze from his body. What was the *matter* with her? She had grown up in the middle of a large, closely knit extended family unit, where the sight of the male body at every stage of its development, from babyhood right through adolescence, young manhood to middle age and beyond, had been so commonplace that until she had formed her crush on Saul she had been openly derisive of other girls' embarrassed and curious interest in the unclothed male form.

And yet here she was, breathing too shallowly and too fast, with a face that felt too hot and a potently explosive sensation low down in her body threatening her composure to the extent that she was having difficulty forming even the most basic coherent thought—and just because she had seen Gareth Simmonds wearing a pair of swimming shorts!

'Look, let's go inside, where it's cooler, and you can tell me exactly where your car is and I—'

'No. No, I'm all right,' Louise started to protest, but it was too late. He was already walking purposefully towards the open doorway to the house, leaving her with no alternative but to follow him inside.

If she had doubted that he might be telling the truth about his family, the number of photographs that crowded the flat surfaces of the heavy solid wooden furniture in the comfortably sized sitting room would soon have put her right. Even without studying them too closely Louise could immediately see the resemblance to him in the happy, affectionately close groups of people featured in the photographs. Her mother's small sitting room and her aunt Ruth's elegant small drawing room were similarly adorned with photographs of her own family, but that knowledge did nothing to alleviate the sense of anxious wariness that had gripped her ever since she had realised just whose territory she had unwittingly strayed into.

'The kitchen's this way,' Louise heard Gareth informing her as he led the way to the rear of the villa and the large, traditional farmhouse-style Tuscan kitchen.

'Sit down,' he instructed her firmly, pulling a chair

out from the table and then beginning to frown as she hesitated. To get to the chair she would have to move closer to him—*too* close to him, Louise recognised. He really had the most sexy and masculine-looking arms. The kind of arms you could just imagine locking tightly around you and holding you…the kind of arms…

'Louise.'

The sharp way he said her name penetrated the totally alien fog of shockingly unexpected feminine arousal that had momentarily swamped her.

What on *earth* was happening to her? It must be the heat or something, Louise decided hastily, still refusing to sit down as she repeated huskily that she was perfectly all right.

'If I could ring my father and explain to him about the car…' she told him.

'It might be easier if I took a look at the car first,' Gareth Simmonds argued, and Louise's face flamed, not with embarrassed confusion at her own inexplicable awareness of him this time, but with quick anger that he should dare to imply that she had not properly diagnosed the problem with the car herself.

'*You* won't be able to start it,' she warned him immediately, but she could see that he didn't intend to let her put him off.

'It's halfway up the hill,' she informed him. 'I'd stopped to sketch the shrine there…'

'Oh, yes, the Madonna. I know where you mean. Look, why don't you wait here, out of the heat, while I go and take a look?'

Dearly as she wanted to go with him, and see his expression when he discovered that she was right and the Fiat wasn't going to start, a small, inner, unexpectedly cautious voice warned Louise that she might be better advised to stay where she was. Even more unexpectedly, she actually found herself not just listening to it but actually agreeing with it as well.

She wasn't sure what malign fate had brought her here to be confronted by the person who, after Saul, she absolutely least wanted to see, but she *did* know that, given her extraordinary reaction to him just now, it would be extremely unwise of her to insist on doing *anything* that kept her in his company.

In fact, she knew that if she could just have summoned the strength to argue with him she would far rather have insisted on ringing her father and begging him to come over to fetch her just as soon as he possibly could.

Once Gareth had gone, having assured her that she was free to make herself as at home as she wished in his absence, she acknowledged that it was a good deal more comfortable inside the pleasant shade of the villa than outside in the full heat of the hot summer's day.

There was a bottle of Chianti on the table, and she was tempted to pour herself a glass, but, remembering what had happened the last time she and Gareth Simmonds and a bottle of wine had come together, she opted instead to pour herself a glass of water.

Taking it with her, she wandered back through the house, pausing to study the photographs in the sitting room. There was one there of Gareth Simmonds as a young boy, flanked by his parents, his grandmother and his older sisters. Hastily Louise looked away from it.

Outside, the water in the swimming pool glittered temptingly in the sunlight. If their own villa had one drawback, it was that it didn't possess its own pool;

they had to share one with two other villas situated close by.

Louise licked her suddenly dry lips. With any luck Gareth Simmonds would be gone for quite some time. He hadn't struck her as a man who could ever give in easily to anything, and she judged that he would be determined not to come back until he could prove her wrong in asserting that the car wouldn't start.

Beneath the cotton fabric of her chino shorts and her top, her skin itched with heat and dust. The swimming pool looked so very, very tempting.

Narrowing her eyes, she looked longingly at it and then, recklessly dismissing the cautious voice that warned her that what she was doing was dangerous—when had that ever put her off anything?—she walked very deliberately towards the pool and quickly stripped off her shorts and top.

The weight she had lost in the months she had ached for Saul had left her looking fragilely fine-boned. Too thin, according to her mother, who had been shocked when she had first seen Louise out of her baggy shirts and in her more revealing shorts and T-shirts. She was certainly too thin for Tuscan male tastes, although she had noticed that that had not stopped Giovanni, Maria's nephew, from making an increasing number of excuses to come up to the villa and flirt heavily with both herself and Katie.

Her skin, nowhere near as tanned or healthy-looking as Gareth Simmonds', was just beginning to lose its British pallor, but was more pale honey than rich gold. Beneath her shorts she was wearing a pair of plain white briefs, and under her top—nothing. Her breasts, firm though they were, were still femininely full, their shape disguised by the looseness of the top she had been wearing. A quick glance around the pool assured her that she had the place to herself. Gracefully Louise dropped into the water, deliciously cool against her hot skin.

Blissfully she floated lazily for a few seconds, and then started to swim. One length and then another, checking at each turn that she still had the place to herself. She was bound to hear Gareth Simmonds returning. The sound of a car engine would carry perfectly on the clear hot summer air.

She did another length, and then another, and then floated again for several seconds before some sixth sense abruptly made her roll over and flounder for a few seconds in the water as she opened her eyes.

Gareth was standing at the end of the pool, watching her. Cautiously she swam to the far side, where she had left her clothes and the towel which *he* had discarded earlier. How long had he been standing there? Not long—he *couldn't* have been.

As she pulled herself out of the water she could see him starting to walk towards her. Quickly she enveloped herself in the wet towel, shivering as it touched her damp skin.

'Take this one. It's dry.'

He was standing far too close to her, Louise acknowledged as she fumbled with the damp folds of the towel wrapped around her.

As she reached reluctantly to take the dry towel from him she could feel the one wrapped around her body starting to slide away. Quickly she made a grab for it, but it was too late. She could feel the heat flushing her face as Gareth's sharp eyed navy blue gaze thoughtfully studied her nearly naked body, but it wasn't her breasts his glance lingered the longest on, Louise noticed; it was her ribs and the narrow over-slenderness of her waist.

'You're still too thin,' he told her curtly, and before she could stop him, much to her chagrin, she felt him swiftly and practically envelop her in the dry, sun-warmed towel which he briskly fastened round her.

'I am *not* thin. I'm *slim*,' Louise retaliated through gritted teeth.

'You're *thin*,' Gareth countered grimly. '*And* you know it, otherwise you wouldn't be so defensive. I take it that your...that Saul isn't here on holiday with your family.'

Louise stared at him, her embarrassment over the fact that he had seen her virtually naked body forgotten as she marvelled not just at his memory but also his tutorial ability to make her remember that she was still his erring student.

'No, he isn't. *Not* that it's *any* business of yours,' she reminded him sharply.

'No? In so much as you are still one of my students— a student whose standard of work has dropped lamentably—it is *very* much my business. You were right about the Fiat. It won't start,' he added, before she could catch her breath to argue with him. 'I'll give you a lift home.'

'There's no need for that,' Louise protested. 'I can ring my father...and...'

'I'll give you a lift home,' Gareth reinforced as though she hadn't spoken. 'Give me five minutes to shower and get changed.'

'You might *think* you're a woman, Louise,' he told her astoundingly as he turned to go. 'But in fact, in many ways you're still very much a child—as you've just proved,' he told her as he glanced from the pool to her towel-wrapped body.

To Louise's chagrin, when Gareth drove up to the villa with her, her parents were standing outside, quite plainly having just returned home themselves. It naturally followed that she had to introduce Gareth to them, and explain not only what had happened to the Fiat but who he was.

'You're Louise's professor!' her mother exclaimed with a smile. 'Oh, poor you, coming all this way and then having your privacy invaded by one of your students.'

'I rather think that Louise believes if anyone is deserving of commiseration for the coincidence, then it's her,' Gareth advised her mother dryly.

Hospitably her mother offered Gareth a drink—but he hadn't had to accept, Louise fumed an hour later, as Gareth was still chatting, apparently quite happily, to her parents while *she* sat in silent resentment beside her mother. That was bad enough. But when her mother invited him to join them for dinner, and Gareth accepted, Louise wasn't sure which of them she disliked the most. However, a welcome diversion was fortuitously provided when Giovanni slouched round the corner of the villa, his face lighting up when he caught sight of Louise.

'Here comes your admirer,' she heard her father warning her. Louise tossed her head, suspecting that Giovanni was even more astonished than her father when, instead of irritably rejecting his unwanted and quite obviously sexually intentioned advances as she normally did, she not only responded to his soft-eyed looks and flowery compliments, but actively encouraged them.

'Oh, dear, Louise, was that wise?' her mother sighed once he had gone. 'Maria was telling us only this morning that his family are trying to encourage a match between Giovanni and his third cousin.'

'I wasn't actually thinking of *marrying* him, Mum,' Louise told her mother meaningfully, adding pointedly, just in case anyone listening—including her wretched and far too watchful tutor—had missed the point, 'He's got the most terrifically sexy body, though, don't you think?'

'Oh, Louise…' Jenny protested, but over her daughter's downbent head she gave her husband a rueful, slightly relieved look, which Louise caught out of the corner of her eye. She knew very well how concerned her family, especially her parents, had been about her crush on Saul, and they weren't to know that her pretence of being physically attracted to Giovanni had nothing to do with Saul but *everything* to do with the impassive and unwanted presence of the man seated next to her mother, silently watching the small piece of theatre being played out in front of him.

'I think I'll just go and see what Maria's planning for supper,' she told her mother airily, standing up to follow Giovanni who had disappeared in the direction of the kitchen and his aunt. 'Suddenly I'm rather… I'm… hungry…'

Tossing her head, she left her startled parents to exchange surprised looks as she stalked ferociously after her prey.

Once inside the kitchen, though, it was a different matter. Under Maria's stern eye, Giovanni's earlier swaggeringly macho display of flirtation quickly turned into bashful silence, and while Louise herself had been happy enough to encourage him while Gareth was

looking on—how dared he imply that she was little
more than a child?—now she lost no time in making it
plain to the young Italian that she simply wasn't interested.

In the days that followed Louise very quickly came to
regret not just encouraging Giovanni, who had now
taken to following her around at every opportunity, but
even more importantly running into Gareth.

An easy, relaxed friendship had very quickly developed between her parents and her tutor—even Joss and
Jack seemed to enjoy his company, going off on long
walks with him to explore the Italian countryside—and,
whereas normally Louise would have been able to give
vent to the pent-up irritation his almost constant
presence in their family circle was causing her to Katie,
there was a certain amount of distance between her and
her twin still, a small and as yet not totally healed sore
place from the quarrel they had had at Oxford—the
quarrel of which Gareth himself had initially been the
cause.

When her cousin Olivia, her husband and their little
girl came to join her own family the situation, at least
in Louise's eyes, became even worse.

Like Gareth, Olivia's husband Caspar was a university lecturer, and the two men very quickly hit it off, so
that while technically Gareth was the one who was the
outsider in their family group it was Louise who often
felt on the outside of the comfortable closeness that
everyone else was enjoying sharing.

Part of the reason for this was that she couldn't
quite bring herself to forget that Olivia was a close
friend of Tullah's. Tullah, who had taken the place in

Saul's heart and Saul's life that she, Louise, had so desperately wanted for herself. And, worse, Olivia had been there on that ill-fated evening when she, Louise, had behaved so stupidly and so…so dangerously, tricking Tullah into following her into the maze and leaving her there so that she could spend the evening with Saul. Only it hadn't worked out like that, and instead…

Watching Olivia and Caspar sitting with her father and Gareth in the sun one afternoon, Louise couldn't help wondering if Olivia had told *Gareth* about what she had done.

'Lou, why don't you come and join us?' Olivia called out cheerfully. 'I could do with some female support among all these men.'

For a moment Louise was tempted. She had always liked Olivia and, yes, even admired her—and, oddly, perhaps, for someone with her relatively competitive and ambitious nature, Louise had a very definite soft spot for small children, especially Olivia's little girl, Amelia. Louise had often gladly given up her own free time to occupy Amelia so that Olivia and Caspar could have some time alone. But today, seeing the way that Gareth broke off his conversation with Caspar to look at her, she fibbed quickly, 'I can't…I…I'm seeing Giovanni. He's taking me out for a drive…'

'Giovanni?' Olivia gave her an old-fashioned look, and Louise could see that she was surprised.

'Careful, Lou,' Caspar teased her. 'These young Italians can be hot stuff, and they aren't—'

'Will you all please stop telling me what to do and trying to run my life for me?' Louise interrupted him angrily, her anger caused in reality far more by the fact that Gareth was an unwanted witness to Caspar's teasing than what Caspar had actually said.

'First you tell me to keep away from Saul, and now you're telling me to keep away from Giovanni. I *am* over eighteen, and who I choose to…to be with is *my* affair and no one else's,' she finished in a fierce voice, before turning on her heel and starting to walk away.

She was almost out of earshot when she heard Caspar saying, 'Phew…what did I do?'

'She still must be feeling very…sensitive about Saul,' she heard Olivia telling him. Bunching her hands into angry fists, Louise almost ran the rest of the distance to her bedroom.

No doubt by now Olivia and Caspar would be regaling Gareth with the full details of her wretched stupidity. Her cheeks burned, and to her chagrin she discovered that hot angry tears were splashing down her face.

Why, oh, why had she had to bump into Gareth like that? And why did he have to keep on coming round here? The rest of her family might have made him welcome, but surely he could see that she…

Since she didn't, in reality, have a date with Giovanni and since in reality dating him was the last thing she wanted, she was forced to spend the afternoon sulking in her room hoping that no one would realise that she was there.

CHAPTER FOUR

It was during the last week of their stay in the villa that things finally came to a head.

Caspar and Olivia had already returned home. Katie, with whom Louise had still not totally made her peace, had gone out for the afternoon with the rest of the family, who had wanted to visit the local monastery, so that Louise was on her own. Even Maria was having a day off, which was no doubt why, she realised later, that Giovanni had decided to pay her an unexpected and unwanted visit.

She was lying on the sun-baked patio when he arrived, her bikini top untied and her eyes closed as she soaked up the hot sun and the even more welcome peaceful solitude.

The first intimation she had that Giovanni was there was when she heard his liquid voice asking if she would like him to put some suntan oil on her bare back.

Startled by his presence, she immediately turned over, and realised her mistake when she saw the way he was staring appreciatively at her naked breasts.

Immediately she reached for her bikini top, telling him at the same time that his aunt was not there and that he had better leave.

'I know she is not here, *cara*,' he told her crooningly. 'But that is why I am here. So that we can have some time together alone. I have wanted to be alone with you for a very long time, and I know that it is the same for you. Your eyes have told me so,' he teased her.

His own eyes were liquid with something that Louise judged had been ignited more by physical lust than tender emotion, but either way she was simply not interested.

'Giovanni…' she began warningly as she scrambled to stand up, but either he had misread the tone of her voice or he had decided to ignore it, because instead of giving her some distance he made a grab for her.

Thoroughly outraged, Louise tried to break free of his hold, but he was a strongly built young man, much taller than her and much, much heavier, and it suddenly struck her with a sharp thrill of fear that if he should choose to do so he could quite easily physically overpower her.

'Giovanni,' she began again, but this time, as she was all too uncomfortably aware, her voice sounded rather more hesitantly pleading than firmly assertive.

'Louise…what's going on?'

Never had she thought she would be so grateful to see Gareth Simmonds, Louise admitted as Giovanni immediately released her and started to say something to Gareth that she felt too shaky to catch.

Her hands, as she reached down for the skimpy top of her bikini, were trembling so much that it was impossible for her to fasten it, and instead she could only hold tight to it while wrapping her arms protectively across her naked breasts as Gareth told Giovanni curtly that he wanted him to leave.

'You *do* realise what could have happened, don't

you?' he asked Louise sharply, once the noise of Giovanni's battered Vespa had died away.

Both his expression and his tone of voice immediately set Louise's back up. He was behaving as though he were her father, or her brother, as though he had a *right* to tell her what to do, to bully and correct her.

'Yes, I do,' she answered, her voice shaking as she added, completely untruthfully, 'And, for your information, I *wanted* Giovanni to make love to me…'

'To do what?' Gareth's voice dripped with cynical contempt. 'I doubt that *love* had very much to do with what he'd got in mind…' he told her derisively.

Louise's chin tilted dangerously.

'So he wanted to have sex with me. Is that so wrong?' she challenged him, tossing her head. 'After all, I've got to lose my virginity somehow, become the woman you're so keen to tell me I'm not. And since, as I'm sure you're now very well aware, thanks to my cousin and my loving, loyal sister, I can never share that experience with the one man…the *only* man I…'

Pausing, Louise bit down hard on her bottom lip. Why on earth had she got involved in this conversation, embroiled in this situation? Just thinking about Saul had made her heart ache, and filled her eyes with treacherous tears. Fiercely she fought to suppress them.

'It doesn't matter to me who the *hell* it is—who *he* is any longer.' Louise virtually spat at him. 'I just don't care…'

She had said more, far more than she had ever intended to say. Much more…too much, she acknowledged shakily. But instead of taunting her for her immaturity, instead of talking down to her as he had been doing all these last unbearably long weeks, she heard him saying in a voice that shook almost as much with anger as her own had done, 'Are you *crazy*? Have you *any* idea just what you're saying? Of course it damn well matters.'

'Not to me it doesn't,' Louise told him savagely. 'Why should it?'

Before he could stop her she turned on her heel and ran through the villa, up to the bedroom she shared with her twin.

From its windows it was possible to see the village, with its red-tiled roofs and the hillside beyond, but it wasn't the view that held Louise's attention, her eyes widening as she realised that Gareth had followed her upstairs and was now standing just inside her room.

'You dropped this,' he told her gruffly, handing her her discarded bikini top.

Automatically she reached out to take it from him, and then stopped as she saw the way he was looking at her.

'Keep away from Giovanni, Louise,' she heard him advising her grimly. 'He isn't…'

'He isn't what?' she demanded, anger flaring again. 'I don't *care* about what he isn't. I only care about what he *is*… He's a man, isn't he…a male? And he can… I'm tired of being told I'm still a child…not a woman. What does it take to make me a woman? As if I didn't know.

'I just want to have sex,' she told him defiantly, 'and I don't care who it's with…not if I can't have Saul…If I can't have Saul then it might as well be anybody…'

'You don't mean that,' she heard him contradicting her flatly. 'You don't know what you're saying…'

'Stop patronising me…' Louise was practically howling at him now, so driven by the combination of her own feelings and his resented, unwanted presence that her reactions were no longer fully under her own control. 'I do mean it…'

'Oh, no, you don't,' Gareth was telling her sharply. 'And I'll prove it to you.'

Before she could even guess what he had in mind he had slammed her bedroom door closed and was standing between her and it—her and freedom. An ominous sense of things having gone too far began to trickle like icy water into her veins, but Louise wasn't going to give in to it and risk losing face in front of him.

'*I* lost *my* virginity to a friend of my youngest sister,' she heard him telling her coolly as he started to unfasten his shirt. 'She was twenty; I was just seventeen.'

Louise couldn't take her eyes off his body, his shirt…his hands… In appalled, paralysed fascination she watched as he finished unfastening it and shrugged it off. Calmly he started to reach for his belt.

Nervously Louise moistened her suddenly dry lips.

'What's wrong?' she heard Gareth taunting her. 'Having second thoughts…?'

'You…you can't mean this. You don't know what you're doing…' she whispered shakily.

'Yes, I can, and yes, I do. You said you wanted to lose your virginity. *You* said you didn't mind *who* you lost it to. I'm here, and I can promise you, Louise, that I'm perfectly willing and able to assist you. After all, it might as well be me as Giovanni, mightn't it…? *You* don't mind which of us it is, after all, do you? And forgive me, but it is quite some time since I've had sex, as the sight of your extremely attractive naked breasts has just rather forcefully reminded me.

'Men are *like* that, you know,' he continued conversationally. 'There's something about the sight of a pair of pretty, pert bare breasts that just naturally turns a man's thoughts to how those same breasts would feel filling his hands, how they might taste when he could get to suckle on them, how the *woman* they're a part of might react if he showed her…'

When he heard Louise's small shocked gasp he asked her quietly, 'What is it? I'm not embarrassing you, am I, Louise? After all, *you* were the one who said that it didn't matter *who* you had sex with, and, like I've just said, I'm more than willing to oblige you… *More* than willing… Here, feel,' he commanded, reaching out for her hand.

Louise stared at him in horrified fascination. What on earth did he think he was *doing…saying…*? He was her *tutor*. He was… She closed her eyes and then flicked them open again as, shockingly, she had a sudden explicitly clear mental image of him the way he had been that first day she had seen him climbing out of the pool at his own villa. Then she had been very much, if unwontedly, aware of the fact that he was not *just* her tutor but also very, very much a man, and now, suddenly and inexplicably, she was aware of it again.

'Did you…did you love her…your sister's friend?' she managed to ask him jerkily as she tried to drag her appalled gaze from his face. She did not *dare* to look at his body now that he had removed his shirt and was, it seemed, in the process of removing the rest of his clothes as well.

'I dare say I *believed* that I did,' he told her coolly. 'But at seventeen…I was *just* seventeen. What's wrong…? Louise, have you changed your mind…?'

Oddly, despite the fact that he had been talking to her for several minutes, he had still not unfastened his belt, and yet it had taken him no time at all to unfasten and remove his shirt.

Just for a second Louise was tempted to give in and admit that, yes, she had most certainly changed her mind, but her pride, always one of her own worst enemies, refused to let her. Give way, give in, and to him…? No… No… Never… And besides—besides, she knew perfectly well that he was only bluffing, and that he would never… Well, *she* could play that game just as well as him, and probably even better.

Her confidence returning, she gave a small toss of her head and told him firmly, 'No. I haven't.'

She pursed her lips and forced herself to make a thorough visual inventory of what she could see of him, determinedly lingering as long as she dared on the bare, bronzed expanse of his torso before quickly skimming over the rest of his, thankfully, still clothed body and returning her gaze to his face, saying, as disparagingly as she dared, 'You aren't as…as macho as Giovanni, but I suppose you'll still do.'

She saw at once that she had touched a raw nerve. A muscle twitched warningly in his jaw, but she willed herself to ignore it.

'By rights I ought to put you over my knee and…'

Widening her eyes, Louise willed herself not to blush as she asked him provocatively, 'Ooh, is that some special kind of position? I don't have your experience, of course, and—'

'You really are asking for it, Louise,' she heard him warning her, but she wasn't going to give in.

Shrugging, she told him tauntingly, 'Well, yes, I suppose I am… You needn't worry about me getting pregnant, by the way—I *am* on the pill…'

Her doctor had prescribed it several months earlier, when her emotional trauma had begun to have a disruptive effect on her normal monthly cycle.

'Very practical of you,' she heard Gareth commending her curtly. 'No doubt that was for Saul's benefit, was it? You do surprise me. I should have thought that deliberately encouraging, if not inciting the kind of "accident" that would have forced his hand and made him offer you and his child the protection of his name would have been more in keeping with the high drama of your infatuation with him.'

Louise's face blazed with angry colour.

'How *dare* you?' she breathed taking an impulsive step towards him. 'I would *never* try to trap a man like that,' she told him with fierce pride—and meant it.

'Louise,' she heard him saying almost wearily as he raised his hand and cupped the side of her face. To tell her what? Something she really didn't want to hear, she was pretty sure of that, and so far as she knew there was really only one sure-fire way to stop him.

Without stopping to consider the consequences of her actions, desperate only to silence him and have him stop dragging up the still raw pain of her loss of Saul, she quickly closed the distance between them, placing her mouth against his as she whispered, 'Save the lecture, Professor; *that* isn't what I want. What I want—'

She never got to finish her sentence, because suddenly and totally unexpectedly she heard Gareth groan deep down in his throat, and the next minute she was being dragged tightly against his body by his free hand as his mouth opened over the prim closed shape of hers and he proceeded to kiss her in a way she had previously only experienced at second hand, via the television screen.

She had known, of course, that people did, *must* kiss like this—had even dreamed and fantasised about Saul kissing her with just this kind of intimacy and hard male heat—but the reality of having a man's body pressed up hard against her own, the bare flesh of his torso hard and firm and hot against the nakedness of her breasts while his hand cupped her face and his mouth moved against hers with devastating expertise and determination, was like comparing watching someone else screaming through the air on some wild fun-park ride with being the one sitting there in the seat feeling that experience for oneself.

But no big-dipper ride, however terrifying, appalling and thrilling, could come anywhere near making her feel what she was feeling right now, Louise acknowledged as she felt her whole body submit to an avalanche of feeling—of sensation—of reaction—she had *never*, ever guessed it *could* possibly feel.

She couldn't even control her body's urgent, hungry response to the skilled sensuality of his kiss, never mind do anything about the way her breasts, her nipples were already aching so tormentedly for the kind of caresses and intimacy he had described to her only minutes earlier.

Briefly, bravely, Louise tried to fight what she was feeling, to withstand the dizzying surge of hormone-drenched arousal that swamped her, but it was a lost cause, her brain no match for the clamouring hunger of her body. Weakly she clung to the only solid thing she could find to cling to, her nails digging unwittingly into the hard muscles of Gareth's upper arms as she hung onto him for support.

'Louise.'

She heard Gareth protesting warningly against her mouth, as though he could feel what was happening to her and was urging her to resist it, but Louise *couldn't* resist it; she didn't *want* to resist it and she didn't want him to tell her to.

'No. No-o-o...' she moaned, pressing tiny pleading kisses against his lips, his jaw, his throat. 'No... Gareth... No, don't stop. Don't stop now...' she begged him, lost to everything. 'No, you can't. You can't...'

And to prove her point she pushed her body even closer to his, moving frantically against him, bestowing eager, feverish kisses against whichever bit of him she could reach.

'Louise. Louise... No. You...' She could hear him protesting, but at the same time his hand was reaching out to cup her breast.

Louise shuddered wildly in sensual delight as he touched her, urging him huskily, 'Do what you said you would do before... You said you wanted to taste me... them...' she reminded him, her voice sensually soft and slurred, her eyes bright with shocked passion, dilating in betrayal of her need as she focused blindly on him. And as she saw him hesitating she moved invitingly against him, arching her body against his, showing him the need she could feel pulsing so strongly through her veins and her senses.

The rest of the villa was empty, silent, the air in her room hot and languid from the afternoon sun. Louise could see a tiny bead of sweat forming on Gareth's throat. She watched it in fascination as he tensed, his throat muscles rigid. Each second—each breath she took—seemed to stretch out for ever. Time itself felt as though it was standing still. She could see, hear, almost feel Gareth trying to swallow; the small bead of sweat moved. She reached out with her fingertip and caught it, holding his gaze with her own as she very deliberately transferred it to her tongue.

His whole body seemed to be caught up, galvanised by the fierce shudder that racked him. His hands cupped her breasts; his mouth covered hers. Louise shuddered in intense pleasure as wave after wave of sensual response flooded over her.

She could feel Gareth's hands, firm, broad, his fingers long and supple, shaping her as they slid down the silky hot flesh of her back before coming to rest on the rounded curves of her bottom. He bent his head, his hair brushing against her naked skin softly, in the most tenuous and spine-tingling kind of caress. She could feel the heat of his breath against her breast, and the delicate shivers of sensation down her spine became fierce, gutwrenching, arousal-drenched waves of female need. He was caressing her breast with his mouth, gentle, slow, deliberately explorative kisses that drove her into a fury of impatience and longing.

Overwhelmed by her own need, she moved frantically against him. His mouth brushed her nipple, stiff and aching with the hunger that he himself had conjured up with his shockingly explicit verbal descriptions earlier.

She felt him hesitate, and her frustration boiled up, bursting past what was left of her self-control and ability to think and reason logically.

Her hands found his shoulders, the flesh hot, and stroked the muscles and bone beneath, and their sensory message of his alienness, his total maleness, made her groan deep down in her throat—the same kind of feral yearning sound a hunting lioness aching for a mate might have made.

Her hands reached his back, strong and sleek, and urged him down towards her body. She felt the heat of his expelled breath against her nipple and shuddered uncontrollably beneath its impact. So might the hot peaks of a desert sand dune feel, when lashed by the scorching burn of the hot sirocco wind, the sensation both at once an unbearable aching pain and the promise of an even more intense and untenable pleasure.

'Do it… Do it…'

Not even hearing herself breathing the thick, urgent, guttural words had the power to shock or silence her, and the sensation that rolled through her as he gave in to her female command was not one of triumph or any kind of cerebral pleasure. Rather it was a form of relief so exquisite that she felt as though her whole body, her whole self was being drenched in a sensation so acutely intense that it was almost beyond her to bear it.

Rhythmically she moved herself against him, her hands going out to hold his hand as he drew her nipple deeper into his mouth, his earlier delicate, tentative suckling giving way to a fierceness, an urgency, that sent her delirious with reciprocal pleasure.

'Yes. Oh, yes… Yes…' she heard herself beginning to chant as her body writhed helplessly, no longer within her own mental control but totally and completely responsive to the male allure of his.

She was the one who reached for the fastening on his belt, and it was *she* too who urged and demanded that he remove the rest of his clothes.

'I want to see you, all of you,' she insisted to him. 'I

want…' And then her voice and her body, her hands, grew still when she saw that he had given in to her pleas. Her whole body stiffened, a massive visible shudder running right through it as she gazed wide-eyed at him, slowly absorbing the visual reality of his body.

No need to question whether or not he wanted her; she could see perfectly well that he did. Tentatively she reached out and let her fingers slide down the soft arrowing of hair that neatly bisected his body. When she reached his stomach she could feel his muscles start to clench, but he didn't try to stop her.

The hair around the base of the shaft of his manhood was thick and soft. It clung to her fingers as though wanting to encourage her touch. Gravely Louise allowed herself to linger there a while, exploring the springy strength of the dark curls. Above her downbent head she heard him groan, and her naked breasts, her inner, secret womanhood throbbed urgently in a silent echo of the need he was expressing.

Her hand trembled slightly as she reached out to touch the hard, erect strength of him—her tremor wasn't caused by any feeling of trepidation or apprehension, it was simply her body's warning to her that it was as close to losing control as his low, raw groan told her that his was.

Delicately and slowly she explored the full length of him, her lips parting on a soft, heavy breath of con-centration.

Beneath her fingertips his flesh burned, his body rigid and hard. The sensual scent caused by the heat of their bodies filled the small, hot room, making her feel dizzy with longing.

Drawing back from him, she looked towards the bed

and then at him, but before she could say anything he was removing her hand from his body and telling her thickly, 'You *know* me now, Louise, and now it's my turn to know you.'

Like someone trapped in a dream, without the power to move her limbs, Louise simply stood there while he removed her bikini bottoms. The sensation of his hands sliding down her thighs to remove them and then moving back up over them far more slowly and exploratively made her feel as though she was melting from the inside out. As she closed her eyes he stood up and picked her up in his arms, carrying her over to her bed. Laying her carefully on it, he started to touch her, caress her, licking her breasts. First one and then the other was given the moist attention of his tongue, and then his lips, suckling gently at first and then far more urgently on her nipples while she writhed and protested incoherently that what he was doing to her was too pleasurable for her to bear.

Slowly he kissed his way down the length of her body, his hands firmly parting her legs so that he could kneel between them, his fingertips stroking gently up the inside of her thighs. A soft, tormented moan escaped from Louise's throat, and her whole body started to tremble eagerly, helplessly snared in the unbreakable grip of her own arousal.

When his hands cupped her sex, and slowly and very deliberately started to explore it, laying it bare, not just to his touch but to his sight as well, Louise closed her eyes. Not because she felt self-conscious or inhibited, but simply because the sexual excitement exploding through her was almost too much for her to bear.

Within its intensity she could sense not just her own

desire to push back the boundaries of her sexual knowledge and experience, but also her extraordinarily powerful female anger against herself, against Saul, against nature itself almost. Anger and love, love and anger—which of them was the stronger? Her body quivered feverishly beneath his touch, so delicate and yet at the same time so…compulsively needed, so…so addictive to her senses.

Inside her the desire tensed and coiled. Urgently she opened her eyes. He was bending his head towards her. She could feel herself hovering on the edge of a precipice, carried there, *hurled* there by the ferocity of her own need. Frantically she reached for his shoulders, whispering thickly, the words almost lost against his chest, 'Yes…oh, S… Now…now… I want you now.'

Her body was already quivering in the grip of its first pre-climax spasm of warning, and she whimpered beneath the force of it. He was moving onto her, *into* her, slowly—too slowly, her aroused senses recognised, and her flesh surrounded him with eager complicity, the jerky movement of her hips setting a fast and urgent rhythm that she could feel him trying to resist. Her hands slid down his back, urging him to thrust deeper within her. She felt him pause, resist almost, but her body wouldn't let him. Moist and urgent, more erotic and arousing, more *irresistible* by far than any practised sensual persuasion, it finally overcame and overwhelmed his attempt to hold back from her, and he began to move far more deeply and strongly within her.

It was like hearing her favourite, most emotion-arousing piece of music, looking out of her bedroom window at home on Christmas Day to see the countryside deep in an unexpected blanket of snow; eating her favourite food; having her emotions and her senses touched in every single way that aroused them, and all at the same time. It was all those things and more. All those things intensified a thousand—no, a hundred thousand times over, a sensation, a feeling, a *being* so, so intense, so perfect, almost beyond her capacity to bear its delight, that she thought when the fiercely strong climactic contractions surged through her body that the relief would cause her to break apart.

Afterwards, lying in Gareth's arms, crying and clinging to him as she fought for the words to tell him how magical, how mystifying, how awesomely unbelievably wonderful she had found the experience in between her emotional tears she could hear him telling her hoarsely that it was all right, that she was safe, that he was sorry. Somewhere between registering what he was saying and trying to respond to it she fell asleep, and when she woke up it was dark and Gareth was gone, leaving her tucked up in her bed, her bikini neatly folded on her chair beside her.

Downstairs in the villa she could hear her parents' voices, and then Katie came rushing into the room calling out urgently, 'Lou, wake up. We've got to pack. There's been some sort of emergency at home and we've got to go back. Dad's got us an early-morning flight…'

'An emergency… What…?' Louise demanded groggily, her thoughts automatically turning protectively to Saul.

'I don't know. None of us do. All I know is that Mum was on the phone to Maddy for simply ages.'

In the rush to pack up everything and make it to the airport to catch their flight, Louise simply didn't have the time to dwell on what had happened with Gareth, and anyway her lethargic, sensually sated body felt too complete and satisfied at that stage, too well pleasured and indolently disinclined to take issue with her mind about what had happened for her to do anything other than secretly luxuriate in the aura of sensuality that still clung to her senses, anaesthetising her against any need to analyse what had happened or why.

That came later, once they were back at home—hours of endless soul-searching and self-cross-examination while she went over and over what had happened, half inclined to give in to the temptation to comfort herself by believing that she had simply dreamed the whole thing. Dreaming about Gareth Simmonds in that way would have been bad enough, but of course she knew it was no dream.

The crisis which had brought them back to Haslewich, as Louise had guessed, involved her grandfather, who had developed a severe chest infection, and Maddy had rushed up from London to be with him.

'Mum is over with Gramps and Maddy. Maddy doesn't look very well herself, though Gramps is over the worst of it now. Joss was very worried about him. You know what he's like?' Katie said, a few days after their return.

'Don't I just?' Louise agreed darkly.

Her brother had caught her off guard only the previous day by asking her if she had heard anything from Gareth Simmonds since their return.

'No. Why should I have heard anything?' she had demanded, red-faced. '*I* wasn't the one who kept on encouraging him to come round to the villa… *I* wasn't the one who went on long, boring walks with him.'

'They weren't boring,' Joss had contradicted her affably. 'He knows almost as much about the country-side as Aunt Ruth. He told me that when he was my age he used to spend his holidays in Scotland, with his grandmother. Anyway,' he had added, returning to her earlier question, 'he is *your* tutor.'

Was. Louise had been on the point of correcting him, but she'd stopped herself just in time. She had already made up her mind that she was going to change courses. The thought of going back to Oxford and having to face Gareth Simmonds now after what had happened made her break out in a cold sweat and shudder with self-loathing. How *could* she have behaved like that…?

While she and Katie were still talking the door opened and Joss came in.

'Could either of you drive me over to Gramps,' Joss asked winningly. 'I thought I'd go and see if there was anything I could do.'

'Why do you want to go over there?' Louise asked him curiously.

'I thought I could go and play chess with Gramps and give Maddy a bit of a break, so that she can go out and do some shopping or something to cheer herself up a bit…buy herself a new dress,' he added, with male vagueness.

'But Mum's over there with her,' Katie pointed out.

Joss shook his head. 'No, she isn't,' he told them. 'She had a meeting of the mother and baby home committee at three. She was just going to call and see Maddy on the way.'

'I'll drive you,' Louise told him, springing up and busying herself looking for a jacket, so that neither he nor Katie would see the emotional sheen of tears in her eyes brought there by the sudden awareness of just what kind of man her younger brother was going to turn out to be.

As she had promised herself she would do, Louise transferred to a different course and a new tutor once she was back at Oxford. Ironically her twin attended Gareth Simmonds' lectures herself now, but every time Katie mentioned him Louise very determinedly changed the subject and blanked her off, telling her quite sharply on one occasion, 'Katie, if you *don't* mind, can we *please* talk about something else, or *someone* else?'

'You don't like Professor Simmonds, I know—' Katie began.

Louise interrupted her, laughing harshly as she told her, 'It isn't simply that I don't like him, Katie—I *loathe*, detest and abhor the man, totally, completely and utterly. Do you understand? I loathe him. *Loathe* him…'

But she still dreamt of him at night that first term of the new year, and into the next—bewildering, confusing dreams involving a kaleidoscope of emotions and feelings from which she awoke in the early hours, her body shaking and drenched in perspiration and her eyes wet with tears.

The phone rang sharply, piercing her thoughts and bringing her back abruptly to the present. Quickly Louise went to pick up the receiver.

'Ah, so you are back. Why have you not returned my call?'

As she listened to the plaintive voice of Jean Claude, Louise reminded herself that she was no longer nineteen, and that she had come a long, long way from the girl who had cried out to Gareth Simmonds to make her a woman.

'When will you be free to have dinner with me?' she heard Jean Claude asking her.

'Not this week, I'm afraid,' she told him firmly.

'But *chérie*, I have missed you. It has been so long…'

Louise laughed.

'Stop trying to flatter me, Jean Claude,' she warned him, ignoring his mock-hurt protests. 'Look, I know very well that there are scores of women besides me in your life, so don't try to tell me that you've been spending your evenings alone and lonely at home…'

She could almost feel his ego expanding as she spoke. Despite his intelligence, Jean Claude was a particularly vain man, and Louise had already discovered that it was always easy to appeal to him through his vanity. That vulnerability in him, though, didn't mean that he couldn't be extremely shrewd and perceptive on occasion. He had already challenged her to disprove to him that the reason she had not, so far, gone to bed with him was because emotionally there was another man in her heart, if not in her life. But she wasn't going to re-surrect *that* particular argument right now.

'My boss has a big meeting in the morning, which could drag on, and then there's a formal dinner at night…'

'The committee which is to look into the fishing rights of the Arctic seas—yes, I know,' Jean Claude acknowledged. 'Our governments will be on opposite sides on this matter, I suspect.'

Louise laughed.

'Perhaps we shouldn't see one another for a while, then,' she teased him. 'Just in case!'

To her surprise, instead of sharing her laughter, Jean

Claude's voice became unusually grave as he told her, 'This is an extremely serious matter for us, *chérie*. Our fishermen need to be able to fish in those waters. Yours…'

Louise could almost see him giving that small Gallic shrug he so frequently made.

'Yours have an area of sea—of seas—to fish which far exceeds the land mass which is your country…'

'A legacy from the days when Britannia ruled the waves,' Louise joked ruefully, but Jean Claude continued to remain serious.

'Such colonialist views are not considered acceptable in these modern times *petite*', he reminded her. 'And if you would accept a word of warning from me I would suggest that you do not voice them too publicly. There are many nations based here in Brussels who consider that they have good reason to resent what they view as British tyranny and oppression…'

It was on the tip of Louise's tongue to point out mildly that the French, along with the Dutch, and the Portuguese, come to that, had all been equally vigorous at some stage of their history in pursuing the acquisition of new colonies, lands and seas over which they staked ownership, but Jean Claude's serious tone prevented her, and besides, as she had often noticed, sensationally handsome and attentive though he was, for her tastes the Frenchman lacked one vitally important virtue: he had virtually no sense of humour.

'It's going to be next week before I can see you, Jean Claude,' she told him instead.

'Very well…then I shall ring you next week. Although we could always be together later…after your dinner is over…' He started to purr meaningfully.

Louise laughed.

'Spend the night with you, you mean… *Non. Non, non…*'

'Now you say *non*, but one day soon you will say *oui*, and not just to spend the night with me,' he warned her, and she could hear the smile of satisfaction in his voice as she laughed and said her goodbyes.

'You're wrong, Jean Claude,' she murmured to herself as she replaced the receiver. Attractive though he was, she was in no danger of being tempted to join his long list of lovers.

'Oh, but you are so cold,' he had complained the last time she had refused him. 'Cold outside, but I think *very*, very hot inside. Very, very hot…' he had whispered as he had attempted to deepen the passion of the kiss they were sharing.

'Why so bashful?' he had added when she had gently, but firmly, disengaged herself from him. 'You are a woman of very great attractiveness, Louise, and I cannot be the first to tell you so—nor the first man to take you to bed…'

'*You* haven't taken me to bed,' Louise had felt bound to remind him.

'Not yet,' he had agreed, adding wickedly, 'But I shall…and very soon.' His voice had deepened as his hand reached out to stroke her breast.

Deftly Louise had manoeuvred herself away from him and opened the door of his car.

He was right about one thing. He was not the first to have wanted to take her to bed, but…

'Oh, no… *No*,' Louise told herself fiercely. 'I'm not going through all that again. I'm not travelling down that road…thinking *those* thoughts…'

Wasn't it one of the first signs of long-term spinster-dom when one started talking to oneself…?

Spinsterdom… It was an old-fashioned, very non-politically correct and out-of-favour word, with all its unkind connotations and in-built prejudices. But a spinster was, after all, what she was, and what she was likely to remain…

By choice, she reminded herself fiercely. By *choice*. By the expression of her *free will* because… because…

'Stop that,' she told herself sternly, reminding herself mundanely, 'You've got to be up early in the morning!'

CHAPTER FIVE

'LOUISE. Good!' her boss greeted her as she hurried into Louise's office. 'I'm glad you're here early.'

'I thought you'd want me to brief you on the possible legal complexities of this proposed change in fishing rights.'

'Yes, yes, I do,' Pam Carlisle agreed. 'But I also want you to accompany me to this morning's meeting. Things have changed rather a lot since we first discussed the matter. For a start, there's been a good deal of political argument brought up by some of the other committee members over the fact that the proposed Chair, Gareth Simmonds, is British, and of course the existing fishing rights are also British.'

'Yes… Yes, so I understand,' Louise agreed tensely, keeping her face averted from her boss as she fiddled with some papers on her desk.

'You know? But how?'

'My sister told me, and as it happens Gareth Simmonds was on the same flight as me. I… He was my tutor for a while when I was up at Oxford,' Louise explained brusquely. There—it was said…out…over and done with.

'Oh, you know Gareth, then.' Pam beamed at her.

'We're most frightfully lucky to have had him agree to accept the Chair, and, as I've already pointed out to the other committee members, they simply couldn't have a chairperson who could be less biased. Well, if he was your tutor *you* must know that. He really is the most— It's just as well I'm a very happily married woman,' she told Louise frankly, with a wide grin. 'I can tell you, Louise, when he smiled at me I could practically feel myself melting. His students must have fallen for him like ninepins, poor man...'

'Poor man? *Why* poor man?' Louise asked, rather more sharply than she had intended, she could see, as Pam gave her a puzzled look.

'Oh, dear, Lou, have I trodden on an Achilles' heel?' She asked, with amusement. 'Did you have a bit of a thing for him while you were an undergrad?'

'No. I most certainly did not,' Louise denied vehemently, her colour suddenly very high and her eyes spitting sparks of anger. 'If you want the truth...' She paused, only too well aware of the danger she was running into.

'Yes...?' Pam prompted.

'Oh, nothing,' Louise hedged. 'Look, I've produced a list of possible points that may be raised, and, of course, there's always the chance that we're going to have that old accusation of colonialism thrown at us...'

'Colonialism...?' Pam raised her eyebrows. 'Well, I suppose you *could* be right, and it's certainly best to be prepared for everything.'

Louise, who knew the situation equally as well as her boss, nodded. 'It's going to be my job to persuade the committee that we need to keep fishing quotas down and retain as much control over our fishing rights as we can. It's not going to be easy...'

'No,' Louise agreed. 'I've read up as much as I can on maritime law, and, of course, all the other legal facts that cover the situation. I've prepared several briefs for you on the subject, and I'm also getting hold of translations of the law and legal histories that the other committee countries are likely to be using as counter-arguments.'

'Mmm…looks like I'm going to be doing an awful lot of reading.'

'Well, I'll condense as much of it as I can, and, of course, if a point is raised that needs further exploration…'

'You'll deal with it. Yes, I know you will, Lou. Have I told you recently, by the way, what a treasure you are? When Hugh first recommended you to me I admit I *was* rather dubious…but he convinced me that you would be up to the job and he was more than right.'

Hugh Crighton was Saul's father, her grandfather's half-brother. Initially a barrister, and now a semi-retired judge, he lived in Pembrokeshire with his wife Ann, and it was from living in a coastal area that he had become acquainted with the European MP Pam Carlisle, for whom Louise now worked.

Originally, when she had been offered the job, Louise had resentfully assumed that this was her uncle Hugh's way of getting her out of his son's life. But at a family gathering Hugh had taken her on one side and told her gently, 'I know what you're thinking, Lou, but you're wrong. Yes, I *do* think it's a good idea for you and Saul to have some distance between you, and for Tullah and Saul to be allowed to build their new life together, but I also happen to think that you're ideally suited for this kind of work. You've got the right kind of fighting spirit it needs.'

'I wanted to be a barrister,' Louise had reminded him.

'Yes, I know,' he had acknowledged. 'But, my dear Lou, you're too hot-blooded and—'

'Too hot-tempered,' she had supplied angrily for him.

'Spirited,' he had amended. 'A crusader…a leader. You need the kind of challenge this work specifically will provide.'

And, of course, he had been right, and if she was honest, the thought of practising law in the dry, dusty courts of the European legal system did not appeal to her any more.

'You just want to be a barrister so that you can prove to Gramps that you're better than Max,' Joss had commented calmly at that same gathering. 'But it's all right, Lou,' he had told her in a kind voice. '*We* all know that you *are* better…'

Better… What did that mean? she wondered now. What had happened to the young woman who had declared that if she couldn't have Saul then all she wanted in compensation was to be materially successful, to make her mark in the world? Why was she suddenly beginning to feel that there might be something missing from her life, that there might be *someone* missing from it?

'Lou? Are you all right…?'

'Yes. Yes, I'm fine,' she assured Pam Carlisle, swiftly gathering up the papers she would need as she prepared to follow her out to the waiting car.

En route to their destination, Louise studied their surroundings absently through the car window. Brussels, despite hearsay to the contrary, was, in fact, a beautiful city; but it was true it *was* a majestic and very proper kind of rigid beauty that perhaps could not always be easily appreciated. But beautiful it was, nevertheless, Louise acknowledged as the driver brought the car to a halt and got out to open the doors for them.

Several of the other committee members and their assistants had already arrived. Louise knew most of them by sight if nothing else. Brussels' political circles were surprisingly small, in view of the number of politicians and ancillary workers and diplomats who worked at the commission.

She was grimly amused to see that the French representative had with him a particularly aggressive and highly qualified legal adviser big-wig, who Louise suspected was far more used to running his *own* committees rather than sitting in a back seat capacity on someone else's. She had never actually met him before, but knew of him by reputation, and, as she whispered discreetly to her boss, it proved how seriously the French were taking the issues that they should have supplied their representative with someone so very senior.

'This is a very serious political issue for them,' Pam Carlisle agreed. 'Even more so in many ways than it is for us. But it's the Spanish contingent we should expect to have the most trouble with.

'Oh, look, there's Gareth Simmonds just walking in,' Pam told her, but Louise had already seen him.

His dark, impeccably tailored suit emphasised the masculine power of his shoulders—and their breadth. Beneath the pristine crispness of his shirt Louise could see his chest rising and falling as he breathed. Was it still bisected by that same dark arrowing of soft, finger-magnetising dark hair? Did he still…?

Angrily, she turned her head away.

'I'd like to have a word with him, but I've been warned to be especially careful. We can't afford to take any risks of having him accused of favouritism,' Pam commented.

'Strictly speaking he shouldn't be in a position to favour *anyone*,' Louise reminded her dryly. 'The issue is to be resolved by sticking to the *law*.'

From the past Louise could almost hear Gareth Simmonds' voice as he lectured them on the finer points of European law, his tone becoming increasingly passionate as he pointed out to them that the way ahead lay not so much in the British law courts, but in those of the new European parliament.

'New community laws will be written which will supersede the old, nationalistic laws, and the responsibility for making those laws could well lie in your hands…'

The meeting was being called to order. Out of the corner of her eye Louise watched Gareth. He was deep in conversation with a stunning blonde whom Louise recognised as one of the phalanx of legal advisers attached to the German embassy—Ilse Weil. From her body language, it was quite plain that it wasn't just Gareth's attention as the chairperson of the committee she was courting, Louise decided derisively. And, what was more, Gareth Simmonds didn't seem to be doing anything to put a less intimate distance between them.

Abruptly, she turned away. If Gareth Simmonds chose to respond to another woman's sensual come-on, then that was no business of *hers*. No business at all. Nor was there any way she would ever want it to be.

'Thanks, Lou… I appreciate the way you handled everything. We were faced with some pretty tricky questions, and I could be wrong, but I've got a gut feeling that one or two people were quite definitely caught off guard by the answers you were able to come up with.'

'Mmm… I wouldn't be *too* optimistic,' Louise warned her boss, adding dryly, 'We *are*, after all, dabbling in pretty murky waters…'

'Murky, maybe, but hopefully legally within our territory,' Pam responded with a grin. 'You haven't forgotten we've got this wretched dinner tonight as well, have you?'

Louise shook her head.

'I must say that I'm not particularly looking forward to it—all that boring small talk. *Why* is it that diplomatic small talk is even worse than any other kind?'

Louise laughed. 'Cheer up,' she consoled her boss. 'Only another few days and then you'll be going home.'

Her boss had some leave she was due, which she had decided to take to coincide with her husband's early retirement from the local government department he headed.

'Once Gerald has retired, at least we'll be able to spend a bit more time together. Although I'm not sure how well he's going to adapt to living here in Brussels,' she confessed.

Louise suspected that it wasn't so much Brussels her boss was concerned about her husband adapting to as the fact that he would be living there rather in her shadow.

The nature of her job meant that Louise rarely worked normal office hours, and so she had no qualms about her plan to head straight back to her apartment now the meeting was over. She had some reading up she wanted to do, and one or two other things. A couple of points had been raised at the meeting that she wanted to check up on, and then, she decided luxuriously, she would probably go for a swim. The apartment block where she lived had its own gym and in-house swimming pool facilities, which Louise used as regularly as she was able.

Ilse Weil had collared Gareth Simmonds again, she noticed as she started to collect her papers together. Much as it went against the grain for her to have to admit it, he *had* chaired the meeting extremely well. She had almost been able to see the committee members' respect for him growing as he'd dealt courteously but firmly with some of their more outrageous claims and counterclaims.

From a legal point of view, of course, his grasp of the subject would be absolutely first class.

Out of the corner of his eye Gareth watched Louise turn to leave.

He had known, of course, that she was working in Brussels, and it had been perhaps inevitable that they should run into one another. It hadn't been altogether welcome news for him to discover that the British representative on the committee had Louise working for her as her assistant, but by then it had been too late for him to back out.

Seeing her on the plane had been a shock that he hadn't been expecting, and he could still feel the aftereffects of the jolt that had hit him like a surge of electricity when he had stood up and seen her.

Ilse Weil was still talking to him. He bent his head towards her and smiled politely. She had long blonde hair and good skin. Beneath the fine wool of her top he could see the firm jut of her breasts, her nipples discreetly outlined. Male instinct told him that she would be far from cool in bed, but his body refused to be impressed—or aroused.

Louise… She had had her hair cut short, a gamine crop. It suited her, revealing the perfection of her delicate bone structure, making her look somehow more feminine and fragile than she had done with it long. Her clothes, unlike Ilse's, did not reveal the curves of her breasts, and there was certainly no suggestion of any tempting thrust of an aroused nipple beneath the shirt she was wearing under her suit jacket. He had seen the flash of dislike in her eyes when she had seen him earlier, just as he had seen it on the plane. She had quite obviously still not forgiven him for what had happened that summer in Tuscany.

'Gareth?'

'I'm sorry, Ilse. I missed what you were saying.' He was forced to apologise as she placed a smooth white hand on his arm. Her nails were painted an immaculate glossy dark red. They were long and elegantly manicured. Louise's nails were short and unpolished, or at least they had been that summer in Tuscany. But they had still been long enough to leave long, raised, passion-driven weals in his skin, on his arms and his back where she had raked him with them in the frantic intensity of her sexual passion—but not for him. *Her* passion had not been for him. His mouth hardened. Had it been deliberate, the way she had tangled his name with another man's as she'd pleaded with him to satisfy her, to take her, to…?

'I'm sorry, Ilse. I really must go.' He interrupted his companion.

Immediately she pouted, her finger curling round the cloth of his sleeve.

'Oh, but I hadn't finished… But then I shall see you tonight at the dinner.' She gave him a flirtatious look. 'Perhaps I might even arrange for you to sit next to me…'

'I rather think the other members of the committee will have something to say if they think I'm paying you too much attention,' Gareth told her gently, before retrieving his arm.

An affair with a woman who threatened to be as tenacious as Ilse was obviously the last thing he wanted. An affair with *anyone* was the last thing he wanted… He closed his eyes for a moment and leaned against the wall. What he *wanted*…what he wanted was, ironically, what his mother and his married sisters were continually telling him he *needed*. A wife, children…a family… Louise!

All of those things, those life fulfilments, were denied to him, though, and had been denied to him since that fateful summer's day in an Italian villa when he had wilfully, stupidly, and for ever and ever, heart-achingly, life-challengingly allowed his emotions to overrule his intelligence.

Now, for him, there could be no happy-ever-afters. How could there be when he knew, had known, from the moment he touched her, that any other woman than Louise could only and for always be second best? And that any children he might have with her, no matter how much loved, would always stand in the shadow of the children he might have had with Louise.

He had known, of course, all along, that she had not shared the explosive, mind-shattering moment of stark truth and self-knowledge he had been forced to endure, that for her there had been no savage, searing pain of recognition for the emotional significance of what was happening, no realisation that here was something that wasn't going to remain hidden by the anger he was using to mask it, and that he was deluding himself by trying to convince himself that his reaction to her was merely physical.

He had been under no illusions; she had simply been punishing herself, trying to destroy her love for another man in the fierce heat of what they had shared. She had not emerged from the inferno of their lovemaking with her emotions transformed, transmuted, from the base metal of lust into the pure gold of love—but he had. Oh, yes, he most certainly had.

He had tried to contact her the following day, telling himself that it was the right thing to do, the responsibly aware thing to do, but when he had initially telephoned and then called round at the villa he had found it empty. It had been another day before he had been able to make contact with Maria and discover that an emergency had taken the family home.

On his own return to Britain he had tried again—telephoning Louise's home in Cheshire. Jenny had answered the telephone, her voice warm with recognition as he'd explained that he had learned from Maria that they had had to leave before the end of their holiday.

She had thanked him for telephoning and had written down his number when he had proffered it—'just in case Louise wanted to have a chat with me before the new term starts'.

There had been a brief but very significant pause before Jenny had told him a little uncomfortably that Louise had told her parents she had decided to change courses.

He had known then, of course, that what had happened between them was something that Louise didn't want to pursue. And he had told himself firmly that he was a mature, thinking man and that he would somehow get over what he was feeling.

And in a way he had. He no longer woke up every morning longing for her, and the memory of the time they had spent together was something he only allowed himself to relive very, very occasionally—or at least it had been.

His family thought the reason he hadn't married was that he was too choosy…too dedicated to his work.

'If you're not careful, you're going to end up a lonely old man,' they had warned him as, last Christmas, they'd plucked a miscellany of small children and large animals from his prone body.

'If you're not careful I shall be a *grandmother* before you're a father,' his eldest sister had told him direfully.

Since her eldest child, a girl, had not yet reached her teens, Gareth had felt impelled to deny this statement, but the truth was that, much as he would like to be married, to have for himself the obvious happiness and contentment that existed for his sisters with their partners and their families, there was one vital component missing from his life that made this scenario impossible.

He needed to find *someone* he could *love*—someone who would love him in return. He was a long way past the age when the excitement of mere sexual lust, no matter how strong, was enough to convince him that it was a sound basis for a long-term relationship.

'Please don't blame Lou for…for… She can't help it,' her twin sister Katie had told him, her voice trembling slightly as though she could feel an echo of her sister's pain. 'It's because she's in love.'

In love… Oh, yes, Louise had been in love…!

'If I can't have Saul then it might as well be anybody…' she had told him passionately, when he had pointed out to her the consequences of her flirtation with the young Italian nephew of the villa's house-keeper.

Anybody… Even *him…* Wearily Gareth bowed his head. There was pain and then there was guilt, and of the two of them…which did he find it hardest to bear? The knowledge that he couldn't control his emotions, or the knowledge that he couldn't control himself? Both were spirit-crushing, heart-numbing emotions, but of the two… He looked again at Louise, and for some reason she stopped what she was doing and looked back at him. Even at this distance he could see the rejection and the dislike in her eyes. What would she say, he wondered, if he were to go over to her and tell her…take her…?

Having watched Gareth lever his shoulders away from the wall on which he had been leaning, Louise looked abruptly away from him. When she picked up the last pages of her notes she saw that her hand was trembling. Stuffing the pieces of paper into her case, she warned herself that she couldn't afford to give way to her emotions.

She hated the knowledge that he had about her, the fact that she could *never* take back the power she had given him over her, the fact that she could *never*, ever forget or wipe out what had happened between them. Even now there were times when she came awake from her dreams with his name on her lips, when she could hear an echo, the sound of her own voice calling out to him in the throes of her agony of sexual need. She had been a virgin, and yet, in the space of those few hours, her body had flowered, burst into full womanhood in a way that had left her feeling as though she hardly knew herself at all.

All her dreams of sex with Saul had centred on the thrill of finally having him to herself, of *his* desire for *her*, *his* arousal, *his* need. Naively she'd visualised him begging her to allow him to touch her body. It had simply never occurred to her that *she* might be the one doing the begging, that *her* emotions, *her* desires might be the ones that were out of control, that *she* might…

But in the end it hadn't been Saul who had heard those shaming cries, who had seen…felt…*known* her body's urgent need for fulfilment.

She could feel her body starting to grow hot, and she had an urgent desire to run out of the building and away from Gareth Simmonds just as fast as she could. But of course she couldn't give in to such a childish temptation. Instead she held her head high and walked as calmly and quickly as she could towards the exit.

'I'll see you tonight,' Pam told her when the car stopped outside Louise's apartment building.

'Er…yes,' Louise agreed, before climbing out of the car.

Her telephone was ringing as she let herself into her apartment. Picking up the receiver, she was surprised to hear her twin's voice on the other end of the line.

Their mother's habits of good housekeeping and thriftiness had, as Katie had once ruefully confided to Louise, proved almost as beneficial in her career as her Oxford degree, her boss at the charity for whom she worked being profoundly impressed by Katie's firm grip on their departmental budget. As Louise was well aware, Katie was not given to making expensive overseas telephone calls merely for the self-indulgence of hearing her sister's voice.

Knowing this, her response to her twin's warm greeting was coloured by a little bit of anxiety as she asked her, 'What is it? Why are you ringing? Has something happened to Gramps or…?'

'No. Everything's fine.' Katie quickly reassured her. 'I just wanted to make sure you'd got back all right and that everything was…er…okay.'

There was a photograph of her sister, of both of them, in fact, in their university gowns, on the table just in sight of where Louise was standing, and she frowned suspiciously into her twin's smiling features now as she quickly mentally ran over all the various interpretations that could be put on Katie's comment.

'Why did you leave it until my flight to tell me Gareth Simmonds would be in Brussels?' she demanded quietly.

'I *wanted* to tell you,' Katie admitted guiltily. 'Don't be cross, Lou,' she coaxed. 'I just didn't want to spoil the weekend. Are you angry?'

Louise closed her eyes and then opened them again.

'What's to be angry about?' she asked as carelessly as she could. 'With any luck I shan't have to have very much to do with him.

'How much longer are you working on your current project?' Louise asked her twin, firmly changing the subject and at the same time trying to banish from her mind the annoying image that would keep on forming there of Gareth's dark head inclined attentively towards Ilse's bright blonde one.

'I'm not quite sure,' she heard Katie telling her.

'Well, don't forget you promised you'd try to get over here soon if you can.'

'I will try,' Katie agreed. 'It was lovely seeing

everyone at home—so much has happened while I've been away working in London that there was simply masses for me to catch up on with everyone. What with Tullah and Saul's new baby—and I couldn't get over how much Olivia and Caspar's two have grown—and Mum and Aunt Ruth have done wonders with their fund raising for their mums and babes. Mum told me that she and Aunt Ruth are going to try to buy an older house for conversion into flatlets for single mothers.

'Aunt Ruth was saying that the stable block at Queensmead would make a wonderful potential conversion, and that its setting would be perfect...'

'Gramps would never agree to anything like that,' Louise laughed, her face breaking into a wide grin as she pictured her irascible grandfather's reaction to the news that his sister wanted to turn the stable block of his large mansion into homes for the area's single mothers and their babies.

'No, I know, and so, of course, does Aunt Ruth. I sometimes suspect that the only reason she pretends to Gramps that she's serious about it is because she knows how much he loves to have something to get angry over and to fight about. He's just not been the same since Uncle David disappeared...'

'No. He hasn't,' Louise agreed, and for a second both of them were silent as they thought about their father's twin brother.

'Do you think we will *ever* hear anything from him again?' Katie asked Louise slowly, eventually.

'I don't know. I suspect that for Gramps's sake, if nothing else, Dad hopes that he will get in touch, and it must be strange, too, for Olivia. Her mother has another man in her life, and Olivia only sees her when she and

Caspar go down to Brighton to stay with Olivia's grand-parents. David doesn't even know that Caspar and Olivia are married, never mind that they've got two children.'

'I know… I can't imagine what it would be like not to have Mum and Dad, can you?' Katie asked.

'No. I can't,' Louise agreed.

Katie suddenly interrupted their discussion about their family life to ask her with unexpected urgency, 'Lou… It isn't bothering you *too* much…about… about Gareth Simmonds being there in Brussels is it?'

'No. Of course it isn't,' Louise denied. 'Obviously I would have preferred *not* to have had him working in the same arena, but because the Commission is so closely interwoven the fact that he *is* working here would have meant that we would have been bound to run into one another sooner or later, even if he hadn't been heading the same committee that Pam is on. After all, why *should* it bother me? I don't like him, it's true, but I can live with that.'

There were some things too private to discuss even with someone as close to her as her twin was, and her real feelings about Gareth Simmonds and his presence in Brussels was quite definitely one of them.

'Look, I've got to go,' she told Katie. 'There's a big official dinner this evening, and I've got some reading up I need to do.'

These official Commission dinners, which in the early stages of her new job had filled her with such trepidation and seemed so daunting, had now become boringly familiar.

The dinner-table talk would be all the usual gossipy stuff, unleavened by anything genuinely worth talking about, Louise decided later, as she quickly showered and got herself ready, automatically pulling on the first of her wardrobe's three smart black dresses which she and Katie and Olivia had chosen on a weekend shop in London before Louise had taken up her new post.

The dresses, two of which had been bought as a bargain from a designer shop in Bond Street in its end-of-season sale, had more than paid for themselves, and in fact drew compliments every time she wore them. In matt black jersey, they were easy to wear and even more practical. They could actually be washed—a bonus indeed in view of the number of times Louise had to wear them. The one she had chosen to wear tonight was sleeveless, with a wide slashed neckline, the fabric fitting sleekly to her body and draping flatteringly over one hip.

Her urchin-short haircut needed little attention other than a fiercely expensive reshape every few weeks, and she had never favoured more than a minimal amount of make-up—eyeshadow in subtle smoky shades to emphasise the shape and depth of her eyes, blusher, and lipstick which discreetly played down the fullness of a mouth that caused members of the male sex to stop and look again with speculative interest.

Both she and Katie had inherited their father's lean, elegant frame. Louise had never minded being tallish, but she had on occasions during her teens wished that her body was a little more curvaceously rounded. Time had granted her that wish, and although she was still enviably slender, according to her female friends, she had the kind of distinctly feminine curves that made the black jersey cling to her body with loving fervour.

Black shoes and a handbag large enough to hold a

small notebook and a pen—things she never went anywhere without—and she was ready, with five minutes to spare before the car arrived.

Irritatingly her last thoughts as she stepped into the waiting car were not of her recent conversation with her twin, and Katie's promise to fly over to Brussels, or even of the conversational pitfalls she might be called upon to face regarding this morning's committee meeting at tonight's dinner, but instead were focused ominously and exclusively on the man who had headed that committee meeting.

Gareth Simmonds. Hadn't she *already* wasted enough, indeed far too much emotional energy on him?

One of the first things she had done when she had originally come here to Brussels to work was to tell herself that she was not going to allow any events from her past to cast dangerous shadows over her new life—and one of the darkest and most dangerous shadows in her life then had been the one cast by her ex-tutor…her ex…

Her head jerked up as she instinctively fought to deny even allowing herself to mentally frame the word 'lover'. They had *not* been lovers. Not in the true sense. Not as she interpreted the word.

Was there a woman in his life now? Pam, her boss, had made mention of the fact earlier that he was a single man, and as such would no doubt be in great demand socially.

'And not just single either,' Pam had commented admiringly. 'He's stunningly attractive and hunky with it…'

'Is he?' Louise had retorted in a clipped, short voice. 'I really hadn't noticed…'

Not noticed. When her brain had already faultlessly

recorded and remembered the sheer thrill of female awe she had felt that first time she had seen him fully naked.

The car had stopped and the driver was, she realised belatedly, waiting for her to get out.

CHAPTER SIX

HOLDING her hand over her still half-full glass of wine, Louise shook her head at the circulating waiter, refusing his offer of a fresh glass.

It paid to keep a clear head at these affairs, and she had never been very good with alcohol.

Formal affairs such as this reception and the dinner which would follow it were really very much more Katie's strong suit than her own, and it had been brought very sharply home to her, not long after her original arrival in Brussels, that despite the fact that everyone close to her, including herself, always thought of *her* as being the stronger and more independently minded of the two of them it was Katie who had that nice degree of social confidence and easiness. She, as her twin, had developed the habit of allowing Katie to attend to all the social niceties that attended such conventional gatherings for *both* of them.

It had brought her rather sharply down to earth and humbled her a little to recognise how much she had depended on her twin in formal social situations, and indeed how much she had abused Katie's willingness to chat politely to ancient aunts, indeed to anyone whom she personally had deemed dull or boring, leaving her free to behave with unrepentant selfishness and very much please herself as to who she talked to and who she didn't.

A few months in Brussels had very quickly changed all that, and now Louise was adept at simulating interest in even the dullest of subjects—which didn't mean that she enjoyed it any more, she acknowledged ruefully as she directed a polite social smile towards the Commissioner paying her heavy compliments before excusing herself by saying that she thought her boss would be looking for her.

Louise made her way over to where Pam was deep in conversation with a fellow British Euro MP.

'Hello, Louise.' Pam welcomed her to her side.

'How is your aunt Ruth keeping, Louise?' the man Pam was in conversation with asked warmly. 'The last time I saw her she gave me the most fearful lecture on the damage she believes is threatening the British countryside from the volume of articulated lorries we're getting.'

Louise laughed. She knew John Lord quite well, since, in addition to being a Euro MP, he was also one of their close neighbours.

'Aunt Ruth is campaigning vigorously for a bypass for Haslewich, and she does have a point,' she conceded. 'The new business park outside the town *has* brought in an increased volume of traffic.

'I was just at home for the weekend, and my younger brother, Joss, was full of the fact that an Italian lorry driver had missed his road and got his artic stuck right in the middle of town, wedged solidly in between two listed buildings. Apparently it took the police five hours to unblock the traffic and get things back to normal.'

'It is a problem, I know,' John Lord agreed. 'The

town does need a new bypass, and under one of the new EC agreements community funds should be provided to help pay for it.'

The conversation moved on and Louise excused herself to go and circulate. It wouldn't do any harm to pick up as much feedback as she could after this morning's meeting.

Ten minutes later, just as she was discreetly checking her watch to find out how much longer it would be before they went in for dinner, she heard a familiar and very sensual voice behind her.

'Aha, there you are *chérie*…'

'Jean Claude.' She turned round immediately to smile up at him. He really was the most wickedly handsome-looking man, but oddly enough his almost film starish good looks did very little for her in any personal sense. Jean Claude was the kind of man who, while laying siege to one woman, would always be secretly looking over her shoulder to check out another potential victim. Louise suspected that her knowing this, realising that for him sex, seduction, relationships were all simply part of a very enjoyable but never serious game that he revelled in playing, automatically protected her, and prevented her from taking him too seriously.

'When are we going to get together?' he whispered to her as he skilfully drew her slightly away from everyone else. 'I have some leave owing to me. We could spend it together,' he suggested meaningfully. 'I could take you to Paris, show you things that only a person with experience could show you.'

Louise laughed and shook her head.

'Impossible, I'm afraid…'

'Ah, you are no doubt busy rushing to find laws to

protect your cold northern seas. They are almost as cold as your heart, *chérie*…'

'And *both* are very well protected,' Louise informed him firmly, then smiled at him. This situation over fishing rights had never been one it was going to be easy to resolve, but she knew better than to respond to the lure that Jean Claude was trailing in front of her.

He might be a man who very much wanted to take her to bed, but he was also a Frenchman, with a vested interest in seeing his own country increase its allocation of the existing fishing rights. *She* wasn't powerful or important enough to influence the outcome of the newly formed committee in any shape or form, but it would be very easy for a woman who was emotionally vulnerable or not quite wary enough to be tricked into giving away information which *might* be useful to an opposing party, and Louise was very much aware of that fact.

Several yards away Gareth, who had been adroitly and very determinedly annexed by Ilse Weil virtually from the moment he'd arrived, frowned as he saw the way Jean Claude's hand lay possessively on Louise's arm, his body language making it plain that he would permit no other man to break into their intimate conversation.

Ilse, following his glance, raised her eyebrows.

'Oh, dear, I see Jean Claude is up to his tricks. It is well known here in Brussels what he is about,' she told Gareth with a dismissive shrug. 'And it is also rumoured that one of the reasons the French are so well informed is *because* of Jean Claude's skill in persuading his lovers to confide in him.'

She gave Gareth an arch look and made a purring

sound deep in her throat as she told him, 'I'm afraid when *I'm* in bed with a man I lose myself so completely in the sex that the last thing *I* want to do is to talk politics…'

'I know what you mean,' Gareth agreed gravely. 'I too have a rule about never mixing business with pleasure…'

He was saved from having to say any more by an announcement requesting everyone to go in for dinner. Louise, he couldn't help noticing, seemed particularly reluctant to end her conversation with her companion.

'Louise.'

Louise tensed as she heard Gareth saying her name. The dinner had finished ten minutes ago, and she had hoped to slip away early, but now Gareth was bearing down on her, making it plain that he wasn't going to allow her to escape until he had said whatever it was he wanted to say to her.

'Gareth.' She acknowledged him curtly, glancing politely at her watch and then at the door.

'I saw you talking to Jean Claude le Brun earlier,' Gareth informed her, equally pointedly ignoring her attempts to show him that she was anxious to leave. 'You may not be aware of it, but it seems that he has something of a reputation in Brussels.'

Louise stared at him, her hackles immediately starting to rise as she caught the drift of Gareth's warning.

'A reputation for what?' she challenged him angrily. 'For being a good lover? What *is* it *exactly* you're trying to ask me, Gareth? Whether or not it's well deserved?'

'What I was trying to *warn* you against was the danger of putting yourself in a position where you might inadvertently discuss certain sensitive subjects,' Gareth corrected her grimly.

Louise's eyes widened and then darkened, first with disbelief and then with anger, as she drew in a sharply outraged breath.

'Are you *seriously* trying to suggest that Jean Claude is trying to lure me into some kind of sex trap, like…like someone out of a James Bond film?' she demanded scornfully. 'How ridiculous and how *typical* of you, Gareth. There *are* men who want to go to bed with me simply for the pleasure of doing so,' she informed him with angry scorn. 'They aren't all like you, and—'

Abruptly she stopped, mentally cursing herself for allowing her emotions to get the better of her. But it was too late. Gareth had quite obviously heard her and equally obviously wasn't going to let her escape.

'They aren't all like me and what?' he challenged her silkily.

Furious with herself, and with him, Louise immediately took refuge behind the ploy of quickly changing the subject.

'My private life has absolutely *nothing* whatsoever to do with you,' she informed him, and then added for good measure, 'You have no right, no right at all, to dare to suggest to me that—' She broke off, and then continued furiously, 'How would *you* like it if I suggested to you that *you* should take care not to be lured into bed by Ilse Weil? After all, *your* position as head of the committee into the fisheries question surely makes you far, *far* more vulnerable a target for someone to try to influence your decision than me.'

She had a point, Gareth had to admit, but what he couldn't admit—at least not to her—was the fact that it wasn't merely concern for matters of diplomatic delicacy that had prompted his warning to her...

'You have no right to dictate to me *how* I live my private life,' Louise continued fiercely. 'You're not my tutor now, Gareth. You have *no* control over my life or my future. You might have been able to punish me for what you decided...for loving Saul, but—'

'To *punish* you?' Gareth interrupted her sharply. 'Louise, I promise you I—'

'You what?' she interrupted him shakily. 'You weren't responsible for the fact that I didn't get my first? It wasn't because of you that I—'

'You're not being fair.' He stopped her quietly. 'And neither are you being very logical. I wasn't your tutor and I—'

'No, you weren't,' Louise agreed. 'But...' She stopped. How could she admit to him that it had been because of her confused feelings for him, her fear of what those feelings actually were, that she hadn't been able to give her full attention to her work for her remaining time at university—that her thoughts of him had come between her and her work, that the sheer effort of denying them had drained her of the energy she needed for her study?

She was, she discovered, shamingly close to tears. The sheer intensity of the anger she was feeling was unblocking memories she had thought locked safely away.

Not once during her years at school had it occurred to her that she wouldn't always be the praised, clever student, and the shock to her pride and her self-esteem, never mind her plans for her future, when her work had been criticised had been very hard for her to come to terms with.

Yes, maybe *now*, with hindsight in a very small corner of her mind, she was just about beginning to admit that the life she was making for herself, the cut and thrust of the European scene, was far better suited to her passionate nature than the much more sterile atmosphere of the upper echelons of the British legal system would have been. But it was a very, very reluctant admission, and certainly not one she was prepared to share with Gareth Simmonds.

'I'm sorry if I said the wrong thing,' Gareth began quietly. 'I was simply trying to warn you.'

'Why warn me? What makes you think that *I'm* particularly in need of that kind of warning? Or can I guess? Just because I made the mistake of…of loving the wrong man…' She stopped and swallowed, and then told him bitingly, 'The relationship I choose to have with Jean Claude—*whatever* that relationship is—is no one's business but mine.'

'In one sense, no,' Gareth agreed. 'But in another… You don't need me to tell you that Brussels is a hotbed of gossip, and—'

'No, I don't,' Louise agreed tautly.

She had had enough of listening to Gareth lecture her. More than enough. Abruptly she turned on her heel, walking smartly away from him before he could say or do anything to stop her.

She was still seething over her run-in with him over an hour later, back in her flat, as she read through some notes while preparing for bed.

What right had he to dare to question the wisdom of her relationship with Jean Claude?

But it wasn't so much his assumed right to warn her that was making her so furiously angry—and not just with him but with herself as well—as the thinking she knew lay behind it. No doubt *he* was remembering her as the girl who had fallen so foolishly in love with a man who didn't want her, and who had then recklessly compounded her folly by inciting another man, who *also* didn't love her, to relieve her of her virginity—another man whom she had realised too late that she—

Those memories, that knowledge, and seeing Gareth, had reminded her of that hurt, and of her own foolishness.

Waking up early, unable to get back to sleep, Louise went down to the basement of the apartment complex which housed the gym and the swimming pool. At this hour of the morning she had the pool to herself, and the energy it took to make herself complete a punishing sixty lengths thankfully robbed her brain of the ability to concentrate on anything other than gritting her teeth and forcing herself to meet that target.

The last five lengths hadn't been a very sensible idea, she acknowledged when she eventually tried to haul herself out of the pool and discovered that she was too weak to do so. Instead she had to swim tiredly over to the steps and then climb them on legs that trembled with over-exertion and exhaustion.

Her short hair clinging sleekly to her scalp, her eyes momentarily closed as she willed herself not to give in to the jelly-like urging of her legs to simply sit down and rest, she was unaware of the fact that she was no longer alone in the pool area until she heard an unwontedly familiar voice demanding curtly, 'Louise? Are you all right...?'

Gareth Simmonds. What on earth was *he* doing here? Or was she simply hallucinating, dreaming him up in some insane desire to inflict even further punishment upon herself?

Groggily she opened her eyes. No, she *wasn't* dreaming. Despite the fact that the pool area was almost tropically heated, her skin suddenly broke out in a rash of goosebumps, and she started visibly to shiver. Gareth was standing less than a yard away from her, wearing a pair of businesslike black swimming shorts. The rest of his body…

Louise swallowed and gulped, then tried to draw extra oxygen into her suddenly starved lungs, a hot flood of perspiration drenching her skin despite the fact that she was actually trembling as though she was icy cold.

The sight of him brought down an avalanche of memories for which she was totally unprepared, against which she had absolutely no defences, and she could feel her knees starting to buckle under their crushing weight.

In Tuscany he might have been more tanned, but so far as she could see nothing else had changed. His body was still the same male powerhouse of energy and sensuality, and, yes, he *did* still have that same arrowing of dark hair, so very masculine and dangerous to look at, but so soft and sensually stirring to touch.

'Louise…'

She could feel the strength starting to leave her legs as the blood roared in her head and her heart pounded with sickening force.

'No.'

Automatically she put out a defensive hand as she saw Gareth coming towards her, but he ignored it, catching hold of her by the shoulders, his face, his eyes, expressing an unexpected and unfamiliar look of concern as he demanded urgently, 'What is it? What's wrong? Are you feeling ill…?'

'Let…let me go,' Louise demanded, frantically struggling to pull herself free of his grip, but the tiled surround of the pool felt slippery beneath her wet feet, and she could feel herself starting to lose her balance, so that instead of pushing herself free of Gareth she had, instead, to cling onto him for security. This close she could smell the heat of his body—not, this time, as strongly musky as it had been on that fateful Tuscan day—and mingling with it a hint of lemon freshness from his soap…or aftershave…?

Louise wasn't even aware she had asked such a question until she heard him reply, his voice disconcertingly close to her ear, 'Shower gel. My eldest niece's choice—a Christmas present.'

'In Italy you smelled of…'

What was she saying…thinking…betraying…? She cursed herself mentally in desperation, but it was too late; Gareth was already holding her slightly away from him so that he could look down into her face, her eyes…

Louise blinked and tried to look away from him, but it was impossible. She felt her breath rattle in her lungs as their glances locked, clung, refusing to let go, like lovers' bodies.

'In Italy *you* smelled of sunshine and heat and of being a woman,' Gareth told her softly, as though he knew exactly what it was she had been about to betray herself by saying.

Louise opened her mouth to protest that what he was saying was wrong, that he was speaking the unspeakable, the unimaginable, the forbidden, but no words came out, and instead she discovered that she was focusing blindly on his mouth, studying it, staring at it as though she was starved for the…

'Louise…'

Afterwards she would ask herself why on earth her brain interpreted the way he said her name as an invitation to do what she did—to close the gap between them and to press her mouth against his, not so much in a kiss, more in a compulsive, instinctive response to a hunger that demanded far, far more than the mere meeting of their lips.

What she was doing was wrong, crazy…insane. But it was too late. She had already done it and Gareth… Gareth…

Heavily she closed her eyes as she heard him repeating her name over and over again, before he started to kiss her.

Her body trembled violently beneath his hands, but she made no move to stop him when he wrenched down the top of her swimsuit, baring her breasts to his touch. Against her body she could feel the hardness of his, and her own flesh leapt in immediate response, immediate recognition of its first…its *only* lover.

Heedlessly, ruthlessly, it laid waste to all the barriers she had painstakingly erected between herself and…and this… And instead of repudiating him, as she knew she must, Louise heard herself moaning his name, sobbing it aloud almost as she hung helplessly in his arms, her body no longer her own to command or protect, responsive only to what he might tell it or arouse within it.

She could feel the heat of his chest against the naked dampness of her breasts, and it was as though their first coming together had only been yesterday. As though she had learned *nothing* in the time since—as though all the resolutions she had made for herself in those long, agonising weeks and months afterwards, when she had finally realised just what was happening to her, just what *had* happened to her, had never been. As though this man had never caused her so much pain that she had sworn she would *never*, ever forget the agony of the lesson she had learned through him.

A sound, a long, tortured, aching sob of need and longing, tore at her throat. Beneath Gareth's hands she felt her body tremble and burn; beneath his mouth she felt herself melt, yield, yearn, until the intensity of her own hunger threatened to devour her.

All sense of place or time had long since left her. They could have been anywhere; she really didn't care. All that really mattered, all that was actually real, was what she could feel. Eagerly she pressed herself against Gareth, and felt the answering hardness in his own body.

Somewhere in the distance a door slammed, and abruptly Louise came back to reality. Immediately she pulled back from Gareth, covering her exposed breasts with her hands and then turning her back to him as she frantically struggled with the straps of her swimsuit.

'Louise.'

She could hear him saying her name urgently, but she shook her head in denial of whatever it was he might want to say to her, not even daring to turn round, knowing she couldn't allow herself to look at him as she denied him fiercely. 'No. No! Just leave me alone, Gareth… *leave me alone.*'

And without giving him the chance to stop her she started to walk away from him, and then to run.

Silently Gareth watched her go. What was there, after all, that he could say? What explanation, apology could he make for what he had done? To admit that he had momentarily lost control would make matters worse rather than better, and as for pointing out to her that she had been similarly vulnerable...

To see that tormented hurt in her eyes, to feel the need coursing through her body, to sense the longing she was so obviously struggling to repress and to know that she was repressing it because she still wanted, still loved another man, a man she could not have, had been like receiving a death blow, which was ironic when he had long ago assured himself—and believed those assurances—that he had come to terms with the knowledge that she loved someone else.

In Italy he had told himself initially that it had been anger, irritation, impatience with the way she was so wantonly and childishly destroying the pleasure of sharing herself with a partner who genuinely cared about her that had driven him to do what he had done. But he had known the moment he touched her that he was lying to himself, that he was just as guilty, just as burdened by inappropriate emotions for someone who did not want him as she was herself.

He might not have called those emotions love—not then—but he had known for sure what they were when he had held her in his arms and heard her cry out another man's name while *he* loved her.

Gareth closed his eyes. The Louise he had fallen in love with had been a mere girl, and he had derided himself for having done so, telling himself it was the classic tale of the mature tutor falling for his youthful pupil, hoping to recapture his own youth through her. But they were tutor and pupil no longer, and Louise was now a woman in *every* sense of the word. And his

feelings hadn't changed, merely deepened, strength-
ened. But then he hadn't needed anyone to tell him that.
He had known it the moment he saw her on the plane.
Had known it even before then.

Had known it at Christmas, when his family had
teased him about his lack of a wife and children of his
own. Had known it and ached for it as he'd held his
youngest nephew in his arms and known beyond any
kind of doubt that the only mother he wanted for *his*
children was Louise. How had it happened? He didn't
know. And when? Before Italy? What did it matter now?
All that mattered was that quite obviously for Louise
nothing had changed, and she still loved her cousin
Saul.

Even though she had had a hot shower to warm her cold
body, and drunk a mug of coffee, she was still shivering, still shaking with reaction to what had happened
down by the pool, Louise acknowledged. And no
amount of water, no matter how piping hot, could wash
away the scent of Gareth that still clung somehow to her
own skin, which had embedded itself for ever in her vulnerable senses.

Gareth.

When had she known just how she really felt about
him? In Italy, when she had fought to deny it with a
ferocity that should have warned her just how frightened
she really was? At home that Christmas when everyone
had tiptoed around her, afraid of mentioning Saul's
name or the fact that he and Tullah had now set a date
for their marriage, when in reality Saul and what she had
once felt for him had paled to the faintest of shadows?

Gareth.

She had denied for as long as she could what had happened to her, telling herself that she was just over-reacting, that it was the classic virgin's response to her first experience of sex to imagine she was in love with the man who had been her partner, reminding herself with bitter scorn of how pathetically trite it was for a student to fall in love with her tutor.

You don't even like him, she had told herself over and over again. You're just transferring your feelings to him from Saul... He doesn't really mean anything to you, and you certainly don't mean *anything* to *him*.

The last part of that statement might have been true but the rest of it certainly hadn't.

And so she had transferred to another course, had told herself bitterly that she was *glad* that Gareth no longer taught her, had done everything and *anything* she could to make sure that she never came into contact with him. But, while she might have been able to control her daytime waking thoughts and responses, at night in her dreams it had been different. At night in her dreams she'd ached for him, yearned for him, clung to him while her body desperately tried to relive the pleasure he had given it.

The pain, the agony of waking each morning to the reality of knowing that he didn't want her, that he *wasn't* a part of her life, had shown her more clearly than anything else just how childish and adolescent her feelings for Saul had actually been.

With Gareth there had been no question of her trying to pursue him, to convince him that he really wanted and loved her, no adolescent fantasising that against all the evidence to the contrary she could make him love her.

Finally, she had grown up.

She was still shivering, and her head had started to pound with sick intensity, a sure sign that she was about to suffer one of her fortunately rare migraine attacks. It was pointless even thinking about trying to go to work. Dizzily she picked up the phone and dialled her boss's number.

'A migraine!' Pam exclaimed when she had explained how she felt. 'Don't even *think* of trying to come into work. I know how bad they can be.'

By now the pain was so intense that it was all Louise could do to croak a disjointed response before she replaced the receiver and somehow managed to drag herself into her bedroom.

Gareth Simmonds. Why had fate so cruelly brought him back into her life? Why?

CHAPTER SEVEN

LOUISE woke up abruptly. Her migraine had gone and someone was knocking very loudly and impatiently on her apartment door. Pushing back the bedclothes, she swung her legs onto the floor, grimacing as she realised she had gone to bed still wearing her swimsuit.

As always in the aftermath of one of her migraines, she felt mercifully pain-free, but somehow slightly unfocused and not quite together, her body and her brain both working slowly as she reacted automatically to the continued knocking and went to open the door.

'Joss! Jack! What on earth are you two doing here?' she exclaimed as she saw her younger brother and cousin.

Whoever she had expected to find outside her door it had certainly not been them.

'Lou, Jack isn't feeling very well,' her brother announced urgently, ignoring her question as he put a comforting, protective arm around his cousin's shoulders and ushered him into Louise's apartment.

'He was sick during the Channel crossing and…'

'Sick…'

As Louise inspected the slightly green and heavy-eyed face of her younger cousin she recognised that he was indeed looking extremely unwell.

'Jack...' she began in concern.

But he shook his head and told her wanly, 'I'll be fine... I just need to lie down for a while...'

'The bedroom's this way, Joss,' Louise informed her brother, leading the way as Joss guided his cousin across her small living room and into the inner hallway that gave on to the apartment's single bedroom.

Quickly straightening the bed before Jack virtually fell down on top of it, Louise frowned. What on earth were the two boys doing here?

Jack, Olivia's younger brother, had made his home permanently with Louise's parents following his father's disappearance some years earlier, and was now looked upon by Louise as more of another brother than a cousin.

His mother, never particularly maternal and suffering from an eating disorder, had announced that the last thing she felt capable of doing was single-handedly looking after a teenage boy—and one, moreover, who had already spent far more of his time with her brother-in-law and his wife than he had with her—and Olivia, his elder sister, while more than willing to give him a permanent home, had allowed herself to be persuaded by Jenny and Jon that it was in Jack's best interests for him to remain where he was, living under their roof, instead of being subjected to even more changes.

It was an arrangement which worked very well. At fourteen, Joss was two years younger than Jack, and they were not just close in age but close in other ways as well—more so than if they had actually been brothers, Jenny often said. And to Louise and Katie, growing up in their parents' comfortable family home, Jack had simply been accepted as though he were an extra sibling.

There had been some talk of Jack going to Brighton to live with his mother and his maternal grandparents once his mother's health had recovered, but when offered this option Jack had declared very firmly that he wanted to stay where he was.

An extra mouth to feed, an extra child to love and nurture was, as Louise knew, no problem to her parents, and if anyone had ever asked her she herself would have said quite honestly that she'd never thought of Jack as being anything other than a very close member of her intimate family, and she knew that her twin would have said exactly the same.

Within the family Joss and Jack were known collectively as 'the boys', just as she and Katie were referred to as 'the twins', but she hadn't missed the way that Jack had withdrawn from her just now, when she had gone to give him the same swift and automatic hug of greeting she had given to Joss, nor the way he hunched his body away from her as he lay on her bed as though somehow in rejection of her.

As she closed her bedroom door she beckoned to her brother to follow her into her small kitchen, where she automatically filled the kettle with water and, much to her own wry amusement, heard herself taking on a role which she had hitherto assumed belonged exclusively to women like her mother as she asked him, 'Are you hungry. I don't have much in, but I can rustle up some sandwiches, I expect.' And then, without waiting for a response, she continued firmly, 'What on earth is going on, Joss? What are you doing here? Mum never rang to say you were coming. I don't even have a spare room to—'

'Mum doesn't know.'

Louise, who had been just about to start slicing some bread to make him some sandwiches, stopped what she was doing and turned to face him, putting the knife down on the breadboard.

'What do you mean, Mum doesn't know?' she demanded suspiciously. There was a small silence while her brother looked down at his feet and then at the kitchen wall.

'That's one of the sketches you did in Tuscany, isn't it?' he asked her. 'I—'

'Joss.' Louise warned him.

'I've left them a note…explaining.'

Louise's eyebrows rose.

'Explaining what?' she asked warily.

'Well, I couldn't tell them what we were doing—they would have stopped us.'

'Oh, now, surely not,' Louise protested dryly. 'I mean, why on earth should she? You're only fourteen. I can't think of any reason on earth why the parents should possibly object to the pair of you doing a disappearing act…'

Joss gave her a sheepish look.

'I know. I know…' he conceded. 'But I had to come. If I hadn't…I tried to persuade Jack that it wasn't a good idea, but he just wouldn't listen, and the mood he was in I was afraid he would just up and leave anyway. At least this way I was able to come with him and persuade him that we should come here to you. He didn't want to, and it took me ages to persuade him that you might be able to help…'

'To help with what?' Louise demanded, exasperated.

'He wants to find David…his father,' Joss told her simply.

There was a brief silence while brother and sister looked at one another, and then Louise picked up the bread knife and reached for the loaf, telling Joss quietly, 'I think you'd better tell me the whole story.'

Ten minutes later, when she and Joss were sitting opposite one another in the small sitting room, Joss biting appreciatively into the sandwiches she had just made, he told her with a grin, 'Do you know, you sounded just like Mum back there in the kitchen?'

He was growing up fast, Louise recognised as she studied his lanky frame. Once he filled out a bit more he would probably top Max's six-foot frame, and maybe even grow taller than the Chester cousins, the shortest of whom was a good six feet two.

'Mmm…maybe. But don't expect me to listen as indulgently to whatever piece of mischief the pair of you are up to as she would,' Louise warned him, adding, 'You're lucky I was here. I *should* have been at work. If I hadn't had to go back to bed this morning with a migraine…'

'Yes, it was lucky,' Joss agreed, happily munching on another sandwich. 'I *was* a bit worried about how I was going to persuade Jack to hang around if you weren't here. When we hitched a lift from the ferry terminal he was all for going as far as Spain before we stopped.'

'Spain?'

'Mmm…He said that Uncle David once sent Gramps a card from there. Jack saw it when he went round. It was on Gramps' desk, apparently, although he couldn't get a proper look at it, and he says that when he went back to try and read it *properly* it had gone.'

'To read it *properly*? He had no right to be even thinking of doing such a thing,' Louise told him severely, wisely forgetting all the times she had been guilty of attempting to read her school reports upside down on her father's desk.

'Uncle David *is* his father,' Joss pointed out with unanswerable logic.

'Yes. I know,' Louise agreed. She started to frown. What she had initially assumed was just some boyish prank was beginning to take on a much more ominous perspective. So far as she knew, Jack had been happy— very happy—to make his home with her parents. She couldn't remember ever having heard him *mention* his father, never mind expressing a desire to see him. Olivia, she knew, had very ambiguous feelings about both her parents, and had once remarked to her that she found it was much, much easier to think charitably of them now that they were not a part of her day-to-day life.

'I know that Uncle David is Jack's father,' Louise repeated. 'What I *don't* understand is why Jack should have decided he needs to see him so urgently that the pair of you have to set out to do so without first discussing it with Mum and Dad. Has there been a problem at home— a row about something…bedrooms not being kept tidy, homework not being done, that kind of thing?' Louise asked, mentally casting her mind back to her own adolescence and the areas of contention between herself and her parents then that might have led to her taking the same kind of action. Although, to be fair, she couldn't actually remember ever having wanted to leave home.

'No, it's nothing like that.' Joss shook his head, his answer so immediate and so positive that Louise knew he was telling her the truth.

'Then what *is* it?' she asked him.

'Not what, but *who*…' Joss corrected her, explaining, 'It's Max. He was in a foul mood when he was home last time. I think he must have quarrelled with Maddy because I saw her crying in the kitchen. Max had wanted Dad to play golf with him, but Dad said he couldn't because he'd already promised to take Jack fishing. Max probably wanted to borrow money off him anyway—you know what he's like.'

'Go on,' Louise encouraged him when he paused to wolf down the last of the sandwiches. She would have to go out and buy some extra food. There was no way she had enough in her meagre store cupboards to fuel a pair of appetites like her brother's and her cousin's.

'Well, I don't know exactly what Max did say to Jack, but…' Joss pulled a face. 'All Jack would say was that Max had called him a cuckoo in the nest, unwanted by his own parents, and asked Jack if he had any idea how much his school fees were costing Dad. Not that it's—'

'He did *what*? Do the parents know about any of this?' Louise asked her brother acerbically.

Joss shook his head. 'No. I wanted to tell them but Jack wouldn't let me. I think he's a bit afraid that Max might be right and that—'

'Right? Of course he isn't right. Mum and Dad look on Jack as one of us,' Louise protested indignantly. 'They'd no more begrudge the cost of Jack's school fees than they would yours. Less…'

'No, I know that. But you know how Max is about money…'

'Yes. I do know,' Louise agreed. It was an unfathomable mystery to her how she and the rest of her siblings, her cousins, could ever have come from the same gene pool as Max.

'I suppose one of the things that makes Max so horrid is that, deep down inside, he must know that no one likes him,' Joss suggested.

Louise gave him a surprised look.

'If only! If you're trying to drum up my sympathy for Max you're wasting your time—and putting the cart before the horse. The reason no one likes *Max* is because he is the way he is, not the other way around. Look at the way he treats poor Maddy—'

Louise broke off, wondering belatedly if her mother would approve of her discussing such a subject with her younger sibling. But Joss didn't look in the least disconcerted by her comment.

'Aunt Ruth says that Maddy is a bit like a sleeping beauty, and that she doesn't do anything because she hasn't woken up to her own true potential yet. Aunt Ruth says one day she will, and that when she does Max had better watch out,' Joss told her simply.

'Jack says that he doesn't want to be a burden on the parents any longer,' he added, 'and that he intends to find his father and make him repay Dad for everything that he's spent on him. *And* he says that if he can't then he'll have to forget about university and get a job so that he can earn some money to repay them himself…'

'Oh, Joss,' Louise protested emotionally. 'That's the last thing Dad or Mum would want him to do. Why on *earth* didn't he talk to them about this instead of…?'

'He said he couldn't because he knew that they would deny everything,' Joss told her.

'They would deny it because it simply isn't true. They love him just as much as any of us,' Louise protested.

'I *know* that,' Joss agreed. 'But I don't think that Jack does. It must be hard for him, though, because in a way Max was right about one thing. Uncle David and Aunt Tania didn't really want him and Olivia... Not like Mum and Dad want us.'

Louise bowed her head, knowing that there was nothing she could say.

'Different people have different ways of loving,' she informed her brother gruffly. 'Just because Uncle David and Aunt Tania weren't as good at parenting as the folks, that doesn't mean that Olivia and Jack weren't loved and wanted.'

Joss looked steadily at her. 'Aunt Ruth says that having truly loving parents is like having a hundred fairy godmothers—only better!'

Louise gave her brother an old-fashioned look.

'All right, now I know why Jack is so determined to find his father—although how on earth he hopes to do so when Dad's tried without success I *don't* know. But what I don't fully understand is exactly what *you* are doing with him...'

'I couldn't let him go on his own,' he told her simply. 'Anything could have happened to him. So I thought if I could persuade him to stop off here with you, you could...'

'I could *what*?' Louise prompted, firmly ignoring the sharp tug of emotion she had felt as she listened to him. Her brother had enough admiring fans already without her adding herself to the list.

'Well, I told Jack that you might be able to find something out for him...what with Brussels being the headquarters of the European Union and everything, but...'

'I understand what you're saying, Joss,' Louise agreed. 'But you do know, don't you, that Mum and Dad will *have* to be told where you are, and that they'll insist that the pair of you go straight back to school?'

'Yes, I know.'

Louise looked at him. She had a pretty shrewd suspicion that Joss had known exactly what would happen in stopping off to see her, *and* she suspected that he had deliberately manipulated events so that a full stop would be placed on Jack's expedition before it took them too far from home.

'You stay here with Jack,' she told him. 'I need to go out and do some shopping if I'm going to be able to feed you. When I come back I think a telephone call to home would be in order, don't you?'

Gareth paused in the foyer to the apartment block. He had had to call in to see Pam Carlisle earlier in the day, to check on a couple of points she had raised in the committee, and during the course of their conversation she had happened to mention that Louise had been struck down with a bad migraine. He would be the last person she would feel like seeing. He knew that, especially after this morning. But it hadn't been difficult getting her apartment number from her boss, though he had to admit he had felt a small stab of guilt over the way he had described himself to her as an old friend of the family.

'Oh, really? Louise never said,' she had responded, obviously rather puzzled.

'It probably slipped her mind,' Gareth had responded.

No, *she* wouldn't want to see *him*, but he wanted... *needed* to see her. This morning... He closed his eyes. Damn it, his body still ached unbearably for her, but that was *nothing* compared with the agony of deprivation and loss that was affecting his emotions.

Joss answered the door to his knock, recognising him straight away and welcoming him in.

'Louise's just gone out for reinforcements... food...' he explained with a warm smile.

'I was just going to make a cup of tea for Jack,' he explained as he led the way to Louise's small kitchen. 'He didn't feel very well on the ferry and he's lying down. Can I make one for you?'

Gareth smiled his acceptance, his attention briefly caught by Louise's sketch of Tuscany.

'Louise drew it,' Joss remarked as Gareth studied the sketch of the small shrine on the road to his family's villa.

'Yes,' Gareth agreed, without removing his attention from the sketch.

'She's not the world's best artist,' Joss elaborated. 'Strictly speaking her perspective could be improved upon.'

'Strictly speaking,' Gareth agreed urbanely.

'But of course I expect *you* see it with rather different eyes,' Joss commented simply.

Gareth swung round to look properly at him.

He had got to know Louise's family well during the summer in Tuscany. Joss had been rather younger then, of course, but Gareth had very quickly picked up on the fact that within his family he already had the reputation of being something of a prophet and a seer, and was blessed with, if not exactly foresight, then certainly twenty-twenty emotional vision. Bearing in mind all this, Gareth resisted the temptation to probe more deeply into the reasoning behind his statement and said calmly instead, 'Yes. I believe I do. Are you and Jack planning a long stay with your sister?' he asked conversationally, determinedly changing the subject.

'Er…no… The thing is, she wasn't *really* expecting us at all. She's only got one bedroom…'

Gareth had enough experience from dealing with his nieces and nephews, not to mention his students, to know when someone was being evasive, and it wasn't very long before he had managed to coax the full story out of Joss.

'What makes Jack believe his father might be found in Spain?' he asked him, when he had finished.

Half an hour later, when Louise eventually returned to the apartment, weighed down by several bulging carrier bags, it was to discover that not only had Gareth apparently made himself very much at home in her apartment, but that it had additionally been arranged that her brother and her cousin were going to be staying with him, and not, after all, with her.

'Gareth says he doesn't mind, and since he's got a spare bedroom it seemed the sensible thing to do,' Joss informed her as the three of them deftly relieved her of her heavy shopping.

On the point of informing Gareth in no uncertain terms that there was absolutely no need for him to involve himself in what, after all, was a purely personal family affair, Louise looked across her small and now very crowded sitting room, which seemed to be filled with very big males, and hesitated.

'I promise you, they'll be perfectly safe,' Gareth informed her quietly.

Louise frowned as she looked from his clear, intent gaze to her brother and then her cousin who was now out of bed and looking better, correctly interpreting the message both in Gareth's words and his expression that he knew what was going on.

While she had been rushing round the supermarket snatching up food she had acknowledged that the first thing she needed to do was to speak to her parents—something it would be very difficult for her to do with Jack in the apartment with her. If Gareth took both boys back to *his* apartment with him she would at least have the opportunity to speak openly to her mother and father, and she knew, too, that they would both be safe in Gareth's hands, that she need not worry that he would somehow allow Jack to do a disappearing act on them. In fact, if she was honest, it was almost a relief to have Gareth there, if not to take charge then certainly to play a supporting role in the small mini-drama which had erupted into her life.

A relief to have *Gareth* there? She could feel herself starting to stiffen with inner apprehension at the thought, but oddly, instead of telling him that his help most certainly wasn't needed, she found herself turning instead to Jack and asking him gently, 'Are you feeling okay now?'

'Yes,' he responded. 'It was the ferry and then the jolting of the lorry ride…it made me feel really sick.'

'I told you you shouldn't have eaten that curry,' Joss remarked severely.

'I was hungry,' Jack countered. 'And anyway, *I* wanted to go straight to Spain, not come here first and—'

'Look, why don't we argue out the pros and cons of this later?' Gareth interposed, pushing back his sleeve to look at his watch as he announced, 'It's almost six p.m., and I don't know about everyone else, but I'm getting hungry. What do you say to you two coming round to my flat with me, where you can have a shower and get yourselves sorted out, and then, say at seven o'clock, we'll come back for Louise and the four of us can go out for something to eat?'

Louise opened her mouth to object, to say that she was perfectly capable of making her own arrangements, not just for the boys' welfare but for her own supper as well, but quite unaccountably she discovered that she was closing it again without a word of protest being uttered.

Both boys had brought haversacks with them, and with truly amazing speed Gareth soon had them and their belongings organised and marshalled at the door of her apartment.

'Is seven o'clock all right for you?' he asked Louise as Joss opened the door.

'Yes…it's…it's fine,' she agreed. The close confined space of her small hallway made it impossible for her to move away from him. Was it really only this morning that he had held her in his arms and she had…? Shakily she closed her eyes, unable to bear the burden of the memories she was reliving.

'Are you all right? Is it your migraine…?'

Her *migraine*… How did *he* know about that?

Louise's eyes opened abruptly.

'I'm fine,' she told him curtly. How would it feel to be the woman Gareth loved, the woman he wanted to cherish and protect, to spend his life with, to have his children with? She could feel herself starting to tremble deep down inside, and it was several minutes after they had gone before she felt able to walk to the telephone and dial her parents' telephone number.

Her mother answered the phone almost immediately, and Louise could hear the anxiety in her voice as she did so.

'It's all right, Mum,' she told her quickly. 'They're here with me.'

'They're *what*?' She could hear the astonishment in her mother's voice. 'But what…? Why…?'

Quietly Louise outlined the details of the story Joss had told her.

'Oh, no,' her mother protested when she had finished. 'I can't believe that Jack could ever think we felt like that. Neither your father nor I have ever…' Her mother stopped speaking for a moment as her emotions overwhelmed her.

'And you say Joss told you that it's because of what Max said to him that Jack has decided that he's being a burden on us…?'

'Well, yes, at least according to Joss. But I was wondering, Mum…' Louise paused and nibbled thoughtfully on her bottom lip. 'He's at a very sensitive age, and no matter how much you and Dad love him you *aren't* his mother and father. There are bound to be times when he wonders about them, when he feels angry and hurt and rejected by what they've done, and perhaps…'

'Yes. I understand what you're saying,' her mother agreed quietly. 'Olivia and Ruth both think that we…that all of us might have been over-compensating to him for the fact that David and Tania aren't here, and I think they're probably right. Thank goodness Joss had the good sense to come to you…'

'Mmm…' Louise agreed, and then added warningly. 'I don't want to sound pessimistic, but it seems to me that this isn't something that's going to go away very easily. All right, *this* time he's here, but…'

'I know what you mean,' her mother acknowledged swiftly. 'And it isn't even a matter of ensuring that he doesn't take off to go looking for his father again. There are quite obviously some very important issues concerning his parents troubling Jack. Issues which he no doubt thinks can only be resolved by discussing them with his father face to face. Right now Jack needs David, and I only wish it was possible for him to have him here. Since he disappeared your father has tried very hard to trace him, but without any success. Your grandfather has received the odd card from him, just telling him that he's safe, but that's all. Where are the boys now, by the way?' her mother asked.

Louise hesitated.

'Well, actually, they're with Gareth Simmonds,' she told her, trying to sound as casual as she could, but horridly aware that her voice sounded just a little too high-pitched and strained. 'You remember him, don't you, Mum? He was in Tuscany when—'

'Gareth? Of *course* I remember him,' her mother agreed. 'Katie said that he was working in Brussels, and I wondered if the two of you would bump into one another.'

'Well, he has an apartment in the same block as me, and since he has a spare bedroom, and I don't, he's offered to put the boys up there. I was glad, really, because it's given me an opportunity to ring you and speak to you without Jack being here. You'll have to let me know what arrangements you want me to make for sending them home—always supposing that Jack can be *persuaded* to go home voluntarily...'

'Mmm. I know that could be tricky. Look, let me speak to your father, and to Olivia as well. After all, Jack is her brother. Can I ring you back later?'

'Yes, that would be a good idea. Gareth and the boys are coming round for me at seven, and we're going out for something to eat.'

'Well, give them both our love, and thank Gareth on

our behalf for being so helpful, will you, please, Lou?'
her mother asked, before ringing off.

Thank Gareth for being so *helpful*. Oh, yes, and
perhaps her mother would like her to fling herself into
his arms and give him a big kiss as well...

Involuntarily Louise discovered that she was curling
her toes into her shoes, her whole body threatening to
tremble with aching longing.

It had been several years now since she had forced
herself to make a constructive critical analysis of herself
and to recognise certain self-destructive personality
traits, chief among which had to be her self-willed stubbornness—the stubbornness which had kept her locked
in the belief that her teenage crush on Saul was the kind
of love that made them matched soulmates and him the
only man she could ever love or want.

By the time she had learned that real love was a far
more complex and sometimes less easily recognised
emotion it had been too late. The damage had been
done.

Now, with the benefit of hindsight, it seemed incredible to her that she had never stopped to question
just why she had been so determined, so eager, to go to
bed with Gareth. Simply to shed the burden of her virginity? No! Oh, no. Somewhere all along, even though
she had refused to recognise or acknowledge it at the
time, among the anger, the resentment, the sense of
furious anguished pain, there had been something else,
something which had not merely been sexual curiosity
or even physical attraction.

It hurt her to acknowledge even in the privacy of her
own most secret thoughts that a part of her had wanted,
needed, ached for Gareth all along—for Gareth himself,

not just as a substitute, any substitute, for the intimacy she'd been denied with Saul. And of course Gareth himself must surely, at some level, have recognised that fact—he was, she suspected, far too intelligent not to have done so, which no doubt explained why he had been only too pleased for her to distance herself from him.

After all she had learned from her unwanted pursuit of Saul, she had been proudly determined she was not going to repeat that mistake with Gareth. She was not going to offer her love, *herself*, and be rejected—but oh, how she had ached for him to want her, to love her, and to show and tell her so. Stupid, impossible dreams of course!

'Gareth telephoned…' her mother had said, shortly after their return from Italy, and her heart had stood still while she fought to stop her body's physical reactions from betraying what she was feeling, from giving away any trace of that huge, weakening surge of need and longing that had swept over her.

'Mmm…' her mother had continued. 'He'd heard from Maria that we'd been called back unexpectedly, and he was just ringing to see if everything was all right…'

To see if everything was all right… Not to see if *she* was all right, not to speak to her…not to say, to ask… Fiercely she had swallowed back her tears, clenching her hands into tight fists.

Please God, not again…not a second time. This time she was not going to make a fool of herself by showing her feelings… This time…this time she was a woman, Louise had recognised painfully. This time she was not going to cry for a man who didn't want her, like a child crying for a denied need. This time she wasn't even going to let herself acknowledge her feelings. What feelings? She had no feelings—at least not where Gareth Simmonds was concerned. Why should she have? After all, he had no feelings for her!

'Anyone want more coffee?'

To Louise's initial chagrin, it had been Gareth who proved to be the more knowledgeable about the city's restaurants, despite the fact that she had lived there for much longer.

'I'm only going on what I've been told,' he had volunteered when Louise hadn't quite been able to conceal her reaction to his expertise.

The square where they had eaten was surrounded by streets on which fish vendors and restaurants displayed their wares on open stalls.

Predictably, it had been the more visually unappealing species of fish—to Louise's eye at least—which had caught the boys' enthusiastic attention.

'Ugh…it looks horrid,' Louise had objected when Joss had drawn her attention to a particularly vicious-looking glassy-eyed monster.

'Mmm… I don't know whether or not it's a sign of getting old, but I must say that these days I prefer not to be able to recognise the food on my plate in its original life form,' Gareth had calmly responded to the boys when they had derided her for her squeamishness. But Louise had been ruefully amused to notice that neither of the boys had taken the restaurateur up on his offer to go and choose their fish as they swam in their tanks.

The streets around the square were busy and bustling, creating an almost holiday-like atmosphere—which must be the reason she was feeling so dangerously happy, Louise decided as both boys declared themselves satisfactorily full in response to Gareth's question.

The ambience of the square was one of relaxed enjoyment and a warmth that one might more readily have associated with Paris rather than Brussels, with its unfairly 'staid burgher' reputation. Because of its present-day association with the Common Market and modern politics, one sometimes forgot that Brussels was a city with a long and distinguished history.

Louise also shook her head in response to Gareth's offer of more coffee. The evening had gone surprisingly well. It had amazed and, yes, if she was honest, piqued her just a little to see how quickly Gareth had re-established a very strong rapport with both her brother and her cousin.

Of the four of them she was probably the one who felt the most self-conscious and wary, she recognised, and that was because... She bent down to reach for her purse, determined to ensure that she paid for her own and the boys' meal.

There had been moments during the evening when she had found herself joining in with the boys' laughter as Gareth told them a particularly funny story about his own family, but her laughter had quickly been replaced by a feeling of envious sadness. *She* would never be a part of his life. *She* would never be special to him, as his sisters and his nieces and nephews so obviously were. He would *never* love her the way he loved them; his eyes would *never* light up warmly when he spoke of her, thought of her. If he had cared he would never have ignored what had happened between them—and ignored her!

'Well, if everyone's ready, I think we'd better be going,' Gareth announced as he glanced at his watch.

To Louise's relief he made no objection to her statement that she intended to pay their bill.

Jack, she was relieved to see, was looking much happier than he had done at the beginning of the evening. Louise ached to be able to reassure him that whatever Max had said to him, however hurtful it must have been, could never be a true reflection of what the other members of their family felt, but she could sense that he would close up on her if she did, and that he was still feeling too sensitive for the subject to be easily broached. And besides, she guessed intuitively, it wasn't so much *her* reassurance he craved and needed, nor even that of her parents, but rather that of his own parents, and most especially his father.

As they left the restaurant Louise discovered that the boys were walking ahead of her while Gareth fell into step beside her. Instinctively she started to walk a little bit faster, but Gareth kept pace with her. In her haste to make sure that she wasn't left on her own with him, she almost stumbled.

Immediately Gareth's hand shot out to steady her, his body offering a bulwark for her to lean into while she got her balance. Weakly Louise closed her eyes. The evening air was heavy with the scent of the traffic and the city, but stronger by far was her awareness of the sensual warmth of Gareth's body, its scent dizzying her, robbing her of the ability to fight her desire to move closer to him, her illusion that he *wanted* her to move closer.

To her chagrin she discovered that her hand was resting against his chest. No, *clinging* almost to his jacket, she recognised, her head inclining helplessly towards his shoulder.

'Are you all right? Your migraine hasn't come back,

has it?' she heard him asking her, his voice almost short and terse, as though… As though he was uncomfortable with the way she was practically leaning against him, Louise decided. But when she struggled to pull herself away he wouldn't let her. The boys had stopped several yards ahead of them to study a sculpture in the centre of the small square they were walking through, their faces absorbed.

'It must have been a shock for you to have the pair of them turn up on your doorstep so unexpectedly,' she heard Gareth saying to her as she weakly allowed herself to relax back into the warmth of his body, and the arm he had placed so securely around her. 'I must say I think you've handled the situation very well.'

'Er…thanks for stepping in the way you did,' Louise responded. 'My parents said to give you their thanks as well, by the way. I spoke to my mother after you'd gone. She's going to ring me back later to discuss what arrangements they're going to make to get the boys home…' She paused, and looked worriedly across at her brother and her cousin.

'Has…? Did…? Jack wants to find his father… and—'

'Yes, I know.' Gareth interrupted her gently. 'I take it that no one does know where he is?'

'Dad's tried to find him,' Louise told him, 'but without any success. Oh, I could wring Max's neck. He must have *known* how upset Jack would be by what he said. He really is the most selfish, thoughtless…'

'Unlike the rest of his family, who, from what *I've* seen of them, are extremely caring and concerned for one another,' Gareth told her.

It was impossible for her to see his expression

properly now that it was dark, but Louise could hear an intensity of emotion in his voice that surprised her.

Gareth looked down at the top of her head. Protecting one another obviously came easily and naturally to most members of the Crighton family.

He could still remember how determined to protect her twin her sister Katie had been, when she had explained to him just why Louise was skipping so many lectures.

'Louise…about this morning…'

Immediately he could feel her tensing, and starting to withdraw from him.

'I don't want to talk about it,' she told him quickly. 'I…it shouldn't have happened. I…'

Cursing himself under his breath, Gareth immediately let her go. What a fool he was. Just because for a few moments she had relaxed in his arms, that didn't mean… Mind you, he derided himself inwardly, it was probably just as well she *had* put some distance between them. Another few seconds of standing close to her like that and she would surely have discovered exactly what kind of effect she was having on him.

He saw the way she was studying Joss and Jack and, guessing what she was thinking, tried to comfort her.

'Try not to worry,' he advised her. 'I'm sure your parents will find some way to reassure him.'

'I hope so,' she agreed. 'But they can't…they aren't… I was thinking earlier, when we were in the restaurant…trying to imagine how *I* would feel if I were Jack. It must be hard for him, and I can understand *why* he would want to find Uncle David.'

'Yes,' Gareth agreed quietly, 'but there are other,

more effective ways of doing so than giving up his studies and hitch-hiking all over Europe…as I'm sure your father will be able to explain to him.'

It was an odd and very disconcerting experience to have Gareth trying to comfort her instead of criticising her. Somehow it had been a lot easier to try to cope with her feelings when they were antagonists.

At Gareth's insistence he and the boys saw her back to her own apartment, and Gareth even insisted that she open the door and go inside before they left her.

Impulsively Louise turned to hug first her brother and then Jack.

'Thanks for everything, Lou,' he told her gruffly, returning her hug with teenage embarrassment.

'There's nothing to thank me for,' Louise told him, ruffling his hair. 'You're my…you're family.'

Quickly blinking back the tears she knew he would be embarrassed to see, she turned to thank Gareth once again for his help, and then gasped back a small sound of shock, as instead of keeping his distance from her, he was actually taking her in his arms and hugging her just as fiercely as Jack had done. But the sensations she felt in *Gareth's* arms were a world apart from those she had experienced when hugging her cousin.

'Gareth—' she started to protest, but he was already dropping a light kiss on her forehead, and then a far less light, breathtakingly intimate and far too brief one on her startled parted lips.

'Goodnight,' he whispered against her mouth. 'Sleep well and don't worry… They'll both be safe with me and I'll bring them over in the morning.'

He had turned to go, marshalling the boys in front of him, before she could say or do anything.

Her hands, she discovered as she locked and barred the door after them, were trembling slightly, and her heart was racing as though she had just sprinted a hundred metres.

Why had he kissed her like that? Simply as an automatic reaction following the boys' example? But *his* kiss had not been… His kiss. His *kiss*. She closed her eyes and felt her face start to burn.

In the sitting room her telephone had started to ring. Quickly she pushed the memory of Gareth and the unexpected, heart-jerking, sweet tenderness of his brief kiss out of her mind, and went to answer its summons.

CHAPTER EIGHT

'LOU, it's me,' Louise heard Olivia announce herself. 'Your mother's told me what's happened. Where are the boys now? Are they…?'

'Gareth has taken them back to his flat with him for the night. I don't know whether or not Mum mentioned to you that he's working here in Brussels now, and—'

'Yes, yes, she did.' Olivia interrupted her quickly. Louise knew that Olivia would have remembered Gareth from Tuscany, and guessed that her cousin was far more anxious to talk about her brother than to discuss past acquaintanceships. She knew that she was right when Olivia cut across her to ask her worriedly, 'Lou, how is Jack? Is he…?'

'He *seems* fine,' Louise told her cautiously. 'He was sick after the travelling, but he's over that now, and he seemed chirpy enough this evening. The four of us went out for a meal—my apartment isn't really equipped for any serious cooking, but…' She hesitated.

'But what?' Olivia pressed her.

'Well, he *seems* okay, Livvy, but, easy as it would be to put all the blame for his upset on Max's shoulders, I can't help thinking that there's more to the situation than that. Jack is a sensible enough boy. He knows how Max is, and he knows as well how much my parents love him. I can't help wondering if this desire to find your father is perhaps something he's been brooding on in secret for some time.'

'You've just put into words exactly what *I've* been thinking,' Olivia agreed. 'I feel *so* guilty, Lou. I should have seen…*guessed*. But I've been so tied up in my own life, the girls and Caspar. And Jack seemed so happy, and well adjusted to the fact that Dad and Mum were no longer on the scene, that I'm afraid I just assumed that he felt the same way about the situation as I do. But of course I was an adult when it all happened. Jack was only a child.'

Louise knew, without her cousin having to explain, what she meant by 'when it all happened'. She was referring to the disappearance of her father.

Louise's own father had tried to trace him, and so too had Olivia and Jack's mother, who was now divorced from him and remarried.

'Mmm… I was thinking about…everything…this evening while we were out,' Louise told her. 'Do you think, Livvy, that by trying to protect Jack from the truth we've perhaps made the situation more difficult for him to cope with? He's an intelligent boy, and from what Joss has let slip I get the impression that the pair of them have a pretty good idea of what actually happened. Of course your father's disappearance is bound to have left Jack with an awful lot of unanswered questions—and an increasing number of them, perhaps, as he grows up. After all, looking at it from Jack's point of view, he perhaps feels that when your father disappeared he took with him the answers…'

'You're very perceptive, Lou,' Olivia told her. 'I must admit I hadn't put myself in Jack's shoes and tried to see things from his point of view. When Dad took off, to be blunt, I was so shocked and traumatised by the discovery that he had virtually stolen someone else's money that I was glad he'd disappeared. I don't know *how* I would have dealt with the situation if he hadn't… By going he relieved me of the necessity of having to do anything other than let your father and Aunt Ruth clear up the mess that he had left behind.'

'I think you're being too hard on yourself, Livvy,' Louise protested. 'I don't know how I would have coped in your shoes. I have to admit that I can't help sympathising with Jack, though. I know that *this* time we've managed to nip his plans in the bud, but—'

'But what happens next?' Olivia interrupted her wryly. 'That's what's been worrying me…'

'Well, I've had a thought,' Louise began hesitantly. 'And it *is* only a thought, that's all…'

'Go on,' Olivia commanded.

'Well, perhaps if Jack felt less isolated, if my father could involve him in his own enquiries to try and locate your father… If Jack could be *involved*, somehow, that might at least stop him from bunking off school and help him to feel he has some say, some control in things.'

'I hear what you're saying,' Olivia told her. 'And, yes, I think you could be right. I'll talk to your father about it, *and* to Jack. Which reminds me. The reason I'm ringing is to tell you that Saul will be flying over to collect both boys. He was due to come over on business anyway, apparently, and he says it's no trouble for him to bring Joss and Jack back with him.'

'What…when will he be arriving?' Louise asked her quietly.

'He's advanced his meeting and he's leaving first thing in the morning; he says his business should be over by mid-afternoon. Look, I must go; I can hear Alex crying. Thanks again, Lou…I'm *so* grateful to you. It was such a shock when your mother rang to tell me what had happened.'

'I know what you mean.'

Olivia paused. 'Lou, it won't be a *problem*, Saul coming to collect the boys, will it?' she asked tentatively.

'Not in the least,' Louise replied promptly and truthfully—meaning it.

'No…that's what Tullah said,' Olivia agreed after another small pause, and Louise knew that it was a measure of how far she had come that she felt not the least degree of chagrin or resentment at the thought of her cousin and Saul's wife discussing her.

Another measure of her maturity, she acknowledged with far less pleasure, was that she did not have the least inclination to confide to Olivia just *why* it was that she knew so positively that her feelings for Saul were no more than those of a cousin—and had been for a very long time. Since Tuscany, in fact…

Louise opened her eyes abruptly. She had been asleep, dreaming about Gareth. In her dream she had been trying to reach out towards him, to hold him and kiss him, but every time she'd tried to do so he'd moved away from her.

A glance at her alarm clock warned her that it would soon be time for her to get up. Not that she particularly *wanted* to go back to sleep. Not if she was going to have *those* kind of dreams.

After a quick breakfast, she rang her boss at home, explaining to her what had happened and asking if she might have the day off to look after the boys until Saul arrived to collect them.

'By all means,' Pam Carlisle assured her. 'How's the migraine, by the way?'

'Gone,' Louise told her. 'Fortunately.'

After she had finished talking to Pam she cleared away her breakfast things, wondering what time Gareth would bring the boys round, and what she was going to do with them until Saul arrived.

She had just finished tidying up the kitchen when she heard Gareth and the boys arrive. Going to the door to let them in, she was relieved to see that Jack was smiling.

'Thank you for giving them a bed for the night,' she said to Gareth as he followed them into her flat.

'I've been on the phone to the parents,' she informed both boys as she ushered them into her living room, a little disconcerted to realise that instead of leaving Gareth had closed the door and joined them. 'And Saul will be calling round later to take you both home.'

'Saul?' All three of them repeated his name with varying degrees of emotion, but it was Gareth's quick, sharp demand that overrode the other voices as they made eye contact and she saw the critical condemnation in his look.

She could see that Jack was beginning to look slightly uneasy, and quickly she reassured him.

'It's all right Jack,' she told him. 'Mum and Dad *do* understand. You should have told them that you wanted to find your father,' she pointed out gently to him, and when she saw that he might still be determined to head off for Spain, added, 'And maybe Dad has been a little at fault in neglecting to keep you informed of…things. He *has* tried to find your father, you know, and—'

'Is it true that Dad will have to go to prison if he comes back to England?' Jack blurted out, his face going scarlet as he focused anxiously on Louise.

'Who on earth told you that?' Louise asked him, shocked.

Jack shook his head.

'No one…at least not in so many words. But Max…'

'Max is a trouble-maker. He's like—'

'Like my father,' Jack interrupted her.

Louise bit her lip in consternation. Gareth was still there and showed no sign of planning to leave, but this was not a conversation she particularly wanted to have with him as an observer—a critical observer, no doubt, she decided irritably.

'So far as I know, Jack, your father *has* never been, *was* never motivated by malice, which I have to be honest and admit Max very often is. But it's true that your father and Max do share certain personality traits…'

'Uncle Jon once told me that the reason Dad was the way he was is because…because Gramps spoiled him…' Jack told her uncertainly.

'Gramps *did* spoil him,' Louise agreed. '*And* he has spoiled Max too…given him…given them both the impression that they have the right to put themselves first.'

'Uncle Jon told me as well that no one should blame Dad completely, because Gramps' expectations of him had put him under a lot of pressure…'

'Yes, Gramps does have very, very high expectations of his favourites,' Louise agreed dryly.

'Dad can't have loved *us* very much, me and Livvy, can he?' Jack asked her huskily. 'Not and have done what he did. Uncle Jon would *never* disappear and leave all of you…'

'I'm sure that he *does* love you, Jack,' Louise contradicted him. 'The fact that he disappeared isn't a reflection on you, you know, and it *certainly* doesn't mean he doesn't *love* you. In fact, I expect that one of the reasons he left was because he *does* love you both, very, very much.'

She saw the look that Jack was giving her, and explained quietly, 'By leaving, he probably thought that he was helping to protect you.'

'Do you really think so?' Jack questioned her uncertainly.

'I'm sure of it,' Louise confirmed, sure now that Jack would return to Haslewich, and the loving family awaiting him.

'What time's Saul arriving?' Joss interrupted.

'He has some business, which will take him until after lunch, so I doubt that he will be here until late afternoon,' Louise informed him. 'Is there anything that either of you would like to see or do while you're here? I've taken the day off work so…'

'Gareth's going to take us to this place where we can surf the net,' Joss informed her excitedly.

Louise opened her mouth to point out that Gareth had no right to make any such arrangements without checking with her first that it was all right, and then closed it again.

'You can come with us if you want to. Can't she, Gareth?' Joss added.

'Gee, thanks,' Louise drawled as she looked across at Gareth, half expecting to see him sharing her amusement that Joss should think she might consider this a high treat.

But instead of smiling Gareth was frowning, his voice curt and terse as he demanded, 'I take it it was *your* idea that Saul should be the one to come for the boys?'

Louise looked at him.

'No, as a matter of fact, it wasn't—' she began.

But before she could finish he cut across her and said sarcastically, 'I see. So it was just a fortunate coincidence, was it?'

Louise looked across to where Joss and Jack were too deep in a highly technical discussion about some new computer technology to be aware of what was going on between Gareth and herself.

'I don't know *what* you're trying to imply,' she began in a heated, low-pitched voice, 'but for your information Saul is—'

'I know *exactly* what Saul is to you,' Gareth interrupted her savagely. 'My God, haven't you—?'

He stopped abruptly as Joss looked across at them both questioningly.

'I'd better get my coat,' Louise informed Gareth. 'How far is this place? Can we walk, or…?'

'No. I'll drive us there in my car,' Gareth informed her brusquely.

'If you've both finished, I think we ought to be heading back to the flat,' Louise informed Joss and Jack as she glanced quickly at her watch. Gareth had insisted on taking them for a late lunch at a small trattoria close to where they had spent the morning, and now, as they all stood up, Louise gave him a dismissive smile and told him, 'There's no need for you to drive us back. I'll get a taxi.'

All day she had been conscious of a very definite brooding hostility in his attitude towards her, and despite her determination not to let either him or the boys see how much it was affecting her the strain was beginning to take its toll.

She already knew, of course, that he neither liked nor approved of her, but the contempt she could feel emanating from him today had brought home to her just how very vulnerable she was where he was concerned.

'We can't go home without going to Gareth's flat to collect our stuff,' Joss reminded her practically.

Louise's heart sank. But he was right, of course. However, when they arrived at the apartment block, a little to Louise's consternation they discovered that Saul was already waiting in the foyer for them.

'Saul, I'm so sorry,' she apologised. 'I didn't think you'd be here until later.'

'Don't worry,' Saul reassured her as he smiled at her, and then looked thoughtfully towards Gareth. 'My business was completed earlier than I expected.'

'You must be Gareth.' Saul smiled, extending his hand towards the other man. 'I'm Saul Crighton, Louise's cousin…'

'And ours,' Joss added.

'Yes, I know,' Gareth acknowledged tersely, ignoring Saul's outstretched hand and turning instead to the two boys, reminding them, 'Your things are still in my apartment. I'll—'

'Oh, yes. You'd better go with Gareth now and get them,' Louise interrupted him quickly, seizing the opportunity to ensure that she had a few moments of privacy with Saul to put him fully in the picture just in case Olivia hadn't already done so.

Over the boys' heads Gareth sent her a corrosively contemptuous look. Her face burning, as much with unhappiness as anger, Louise looked away from him.

'Not exactly the friendly type, is he?' Saul commented dryly once he and Louise were on their own.

'You mean Gareth?' Louise asked, fumbling with the key as she started to unlock her apartment door. 'It's my fault... He... I...'

She stopped.

'He thinks I'm trying to manipulate the situation so that I can have some time on my own with you,' she told Saul with painful honesty as she pushed open her apartment door and beckoned to him to follow her inside.

'He...he was my tutor that time when...the time of the masked ball, and...' She stopped. 'In a way he's right I *did* want to have some time on my own with you, but not for the reason he suspects. I wanted to have a private word with you about Jack, Saul. I don't know how much Livvy has told you.'

'Not much at all...only that Jack has taken it into his head that he wants to find David.'

'Yes, that's right, he does. I've tried to talk to him, but I'm worried about him, and I wondered if perhaps you... He *needs* someone to confide in, someone he can talk to who he can trust.'

'I'll do my best,' Saul promised her gravely.

'He thinks his father didn't love him.'

Saul was starting to frown, and to her chagrin Louise suddenly felt her eyes fill with tears.

When he saw them Saul's frown deepened with concern.

'Lou...' he began. But she shook her head trying to smile as she told him huskily, 'Saul, I'm sorry... It's just… I can't understand why I'm such a fool. You'd think after the lessons I learned through having that fearsome crush on you that I'd know better than to risk loving a man who doesn't love me back. But…'

'A man who doesn't love you back… Are we talking about your extremely unfriendly friend and ex-tutor Gareth Simmonds, here?' Saul asked her dryly.

Louise shook her head, but it was no use; the strain of the last twenty-four hours was having its effect on her, and the next thing she knew she was in Saul's arms, her head pressed firmly against his shoulder while he comforted her in much the same way he had done many years ago, when she had still been a child suffering from the pain of a scraped knee. But broken skin could in no way be compared to the agony of a broken heart, and she wasn't a child any more but a woman, Louise reminded herself.

'I'm being an idiot. I'm sorry,' she apologised, blowing her nose firmly on the handkerchief he proffered as she gave him a frail smile.

She was still smiling up at him, and still held securely in his arms, several seconds later as the sitting-room door burst open and Joss and Jack, followed by Gareth, came in.

The sight of Louise in Saul's arms was plainly of no interest to either Joss or Jack, both of whom, in their different ways, were anticipating their return journey to Britain in Saul's charge with a certain amount of trepidation.

Gareth, though, reacted completely differently, coming to an abrupt halt only feet away from them and saying with open contempt, 'I'm sorry if we're interrupting something…private.'

Automatically Louise started to move away from Saul, but to her consternation, instead of letting her go, Saul kept a firm hold on her arm, his other hand giving her a small warning pinch out of Gareth's sight as he countered dangerously, 'Yes, so am I.' He turned his back on Gareth, so that his view of Louise's face was blocked as he told her tenderly, 'I meant what I said the last time we met, you know. You'll always be very… special to me, Lou…'

Louise gawped at him. What on earth was Saul trying to do? He must know the interpretation that Gareth would put on his comments after what she had just told him, and now here he was, quite deliberately, or so it seemed, adding some volatile and combustible material to the flames fuelling Gareth's suspicions.

'Come on, you two,' he instructed the boys, in a much firmer tone of voice, before turning to Gareth and telling him formally, 'It seems I owe you a debt of thanks…' And then, to Louise's bemusement, he lifted her hand to his mouth and gently kissed her fingers, before very firmly and expertly drawing her into his arms and holding her there intimately for a few long seconds.

Louise didn't offer to go down to the foyer to see Saul and the boys off; her legs felt as though they wouldn't carry her as far as her own front door, never mind the foyer.

What on *earth* had got into Saul to make him behave so…so outrageously? It must have been as obvious to him as it had to her that Gareth was not in the least amused by his behaviour. Shakily she closed her eyes and put her hand on the back of her small sofa to steady herself as the apartment door banged shut behind them all.

CHAPTER NINE

'HAVE you gone completely out of your mind? He's a married man, for God's sake, and no matter how much he might feel like having a bit of sex on the side with you, right now I'll bet that's *all* he's got on his mind. Have you stopped to *think* that if he really wanted you, if he *really* cared…if he *really* had the least degree of respect or affection for you, he would never…?'

'Gareth.' Weakly Louise opened her eyes. 'I thought you'd gone. What…?'

'For God's sake, Louise. He *might* be your cousin… you *might* still love him, but—'

Louise had had enough—more than enough.

'No, I don't,' she corrected Gareth flatly. 'Or at least I don't love him in the way that *you're* trying to imply. And even if I did…' She pushed her hand tiredly into her hair.

'If you don't love him then what the hell were you doing in his arms back there?' Gareth demanded furiously.

'He was just holding me…comforting me…' Louise told him wearily.

'Comforting you? Oh, my God, now I've heard everything—'

'That's right,' Louise interrupted him. 'You *have*. Or at

least you've heard all you *are* going to hear and if you want the truth, Gareth, what I've *heard* is too much…much too much from *you*. I want you to leave,' she told him. 'You have to leave,' she added with quiet desperation. 'You have to leave, Gareth, because if you don't…'

She stopped, unable to say any more as one bright tear and then another filled her eyes and splashed down onto the hand she had lifted to wipe it away.

'Oh, God, Louise, how *can* you love a man who…?'

'Who doesn't love *me*?' Louise supplied for him, when, instead of obeying her command, Gareth took a determined step towards her.

'A man who isn't *worthy* of your love,' Gareth corrected her gruffly. 'I know how you feel about me, Lou. I know how much you dislike and resent me…'

He stopped as Louise gave a small strangled yelp of mingled pain and laughter deep in her throat.

'No, you don't,' she told him bravely. 'You don't know how I feel at all…because if you did… Gareth, please, I just can't *cope* with this. You *have* to leave,' she begged him.

But inexplicably, instead of obeying her, he was suddenly reaching out for her and taking hold of her and telling her hoarsely, 'I may not know how *you* feel, Lou, but I certainly know how *I* feel, and how I've felt for one hell of a long time. It's tearing me apart, thinking about you wasting your love, your life, on someone who…on a man who… I *know* he's your cousin but…'

'For the last time, Saul is *not* the man I love,' Louise told him, her self-control finally deserting her. 'You are that man, Gareth. *You* are the man I love, the only man I have *ever* properly loved, and the only man I am *ever* likely to properly love. The reason Saul was holding me in his arms when you and the boys walked in was because I had just been telling him about you, and—'

'Gareth! Gareth! Let go of me,' Louise demanded breathlessly as she lifted her hands to push him firmly away from her.

But it was too late, and besides, Gareth quite obviously had absolutely no intention whatsoever of letting her go. Instead he was demanding thickly, 'Say that again... You love *me*...? When...? How long...? Why...?' he began, and then stopped, closing his eyes and taking deep breaths before muttering something under his breath that Louise couldn't quite catch.

When he opened his eyes Louise felt her heart lurch dangerously against her chest wall as she saw the way he was looking at her.

'We can *talk* later,' Gareth informed her softly, barely breathing the words so that she automatically had to move even closer to him to hear what he was saying.

'Right now there's something far more important I need to do...far more important and far, far more pleasurable...'

'Gareth...' Louise protested weakly, but it was too late. His mouth was already moving over hers and she was responding to him, her body melting against his as his mouth moved more determinedly over hers, his tongue tracing the shape of her lips and then gently probing them apart.

'No,' Louise whispered, but the word was more a soft sigh of pleasure than any kind of real denial.

It was the longest, sweetest, most loving, cherishing kiss she had ever known, Louise decided dreamily as Gareth continued to caress her lips, his hand cupping her face, stroking her skin, his heartbeat thudding fiercely beneath the hand she had originally lifted to fend him off and which had now stayed to curl possessively into the front of his shirt. She felt dizzy, light-headed almost, with a mixture of desire and disbelief, unable to comprehend properly that this was actually happening, that *she* was *here* in Gareth's arms, that *he* was holding her, kissing her, loving her, as though he actually meant it.

'Have you any idea just how much I've been wanting to do this?' he was whispering against her mouth. 'How much I've *ached* to touch you…kiss you…*love* you, Louise?'

'I thought you despised me…disliked me,' she whispered back.

'Despised *myself*, disliked *myself*, yes. But *never* you,' Gareth groaned. 'When I came to the villa that morning…the morning after and found that you'd all left…I thought at first that it was because…that I'd…that you'd been so affected by what had happened, that your parents… But then Maria told me that there was some problem at home.'

'I *was* affected by what…what we did. But not in the way you mean,' Louise told him truthfully, shivering in delicious pleasure as his lips started to caress the soft curve of her throat.

'I knew that I'd…enjoyed…what happened, and that you'd made me feel things…do things…I'd no idea I could feel or do. But it wasn't until the following Christmas that I realised what had happened to me. I'd told myself that I hated you, that I was glad you weren't my tutor any longer and that there was no contact between us. I even managed to persuade myself that I was still in love with Saul, that I had simply transferred what I felt for him into a physical response to you…'

'Well, you certainly had *me* convinced,' Gareth interrupted her hoarsely. 'You called out his name when I…'

'I didn't even know I had…it must have been a protective reflex,' Louise told him softly, achingly. 'A way of trying to pretend to myself that you weren't…that I wasn't…' She stopped, and her eyes widened in fierce response as he ran his fingertip around the neckline of her top and her breasts immediately started to ache wantonly for his touch.

'Last time, when I went home, Saul and Tullah were both there. Everyone was tiptoeing around me as though I was an unexploded bomb. I admit I had been dreading seeing them myself, but when I did…' She looked up into his eyes. 'He was just Saul again,' she told him simply. 'Just my cousin. There was *nothing* else, and I couldn't really understand how I had ever thought… felt…wanted…

'Ever since Tuscany I have been having these dreams about you… Dreams when I…we… I thought it was simply because you were the one who…' She paused, flushing, and then laughing as she shook her head. 'I was so naive…naive and stubborn. I didn't *want* to admit the truth to myself, but I looked at Saul and I ached for you so badly…wanted you so badly…'

As her eyes filled with tears at the memory of the shocking fierceness of the pain, Gareth's eyes darkened in protective love.

'I was thinking about *you* as well,' he assured her. 'Wondering what you were doing…and who you were with…wishing it was me and wishing to hell that I hadn't been stupid enough to give way to feelings that I knew then were dangerous…'

'But you didn't *love* me when we…when you… You didn't *love* me. Not then,' Louise protested.

Gareth looked steadily at her.

'You're right. You *were* naive,' he told her huskily. 'Of course I damned well loved you. You don't think for a single solitary moment that I would actually have… that a man who didn't love…? You couldn't really have believed I could be so unprincipled as to…?'

'I thought you did it because you were angry with me,' Louise told him simply. 'I thought it must be a male reaction thing.'

'"A male reaction thing."' Gareth laughed huskily and closed his eyes. 'Oh, it was certainly that, all right,' he assured her. 'A *very* male reaction thing. The kind of male reaction thing that happens when a male, a *man*, falls deeply and passionately in love.

'I could have killed you when you told me that you were planning to lose your virginity with Giovanni. Do you know that?' he asked her lovingly.

'Well, you certainly made it plain that you didn't think it was a very good idea,' Louise agreed demurely. '*When* did you fall in love with me…?'

'It started one afternoon in my rooms. You were arguing passionately about something. I can't remember what. I looked at you and suddenly…' He paused and shook his head. 'It just happened. I told myself not to be a fool. I even reminded myself of all the reasons why it wouldn't work. And then you started skipping lectures, getting Katie to sit in for you instead…'

'Katie *said* you knew about that.'

'Of course I knew,' he told her lovingly, adding wryly, 'And so, too, did my body. It never reacted to Katie the way it did to you. And then, when I found out that you were in love with someone else…' He paused and shook his head. 'That day when I came to your room and found you there half-drunk…'

'I felt so humiliated that you'd seen me like that,' Louise whispered. 'And then you turned up in Tuscany…'

'I wasn't too pleased either. I'd gone there hoping to get things in perspective, to get my emotions under control, and instead…'

'Why didn't you *say* something…tell me how you felt?' Louise asked him.

'How *could* I when you'd already told me that the only man you could ever love was your precious Saul?'

'I knew in Tuscany that it was just a silly crush that had burned itself out, but I'd made such a big drama out of it that I couldn't bring myself to let it go. And then you took me to bed and I realised that you were right…that I had just been a girl…but after our afternoon together I woke up a woman, and it was as a woman that I began to realise that I loved you,' Louise told him softly.

'I couldn't repeat all the mistakes I'd made with Saul…I couldn't embarrass you and humiliate myself by putting you through all the stupid things I'd done to try and get Saul's attention—I didn't even *want* to. I could see just how ridiculous…how selfish and, yes, childish in many ways my behaviour had been. I knew then how different real adult love was from my teenage fantasy of what love was, which I had woven around my feelings for Saul.

'I'd believed that if I just tried hard enough I could *make* Saul love me. With you… With you I *knew* that the only way your love could be mine was if you gave it to me freely, and I knew you would never do that…'

'You knew wrong, then, because you already had it,' Gareth whispered rawly to her. 'Oh, Lou, when I think of the time we've wasted, the days, the years, the nights we've spent apart when we could have been together.'

'Especially the nights,' Louise agreed wickedly, her

mouth curling up at the corners, but she still blushed a little bit as she saw the way he was looking at her.

'It's been a long time,' he told her huskily. 'And there hasn't been anyone else for me since then, Louise…'

'There hasn't been anyone else for me either,' Louise told him a little shyly, adding shakily, 'What you…what we did…the way I felt, was so…so good…so right… that I couldn't…I didn't… I was afraid of spoiling the memory of it, because I knew no one else could ever make me feel the way you had done.'

'No one else?' Gareth quizzed her gently. 'Not even Jean Claude…?'

Louise burst out laughing.

'No one else,' she confided. 'And *especially* not Jean Claude…'

'Gareth, what is it? What are you doing?' she demanded as he suddenly turned away from her and reached for the telephone, quickly pushing the buttons and wrapping his free arm around her to stop her from moving away from him as he started to speak into the receiver.

'Paul, it's Gareth Simmonds here. Look, I'm not going to be around for the next few days—an urgent family matter… Yes… Well, the committee doesn't have another meeting until next month, I know… Can you check through my diary and cancel all my appointments for the next week, please? Oh, and by the way, can you ring the airport and book me two seats on the first available flight for Pisa? You can ring me back on this number,' he added quickly, giving Louise's telephone number and then replacing the receiver before she could say a word.

'Tuscany,' she said, her eyes starting to shine.

'Tuscany,' he agreed.

'But Pam…'

'No buts. Pam will be able to manage without you for a couple of days.' Gareth informed her masterfully, and then groaned as he added ruefully, 'I'm not quite sure how *I'm* going to manage to keep my hands off you until we reach the villa… You do realise, don't you, that it's a good two-hour drive from the airport and—?'

'The *villa*… But it might not be empty, and you could—'

'If it isn't empty then I shall bribe whoever is staying there to move out,' Gareth informed her determinedly. 'And besides…*my* family's villa *is* empty at the moment. It might not be quite the same—'

'*Your* family's villa? With the pool…' Louise interrupted him. 'The pool where I saw you swimming that day the Fiat broke down…?'

'Uh-huh…the very same one.'

Louise closed her eyes and gave a small, femininely ecstatic sigh.

'I want to go *there*,' she told him happily. 'Oh, yes, I want to go *there*, Gareth. I want it to be *there*… please…'

'Of course… But why…?'

A small smile curved her mouth as, leaning forward, she whispered to him, 'Because that's where I realised for the first time just what a very, very sexy man you are, and that's where, when I saw you getting out of the pool in those trunks, I couldn't help wondering just how you'd look without them, and that's where…'

'Okay, I think I get your drift,' Gareth told her softly.

'Well…?' Gareth asked Louise lazily, smiling sexily at her as he leaned over her sun lounger to kiss her awake.

'Well, what?' she asked him, sitting up and taking the drink he had brought her.

They had arrived at the villa in the early hours of the previous morning. Louise had wanted to go straight to bed, but Gareth had demurred.

'Let's wait until this afternoon,' he had suggested meaningfully, and, her stomach knotting with sharp, sensual excitement, Louise had agreed.

It…*he*…had been worth waiting for…*more* than worth waiting for, and today her body still felt relaxed and softly heavy with sensual satisfaction.

'Well, do I look just as good without my shorts as you hoped?' Gareth teased her.

Louise laughed.

Last night Gareth had persuaded her to go skinny-dipping with him, and afterwards they had made love beside the pool in a tangle of damp limbs and soft, warm towels.

'Oh, every bit as good…' she confirmed. 'But you can always prove it to me again if you want to,' she teased him provocatively.

'Oh, I *want* to,' Gareth assured her.

'I hope everything is going to work out all right for Jack,' Louise murmured, her eyes darkening a little as she thought about her young cousin. 'I feel that we've *all* been guilty of not realising how much his father's disappearance has affected him.'

'It *must* have been difficult for him,' Gareth agreed sombrely. 'But you handled the whole situation very well. You're going to be a very good mother, Lou…'

'But not yet,' she told him. 'Or at least not until we're married…'

'No, not until we're married. You'll make a lovely winter bride with your colouring…'

'A winter wedding…' Louise murmured.

'I have to warn you that I have at least a dozen nieces who will all want to be bridesmaids…'

Louise giggled. 'Oh, not a dozen, surely!'

'Well, four,' Gareth amended. 'You *do* want to marry me, don't you, Lou?' he asked her, his face and voice suddenly very serious.

'Oh, yes,' Louise assured him huskily. 'Oh, yes, Gareth. Yes…yes…yes…' she moaned, as his mouth covered hers and the sun lounger rocked perilously beneath their combined weight.

'Louise is going to marry Gareth Simmonds,' Joss informed his great-aunt Ruth solemnly as he sat in her drawing room eating the fresh scones she had just baked.

'So I understand,' she agreed, smiling over his head at her American husband, Grant. They had only been married a few years themselves, even if their love went back over several decades.

'I like him. He understands things…' Joss told them seriously. 'Maddy was crying again yesterday, when I went to see Gramps. Why does Max have to be so horrid to her?'

Ruth sighed as she looked at him.

'I'm afraid that Max is just like that, Joss,' she informed her great-nephew sadly. 'Some people are, and when they are I'm afraid it takes a miracle to change them.'

'But miracles do happen,' Joss pointed out gravely. 'Look at you and Uncle Grant.'

'They do, yes,' Ruth agreed.

'I hope one does happen to Max…for Maddy's sake,' Joss added.

Ruth looked at him calmly.

'I shouldn't build your hopes on it, Joss,' she warned him. 'Not where Max is concerned.'

'I still can't totally believe it,' Katie told her twin, shaking her head slightly. 'You and Gareth in love and getting married…'

'What Mum finds harder to believe is that I'm going for the whole traditional wedding bit, complete with dress and bridesmaids,' Louise informed her sister wryly. 'We're getting married Christmas week, and spending Christmas Day at home with the family. Then New Year in Scotland, with Gareth's family, before we go off on honeymoon.'

Katie was in Brussels with Louise, and Gareth had promised to take them both out for dinner.

'You like his family, then?' Katie asked her twin.

'Oh, yes,' Louise confirmed enthusiastically. 'A small part of *me* still can't quite believe it, either, Katie, I feel so…so special…so…so lucky… so…'

'So loved?' Katie suggested gravely.

Louise frowned. Was that a small shadow she could hear in her twin's voice, see in her eyes, and, if so, why?

'Katie…' she began, but her sister was already getting to her feet and picking up their empty wine glasses.

'It's six o'clock,' she warned Louise. 'We're going to have to start making a move if we're to be ready for Gareth when he calls for us at seven-thirty.'

'You are going to be there, aren't you?' Louise demanded as she followed her into the kitchen. 'At the wedding, I mean… No last-minute trips to the back of beyond to inspect some irrigation scheme or anything…'

'It's documents that I inspect, Lou, not irrigation schemes,' Katie reminded her lightly. 'And, yes, I shall be there.'

She was glad that she had been alone when she had taken Louise's ecstatic telephone call to tell her that she and Gareth were going to be married. Louise had put her silence down to the fact that she had been so surprised by her news... Well, she *had* been surprised, but...

Louise wasn't the only one who could love inappropriately and unwontedly. Not that Katie had ever imagined that Gareth might feel something for *her*, but then neither had she suspected that he was actually in love with her twin.

Anyway, whatever foolish dreams she might once have had had been packed away quietly and for ever now, along with all the other things that belonged to her childhood and the past. And, yes, of course she would be at their wedding, and she would smile for them and *with* them. How could she not? How could she not be happy for her twin? And how could she not grieve a little for herself?

'We'll never be alone, Katie,' Louise had once told her. 'We'll *always* have each other.'

But Louise had been wrong and now she *was* alone. Alone and lonely and hurting.

'You know that Gareth actually knew right from the start when you attended his lectures in my place that you weren't me?' Louise burbled happily as Katie quietly washed her used glass. 'He could tell the difference between us because he loved me...'

'Yes, you told me,' Katie acknowledged calmly, her hand trembling a little as she put the clean glass down.

'I love him so much, Katie,' Louise told her sister

softly. 'I just wish that you… I want you to be as happy as I am…I want you to have someone to love and be loved by.'

'I'm happy as I am,' Katie told her, and promised herself that one day, very soon, it would be true.